Butcher Boy Blue

By

Paul Hichens

Published by Ardour Publishing

Ardour Publishing is a trading name of Writing Services Limited

Cover by Cherie Fox

ISBN: 978-1-915257-00-0 (print) | 978-1-915257-02-4 (eBook)

First Edition

For more information on the writing and music of Paul Hichens visit www.paulhichens.com

For Ryan Kinnon

Green & Red

It was the moment that would eventually trigger a tsunami of madness, mutilation and murder. Really it merited some kind of God Almighty demonic shriek to announce the approaching Armageddon. An anti-Hallelujah. A thunderclap Eureka antithesis. Apocalyptic horsemen charging and roaring and spewing out fire.

Mo Blenkinsopp could have obeyed the now-doomed woman's demands; he should have legged it. Instead, he just studied the reflection, palmed the scissors and mumbled, 'Mm.'

Chapter One

The blond in the skimpy dress elbowed past the multi-studded goth girl. The lanky ginger lad wobbled in tow. Kell caught the goth's eye, pocketed his phone then reeled the be-metaled waif through to the kitchen with a killer smile and a magnetic wink.

The goth rubbed a skinny pale arm and scowled at the blond. 'What rattled her cage?'

'Says her name's Alex. Wanted to get her claws into me. Offered a moonlit romp in the park to be precise. But I let her down. Not so gently as it happens. Said I'd rather shag a porcupine skunk and threatened to arrest her for soliciting if you must know.'

'Probably explains the tears.'

'Boozed-up glassy eyes more like.'

'Sounds like you were pretty mean to her.'

'Maybe,' Kell scratched his designer stubble. 'I possibly did overreact. But she was pretty mean to my friend Mo first. Gave him the daggers, told him to scram and called him a *square shit*.'

'Hardly a crime. And he *is* dressed like my grandad.'

Kell peered through the throng of partygoers and clocked Alex turn at the exit and snarl at Mo. Her ponytailed bonce juddered with anger, 'Who do you think you're looking at?'

Mo smiled, tapped his temple and muttered something that largely got swallowed up by the Red Hot Chilli Peppers fuelled din.

'You're stunningly gorgeous by the way,' Kell's beam dazzled.

'You're making me blush,' the girl's eyes melted then sparked against a thick mascara backdrop as he poured her a Bacardi with one hand and caressed her waist with the other. 'I'm Kell, ...DC Kell Lilley, in case you were wondering. ...And you are?'

'Er... Natalie,' she snapped out of her reverie and looked over at Mo struggling to don his jacket by the exit. 'So just who is that weird lad? And was it you who bust his nose?'

Kell swung his eyes from the kitchen window and followed Natalie's gaze, 'Ah, that's Mo, ...Mo Blenkinsopp. And no, I didn't thump him. On the contrary, I saved his sorry arse from my *dad of sorts.'*

'Hang on. *Lilley*... Your dad's not that nutter...' Natalie motioned air quotations. '*removals* guy, *Davy* Lilley is it?'

'*Stepdad*, and be careful what you say. There are plenty of hardcases who've ended up in plaster - or worse – and for a lot less than calling him a nutter.'

'Is that what your mate Mo did ...diss him?'

'No. I just caught the back end of the initial rumpus,' Kell said. 'But Davy accused Mo of trying to woo his latest bit on the side.'

'And did he?'

'Who Mo?' Kell laughed. 'He's only got eyes for my colleague and former classmate Debbie Harrison - and he totally blew his one and only shot at her?'

'How?'

'In typical Mo fashion,' Kell shook his head with a crooked smile. 'In an epic public shambles.'

'But if your mate Mo didn't do anything wrong tonight, how come he ended up with a battered nose?'

'Not sure,' shrugged Kell. 'But whatever Mo did or said initially, it's what happened *after* he was thumped that's his biggest worry.'

'Eh?'

'If you'd just been poleaxed by a riled dangerous giant with the order *keep the hell outta my way* ringing in your ears what would you do?'

'Er,' Natalie played with her nose ring. '...*keep the hell outta his way*?'

'So, you wouldn't choose to stagger outside, try to halt his two-ton car with your bare hands then call the police?'

'The police?' the skin around Natalie's eyebrow piercings appeared to stretch as her eyes widened.

'Well, luckily I shut down the call before he filed a complaint, and I also managed to persuade Davy to cool it and beat it - though if he hadn't been on a promise with a voluptuous brunette I doubt I'd have succeeded.'

A gaping Natalie studied the battered Mo as he downed a quadruple vodka straight from the bottle then stumbled outside via a headbutt to the front door.

'And to think I called your stepdad the nutter!'

Chapter Two

Mary Blenkinsopp waited a moment on the landing to catch her breath. She teased up her purple skirt and rubbed the inside of a thigh; semi-permanent chaffing being an uncomfortable drawback of tree trunk legs. At just 35 the stairs shouldn't be giving her so much gyp, but after a bout on the dark side of cancer, years of popping anti-depressants and a lifetime spent largely on her bum, her best stair vaulting days were already well behind her. Truth be told, a sugar-fuelled diet, an off-the-scale BMI index and a forty-a-day habit did little to help either.

It wasn't premeditated, but when she happened to lean on Mo's bedroom door it creaked open. Instinctively, she started to push it back, but then hesitated and let it fall open again. Subconsciously or other she waddled over towards the screensaver illuminating the otherwise dark room that was minimalist not messy, and more monasterial monk than trendy teenager. The solitary poster on the wall depicted Mecca, not Man U, and it was the Quran by the bed rather than sporting albums, guys' magazines, or music DVDs. Not that Mo had ever really been that much into such things. Mary hadn't kicked up any real fuss when he'd told her he was going to become a Muslim. Just the occasional tut, shake of the head and *oh why do you want to join that lot* kind of uttering. And even that had petered out after just a couple of weeks or so. Likewise, when, aged fifteen, he'd said that he wanted to change his name to Mohammed by deed poll, she'd just silently gone to bed, slept on it, and in the morning gave her blessing on the condition that he changed it back to Roland should he ever reconvert.

All in all, she'd been pretty cool as Catholic mothers of teenage Islam converts go. Damned cool. However, as she brushed the mouse, accidentally or otherwise, and a battered sandy urban image lit up, her flushing neck didn't give off a particularly cool vibe.

She snaked the mouse and hovered a finger as the pointer on the screen twitched over a play icon. It was her house, and she knew fine well that she was alone. Even so, she still looked over her shoulder before going click.

She couldn't read a word of Arabic, so the big bold squiggles shouldn't have caused her to catch her breath. They shouldn't have triggered her sweating brow or set her heart pounding like a pneumatic drill either. That particular reaction possibly had more to do with a video launching, and some shemagh-toting geezer wielding a big bloody sword around right in front of her eyes.

***

As night trickled towards daybreak Mary popped a Prozac, checked the plastic clock for the umpteenth time and dragged long and deep on her latest cigarette. She picked up a framed photograph of her in her youth with her long flowing hair that shone red, auburn or even an orangey shade of ginger depending upon the light. Looking at it was always a double-edged sword. Firstly, the teenage waif image not only accentuated the beauty that she had lost, but also the colossal curves that had since ballooned her beyond recognition. Secondly, while she loved, and had even kept, the little patterned dress in the picture, it inevitably reminded her of the time she'd been raped. She could only ever bring herself to give Mo half the story, adding 'attempted' to the rape part – a little white lie to spare him from the unspeakable truth.

She nibbled again on her chewed nails and ran them across the photo, but suddenly stopped as a scraping sound reverberated up the stairs followed by a gentle clunk.

'Mo, is that you?'

The creaks on the staircase punctuated the still night air, ...slow and crescendoed until Mary's bedroom door scraped open and Mo put his mouth to the gap.

'Mam,' Mo's voice was barely above a whisper. 'W... what are you doing up at this time of the night?'

'Me? What about you? Where've you been? And why are you talking through a little gap in the door? ...And it's not *night,* it's almost *dawn* now.' Mary rebounded. 'If you must know I've been fretting about you.'

'Makes a change from me always worrying about you then,' Mo staccato laughed. 'I'm sh... shattered Mam. You should get some sleep too.'

He closed the door with a simple 'goodnight.'

'Don't think you can get out of it that easily. I wanted to talk to you. And I'll want that and answers in the morning,' Mary blustered.

'Whatever,' Mo groaned.

'And I know you've been drinking. And I know you've been up to something. And I know you're hiding something,' Mary barked. 'And don't think I won't find out Mo Blenkinsopp.'

***

An hour and a half later and Mary remained wide awake. She heard movement.

And not for the first time.

Not long after Mo had backed out of her room the stairs had creaked down, then, a few minutes later, creaked up again. Mary had then spent the next half hour gnashing her knuckles while listening to her son's breaths morph to stifled cries then erratic mini snores through the thin wall that separated their bedrooms. She'd re-examined, and re-examined some more, a torn off bit of paper that she had earlier found on the ledge of Mo's open window. Squint as she might, she hadn't managed to make out all the letters and numbers – smudged, no doubt due to the light rain – but she'd certainly got the gist. The first word was definitely *jihad*, and the word *sword* was also clear. There was no doubt about that. Another word was almost certainly *Alexandra*. Then after that came a few numbers and dots that started 82.149 but then blurred like an inky abstract watercolour.

She'd gnawed on trembling fingernails before shoving the scrap of paper to the back of her bedside cabinet drawer, taking a big breath and creaking downstairs herself, as curiosity, fear or whatever it was finally got the better of her.

Rays from the approaching dawn seeped through the landing window and illuminated the staircase as she had puffed her way back up. As she had caught her breath her eyes fell. On white knuckles, white walls and a red streak.

Several trips back and forth to the bathroom later and the walls gleamed and her scrubbed-raw hands stung.

Now, as Mary sat by her window in the post-dawn, curtain-induced darkness, the stairs creaked downwards again. Every so slowly. Every so surely.

Unlike her heartrate.

She'd never been one to intrude in Mo's life. Of course, to some, it appeared like apathy. And if she was apathetic about anything it was other people's opinions. Even so, while the pills and depression quite possibly had the effect of dulling the interfering busybody in her, just as they clouded everything else, she still nevertheless encouraged Mo's independence and had always seemed to back up and show faith in his decision-making.

That said, until a few nights ago he hadn't kept her awake with terrifying shrieks of 'Allāhu Akbar!

And until now she'd never spent the whole night chain-smoking and chewing off the end of a pen as she wondered what the hell to do about it all.

Mary waited until the front door quietly clicked shut before peeking through the curtains – heat soaring up her neck as the colour sapped from Mo's face down below - his eyes bulging in horror as he peered into the wheelie bin.

Chapter Three

'Was it you who rattled scissors through ma letterbox at crazy o'clock this morning?'

'Hang on my shorts are slipping,' Mo wedged his phone between his ear and shoulder and tugged up his new baggy cargo shorts. 'Yes, I borrowed them last night. Sorry if I woke you.'

'You in shorts? That I've gottae see,' Saboor propped himself up against a pillow. 'And yer didnae waken me. Kell and his new girlfriend were in the spare room. He left fae work an hour ago, but they kept me awake half the night – making mae of a racket than the guy hoggin ma stereo did at ma party.'

'I'm glad someone had a good time,' Mo massaged his brow. 'I'm black and blue, had a hell of a night, and my head's pounding with my first ever, monster of a hangover.'

'Welcome tae planet booze,' Saboor nursed his own sore head. 'What happened tae yer anyway? Yer seemed tae vanish not long after yer kamikaze run-in with that vicious gangster.'

'That's what I wanted to talk to you about,' said Mo. 'I didn't want to disturb you earlier, but can you meet me at the park? I've got something important to tell you.'

'What's so important?' Saboor donned his specs. 'And why the park?'

'I won't go into too much detail over the phone,' Mo stopped in his tracks, scanned around 360 degrees and lowered his voice. 'All that vodka, whisky and beer seems to have zapped holes in my memory, but my bones are telling me that something seriously iffy went down last night. The park's ringing a bell - I'm just not sure whether it's memory bells, alarm bells or both.'

‘Oh, so the park visit is nae fae feeding the ducks, it’s you in amateur sleuth mode again. Why dae ye nae just wait on the police tae get back tae yer about yer job application?’ Saboor yawned. ‘And why are yer whispering?’

‘Cos I’ve a feeling someone’s been following me. I sensed it when I left your party last night. I also had this freaky nightmare,’ Mo booted a pebble. ‘Anyway, I’ll wait for you at the par...?’

‘Mo?’ Saboor waited for a response while a bang and a siren reverberated down the line.

Even down the other end of the phone, Saboor identified the sound of knuckles rapping a window. He also recognised the address ‘Oi, Pisswizard!’ accompanied by a voice so deep and thunderous that it ought to have come with lashings of rain and bolts of lightning.

Saboor strained his ears to try to hear what was happening. It sounded like a car slowing to a halt, followed by a vociferous ‘You’re dead!’ threat, then Mo mumbling something out of earshot then a vehicle reversing quickly and doors slamming.

‘Mo, what the hell are yer daein wae Davy Lilley?’ Saboor’s voice tremored. ‘Mo? ...Mo, are yer alright? ...Are yer still there?’

Then the line went dead.

***

‘Hi Saboor, sorry about that. ...Oh Davy? Yep it was him alright. Stood starkers at his fancy woman’s bedroom window he was, threatening me for denting his car. ... Well yes, I could have run. ...Na, I just smiled and waved at him instead. ...Yes really! ...Well, she bobbed down in front of him, and well I guess his priorities kind of changed thereafter. ...Other voices? ...Oh, that’d be the imam and Ishmael, they were driving past, noticed me in a spot of bother and reversed back to see if they could do anything to help. ...What’s that? ...No, they just escorted me a bit further along the road and we had a bit of a chinwag. ...What? ...No, they didn’t mention the perils of the demon drink. ...No, they didn’t rant on about the sin of sodomy like they did with you before – primarily because I'm not the gay one! ...What? ...just because someone at your old mosque in Glasgow tried to coax you into a one-way ticket to Iraq, it doesn't mean to say that Ahmed and Ishmael have similar plans for me! ...No, I'm not telling you. ...Because it's top-secret that's why!'

Mo hung up, stabbed a *'forget the park, I'll go alone!!!'* message to Saboor then picked up pace.

***

Shortly afterwards DS Estelle 'Gran' Grantham surfaced from the footwell that she'd been ostensibly rummaging around during the previous fifteen minutes. She clocked the receding Mo then looked up at the window that had survived Davy's knuckles. She dragged on a roll-up and ran her fingers over the deep-set wrinkles that, alongside her curly grey hair, added another ten years to her actual 51. She tapped her pencil on a blank page in her notebook, seemingly wondering what to write or whether or not to write anything at all. After the tenth tap, she wet the tip of her pencil with her tongue and jotted:

Lilley / ginger lad death threat.

Imam / ginger lad (sounds like) Tall Ships boom!

Chapter Four

It was a still Sunday in mid-April, and the sun was out - if only in short bobbing bursts between occasional gaps in the candyfloss blanket overhead. A vacated unmarked police car party blocked the entrance of Ward Jackson Park as it started to fill up. Swings creaked, ducks quacked, dogs barked, and kids and parents made merry with bikes, scooters and an array of bats, balls and frisbees.

'Yeaaah!' A little blond lad in a Roblox T-shirt snagged his bamboo pole fishing net on something heavy in the pond and strained to yank it up. 'Look Carly, I've caught a whopper!'

A few yards away little Carly fleetingly glanced over to her eight-year-old brother Kaleb then went back to trying and failing to throw bread into the pond from all of three yards.

'Hee hee,' she giggled as ducks jostled for prime position at the water's edge. Until that was, the moment the ducks decided that enough was enough, so waddled out en-masse, congregated around her sandals and started to peck around her toes.

At which point she screamed and burst into tears.

She wasn't the only one, and another scream or two either rang out or echoed virtually simultaneously. Up the hill a little girl suddenly scurried out of the bushes, wailing and sobbing and peeing through her wet panties as she ran. 'Auntie Beth!' she screamed as she flung herself into her aunt's arms. The aunt scooped her up and showered her head in kisses while simultaneously burning her eyes directly into those of the detective responsible. His horrified expression and claims of *looking for a reported flasher* clearly held little sway with the seething auntie. In frustration, the detective swung one of his size tens into the bushes and by chance booted out a gangly ginger teenager. Shorts dangled around his ankles.

As he was being frogmarched to the police car the suspected flasher smiled at the aunt, 'Oh, hi Mrs Lilley,' he remarked almost nonchalantly - and almost as if he hadn't yet joined the dots between her and her husband.

Down at the pond, Kaleb's rod snapped, his net sunk and his eyes bubbled. Carly wiped her own tears, looked around, and hesitated between joining her brother or finding out what all the fuss was about over by some bushes where a woman had screamed just minutes earlier. Folk were now circling around the woman, amid hugs, sobs and an eerie goose-bump aura. Kaleb, in contrast, stood alone, glumly watching his net sink. Lucky for him. His potential trauma vanished with his catch's submergence to the murky depths. The same couldn't be said for little Carly, who not only shrieked at the sight of the purple foot sticking out of the foliage, but who would scream for years to come in gruesome nightmares, remembering the horrific vision of a naked mutilated body spreadeagled across blood-soaked undergrowth.

Blue

Chapter Five

The approaching DI Joe Abraham swerved to avoid the string of wailing squad cars as they hurtled out of the station car park. He ignored his prisoner's question about what the hell was going down and contented himself instead with roughly manhandling the youth out, bundling him inside the station and heftily shoving him into an interview room.

As Mo flung both arms out to stop himself from crashing into the table his loose shorts instantaneously slid back down around his ankles; much to Abraham's amusement. 'I've heard of caught red-handed before, but you're the first weirdo I've apprehended outdoors literally with his pants down!'

'You swine Abraham.'

'Save it,' Abraham said. 'I'm just going to have a word with a colleague. In the meantime, you don't move.'

Mo scowled at Abraham, bent down and took hold of his shorts.

'Are you deaf Blenkinsopp? You're on a serious charge. Your liberty is hanging by slimmer thread than the one in your shorts. And I said don't move!'

As Mo hesitated in his crouched position Abraham swivelled on his heels, banged the door behind him and laughed the whole way up the corridor.

***

Sergeant Matty Black gestured towards a skinny pair of calves in flowery leggings that were just about visible through an ajar door.

'The young lass startled by the flasher.'

Abraham nodded. 'Okay, but what about the blues and twos?'

'Ah,' Matty sighed. 'That's something far more sinister I'm afraid.'

***

After a fast-track conflab with Matty, a very brief natter with the flasher victim and a quick word with DC Debbie Harrison, Abraham re-entered the room chewing gum and all smiles.

'Good news Blenkinsopp. Apparently, the flasher had a distinguishing feature. We should be able to discount you from the investigation if you are willing to cooperate?'

Mo met Abraham's gaze and his eyes whirred. If he was relieved, then it didn't show.

'Apparently the flasher had a tattoo. *A big ugly thing* according to the victim.'

'Great,' Mo sparked up and headed towards the door. 'I don't have any tattoos. Can I go now?'

'Woah, nice try,' Abraham spread his arms to block the exit. 'And aptly in line with your earlier display of bare-bottomed cheek. But even you must understand that we can't just take your word for it. We need proof.'

'Oh right,' Mo twisted his arms, lifted his vest and turned 360 degrees. 'There you go.'

'Ahem,' Abraham coughed. 'We're talking about a flasher remember?'

'Oh!' Sighed Mo looking downwards.

'Tell you what,' Abraham said as he exited the room. 'I'll give you a bit of privacy and some time to think about it. Makes no odds to me whether you want to clear your name or take the rap.'

Mo didn't need any time to think about it. His mind had been made up for him. But he took the extra time anyway and went over to the closed door and banged his forehead against it. Sighing heavily, he trudged back over to the table, tugged off his vest, slid off his shorts and squirmed out of his underpants.

'What the hell are you playing at?'

Mo spun around gasping.

'D...Debbie,' he scrambled to hide his modesty. 'I can see Abraham didn't tell you.'

'Didn't tell me what exactly?' Debbie picked up Mo's vest and threw it hard at him while doing her best to avert her eyes.

'It's not what it looks like. I was just proving my innocence. Abraham said the flasher had a tattoo,' Mo nodded to his nether regions. 'You know, down there.'

'You idiot Blenkinsopp!' It was on his *arm*.' Debbie waved her own arm about in despondency. 'Somewhat uncannily, the victim has no recollection of the culprit whatsoever apart from the fact he has a big ugly tattoo the full length of his lower arm. He could be Martian for all we know. But a Martian with a bloody great tattoo.'

Mo ground his teeth and mouthed '*Abraham*' and something else under his breath.

'Did Abraham tell you to take all your clothes off?'

'Yes!' Spat Mo while making a hash of donning his vest the right way around. 'Oh, hang on. I guess not explicitly. Not in so many words.'

'Oh.'

'But he inferred it!' Mo snorted. 'He sort of made it sound like I had no choice – but without actually saying it.'

'Hm,' Debbie's dark wavy locks spun as she shook her head and tossed Mo his shorts - less forcibly than his vest. 'He's good at that kind of thing.'

Mo sat down and clumsily pulled on his shorts. 'I guess this means I'm free to go.'

Debbie chewed her bottom lip. 'Sorry Mo, but DI Abraham has had to rush off. I did ask him if I could let you go - and he considered it for all of a millisecond before leaving me strict instructions to give you a couple of minutes, then collect you, then lock you in the cells.'

'That's harassment!' Mo banged on the table. 'Why is he detaining me for no rightful cause? And what's so important that he has had to rush off?'

'I shouldn't really say, but you'll find out soon enough I guess,' Debbie sighed heavily. 'There's been a murder.'

'A murder?'

Debbie nodded.

'Surely Abraham doesn't think I'm involved in murder?'

Debbie shrugged.

Mo's mind whirred while his blood coursed and his heart hammered.

Chapter Six

'Who's that lad I saw you hauling in earlier?' Gran asked as they hared down the road, sirens wailing.

'Blenkinsopp, why?'

'Ah, so *that's* Blenkinsopp,' Gran adjusted the seatbelt across her flowery blouse. 'The lad I heard you keep stopping and searching?'

'The very same,' Abraham screeched around a corner. 'He'll trip up one of these days, and when he does I'll have him.'

'So, he's not the flasher?'

'No, but I'm sure he's been up to no good.'

'Funny you should say that,' Gran shuffled her legs amid the confines of her long grey skirt. 'You know you asked me to start keeping tabs on the imam and his henchman yesterday?'

'Yeah, I don't trust those crackpot Quran crunchers.'

'That's a racist comment if ever I've heard one,' Gran, lowered her big blue specs and frowned at Abraham. 'You do know I'm a woman of religion myself don't you patron?'

'I've told you before that you can call me gov' or boss,' huffed Abraham. 'No one else calls me *Pat Ron*.'

'It means *boss*,' smiled Gran. 'I'd have thought that someone of your high standing may appreciate the bestowal of an additional mark of respect patron?'

Abraham eyed Gran suspiciously, but ultimately without objection.

'Anyway, don't be so tetchy Grantham,' he changed the subject back. 'You can't call it racism if I hold bible bashers in equal contempt.'

Gran tutted and rummaged in her bag for a mint before she too changed the subject. 'Anyway, guess who was with Ahmed and Ishmael buying fertilizer?'

Abraham turned to face Gran even though he was flooring it in a 30-mph zone. His cobalt eyes flashed. 'Not Blenkinsopp?'

'Well, he had a different hairstyle and smarter clobber,' said Gran. 'But yes, I'm sure it was him.'

'How many sacks did they buy?'

'Six,' replied Gran. 'But I've only just started watching them. They could have been buying them in dribs and drabs for weeks and have a shed full now by for all we know.'

'And do the imam and Ishmael have big gardens?' asked Abraham? 'Because Blenkinsopp lives in Kathleen Street. His garden will be the size of a postage stamp.'

'Ahmed doesn't even have a garden and Ishmael's would struggle to house a dwarf bonsai,' Gran said. 'And that's not all, Blenkinsopp was with them today, huddled outside the place Davy Lilley was holed up, looking as dodgy as, and whispering.'

'About what?'

'Well, I was straining to hear from twenty yards away through a 2-inch gap in the car's window, but I'm sure I heard the words 'Tall Ships' and 'Boom!'

'I knew it,' Abraham barked excitedly as he screeched to a halt. 'I can feel another stupendous collar with my name on it.'

Gran's grey eyes narrowed. 'Are you thinking of arresting them?'

'Too right,' Abraham boomed. 'It could be a terrorist cell for all we know.'

'If there is a terrorist attack in the offing then we need to stop it,' Gran said. 'But we ought to pass it onto Special Branch. If you think it's possibly a cell then it could be just the tip of the iceberg.'

'That's a good point,' Abraham mused. 'I doubt those three are calling the shots. They'll be the monkeys, not the organ grinders.'

'If indeed it is an actual terrorist plot,' Gran sucked her mint. 'I mean I might have misheard or...'

'Look, I know you come across all happy pills dithering old lady,' Abraham cut Gran off. 'But even just working with you a short time, I've seen enough now to know that underneath that dowdy coat of yours you're pretty damn sharp, and if you say you've heard something then you'll have more than likely heard right. As far as I'm concerned, it's good intel and on our patch, and if those three can lead us to those pulling the strings it'll be *our* stunning collar on News at Ten.'

Gran goggled incredulously at Abraham. 'But if they are planning to blow up the Tall Ships' event when it next comes to town that'd be catastrophic.'

'Agreed, but as far as I'm aware it's not coming to town again this year,' said Abraham. That gives us time to keep tabs on the imam and his cronies. If they can lead us to the ringleaders, then we can blow the whole cell ourselves.'

'But...'

'What else do you know about them anyway?' Abraham cut off Gran.

'Not much yet,' Gran admitted. 'When Ahmed's not imaming – if that's even a word, his day job is as a hypnotist. As for Ishmael, he's unemployed and originally came to the UK as an asylum seeker from somewhere in Africa. Somalia, I believe.'

'Well, make sure you keep a damn close eye on both of them,' Abraham said. 'And in the meantime, we can also have an informal little chinwag with Blenkinsopp when we're back at the station – all casual like. He's not exactly a mafioso master criminal. He might trip up and let something slip. Those three will do a better job of digging their own graves if they think no one is any the wiser.'

***

They arrived at the main park gates just as the few remaining members of the public were being shepherded out. A young PC thumbed towards the pond. 'Down that way sir. In the bushes. You can't miss 'em. Swarming like flies they are.'

'He's not wrong,' Gran panted as she tried to match the athletic Abraham's long brisk strides. 'SOCO has sealed things off and are already at it.'

Abraham looked down the hill at the figures in little white suits crawling around the bushes, combing the area. 'Yeah, but they're more like *nits* than *flies*.'

Just as they approached the crime scene tape someone stumbled over it, fell to his knees, yanked off his mask and vomited all over Abraham's hitherto shiny black shoes.

'Oi you...!' Abraham raised a fist, then froze a moment before uncurling his fingers and crouching down. 'Oh, it's you Kell son. Are you okay?'

Kell spewed a second time. This time in some undergrowth.

'Sorry Dad,' he eventually mustered pointing to a spot by an unusual looking tree with a torn black dress at the foot of its trunk. 'It's just that the body...'

'But you've seen dead bodies bef...,' Abraham followed Kell's finger. His eyes and mouth widening.

'What's up?' asked Gran. 'Have you seen something patron?'

Abraham took a few moments before ignoring Gran, turning back to Kell and finishing off his sentence. 'You've seen dead bodies before.'

'Yes, but not like *that!* God help us. It's a woman. A woman with numbers daubed in blood on her body. A body that's been...' Kell swallowed hard. '...decapitated.'

***

As Abraham and Gran donned crime scene clothing, Kell looked over to where the body lay, below the tree that Abraham had seemed engrossed with minutes earlier - a mature tree with two thick lower branches in the shape of a tuning fork. Out of all the trees in the whole park, the whole world come to that, it was the only one that held any significance for Kell. It still sent stinging shivers down his spine. As a child, Davy had laughingly pointed it out to him once, describing it as his 'punchbag tree', the one where he liked to 'sort out business affairs'. Kell glanced at Abraham then back to the tree that connected the crime scene with Davy. Did Abraham know about the connection? Did he sense something? Or was it more a case of a wild guess or unsupported hunch? Abraham didn't have a reputation as an ace detective for nothing. It *was* possible that this whole tree connection was just a coincidence. It might have nothing to do with Davy. That was one inference. Would Abraham come to any other conclusion?

That arguably depended on whether Kell mentioned it or not.

***

Two miles south, an ex-forces double amputee by the name of Mick Braithwaite scanned around his garden for inquisitive eyes. A siren wailed somewhere in the distance. It seemed to be heading the same way as the ones that had not long preceded it. He gripped either side of the collar of his bloody T-shirt and looked back to the washing machine just beyond his open back door. He craned his neck in the same direction as the siren and hesitated momentarily. Suddenly, he ripped off the T-shirt in one smooth motion, exposing a shaven, tattooed torso rippling with muscle. Only green skin and two lower limbs separated him from the Incredible Hulk. He dropped the T-shirt on top of the other smouldering garments on the bonfire then went inside and pulled an identical one from the linen bin while the cotton frizzled.

Identical, apart from the absence of blood, that is.

***

With his state-of-the-art prosthetic legs stuck behind a strimmer in the shed, Mick clanked into his front room on the bespoke clunky stumps that he'd specially commissioned from an ex-Royal Engineers mate. Protruding strikingly from his ever-present scraggy denim shorts, the crudely cobbled-together heavy metal limbs, with their chunky knobbly bolts, gave off an air of *scaffoldy-armour-meets-Frankenstein*. If they had been designed to get reactions, then they achieved just that alright. Little wonder then that he'd picked up a new middle nickname; Mick '*Who'd you think you're looking at?*' Braithwaite.

As it happened, his new solid appendages weren't as solid, or as crudely cobbled together as first appeared. Mick tugged off the left one, vertically aligned barely perceptible notches in the top three bolts, then depressed the fourth. A soft swoosh and the razor-sharp blade flipped out like a giant flick-knife. Goosey, his innovative Royal Engineers pal, hadn't been that surprised when Mick had revealed that the word was that there was a price on his head, and that he'd therefore wanted some extra-special insurance.

Goosey might have been a bit more shocked however, if Mick had let on that the face behind the word in question was a small, pretty one with a floppy blond ponytail.

***

If the jailor had been any other than Debbie, then Mo would have put up more resistance or have been more vocal with his protestations. As it was, it was he who opened the door and walked voluntarily into the cell - before the rhetorical invite was even issued. Moreover, it was he who actually apologised.

'Sorry Debbie, this must feel rather awkward for you?'

Debbie looked down and straightened out an apparent crease in her skirt. Mo couldn't help noticing that her legs seemed as good as ever; short but athletic, shapely and in his eyes at least - perfectly proportioned. For a moment he completely forgot his predicament.

'Are you keeping up the netball?'

'It's more Zumba these days Mo.'

Subconsciously, Mo's eyes moved up and he pictured Debbie in Latino shake and wiggle mode.

'Well, you're looking fit,' he offered. Realising the ambiguity and potential interpretation of his statement he quickly followed up. 'In a purely sporty way I mean. Not *fit* as in, you know...'

Debbie flashed a brief smile. Her teeth weren't the brightest or the straightest, but for some reason Mo had always found her smile most beguiling.

'I mean I don't want you to think I'm trying to chat you up or anything, because that's not what this is, and if I did ever want to try to chat someone up then I dare say I'd do the actual chatting bit without firstly parading starkers at the local nick. Even *I* know that's not perfect first date material...'

'Look Mo...'

'Sorry Debbie I'm rambling I know. Just ignore me. I think I get like this sometimes when I'm nervous. Not that I've anything to be nervous about. I mean I'm definitely *not* trying to chat you up, and no way am I a flasher. Honestly. Yeah, I know I'm rabbiting on, and I know it looks like I'm nervous, but it's not a *guilty* nervous if you see what I mean.'

'Look Mo,' Debbie eased Mo into the cell and sat him down on the bunk. 'Even if you are a tad nervous it's perfectly natural. Why don't you just have a lie-down and just try to relax if you can? DI Abraham will be back in a while, and we can sort out any misunderstandings and you can be on your way.'

'You think so?'

'Sure,' Debbie's big green eyes both reassured Mo and quickened his heartbeat at the same time.

Debbie clocked Mo's bloodshot eyes and the fresh cuts on his arms. 'Besides, it looks like you've been in the wars and could do with some kip.'

'You can say that again with bells on,' Mo stretched wearily.

‘Why?’ Debbie’s eyes narrowed. ‘What did you get up to last night?

‘I’m not absolutely sure,’ Mo yawned. ‘But a nightmare woke me up after what seemed like just one hour’s sleep, and earlier last night that thug Davy Lilley walloped me on the nose.’

‘Davy Lilley,’ gasped Debbie. ‘Wow, you don’t hang about! Just three years ago you were getting into playground scrapes at our school and now you’ve catapulted straight into the big league - picking fights with Davy Lilley of all people! Whatever possessed you?’

‘Me?’ Mo scrunched his eyebrows. ‘He was the one slathering and pawing all over this lady – who I know wasn’t his wife by the way. All I did was say that if the huge gentleman with the bald head and big red beard was bothering her then to just say the word and I’d escort him off the premises.’

‘Oh Mo,’ Debbie cringed. ‘What happened?’

‘His vicious jab escorted me off the floorboards,’ Mo rubbed his nose. ‘By the time I came to they were outside just heading off in his Range Rover. Almost run me over he did as I staggered out after him.’

Debbie shook her head in disbelief.

‘I actually called your lot,’ continued Mo. ‘But Kell snatched the phone from my hand, rabbiting on about *Davy not being the kind of person I’d want to grass up*. Can you believe that? Him being a policeman himself too.’

‘Kell’s right,’ said Debbie. ‘I’ve seen the aftermath of people who’ve crossed Davy. The word *pulp* springs to mind, and I don’t mean the band. You don’t know what you’re messing with.’

‘No, he doesn’t know what he’s messing with.’ Mo’s eyes found Debbie’s; his defiant glower meandering only fleetingly, to tug up his shorts.

Debbie sighed heavily then looked Mo up and down. ‘So how come you’re not sure about just what happened to you last night?’

'My first dalliance with alcohol has somewhat frothily clouded my memory,' Mo groaned. 'The blanks have been gnawing away at me ever since as it happens.'

'And?' asked Debbie. 'Any luck filling in the gaps?'

'Is this off the record DC Harrison?' Mo smiled crookedly. 'We both know that your boss has it in for me - and that he'll now be on the hunt for murder suspects.'

'If you can't remember what you did last night then how do you know you're *not* the murderer?'

It was casually delivered and off the cuff, but Mo sensed that Debbie's question had a tad of a serious tinge about it.

'I don't,' Mo admitted. 'But I wouldn't want to accidentally incriminate myself by saying something that could be twisted and hung around my neck by Abraham.'

Debbie locked onto Mo's eyes. 'Would you rather disappoint *me* by holding something back?'

A lump caught in Mo's throat, but he coughed and spoke unblinking. 'No Debbie, I'd rather incriminate myself.'

'Well then...?' Debbie's eyes twinkled.

'Hang on, let me think...,' Mo's foot tapped briskly. 'Well, I do remember flashes of bits and bobs. Like a broken bottle and a fight between a man and a woman on Catcote Road.'

'What involving you?'

'Only to try to help the guy up as far as I remember,' Mo's eyes flicked up and to the left. 'A disabled muscleman. ...I think he called me a *faggot* and threw a drunken punch at me, so I left him to it and carried on my way ...Ah yes, ...I then bumped into Ishmael from the mosque. ...He gave me something ...Made me promise to be extremely careful with it...'

'What was it? And where is it now?'

'Dunno,' Mo upturned his palms. 'Guess I must have lost it.'

Debbie shook her head then hovered a finger over Mo's arm. 'Well how about these cuts?'

'They are a mystery too,' Mo sighed.

'Could they have been something to do with whatever Ishmael gave you?'

'Maybe,' Mo rubbed his thumb under his chin and felt a recent nick that he hadn't noticed until now. 'Although, somewhere in the back of my mind I've an image of me clambering over a wall. ...Or was it some railings?'

Debbie's eyes narrowed as they scanned Mo. 'Is that it?'

'Like I say – it's a bit of a blur,' Mo shrugged.

'You've changed Mo, and not just on the trouble finding front. You used to have a razor-sharp mind. And just take a look at you now too, Debbie said. 'When did you get this new waxed back hair, black vest and baggy shorts look? You were always a centre parting, shirt and smart trousers lad.'

'I got this new look just this morning as it happens,' Mo replied. 'The shorts were dirt cheap. I should have guessed there'd be something wrong with them. The drawstring snapped and they fell around my ankles just as I noticed that swine Abraham charging into the park. It's why I scuttled into a bush. I had no idea that the girl was in there too.'

'Does you scuttling into the bushes from him have anything to do with you know...' Debbie bit her lip.

'That night at the school youth club disco?' Mo finished Debbie's sentence off and inwardly screamed. 'You do know that it was an accident don't you Debbie? I just tripped over a bag when I was trying to ask you to dance. I didn't mean to grab your breast as you broke my fall.'

'Yes, I do know that now Mo,' Debbie sighed heavily. 'But at the time I was just 17.'

'And I was just 14.'

'Yes, well whatever, I just panicked and screamed.'

‘And your mate Isobel phoned the cops, DI Abraham collared me at the school gates, and he’s been on my back ever since. Little wonder I wanted to avoid him in the park.’

‘And I’m sorry about that Mo,’ said Debbie. ‘Though in his defence he insists you bit him.’

‘And I certainly did,’ Mo spat. ‘But I bet he left out the fact that he was kneeling on my windpipe at the time, giving me the evil eye and threatening to send me down for five years for serious sexual assault.’

‘I’m really sorry,’ Debbie lowered her eyes then cleared her throat. ‘But talking of sexual offences, DI Abraham asked me to check your phone. Just to make sure there are no incriminating photos – you know, from the park. Hope you don’t mind.’

Mo groaned, dug out his phone, tapped in the passcode and handed it over. Debbie smiled gently then took a step towards the door.

‘Do you have to go?’ There was a croaky crack in Mo’s voice.

‘I could stay here and interrogate you, or I could just leave you, all on your lonesome, but in peace. What would you prefer?’

Mo lay back on the bunk and closed his own eyes. His heart still batted, but more retreating owl wing beats than machine gun woodpecker. Maybe Debbie was right. Maybe this latest nightmare would soon wash over. The cell door clunked shut with a heavy metallic bang. Mo rolled over face down and buried his glassy eyes in the slab of a pillow. Yes, maybe this latest nightmare would soon wash over. That said, if he’d learned anything over the course of his wretched nineteen years it was that the next one wouldn’t be far behind.

***

By the time Debbie next looked in on Mo, just thirty minutes or so later, he was curled on his side and already breathing heavily, ostensibly in deep slumber but with twitchy head, jittery feet and roving fingers subconsciously prodding the cuts on his arms.

Debbie slid the peephole shut as softly as she could then got back to business in one of the interview rooms.

It was probably for the best. If the timing had been different, and she'd checked in on Mo just five minutes later, she wouldn't have just heard the scream that rocked the whole station, but she'd have also witnessed his panicked expression and his desperate gasping utterance.

'Dear Allah the merciful on high, what have I done?'

Chapter Seven

'What do you make of these patron?'

DI Abraham hunkered down next to Gran and silently examined the seemingly random assortment of numbers written in blood on the body.

'98, 12, 14...' Gran postulated. 'Do you think they represent years?'

If Abraham did have any ideas or theories then he wasn't voicing them. Instead, he signalled to Gina Lo the pathologist and together they gently rolled the corpse over.

'No numbers or distinguishing marks on her back sir, apart from two tattoos; the word *vixen* on the right shoulder blade and this cartoon fox tattoo on the left buttock,' she said. 'Beheading with a sharp object seems the likely cause of death, but I'll reserve judgement on that until further examination, and upon retrieval of the head. What is clear is that the victim is Caucasian, probably a blond judging by the colour of her pubic hair, and I'd estimate in around her early-to-mid forties. Notably, there are signs of both forced restraint and recent sexual activity.'

Gina turned the cadaver back over. A worm wriggled out of the gaping neck wound and Abraham suddenly ripped off his mask, tumbled over the body and baulked. He gagged, blundered on all fours to a nearby bush then was sick again.

And again.

'Sorry Gina,' he spat out some last lingering bits of acrid diced vegetables. 'I'm messing up the crime scene.'

Gran raised an eyebrow and shook her head. In contrast, Gina gave Abraham's back a friendly pat. 'It's quite common for the smell of vomit to provoke further sickness in others.'

Sorry about that Gina,' Abraham rose unsteadily to his feet. 'Don't worry, there'll be no more creating a mess or getting in your way.'

Gran called over to a SOCO colleague squatting over a rectangular bit of flattened grass. 'What's that you're looking at Wes?'

'Not sure Gran,' said Wes, the only black face in a white suit. 'Seems like an indentation from a picnic basket?'

'Possibly,' Abraham bent over it and gently ran his finger around the edges. 'But it hasn't been picnic weather lately. Size it up and check around the vicinity will you.'

'Already have,' Wes patted his kit bag then handed a bagged-up phone to Abraham. 'I've also just recovered this from the undergrowth.'

'Cheers,' Abraham took it and headed back to the central crime scene.

Gran turned to Gina. 'What's this about forced restraint?'

'Some marking on her upper arms and both wrists,' Gina replied. 'Not ropes or wires, but marks made by fingers I'd say. Possibly someone heavier and stronger squeezing and pressing down hard on her.'

Gran nodded. 'So, are you suggesting rape?'

'Well, there are clear signs of force and her clothes were scattered about,' Gina gestured over to some of the SOCO team who continued to plod around, bagging up evidence and taking enough pictures to fill the Tokyo Photographic Art Museum ten times over. 'But all I can really do is give you pointers on some of the pieces. You're the ones who have to join all the dots together.'

'Shame,' Gran clocked the back of her boss's shaking head as Abraham crouched in front of the victim's body. 'I've got a feeling that we could use all the help we can get right now.'

'One thing,' Abraham craned his head around towards Gina. 'You mentioned a sharp object. Can you be more specific?'

'Well, I don't want to speculate at this stage,' Gina said. 'But I'll get a clearer picture down at the lab.'

'What are we talking?' asked Abraham. 'A machete?'

'The indications are that the potentially fatal blow was dealt with something longer than the width of a neck,' Gina elaborated. 'And very sharp.'

'Something like a sword perhaps?'

'Maybe,' Gina nodded. 'That isn't out of the realms of possibility.'

***

Gran sighed heavily as they eventually concluded their investigation of the scene. 'Poor wee thing. Beheaded of all things. How dreadful.'

'Yes. Highly unusual,' the still pale looking DI lumbered back towards the park exit. 'If I believed in coincidences, I'd possibly draw conclusions along the lines of religious motive.'

'A particular brand of religion?' Gran probed with another raised eyebrow.

'Well, now you mention it,' Abraham stroked his designer goatee. 'One might postulate a brand of religion taken to very extremist levels. One might also conclude a perpetrator who has already since returned to the scene of the crime.'

'A cliché surely.'

'Most certainly.'

'The question is patron,' Gran lit a roll-up. 'Whether you believe in coincidences, clichéd or not?'

'Oh, I'm a believer alright,' Abraham slicked his black hair back. 'Though of course, we can't just jump to the most obvious conclusion. We still need to weigh up the evidence and carefully consider *all* options.'

'Most definitely,' said Gran. 'There could well be other suspects and other lines of enquiry.'

'Quite...,' Abraham stroked his whiskers. 'But even so, ...I can't help thinking...'

'Don't tell me?' Gran said. '...Whatever it is, does it have ginger hair and baggy shorts?'

'That's an outrageous, highly tenuous and arguably politically incorrect assertion Grantham. The chief super would be appalled.' Abraham let the statement linger. '...But I might just get you some big gold earrings and a crystal ball and set you up with a stall at the next police fête.'

Chapter Eight

Stubby fingers at the end of a thick forearm grabbed the bystander by his suit collar and hauled him out of the way. The arm bore a dragon tattoo, but it was the owner's voice that spat fire.

'Where the hell is he?' growled Mick with a hammering thump of a fist on the counter.

Matty Black rushed around to the other side of the counter, bumped Mick to one side and helped the small sinewy man to his feet. He nodded towards the bulky assailant then turned back to face the man. 'Do you want to press charges sir?'

Mick lurched forward and stuck his big square bristly head in the diminutive guy's face. 'Yeah, how about it? Go ahead, press charges. Let's see where that gets you!'

The man shook his head, wriggled out of Matty's grasp and quickly made a beeline for the exit, just squeezing through as someone else entered.

'That's one timewaster sorted for you sergeant. No need to thank me.' Mick pounded on the locked door that he knew from personal experience led to the cells. 'Now just let me through and we'll call it quits.'

'Still playing the comedian I see Braithwaite,' Matty grabbed Mick's shoulder and tugged him backwards. 'Take one foot through there and it'll be the last one you take this side of the bars for months.'

Mick turned sharply around, fist raised, 'Get your filthy hands off me or I swear to God...'

His sentence trailed off as the colossal figure of Davy swept over them. Davy eased Matty aside with one huge hand and palmed Mick's fist with the other.

'Now yer don't wanna to do that Mick,' Davy boomed. 'It could get yer in all sorts of bother. You toddle off back home. I've got this now. The pervert's mine.'

'Piss off Lilley,' Mick shoved Davy backwards. 'Amy may well be your niece, but she's *my* daughter. This is my business, and *I'm* dealing with it.'

Matty tried pulling Davy and Mick back but got all of an eighth of an inch. 'You haven't even said who you're looking for. Whoever it is they're probably long gone.'

Mick banged on the door and hollered, 'Are you there Blenkinsopp? What have you got to say for yourself? Or are you too much of a spineless creepy faggot to speak up?'

The clattering stopped momentarily as Mick and Davy strained their ears through soundwaves of seething snorts. In his cell, wedged at the corner of the bed between two cold walls, Mo tucked his knees yet further up to his chin. 'Yeah, I'm here.'

Resumption of hostilities was as instantaneous as it was riotous.

'When I get hold of you, I'll punch your teeth out right through your pimply arse!'

'And I'll rip off yer pervy prick and shove it where the sun don't shine!'

'And I'll wring your scrawny neck!'

'I'll eat yer alive!'

The heavy door rattled with each raucous threat and accompanying banging of fists.

Mick took off one of his artificial legs and battered the digital lock with it. He glowered at Matty with blazing eyes. 'Hey copper, open this thing right now. That filthy flasher's due a lesson he'll never forget and I'm not leaving till he gets it.'

'Me neither!' Boomed Davy weighing in with his steel-capped size 15s. He glowered at Matty, pointed at the door and barked, 'Open up! Open up!'

DS Black sighed and clicked on his radio.

'Erm, I think I might need a bit of backup.'

***

Debbie gasped as she opened the door to the heated, and by now cramped reception. The situation had escalated into a testosterone-charged mêlée-stroke-standoff with the incensed Mick and Davy separated from the door to the station's inner sanctums by a wary half a dozen bobbies.

'This way,' Debbie beckoned to the male solicitor and female interpreter who she was escorting to follow her around the back of the policemen to the exit.

'There's no escape Blenkinsopp,' Mick bellowed. 'We're going nowhere.'

Suddenly the solicitor, Usman Ghosh, a small, dark-skinned man in a black pinstriped suit, stopped. 'Blenkinsopp? That isn't *Mohammed* Blenkinsopp by any chance is it?'

'Yeah,' growled Mick. 'What of it?'

'Mr Blenkinsopp is an associate of mine,' Usman announced.

'Yeah well,' Mick inched his mouth up to the shorter man's eyeball and

snarled. 'You'll keep your nose out of it if you know what's good for you.'

'Are you threatening me?' Usman raised his voice, looked around and made sure to catch DS Black's eye.

'Damn right I am! And not just you!' Mick spun around and jabbed his leg at the door to the cells, Zulu spear style, 'Blenkinsopp, I'll snap your legs in so many places you'll have to stagger to Mecca like a spastic!'

While Mick was otherwise engaged, Usman moved quietly over to Matty. 'I'd like to see Mr Blenkinsopp. But, if the chief superintendent is still in his office, I'd like a word with him first.'

***

Ten minutes later the escalating commotion came to a sudden ceasefire as Abraham barged into reception.

'What's all this?' growled the DI.

'What's up with you Abraham?' Davy remarked. 'Your face is as white as that stripe in that poncy hair of yours. Yer look like yer've just seen a ghost. Or are yer frightened that Kell will dump you and come running back to me? Cos he will you know.'

'Want to try your luck Lilley?' Abraham snarled, formed a fist and darted towards the grinning Davy. 'Well come on then!'

'Mes petits-enfants, mes petits-enfants,' Gran chuckled as she squeezed into reception and accidentally-on-purpose bumped Abraham away from Davy and further into the throng of the melée. 'Calmez-vous s'il vous plaît.'

'That means *little kid* doesn't it? I'm no kid,' Mick puffed out his chest and nodded to the gaggle of officers sardined together. 'I'm more of a man than these pansy piglets will ever be.'

'Actually, *petits-enfants* means *grandchildren*,' explained DC Aftab Dehwar.

'Bien sûr, it's *grandchildren* Mighty Mick,' Gran pinched Mick's cheek and laughed. 'I am Gran after all. Now, if you'll excuse me, I'm dying for a wee.'

Abraham put his hands on his hips and snorted as Gran exchanged winks with Davy and slipped through the back of reception, 'Can someone tell me what the hell is going on?'

'I thought you were the famous, so-called *super detective*,' Mick jeered. 'Work it out for yourself.'

'*Super dick* more like,' Davy chuckled. 'We're here to kill that paedo flasher Blenkinsopp if you must know.'

'Except your goons refuse to let us through to his cell,' Mick added. 'And there is no sign of a release on the horizon yet either. Are you going to hand him over or what?'

'Should I hand Blenkinsopp over?' Abraham mused with a tap to a perfect white tooth. He raised his voice in the direction of the cells. 'Sure, take a seat, relax, give me twenty minutes or so and then you can do with him what you will.'

Davy inched up to Abraham, looked down at him with quizzical eyes, chuckled, and then kicked over a plastic chair and slowly eased into it. Mick followed suit and began the process of reinserting his leg.

'But if you *ever* come in here shouting the odds again Davy Lilley,' Abraham bent over and cautioned Davy virtually nose to nose, 'It'll be *me* killing *you*. Have you got that?'

Davy wafted away the lingering smell of vomit emanating from Abraham and blew him a kiss. 'I love it when yer angry Joe.'

'Don't say you haven't been warned Lilley,' Abraham said. 'You'd never see it coming, and I'd still come out smelling of roses.'

'Yeah, yeah super-prick, whatever you say. Just hand over the pervert and we'll be on our way.'

***

'Are you serious?' Gran grabbed Abraham by the elbow as he slipped through to the station's inner sanctums. 'Mick and Davy will rip him apart.'

'Do you want to catch this murderer Grantham?' snapped Abraham. 'As well as get to the bottom of what is potentially a deadly terrorist plot?'

Rhetorical question or not, Gran could do little other than shrug her petite shoulders and mutter, 'Of course patron.'

'Well then,' Abraham hissed. 'Can you think of a better way to loosen Blenkinsopp's vocal chords?'

'Essentially you mean protection in return for information, don't you?'

Abraham winked.

'But what if Blenkinsopp doesn't play ball?' Gran stared. 'You'll throw him to the lions?'

Abraham polished off his shrug with a smirk.

'His choice.'

***

'I saw you winking at Lilley by the way,' said Abraham evenly.

'Nothing gets past you patron,' Gran took off her glasses, wiped them and read a message on her phone.

'Yes, and don't you forget it,' Abraham looked his DS up and down. 'So, what's that all about?'

'Oh, just a little understanding we've come to,' smiled Gran.

'Understanding?' Abraham knotted his brow. 'He's not the one you get your weed from is it?'

'I'm sure I don't know what you mean detective inspector,' chuckled Gran. 'Anyway, I thought the main reason you wanted me on your team was because I got results.'

'Yes. Well, that and your knack for getting crims to come quietly,' acknowledged Abraham. 'But I'm beginning to feel like I've been sold a dud.'

'Intriguing inspector,' enthused Gran. 'Please do elaborate.'

'I know you only transferred here three months or so ago, but really Grantham, your touchy-feely approach and lackadaisical methods are sloppy and slapdash,' chided Abraham. 'That type of thing may have worked in Cornwall and wherever the hell you were in France before that. Euro Disney probably. But I'll tell you this for free, you won't get very far up here unless you come down hard on the lowlifes and show them who's boss.'

‘Thank you for the advice patron,’ Gran rubbed her chin and smiled. ‘By the way, I’ve just had a text – a sure-fire tipoff about that armed robber you’ve been after for the best part of the year.’

‘What? the guy who whacked that pregnant store assistant with the butt of his shotgun?’ gasped Abraham. ‘The word was he’d legged it to Cyprus.’

‘Well, I’ve got an address for him in Hull,’ said Gran. ‘I’ll pass it on to Humberside Police.’

‘Hang on. You still haven’t said how come Lilley was winking at you?’ Abraham scratched his head. ‘He isn’t one of your informers is he?’

‘Well, I’m just a touchy-feely slapdash little old lady. I don’t have your expertise for extracting intel like a DI dentist,’ said Gran. ‘But I do have a knack of getting on with folk – whoever they may be.’

‘I hope for your sake you haven’t been offering to do any favours or look the other way for the likes of Lilley,’ scowled Abraham. ‘Because if you have, I swear to God...’

‘Patron, patron...’ Gran pulled a crooked smile and shook her curly head. ‘I’ve just got a little game going with Davy and a few others. That’s all. Just a few pints, some laughs and the odd curry. Cops and robbers with a couple of tiny twists.’

‘Such as?’

‘Such as a promise to come quietly if I ever catch them red-handed said Gran. ‘And the occasional tipoff when a cad crim oversteps the mark.’

‘What’s in it for them?’

‘Nothing.’

‘There must be something. What’s their *tiny twist*?’

‘Ha. It’ll never happen, but I might have given the impression that I could possibly let something slip if I ever got drunk enough.’

‘Just what the hell have you been telling them?’ snarled Abraham.

‘Nothing,’ smiled Gran. She extracted a hip flask from her handbag. ‘Here, have a swig of this.’

Abraham took a little sniff and immediately recoiled gurning.

‘It’s called *la gnôle* and is 70% proof,’ Gran took a big swig as if it were pop and chuckled. ‘I was weaned on the stuff.’

‘I’ve just had a thought,’ a grin spread across Abraham’s face. ‘When I release Blenkinsopp, Lilley will surely batter him, and if he’s true to his word he’ll then have to hold his hands up and let you cuff him.’

‘I guess,’ Gran played with an earlobe. ‘Unless I dissuade him. I was going to suggest having a word...’

‘You’ll do no such thing,’ Abraham’s eyes sparked. ‘And that’s an order!’

***

Mo held his breath at the sound of footsteps and his cell door lock scraping.

‘Sir,’ clicking heels accompanied the female’s voice down the corridor. ‘The chief super would like a word.’

‘Tell him I’ll be up to see him later. I’m just about to release this prisoner – there are people very eager to see him.’

Mo recognised Abraham’s voice instantaneously. A lump formed in his throat.

A clunk echoed down the corridor as the key did its magic. Abraham yanked the handle only for the young PC to shove the door back shut.

‘The chief super did say that I was to stress *immediately* sir.’

The few seconds listening to Abraham’s heavy snorts seemed like an eternity to Mo before the DI stormed back up the corridor seething, ‘Don’t get too comfy Blenkinsopp, you’ll be reunited with your welcoming party soon ...*real* soon.’

***

Fifteen minutes later Mo held his breath again as his cell door clunked open.

'Usman,' Mo sprung off the bunk. 'What are you doing here?'

'I was already here in my capacity as a solicitor,' Usman took Mo's clammy hand in both of his and shook it firmly. 'But when I heard those thugs threatening you, I thought I'd see if there was anything I could do to help.'

'I suppose you also heard Abraham too then,' Mo's dry voice was higher pitched than some other teenagers. 'He's literally invited Davy Lilley and that other guy, whoever he is, to beat me to a pulp.'

'That's not going to happen,' said Usman. 'The other man is one Mick Braithwaite, the father of the girl at the park. Davy Lilley is...'

'Her uncle,' Mo said sitting up. 'I'm already familiar with him.'

'Anyway, I've had a word with the chief superintendent on your behalf. 'Apparently, it had already been established that you're not the flasher, and they were just waiting for DI Abraham to come back to sanction your release,' said Usman. 'Conscious of the risk of media fallout when dealing with an amputee war hero, the chief superintendent had already given officers instructions to keep Braithwaite and Lilley away from you while simultaneously not aggravating them.'

'So why didn't Abraham tell them that I wasn't the flasher?' seethed Mo. 'He deliberately kept that quiet, fully aware of the consequences.'

'Those were my thoughts exactly,' concurred Usman. 'I said as much to the chief superintendent who assured me most categorically that DI Abraham will *clear up any confusion*.'

***

It took another hour or so before Mo was finally released, but when he stepped back through to reception it was empty, save for Matty Black and Joe Abraham.

Mo, accompanied by Usman, stood in front of Abraham and looked directly into his eyes.

'I'm waiting...'

'Waiting for what?'

'My apology - for wrongful arrest, false imprisonment and your blundering incompetence,' said Mo unblinking. 'In your own time, if you please detective inspector.'

'I don't apologise to the likes of scum toe-rags such as you!' Abraham laughed as he opened the door. 'Go on scram!'

Mo remained statuesque apart from a little tut, slight shake of the head and a hint of a smile.'

'Go on, on your way,' Abraham pushed the door another inch. 'Before I change my mind.'

Mo swivelled on his heels and plonked himself down on a plastic chair. 'I may as well make myself comfy while I wait DI.'

'Wait? For what?'

'Whichever comes first,' Mo leaned back in the chair, stretched his legs out and placed one ankle snugly over the other. 'My apology or the chief super.'

***

The exchange of glances started pretty instantaneously. Between Abraham and Matty, Matty and Usman and Abraham and Usman. As his eyes were closed the whole time, Mo missed all of this. Similarly, he didn't witness the rapid transformation of Abraham's face to poker red either. As such, he wouldn't have been able to try to judge if the dramatic facial metamorphosis was due to something like embarrassment, or rage for example. That said, when it finally arrived, the volume and acrid tone of Abraham's proclamation gave that little game away anyway.

'I apologise for any confusion!' Abraham unfurled his snarl, just the taddiest of tads. '...Mr Blenkinsopp.'

'Tch, call that an apology?' Mo slowly rose to his feet. 'It's hardly heartfelt.'

'It's as good as you're going to get!' Abraham spat his chewing gum in the bin and slammed the door wide open. 'Besides, I'm sure our paths will cross again soon. Now if you don't mind, I have got *other* criminals to catch.'

Mo tutted again as he exited the station – glancing down the street before stepping onto the pavement.

***

'How can you even work like that?'

Aftab tutted and nudged a pencil a tad to the left so it perfectly aligned with his neat jotter as Gran rummaged through the jumble of nick-nacks on her desk. It took a couple of minutes, but she finally copied something from her computer screen onto a scrap of paper and put it face-down on Aftab's desk.

'You don't have a girlfriend, do you?'

'Er... what makes you think that?' Aftab nudged his pencil some more.

'Basic deduction,' Gran tickled Aftab's little triangular moustache, ran a finger through his Brylcreem-greased hair and felt the heat off his cheeks with the back of her hand. 'But there's no accounting for taste, and I've an inkling that you may have an admirer.'

'Me? Who?' Aftab didn't need to feel his own cheeks to check if they were burning.

'The interpreter in reception just now,' winked Gran. 'I noticed her eyeing you.'

Aftab stuffed the bit of paper in his pocket and headed towards the corridor. 'I'm er... just off to the gents.'

'Un petit conseil de femme mon brave,' Gran called after him. 'Some feminine advice... If you do ever arrange to meet her, maybe invest in a razor and some shampoo first.'

***

Gran shuddered as the CID office door slammed and her desk monitor shook. She swivelled in her chair and clocked the DI's volcanic eyes, 'I take it you've released Blenkinsopp then?'

'I had no choice,' Abraham fumed.

'Did you tell the chief super that you wanted to question Blenkinsopp about the murder – *all casual like?*'

'Of course!' Abraham snapped. 'I even indicated how things point to Blenkinsopp.'

'Like returning to the scene of the crime, the possible religious link and Blenkinsopp possibly being up to no good with the imam and his righthand man.'

'Yes, but in addition to reminding me of *community tensions*, the chief super just rattled on about *a lack of any real evidence.* He pretty much warned me off aggravating Blenkinsopp.'

'Ah,' Gran's crinkled brow deepened. 'Is this because it transpires that Blenkinsopp is chummy with that hotshot lawyer Ghosh?'

'It'll be a factor. ...well, possibly,' Abraham snorted. 'Although he also hinted at an awareness of *history.*'

'Oh, by that I take it he means *your history* with Blenkinsopp,' Gran said. 'I've heard about that. So, are you going to lay off him then?'

Abraham ran his fingers through his collar-length swept-back hair. 'For now, I guess. ...But if Blenkinsopp drops his guard and I get even a whiff of his involvement in today's murder - or anything else for that matter - then I swear to God, it's him who'll be history.'

Chapter Nine

Usman parked his Jaguar outside Saboor's bungalow, 'Are you sure here is fine for you? I can take you all the way home.'

'No thanks,' Mo already had a foot on the kerb. 'Appreciate the thought, and your help though. Are you sure I can't give you any money?'

'Certainly not, it's what any friend would do,' smiled Usman. 'If you would like to come to dinner with Fatima, the girls and I one evening then that would be more than payment enough.'

'Thanks again,' Mo placed his palms together and bowed his head. 'I'll catch you down at the mosque again soon.'

***

'Am I glad to see you!' Mo and Saboor said almost in unison.

'I was really worried about yer,' Saboor tapped one of his sticks behind Mo and eagerly steered him indoors. 'Davy Lilley didnae come after yer did he?'

'Well, yes. But not for denting his car,' Mo sighed. 'This time it was for supposedly flashing in front of his niece.'

'What?' Saboor's pearly teeth formed an eclipse of sorts amid his full black beard as he gaped.

'Total misunderstanding of course,' Mo said. 'But par for the course given calamitous recent events.'

Saboor ushered Mo into the living room. 'Wannae elaborate further?'

'Actually, yes,' Mo exhaled heavily. 'I was kinda hoping that I could share something heavy with you.'

Saboor eased his cuddly 15 stone, 5'10" frame onto the sofa, 'Shoot!'

'I don't think you quite understand,' Mo said. 'This is really heavy stuff. The kind of thing you don't want to hear, and you can't un-hear if you do. I really need you to consider that in all seriousness before I go any further.'

Saboor sat up ramrod straight and eyed Mo. 'Mohammed, yer seriously scaring me now. Whatever it is *spill*.'

Mo shuffled to the kitchen. 'I think I could use a drink.' He gulped down some water then splashed the back of his neck. Some hairs on the back of Saboor's neck pricked up too. He shifted his carcass uneasily about the sofa. If Mo was stalling about saying his piece, then Saboor didn't appear in any real rush to hear it.

'You know that thing I said was important?' Mo eventually muttered.

'Aye, but it was pretty hazy, 'Saboor said. 'Something about a nightmare, losing yer memory and thinking yer were being followed. ...Oh aye, and something possibly iffy about the park.'

'Yeah well, I wasn't really sure if it was really important or just something I've been tearing myself into pieces over for nothing,' Mo continued. 'I mean, dreams and nightmares are make-believe right?'

'I guess.'

'It's just that the nightmare I was referring to earlier isn't the only one I've had. There was one a few nights ago, and now I've just had another in my police cell,' Mo elaborated. 'And they're so vivid, so lifelike, that I kind of think they've just *got* to be true.'

'Oh? And?'

'And...' Mo hesitated. 'If there *is* any truth in them then it scares the hell out of me!'

The next few moments passed in silence, save from two sets of heavy breathing and the sound of Saboor wiping his sticky palms on his jeans.

Mo closed his eyes.

'I'm just going to come out with it,' he suddenly opened his eyes and locked them onto Saboor. 'If you subsequently want to tell the police I'll understand. Hell, I'll come with you! But for now, I just need to unload.'

Saboor held his breath and gave the slightest of nods.

'Firstly, Mo drew an invisible number one with his finger. 'The clothes I had on last night have disappeared - like *whoosh* gone! Secondly, I've no explanation for that or much else besides. Maybe that's down to booze-induced loss of memory, but it could also be my mind blocking out something horrific – like some kind of cerebral self-preservation mechanism. Thirdly, I woke up this morning with a bump on my bonce, cuts on my arms as well as a chilling knot of dread in my stomach. And oh, yeah, there was also some blood on your scissors before I cleaned them and returned them to you.'

'Is that yer dream?' Saboor asked.

'No, that's the reality,' the colour drained from Mo's battered face. 'The dreams are even worse!'

More hairs sprung up on the back of Saboor's neck. 'What dreams Mo?'

'Well, the first one involves a jihadi sword attack, the next one a chilling scream in the dark...,' Mo swallowed hard. 'And today I dreamt that I was lying on top of a naked headless lady in the park.'

Saboor breathed a sigh of relief and laughed. 'Yer dimwit Mo, that's just a dream!'

Mo shook his pale, deadpan head from side to side.

'I might have just about bought that myself,' he mumbled. 'If there wasn't mud on my knees and loads of blood all over my hands, face and body when I woke up today.'

Saboor's gape started to reform.

'And if that's not all,' Mo continued. 'I just remembered something on the drive over here.'

'D... dare I even ask?'

'I've...,' a lump formed in Mo's throat. 'I've somehow managed to misplace a bloody great sword.'

***

As Saboor silently hobbled around the back of the sofa Mo sat stock-still - sullen eyes in sunken sockets, staring and seemingly stuck in some chilling personal abyss. Saboor reached out a hand and almost touched Mo's shoulder.

Almost.

Saboor looked over at his phone on the table. Three, four, five seconds. He tried to loosen his shirt collar but the button proved too stubborn. He ripped the damn thing off. Slowly he inched over. He palmed the phone with a clammy hand then chanced a glance at the scissors. The ones that Mo had taken without consent and had bloodied by some means or other.

'How's it even possible that yer got blood on ma scissors Mo?' asked Saboor. 'I use scissors every day in ma computer shop, but I've never cut myself wae 'em – or anyone else fae that matter.'

Immobile, Mo half whispered, half mumbled, 'Dunno.'

Saboor hit the first nine.

'Yer say yer were covered in blood too, but also that yer mind could be trying to protect itself by blocking stuff out,' Saboor cogitated. 'Could yer have deliberately hidden or dumped yer clothes, but yer mind is blocking that out too?'

'Maybe,' Mo shrugged. He reached for the TV remote and punched a button.

Saboor hit the second nine.

The TV flickered into life, firing rays of red and beams of blue across the gloomy room like high-tech ectoplasm. Mo recognised DI Abraham at once, despite the posse of microphones obscuring his face. The self-styled *super-detective* enjoyed celebrity status for an officer of the law around these parts, but even if Abraham wasn't as familiar to Saboor as he was to Mo, then the police station in the background surely was, and especially with Saboor being a recent victim of a hit-and-run. That said, celebrity policeman and familiar building notwithstanding, it was the news flash headline that grabbed all the attention.

'Woman's body found decapitated in park.'

Saboor hit the final nine.

Chapter Ten

'Emergency services. What service do you require?'

'Emergency services. What service do you require? ...Caller, are you there caller?'

Mo sighed, his light blue eyes locked on to the caller's big brown ones. 'I think the word you're looking for Saboor is *police.*'

'Er ...,' Saboor eventually mustered, 'Sorry, wrong number.' The phone fumbled out of his trembling hand and bounced over to Mo who picked it up.

'Wrong number?' Mo knotted his eyebrows. 'Does that mean that you think I'm innocent?'

'No,' Saboor swallowed. 'I daenae know what tae think.'

'I'll do it myself then,' Mo tapped 999.

'Police please.'

***

It was a toss-up as to what surprised Mo the most – Saboor snatching the phone and playing down the call to the operator as a tipsy mistake, or Saboor's, 'I wouldnae put a lot of things past yer ...but murder? Yer *probably* daenae have it in yer' utterance. In most other contexts *'daenae have it in yer'* could have been construed as a slight, a slur, a slap in the face. But in this case, Mo could have taken it as vindication, a vote of confidence or a conviction of innocence.

He could have done...if only he was able to shake the thought that Saboor was loyal, yes, a good friend, yes, trusting yes, but foolish and naïve– absolutely - and in spades.

Chapter Eleven

The forecast was for bright spells and just a slight breeze. Things were looking up. Kids who had been lethargically dragging their heels for weeks suddenly had extra springs in their step and more mischief in their shenanigans as they noisily made their way to school.

'Goal!' Cried a matchstick lad with hanging out shirttails as the quarter-full coke can booted up into the air and clunked on Mo's bonce.

'Whoops, er... soz,' the thirteen-year-old cast sniggered.

Mo didn't even register the can's impact until some of the fizzy brown liquid dribbled to his lips. It was only then that he stopped, looked around and took in his surroundings. Despite the sunshine Mo suddenly found himself shivering. He blew into his hands, scratched the damp sticky bump on his head and tried to fathom things.

Had he really been walking all night? He stared at his watch. The numbers *8:32*, even once deciphered, did nothing to explain what he had been doing over the previous 10 hours or so. He sneezed, and it suddenly dawned on him that it was Monday morning, and he was due to start work, a mile and a half away, in twenty-eight minutes' time.

Work. It was the least of his worries. He knew that much.

An image of the news clip of the park horror scene replayed across his mind for the umpteenth time. It and visions of his nightmare seemed to be on some cruel auto-loop. In the last ten hours he hadn't given even a fraction of a second's thought to work. Legging it, maybe. Handing himself in, definitely. But work? Hell no!

As he prodded the latest bump on his head a police car rolled to a halt at the traffic lights. The driver briefly glanced in Mo's direction. Mo spun on his heels and sharp headed away. Whether his head commanded his feet to stop, or whether they acted independently, after just a few short steps he swivelled around, took a deep breath and strode towards the squad car.

***

As he approached Mo sensed the driver looking at him, *studying* him in the mirror. Her lips jabbered. Possibly just a few words to her colleague in the passenger's seat, but more likely a response to an APB with Mo's name on it.

To Mo's surprise though, when the lights changed to green the car simply accelerated away.

Maybe they weren't hunting him after all.

Or at least not just yet.

Mo nibbled his nails while a niggle or two nudged a neuron or three. Had someone really been spying on him previously? And if so, then why? He scanned around and clocked a twenty-something North African looking guy seemingly avert his eyes. Had he been watching Mo just now? Or before? There was something vaguely familiar about the guy. Had he been at the party? Mo rubbed his bumfluff whiskers and sighed. He hadn't the foggiest. He instead turned his attention to other puzzles - some numbers that kept popping in and out of his conscious - but he couldn't work out why. Also, he only had a vague recollection of the sword, but he was now sure that he'd had one at some point. If so, where was it now? And more to the point, what the hell had he done with it?

He set off walking again. Destination and destiny very much unknown.

***

Twenty minutes or so later the *destination* half of puzzle unfolded as somehow he found himself rubbing his sore calves bang in front of *Shahzad's Halal Butcher's* shop. Surprised and angry with himself, he turned straight back around and marched decidedly away.

Where to?

Somewhat less decidedly, Mo eased up, then stopped dead in his tracks.

He rubbed his tired eyes and snorted.

To hell with it! He swivelled, gathered pace and headbutted his way through the goddamned door.

Chapter Twelve

A mile or so away in the bowels of a red brick building, another door banged on its hinges – this time booted open, Kung-Fu style by a shiny black shoe. Its owner galumphed to a table, flung down a couple of glossy prints, then stood transfixed by the words and blown-up photographs on the whiteboard - oblivious to the shrugs and quizzical glances being exchanged behind him.

'I'm going to have this scum!' DI Abraham abruptly decreed with a snappish swivel and a sudden fling of the whiteboard eraser.

Debbie ducked sharply as the eraser zipped just past an ear.

Abraham fleetingly raised conciliatory hand, like he was shooing away a fly. He kicked a box of marker pens into the air. 'No one does this on my patch!'

Debbie mumbled to Kell, 'Is he always like this?'

'Do you mean when there is a murder?' Kell stooped to gather some of the pens. 'Or just in general?'

'Well, I did mean when there was a murder,' Debbie patted her ruffled hair. 'But, thinking about it, what happens if you leaving the toilet seat up at his place?'

Kell raised his palms and the pens clattered to the floor again. He gaped in mock shock horror. 'Firing squad at dawn!'

Debbie made a gun with her finger and pointed it at Kell. 'Bang!'

'Or on my watch!' Abraham booted the table over, sending the glossy prints spinning.

'Looks like the DI's flipped, not just the table,' whispered Debbie.

‘Seriously though,’ Kell rasped his stubble. ‘Sure, he has a temper - we’ve all seen that - but I’ve never seen him quite like this bef...’ Kell’s eyes trained on one of the prints looping the loop. ‘Is that a picture of Mo? Surely he’s not a suspect?’

‘Oh heck. I think it’s the pic we took of Mo a few months ago when the DI had him in for one of his line-ups,’ said Debbie. ‘Mo did say that he thought your dad would come gunning for him.’

‘For murder?’

‘It sounds mad I know,’ Debbie continued. ‘And especially if it’s just because Mo bit him when he was fourteen.’

‘I doubt it’s just that Debbie, but I still don’t know why the DI is taking it so...’ Kell’s words trailed off as he watched Abraham gather up the prints, hesitate, pocket Mo’s picture, then pin the other one to the board.

‘*So...?*’ Debbie prompted Kell to finish his sentence, then followed his gaze as Abraham stepped to the side, revealing the latest picture on the board. The one depicting a small, thin, smiling blond.

‘...personally.’ Kell gulped as he finished his sentence. He turned to Debbie. ‘Oh my God.’

***

In addition to a few headlines, a shot of the bloated head that had been fished out of the pond, and pictures of the crime scene, the whiteboard housed photographs of distinguishing marks, close-ups of cuts, and the various numbers found on the body.

Abraham cleared his throat, but it still caught as he spoke. He tapped the latest picture with his pointer. The tap resonated despite the crowd in the confined space.

‘I can save you the job of identifying the victim ladies and gentlemen,’ he surreptitiously wiped an eye. ‘Alexandra Hobbs, a forty-one-year-old woman, originally from the area, was an associate of mine.’

Detective Sergeant Audrey Melrose nudged Gran and pulled a crooked smile, '*Associate*?'

'By originally from the area, do you mean that she's been living away?' asked Debbie.

'Yes, but she still has her council flat in town and apparently has been back this last week or two.' Abraham looked towards Audrey.

'That's right,' Audrey continued. 'I called the most recently used numbers on her phone. Her friend Hazel Bond was with her last night and is coming over to give a statement. I've also tried a certain Dean Downing several times, but without luck. Hazel says he was Alex's boyfriend and they've been living together in Aberdeen for a few years. She also mentioned that before Dean, Alex's previous ex is none other than Mick Braithwaite. I'm sure we're all familiar with him.'

'Quite,' snorted Abraham. 'We'll need a word with him too.'

'That'll be fun,' Audrey remarked.

'Quite,' Abraham echoed.

He turned back to the whiteboard. 'As you know, Ms Hobbs' decapitated body was discovered in Ward Jackson Park yesterday morning, and her head was discovered in the pond later in the afternoon. Time of death has been confirmed as between 1.30 and 3 am. It looks like she took a non-fatal bang to the head at some point, but the actual cause of death is decapitation by means of a very sharp object.'

'Is there any news on the weapon?' interjected Kell.

Gran swivelled in her chair to face Kell, 'Possibly a sword.'

'We don't know that,' snapped Abraham. 'It's a possibility, but we need to keep an open mind. The pathologist also indicated the possibility of a second weapon.'

Gran raised an eyebrow. 'What second weapon? That's news to me.'

'There are potentially some inconsistencies with the cuts,' Abraham explained. 'The primary laceration was long and clean, but there is also some indication of secondary cuts. Possibly with a different object.'

'What, like a blunt knife or dagger?' asked Debbie.

'Not blunt,' Abraham shook his head. 'Whatever it was it was very sharp, although possibly not the same blade as the one that delivered the fatal blow.'

'So, like a sharp knife or dagger?' Debbie emphasised her point with a stabbing motion.

'Possibly a knife,' said Abraham. 'We are not ruling anything out at this stage, including the possibility that the cuts could have been made with another side or section of the same object. Essentially, we could be looking for one or possibly two murder weapons.'

'What about the beheading angle?' quizzed DC Aftab Dehwar. 'I can guess what most of you are thinking, but you don't need to spare me on the politically correct front, just because I'm the only Muslim in CID at the station.'

'Wouldn't dream of it Dehwar you big brown dog-faced turd,' Abraham cut a menacing smile. 'I was coming to just that, but thank you for your candid insight.'

Dehwar raised a finger in recognition but his perplexed expression suggested that he was unsure of whether he had just been dealt an insult or a compliment.

'I'm sure we've all seen footage of the likes of Islamic State, read about appalling atrocities and are all too aware of the jihadi threat facing our green and pleasant land and its citizens therein…'

Debbie turned to Kell and mouthed, '*citizens therein*?'

'And believe me Dehwar,' Abraham glowered at the young DC. 'If I find out that Ms Hobbs' murder was down to an Islamic crackpot, I'll come down on him like a ton of brick Mecca-facing shithouses.'

Aftab shuffled uncomfortably in his seat and fanned the top of his chest with his open-collared shirt. His neighbour, Jerzy Masur, a Polish-descent recent transfer from Penrith shot him a shake of the head and a toothy snigger.

'But, even so,' Abraham addressed the room. 'We still need to keep an open mind. The murder could have no religious connotations at all, and even if it does, it could just as well be a born-again Christian fanatic than an Islamic fundamentalist.'

Gran raised an eyebrow but said nothing.

Debbie raised a hand. 'Sir, you said '*him.*' Are you saying that the murderer is a man?'

DI Abraham cleared his throat. 'Thank you, Harrison, I stand corrected. The murderer could be female, we shouldn't rule anything out.'

Debbie allowed herself the briefest of smiles and her blushing cheeks lingered a tad.

'It's just that pathologist indicated that the fatal blow was delivered with some force,' Abraham elaborated. 'And she suggested that the force may be more consistent with that of a man, but as you say it could still be a woman.'

'Anything else?' Gran asked.

'Judging by the angle, the fatal blow was horizontally behind, or vertically above the neck.'

'Meaning?' asked Debbie

'Meaning Harrison, that either the assailant's swing was at neck height, making him – or *her* – significantly taller than Ms Hobbs, or...' Abraham sipped some water. 'Or, he - or she - delivered the blow from directly above Ms Hobbs as she looked downward.'

'You mean like she was forced to kneel down at the killer's feet?' said Aftab. 'Like a ritual jihadi killing.'

Abraham took another lingering sip then set the cup back down.

'That's one possibility we need to seriously consider, yes.'

'Do we have anyone in the frame yet?' asked Aftab.

'The patron thinks Blenkinsopp and a couple of men from the mosque might be involved,' said Gran. 'Blenkinsopp was hanging around the park around the time the body was discovered, and the imam and his sidekick have been acting a bit suspiciously.'

'Don't put words into my mouth Grantham,' DI Abraham shot Gran an icy bolt of double-barrelled iris cobalt. 'I might have mentioned a simple observation out loud about Blenkinsopp and co, but this is a murder investigation, not a garden convention or a gossip column. We can't just jump to conclusions, and we need to do everything by the book. If you have any intel on any person or persons relating to the murder of Ms Hobbs, then I'll be the first in line to hear it. But I'm not interested in half-baked hunches or hedgerow hearsay.'

Gran stared open-mouthed.

'And especially not in the current highly-sensitive political climate,' Abraham continued. 'The chief super has already been bending my ear about that. We need real evidence not potentially misleading guesstimates.'

Gran raised an eyebrow, but nodded.

'Look, I'm not saying that there isn't an Islamic angle. There may well be,' Abraham ran a hand through his hair. 'It's just that if we are going to nail this bastard then we need to do the job properly, leave no stone unturned, gather evidence and cover our arses by doing everything by the book.'

Abraham waited a couple of seconds for a reaction, and when he didn't receive one, he whacked his pointer like a headmaster's cane between the upturned table's legs. 'Got it?'

The assembled officers responded with a mixture of mumbles and crisp 'sir' replies.

'As you will note, ladies and gentlemen,' Abraham tapped on various photographs. 'We have five sets of numbers written in blood on the body.

58 on the left knee, 14 on the left inner thigh, 12 on the right inner thigh, 98 near the left breast and 82 at the base of the severed neck.

'Do you have any thoughts on this sir?' asked Aftab.

Abraham tightened his fist and ground a couple of incisors together. 'Other than we are obviously dealing with a sicko Dehwar, it is unclear at this time what the numbers signify – if indeed, they do signify anything at all.'

'Are you saying they don't?'

'No, I'm saying that some nutcase may be deliberately leading us a merry dance with some random numbers, to put us off the scent or even just for the hell of it.'

Dehwar brushed some fluff from his corduroy trousers and crossed a knee. At 6 foot 3 his legs jutted out further than most of the other seated officers. 'But do you think that is likely?'

'It's a possibility, but for what it's worth, I do suspect that the numbers are significant. I don't know how – *yet* – but in the meantime, it tells us something about the killer, that he...' Abraham caught Debbie's eye. 'Or *she*, is one cocky bastard. Whoever it is, he is – and for the sake of convenience I'm using the royal '*he*' from now on Harrison – whoever he is, then he is not only a depraved sadistic killer, but he is taking pleasure in taunting us.'

'So, we're looking for a deranged arrogant psychopath with attitude,' Gran chipped in.

'*Deranged* is one way of looking at it,' said Abraham. 'Another interpretation is that we are looking for someone of high intellect. A confident sod who thinks they are too clever to be caught.'

'Either way,' Gran said. 'Sooner or later, he'll slip up.'

'That's just the thing,' Abraham warned. 'It needs to be sooner – PDQ sooner. We don't want this escalating into a spate of serial killings.'

'But what are the odds of that?' asked Aftab.

'Oh,' Abraham scrunched up his eyes and gave his face a rough rub. 'I'd say somewhere between 99 and 100 percent.'

***

'What about a telephone number?' offered Aftab. 'The figures on the body could be a jumbled-up landline.'

'Not enough digits,' Abraham raised eight fingers. 'There are only ten numbers, not eleven.'

'What about on the head?' asked Aftab.

'No,' Abraham shook his own nut. 'There were no numbers on the head.'

'It could be a landline or mobile number abroad,' Aftab continued. 'In some countries telephone numbers only have eight digits. Also, in some countries people say the numbers in pairs, such as 14, 16 etc.'

'Yes, I'm aware of that Dehwar,' Abraham said. 'The fact that the numbers are in pairs could be a clue, or it could be just that one long number that has been broken up. As things stand, we just don't know. Yes, it could relate to a phone number, but equally it could indicate a time or date, birthdays, numbers in books, ordnance survey references, national insurance numbers, house numbers, email addresses, an ISPN, bank accounts, postcodes, TV channels, flight numbers, bus routes, roads, passports, an order from Amazon and so on and so forth. Effectively, it's the digital age, and numbers are everywhere. It could be like finding a needle in a haystack the size of K2.'

Aftab exhaled heavily and it made a slight whistling sound.

'That said,' Abraham continued. 'My view is that the killer has deliberately given us a clue – perhaps one that he arrogantly doesn't believe will lead us back to him – but a clue, nonetheless. So, haystack or not we need to get stuck in and try to work out the numbers angle. Do I have a volunteer for this?'

A few arms shot up. Some faster than others. Abraham scanned the room. 'Thank you, DS Melrose. And if you need some extra help, feel free to haul in Kell in.'

'Sir,' Melrose responded crisply and immediately.

'Sir,' Kell echoed, even though his hand hadn't been one of those raised.

'In the meantime,' Abraham rallied. 'We need to try to quickly ascertain Ms Hobbs' movements from Saturday evening into the early hours of Sunday morning.'

'Erm,' Kell coughed. His bicep bulged as he bent his arm to cover his mouth. 'I think I might be able to help on that score.'

All eyes turned towards him.

'And especially since I must be one of the last people to have seen her alive.'

***

'So where was this and at what time?' asked Abraham.

'It was at Saboor Patel's party. If you remember I called you from there that night and mentioned an older woman called Alex offering me a romp in the park. It was roughly around the time she left - 11.30-ish I'd say,' said Kell. 'I was pretty much the last person she spoke to before she left.'

'That makes you a possible suspect Kell,' replied Abraham. 'Don't take this personally, but I hope you have an alibi.'

'Well, I dare say I have,' Kell leaned back in his chair, locked his arms behind his head and puffed out burly pecs. 'And I don't take it personally at all. I'm all for justice, and the guilty - whoever they are related to - getting their fair dues. But a certain Natalie, and the host, Saboor Patel, should be able to verify that I was otherwise engaged all night. By all means check it out.'

'Harrison, check out the alibi please,' ordered Abraham.

Debbie turned to Kell and shot him a wry smile and shake of the head.

'Dirty stop-out.'

Kell replied with a wink.

'You say that you were *one* of the last people to speak to her,' Abraham probed. 'Who was the last person.'

'Oh, I wouldn't really call it speaking,' Kell twisted in his seat, pectorals still pert and pronounced. 'It's just that Mo said something to her before she left – but I doubt she even heard it above the music and all that.'

'Mo?' Abraham exclaimed. 'Mo Blenkinsopp?'

'Yes,' said Kell. 'But it was *me* who Alex was interested in, she hardly gave Mo the time of day. I don't think he took much notice of her.'

Debbie squinted at the whiteboard, scratched her head and wandered over to it, crossing Abraham as he marched over to Kell.

'Blenkinsopp,' repeated Abraham with igniting eyes, 'What did he say?'

'I'm not sure exactly, probably nothing much.'

Abraham sat down on the seat recently vacated by Debbie. 'Think man.'

'Er,' Kell rubbed a couple of fingers back and forth across his forehead. 'I think it was something like *'don't lose your head'*.

'What?' Abraham shot to his feet and maxed the volume. 'Blenkinsopp warns Alex not to lose her head then just hours later she bloody well loses it! Don't you think that's highly relevant?'

'But he probably just said it to calm her down. After all she was pretty pissed off. She'd just suffered a hurtful rejection from er... well me actually.' Kell ran his hand through his dark floppy mane then scratched along the closely cropped bit above one of his ears. 'Besides, I saw him leave *after* her. I was at a window. Alex was just putting her phone back in her pocket when I looked out, she then turned right, so in the direction of Ward Jackson Park, whereas Mo turned left and went the other way.'

'And were you looking out of the said window all night long?' asked Abraham. 'On some sort of party sentry duty?'

'Or a stag party?' Jerzy added with wry smile.

'Well no. I guess wasn't at the window for that long.' Kell continued. 'But I was there for at least a minute or two around the time that Mo left. I wasn't counting.'

'So, Blenkinsopp could have in fact turned around and walked back in the other direction – in the same direction as Alex – and you wouldn't have noticed.'

'I guess not,' Kell shrugged. 'But like I say, he didn't seem to take that much notice of her.'

'Sir,' Debbie rapped the whiteboard with her knuckles. 'Sorry to interrupt, but I've been looking more closely at this photo of Ms Hobbs that you've just pinned up. I think I've seen her somewhere before.'

'And where is that Harrison?' Abraham's voice remained loud and agitated.

'You're not going to believe this,' Debbie said. 'But you know you asked me to check Mo's phone?'

Abraham nodded.

'Well, there was only one solitary picture in his personal photo library, and it was of this exact same person – the victim.'

***

'Grantham, get a move on,' Abraham almost knocked over Kell as he barged through the chairs in his haste to get to the exit. 'Blenkinsopp still lives in Kathleen Street doesn't he?'

Kell steadied himself by grabbing hold of Abraham's thigh. 'Yes, but he won't be there now.'

'What? Okay clever clogs, if you think you know where he is then get your skates on, you're coming with me.' Abraham hauled Kell to his feet with a sharp tug. 'Grantham stand down.'

***

'Come on Kell, shift your arse,' Abraham honked the horn and revved the engine. 'What are you playing at?'

Kell double-timed to the car and piled in. 'Sorry, I was just getting my coat on.'

'It's not even cold,' barked Abraham as they rocketed away. '...Though things are about to heat up big time for Blenkinsopp.'

Chapter Thirteen

They say that owners look like their pets. If Badawi Shahzad wasn't a halal butcher, then some might say he somewhat resembled one of the pigs that (misleading titled) *family* butchers routinely chop up in their shops. The colour of mud, pot-bellied and with a stubby little nose, all he really lacked was a curly little tail and an oink. He did however possess a squeal, and for some reason it was more squealy than usual this morning.

'Mo-ohh! There are two, er...gentlemen here to see you.'

After a sleepless night and with a banging brain, it was as much as Mo could manage just to do his work without losing any fingers, let alone listen out for and decipher shopfront chatter. He raised his knife and, several moments later, happed to notice that it had somehow found its way into a loin of lamb - probably more to do with fatigue and gravity than by force or design.

Abraham, in contrast, knew exactly what he was doing when he forcibly swept Shahzad aside and barged into the back room.

If he had expected Mo to either panic, run or both then he couldn't have been further off the mark.

'Ah, detective inspector Abraham,' Mo yawned. 'What a pleasant surprise. What can I do for you?'

Abraham exchanged quizzical glances with Kell.

'Lambchop? Leg?' Mo raised his butcher's knife and pointed it towards Abraham's jaw. 'Trim of the fancy little beard perhaps?'

'What?' Abraham growled and lurched forward. 'Are you taking the piss?'

Kell moved quickly, grabbed Abraham's arm, and dragged him back. 'Dad, I've got this okay.'

Maybe it was the word *'dad'* that did it, but somewhat uncharacteristically Abraham acquiesced – albeit with a toxic scowl and menacing stare.

Kell stepped forward and motioned towards the knife. 'Ah ehm...'

'Oh right, Kell,' Mo dropped the knife with a clunk. 'Gotcha.'

Kell looked Mo up and down.

'You look like death warmed up,' he placed a hand on Mo's shoulder and eased him towards the shopfront. 'We need a word with you down at the station Mo. Just a few questions. It looks like you could do with a sit-down and nice cup of tea anyway.'

'How kind of you,' Mo stretched his stiff torso up then headed through the shopfront of his own accord. 'Biccies too I hope?'

'Biccies? You're literally taking the biscuit Blenkinsopp!' Abraham snapped. 'You'll be lucky to get life, let alone a custard cream and gingernut.'

'Life? Life? What's this all about officer?' flustered Shahzad. 'And why are you taking Mo?'

'It's nothing Mr Shahzad,' said Mo. 'Just one of DI Abraham's occasional attempted fit-ups. It's always complete nonsense of course. The usual farce normally takes an hour or so, but I'll come straight back and make up the time later.'

'You'll be doing time alright, and plenty of it,' Abraham burnt his eyes into Mo's before turning to Shahzad. 'Mr Blenkinsopp here is likely to be otherwise engaged for the next twenty years or so.'

'What for? Mo tutted. 'Supposedly flashing in the park?'

Abraham motioned for Kell to escort Mo outside to the car. He turned back to look Shahzad directly in his eyes, and deliberately raised his voice. 'No, it's not for flashing in the park this time, nor for the sexual assault incident, or petty theft, fraud or anything else. This time it's for murder in the first degree.'

Abraham left Shahzad to his gawp while he hollered out of the doorway.

'Well done Blenkinsopp, it's been work in progress, but you've finally made the criminal big-league,' He turned to Shahzad, all concerned and supportive, 'You may wish to advertise for a new dogsbody sir.'

Shahzad ruminated for all of a second before shouting after Mo, 'You're fired!'

Kell hurriedly bundled the suspect into the back of the car and clacked the door shut. Mo banged on the window with clenched fist. 'You swine.'

It wasn't clear who the insult was aimed at. Abraham, Shahzad or possibly even Mo himself.

Chapter Fourteen

Debbie signalled Abraham over as Kell led Mo to the interview room for the second time in two days. Kell tipped a thumb and index finger towards his lips.

'For Christ's sake Kell. Give him a cup of tea then,' Abraham moaned. 'But no bloody biscuits.'

'I've called Mr Patel sir,' Debbie said to Abraham. 'Kell's alibi checks out, and Mr Patel says he's happy to give a statement if need be.'

'Is that it?' huffed Abraham. 'Anything else?'

'Yes sir,' Debbie continued. 'I took the opportunity to question Mr Patel about the night in question. He does remember seeing someone fitting Alex's description briefly at the party, but doesn't remember Mo having any altercation with her.'

'When did he say they left?'

'Mr Patel can't be sure, but he thinks Alex left first and Mo followed not long afterwards. He thinks sometime between 11 pm and midnight.'

'So even Blenkinsopp's best friend is essentially saying that he could have followed Alex.'

'That's not quite what he said,' Debbie corrected.

'Don't split hairs Harrison,' sniped Abraham. 'Anything else?'

'Yes, I took the liberty of asking what Mo was wearing,' Debbie said. 'According to Mr Patel it was a blue and white shirt and beige chinos. Mr Patel is certain about this.'

'Kell should be able to corroborate that,' Abraham tapped a tooth in contemplation. 'In the meantime, we should get a search warrant to recover his clothes. With any luck they'll still be in his linen bin. There may also be other potentially incriminating evidence lying about. Blenkinsopp's hardly Professor Moriarty. Can you sort that ASAP Harrison?'

'Actually, I've already gone one better.' Debbie blushed. 'I suggested to Aftab that he just ask Mo's mam politely if it was okay to conduct a search - as such there would be no need for a search warrant. He's there right now with Jerzy. Apparently, she's even been feeding them tea and sandwiches while they ransack the place.'

Abraham pulled a bemused face. 'Wot no biscuits?'

***

Abraham's initial plan of making Mo wait for half an hour or so, just sweating, didn't pan out as Matty Black approached him in the canteen and leaned across the table.

'Looks tasty,' wiry but with the appetite of an ox, Matty couldn't resist nabbing some chips.

Abraham batted Matty's tattooed arm away and bit into his burger. 'What is it Black?' he mumbled through a gobful of beef, bread and ketchup.

'You've a visitor,' Matty said. 'Usman Ghosh. He's demanding to see Blenkinsopp.'

'Stuff him,' Abraham inadvertently sprayed out some crumbs as he spoke. 'He's not his actual lawyer.'

'But that's just it,' Matty moved back a tad. 'He says he is.'

***

'That sneaky Blenkinsopp must have sent Ghosh a text from the back seat of my car,' seethed Abraham. 'I've a good mind to deny access.'

'Yeah,' agreed Matty. 'But you don't want to give Ghosh any grounds to get Blenkinsopp off on a technicality, do you?'

'True, but I could have done with some time with Blenkinsopp on my own first, or at least with just Blenkinsopp and a two-a-penny duty solicitor - because that Ghosh is as slippery as a wiggy, wriggly worm,' Abraham played with his whiskered top lip as he contemplated things. Sighing, he scraped his chair back and rose. 'But I guess you're right.'

***

'How can a kid like Blenkinsopp afford a top lawyer like Ghosh,' Matty wondered out loud as he clacked up the corridor munching his newly acquired leftover hamburger. 'Have you seen his house? His fees must be astronomical.'

'If he's charging any,' stated Abraham blankly.

'I know that lot down the mosque stick together,' said Matty. 'But how many lawyers do you know who put religion before money?'

'Fair point, but Ghosh seems to have a soft spot for Blenkinsopp,' Abraham stopped at the end of the corridor 'Whatever the reason, we're stuck with the slime-ball now.'

'I take it you don't like Ghosh?'

'What, that false, pretentious prick?' spat Abraham as he pushed open the door and stepped through into reception. He took the lawyer's outstretched hand in his and firmly shook it. 'Mr Ghosh... How are you?.... I understand you wish to see your client.... Certainly, follow me please.... Care for a cup of tea? ...How about a digestive?'

***

'Oh Usman, I see you got my text,' the gratitude in Mo's voice was tangible as Usman took Mo's outstretched hand in both of his shook it. 'Thank you so much for coming.'

'Glad to help Mo,' Usman smiled and his thick bushy moustache bowed across his thin dark face. He led Mo into a room that he had conducted numerous previous lawyer-client meetings in, and bade him to sit. 'It's cosier in here and no one is listening.'

‘Oh,’ Mo muttered as he did a 360-degree recce of the room.

‘Aren’t those the same clothes you had on yesterday Mo?’ Usman observed.

Mo looked down at his brown shoes, cargo shorts and black vest and nodded. ‘I guess they are. I never quite made it back to my place last night.’

Mo slumped down on his chair and patted his sticky, matted hair while Usman laid his soft leather briefcase on the table and took out his notebook.

‘DI Abraham tells me that he and DS Grantham are to question you about a murder,’ Usman tipped his head downwards and peered soberly at Mo over his thick black glasses. Mo peered back and noticed that Usman’s plastic spectacles seemed out of sync with his immaculate high-end suit.

Usman extracted his fountain pen from an inside jacket pocket and jotted down a few words. Mo looked at the upside-down scrawl. He briefly tried to decipher the words but soon gave up. His own topsy-turvy life was already doing a fine job of draining his energy reserves, and lexical guessing games were very low on his current agenda.

‘Abraham did mention murder,’ Mo looked down and picked at a fingernail. ‘But he didn’t say who. Although I’m assuming it’s the woman who was found in the park, the one on last night’s news.’

‘He hasn’t enlightened me on that yet either,’ said Usman. ‘He is keeping that up his sleeve for the interview. Mo, sorry to have to ask, but if there is anything you want to tell me, then now is the time.’

Mo looked up, glazy eyed. ‘Do you mean did I do it?’

‘I don’t want to put words in your mouth Mo, and they haven’t arrested you, which at least suggests that they probably don’t have anything concrete on you, because if they had then you’d have been dragged here in handcuffs,’ Usman leaned forward and touched Mo’s bare upper arm. ‘But the fact that they’ve brought you here at all, coupled with Abraham’s smug smirk just now, suggests that they at least think they might have something on you.’

‘Like what?’

'I was hoping that you'd tell me Mo,' said Usman. 'If I'm going to assist you then it helps to have an idea about just what cards Abraham might be holding. If we know that then we can plan and respond accordingly.'

'Do you think I did it?' Mo looked Usman straight in the eye. Usman looked directly back. A few seconds passed before he replied.

'My stock lawyer answer to that question is '*what I think is neither here nor there*,' said Usman. 'But in your case Mo, I'll just come out with not only my gut reaction but what I also believe to be the truth – no, I don't think you did it.'

'That's good,' Mo tapped his temple. 'At least one of us thinks I'm innocent.'

***

Mo banged his fists on the table then stood up. 'Come on, let's find out about these up-the-sleeve aces.'

Usman hastened to his feet. There was a wobble in his voice. 'So, are you saying you're guilty?'

'That's just it,' Mo tilted his head right back and wearily rubbed his face. 'I just don't know.'

'All the more reason to not rush things,' Usman dawdled gathering his things. 'A murder rap is as serious as they come. You could be looking at life. Why not sit back down Mo? We should pre-empt what they might throw at us so we can plan our strategy.'

'*Strategy*,' Mo thought about it for all of two seconds before heading for the door. 'I just want the truth. And if I'm guilty then Allah have mercy on my soul, and I'll take everything that's coming to me.'

'So why am I here Mo?'

'If I'm guilty, I'll thank you for your time but then I'll send you on your way,' Mo held open the door. 'But on the off-chance I'm innocent, I could do with someone in the know who's got my back. You're already aware of my history with Abraham. I wouldn't put anything past him. And that includes setting me up for a fall.'

'Yes, you've told me before about your run-ins with him,' Usman approached Mo and kept his voice low. 'But trying to *'fit you up'* for say shoplifting is one thing. Fabricating evidence in a murder enquiry is a totally different ballgame. In this day and age, he'd be crazy to try, even if he wanted to.'

'I'd be inclined to agree,' admitted Mo as they headed back to the interview room. 'It's just that you haven't seen – no, you haven't *felt* him glare into your eyes like I have. I can't really explain it, but it's like being tasered with ice.'

'Just do me one favour at least,' Usman grabbed Mo's arm and checked him mid-stride. 'Let me do the talking at least.'

'We'll see,' Mo breezed into the interview room. 'Ah, you must be DS Grantham, I'm so glad you could join us.'

Chapter Fifteen

Mo shook Gran by the hand and led her to the table. 'Why don't you sit opposite me DS Grantham. If you and DI Abraham are playing good cop, bad cop then I'd prefer to be facing good cop.'

'Certainly,' Gran sat down precisely where she was told like a ...well, a good cop.

'Don't be shy,' Mo pulled out a chair for Abraham. 'I presume you have no objections to sitting opposite my solicitor?'

Abraham sat down and slowly shook his head, possibly to signal 'no,' but judging by his incredulous stare it probably indicated something else.

'I hear you're a singer these days Joe. Kell told me all about your karaoke duet with him at the policeman's ball. The Clash wasn't it?' Mo cleared his throat and crooned a bar, '*Daddy was a bank rob-ber...*'

'Look...'

Mo interrupted Abraham. 'Though there were some old eighties' music videos on TV the other day, and you don't half look like the singer of The Damned used to. Dave Vanian I think he's called. He had a white stripe in his hair too – although he didn't have a girly little beard.'

Abraham sprang forward, backheeled his chair to the floor and glowered at Mo. His thin lips, narrow nose and neat goatee knotted and contorted as he bared his sharp white teeth, like a wolf.

'For the benefit of the tape,' Mo said. 'DI Abraham appears to be struggling with a thorny bout of constipation.'

'Please take this seriously Mo,' counselled Gran.

‘Ah, but I am DS Grantham,’ Mo replied. ‘DI Abraham has already contrived to deliberately lose me my job today, and I know he’s keen – overly keen – on wanting me to lose my freedom. So just to let you know that my solicitor here will be monitoring you like a hawk to see if we can add ‘false arrest’ to the ‘loss of earnings’ compensation claim.’

‘No one has arrested you Mo,’ pointed out Gran with a good cop smile.

‘Whatever,’ Mo looked at Abraham and both Usman and Gran followed suit. Abraham backed over his side of the table and turned to recover his plastic chair.

‘I’m presuming this has something to do with the lady that was murdered in the park the other night, the one who was tragically decapitated.’ Mo said. ‘Who is she? and just where did you get this notion into your heads that I have anything to do with it?’

‘Ahem,’ Abraham coughed. ‘Mr Ghosh, please remind your client of something.’

‘Yes,’ Usman enquired.

‘That this is *my* interview, and it’s *me* who asks the questions,’ Abraham snapped. ‘Not the bloody suspect!’

Abraham marched over to the recording machine, punched a button and chuntered the usual legal mumbo jumbo about its use in a very loud and clearly irked voice.

By the time he seated himself at the table his heart rate had started to slow back down again, but his wolf stare had resurfaced.

‘Mr...,’ Abraham took a couple of breaths before continuing, as if the word ‘*mister*’ had pained him. ‘Mr Blenkinsopp, can you please recount your whereabouts from 11 pm Saturday evening.’

Usman looked at Mo. Mo didn’t look back.

‘I was at my friend Saboor’s party,’ Mo replied. ‘Kell was there too, you can ask him.’

'Don't worry, we already have,' Abraham smirked. 'He's told us all about it.'

Usman looked at Mo again. This time Mo looked back and shrugged.

'Did anything happen at the party Mo?' asked Gran. 'Anything you want to tell us about?'

'I got assaulted by that nutcase Davy Lilley,' Mo ran a hand over his jaw. 'But I'm not here to make a fuss about that.'

'What about any run-ins with a female at the party?' Abraham probed. 'A blond.'

'Not really,' Mo rubbed his chin. 'Well, there was this blond, an older woman that was giving me the evil eye. She wanted to get her mitts on Kell, and I happened to be in the way. She was downright rude actually.'

'And did you threaten her in any way?'

'You don't have to answer that,' Usman cautioned.

'No,' Mo ignored the caution. 'Anyway, she left. I saw her go.'

'Any parting words to her? You know, above the blurring music and across a room full of witnesses.'

Mo scratched his head. 'Sorry, I got drunk for the first time ever on Saturday and my memory of the evening has been patchy at best, and very hazy in the bits I can actually recall. But let me think...'

'You don't have to answer,' Usman reiterated.

'Oh yes, I think I just muttered it rather than shouted. It was something like '*don't lose your head*,'' Mo tapped on the side of his own cranium and looked pleased with his feat of memory. 'Why?'

'Because,' Abraham rumbled. 'Shortly afterwards she did just that!'

***

'I'd like a word in private with my client,' Usman's slow, unaccented English suddenly fast-forwarded.

‘If you wish,’ Abraham acceded.

‘I don’t wish,’ the skin beneath Mo’s freckles had paled to an even whiter shade than normal, but he leaned forward and opened up. ‘Listen, I know in retrospect it doesn’t appear to have been the most appropriate turn of phrase, but at the time she had been damned rude to me, she was in a bad mood, and she was shaking her head at me like a madwoman with lice. It just seemed a funny thing to say at the time.’

‘It sounds like a warning to me.’

‘That’s pure conjecture on your part detective inspector,’ Usman interjected. ‘My client has given you his answer. It was just an innocent turn of phrase. It wasn’t meant as a warning or anything untoward to the lady in question.’

‘With all due respect, I’d prefer to hear it from the horse’s mouth.’ Abraham eyed Mo. ‘Are you denying that it was a warning?’

‘Of course,’ Mo replied. ‘It was just meant as a bit of a joke. I doubt she even heard. Besides, I had no idea of what was going to happen to her later that night.’

‘Tch,’ Abraham shook his head. ‘Naturally, you would say that, and I’m sure the courts would see it differently.’

‘Really?’ Mo raised his voice and narrowed his eyes. He looked at Gran in the hope that his chances of being believed would increase if he addressed good cop. ‘What happened to her? And who was she?’

‘Alex Hobbs, a 41-year-old mother of two,’ Abraham paused a few moments. ‘Are you claiming you don’t know her?’

‘It’s not a claim, Mo retorted. ‘I’d never met her before Saturday night.’

‘So you say,’ Abraham took out Mo’s phone that he had, for the second time, confiscated upon arrival at the station. ‘So, you wouldn’t have her picture on your phone by any chance, would you?’

Mo pulled an incredulous face. ‘Of course not.’

Abraham got Mo to tap in his passcode then navigated through some screens.

'For the benefit of the tape, I'm showing Mr Blenkinsopp a photograph on his telephone. Do you recognise this person Mr Blenkinsopp?'

Mo stared at the photograph, then turned gaping-mouthed at Usman before swivelling back around towards Abraham. 'It's a picture of *her*, that Alex. How did that get on my phone?'

'Funnily enough,' Abraham smiled at Gran. 'We were wondering the same thing.'

Mo bounced his hand underneath the phone. 'Do you mind?'

Abraham dropped it in Mo's palm. 'Be my guest.'

Mo resized the image and studied it at closer quarters. 'Ah, yes. I can see what's happened now. This was taken at the party. I was actually pointing the camera at someone else, Saboor as it happens. Someone knocked my hand as I clicked the button. A hairy hippie guy with a beanpole girlfriend if I remember rightly. If you look closely you can see Saboor at the edge of the image.'

'I don't see anyone else,' Abraham scoffed. 'Just a very clear picture of the victim taken shortly before her brutal murder.'

'Look, that's Saboor,' Mo pointed at a slither of pink-shirted torso at the edge of the picture. 'Ask Kell if you don't believe me. At the time I had no idea who this Alex was. Her being in this picture is sheer coincidence, nothing else.'

Gran nudged Abraham and they got up and moved to the back of the room.

'Kell should be able to shed some light on that claim patron,' Gran whispered.

'Maybe, but even if the photo is from the party and proves inconclusive, Blenkinsopp could still be lying about not knowing Alex.

Moreover, Patel could be covering for him,' Abraham headed back to the table. 'We're not finished yet.'

'Talking of phones,' probed Abraham. 'You say you didn't know Ms Hobbs.'

'That's right,' said Mo.

'So,' Abraham paused and looked Mo straight in the eye. 'How do you account for you being a contact in her mobile?'

'Eh?' Mo squashed his nose, crumpled his eyebrows and turned to Usman. 'That's nonsense! I barely said a word to her, and I certainly didn't give her my contact details.'

'It's true Mo,' affirmed Gran. 'Debbie was the one who noticed it. Feel free to ask her.'

'What?' Mo creased up his face. 'If Debbie says so then I believe her. It's just that I haven't the faintest idea why this Alex woman would have my details.'

'You mention you saw Ms Hobbs leave the party,' Abraham sat back down and edged forward, his face blank. If he did have some cards up his sleeve, then he was playing poker. 'When did you yourself leave?'

'I didn't notice the precise time,' Mo offered. 'But it wasn't long after she left. Maybe five or ten minutes or so.'

'So, you followed her?'

Usman leapt in. 'He didn't say that.'

'Actually, I think I started off in the other direction.'

'And then you followed her?'

'No, well, not on purpose anyway,' Mo scratched his head. 'I think what happened is I heard a heated argument, so I doubled back.'

'Sounds to me like you took a 50-50 guess, guessed wrong, but when you heard her voice you headed after her.'

'Like I say, my memory of that evening is quite blurred,' said Mo. 'But that sounds like you're the one guessing wrong.'

'Is your loss of memory something to do with the big lump on your head?' continued Abraham.

'Maybe,' said Mo.

'Don't think we haven't noticed that. Or the cuts on your arms,' said Abraham. 'Where did they come from? Did you fall headfirst into the bushes from the railings at the park?'

Mo shrugged. 'Not that I'm aware.'

'Not that I'm aware,' laughed Abraham. 'It's hardly a convincing statement to the contrary.'

'Just now, you also said *not on purpose*,' added Gran. 'That not a convincing argument to the contrary either? Would you care to elaborate?'

'Hang on, let me think,' Mo pensively pinched his lips between thumb and forefinger. 'Yes, it's coming back. What happened is that I was heading the other way, but then I heard an argument between Alex and this guy, so I doubled back.'

'Can you tell us more about this argument Mo?' Gran probed. 'And about this man.'

'Well, it's still a bit sketchy,' Mo tapped a knuckle on his skull. 'But I do remember that he was a big guy. A big bulky guy with artificial legs. And this Alex was attacking him with a bottle.'

'Are you saying she assaulted him?' Gran asked.

'No, she tried whacking him with it after he'd stumbled to the ground, but luckily for him she missed, and the bottle smashed around him. She then scuttled off sharpish,' Mo said. 'The guy slowly hobbled off after her, but not in a straight line. Like me, I think he'd been drinking.'

'And did you chase after Ms Hobbs too?' quizzed Abraham? 'Corner her in the park and brutally slay her?'

Usman opened his mouth but Mo held up a palm, stop fashion.

'I don't remember seeing her at all again that night after she disappeared into the distance.'

'So you say,' Abraham emphasised the word '*you*.' Where did you go after this alleged altercation?'

'Ishmael's house off Rift House Green,' Mo said. 'He's a friend of mine from the mosque. I bumped into him in Catcote Road and we went back to his place.'

Gran nudged Abraham again and they reconvened their discussion by the door. 'That does tie in patron. I myself tailed Ishmael and Ahmed that night. When they split up I followed Ahmed, but Ishmael did head back along Catcote Road towards his place. The time also tallies.'

Debbie's face appeared at the doors' windowpane, 'A quick word if you please.'

The three officers moved into the corridor, closed the door and lowered their voices.

'Firstly, Audrey says she's tried Dean's number about twenty times now with no success.'

'Hm, suspicious,' Gran mused. 'It's often the boyfriend, hubby or lover.'

'Possibly, but we've had a development,' Debbie said. 'A taxi driver has reported seeing an altercation between someone matching Alex's description and a man in Catcote Road roughly around half past eleven on Saturday.'

'Blenkinsopp by any chance?' There was hope in Abraham's voice.

'No, Mick Braithwaite, the witness says he used to drink with him in the Pink Domino before Braithwaite got barred. He's adamant it was him.' Debbie said. 'Not only that but he had another fare around midnight and he saw Mick again, near the top of Burn Valley - just ten minutes or so from the park and heading towards it.'

'Did this witness see Blenkinsopp?'

'Not Blenkinsopp, although he did mention some guy with a *Lebanese or thereabouts* look about him near the park too.'

'So, we can't place Blenkinsopp at the scene, but we can place a person unknown of North African origin, and...' Gran let her words tail off.

'...We *can* place a violent thug with motive and previous.' Abraham finished off the sentence.'

'*Ex's* - I forgot that from my list,' Gran said. 'The murderer is often the boyfriend, hubby, lover or the ex.'

'Do you actually have anything concrete on Mo sir?' Debbie asked. 'It's just that I overheard Matty telling the chief super that Usman Ghosh was here again on Mo's behalf.'

Abraham ground his teeth together, 'Shit.'

Chapter Sixteen

'This is becoming a habit detective inspector,' Usman's moustache crinkled above his ironic smile as everyone headed back through to reception. 'I sincerely hope there won't be a repeat any time soon as my client might have a very strong, genuine case for harassment.'

Mo stifled a snigger, but this didn't go unnoticed and Abraham shot him a scowl.

'If you're expecting another apology, you'll be waiting a very long time,' spat Abraham. 'This is a murder case, and I'll question who I like and whenever I damn well please.'

Out-trumped, Usman turned away from Abraham and pushed open the door. 'Are you sure you don't want a lift Mo?'

'No thanks, I know you are very busy.' Mo held out his hand and Usman shook it before hastening outside.

'Ahem,' Mo turned back to face Abraham. He held his palm out flat. 'My phone if you please detective constable, ...sorry detective *inspector*. I'm thinking ahead.'

Abraham's angular face remained granite, but his eyes turned to ice. Then, after a few seconds they suddenly brightened. He headed back into the station's inner sanctums. 'Sure, just give me a few minutes.'

Mo couldn't put his finger on just why, but all of a sudden, he felt a chill stinging his bones.

***

As Abraham disappeared, Kell entered reception, licking some tomato ketchup off his lips. 'Hey Mo, I'm glad to hear everything has been cleared up. That's great.'

'Yes, everything is just tickety-boo,' Mo sighed heavily and tried to rub some warmth into his bare arms.

'Yeah, I guess you've had quite a turbulent couple of days,' Kell gulped some protein shake, 'What with the flasher mix-up and now this.'

'Not to mention the carry on with your dad,' Mo groused. 'Actually, *dads* plural. Daddy 2 Abraham is trying to wreck my life while Daddy 1 Lilley just wants to wreck every bone in my body.'

'Sorry Mo,' Kell shook his head apologetically. 'I heard about your second run-in with Davy yesterday morning. He was highly displeased about that to say the least. He mentioned something about you '*needing to be taught a lesson for disrespecting him and his vehicle*.'

'Oh, I'm happy to apologise,' Mo yawned. 'Well, to the gruntled vehicle at least. Davy can whistle for his.'

'Look, I never said anything about going as far as apologising,' Kell caught hold of Mo's arm. 'But doing nothing probably isn't the wisest move either.'

Mo held Kell's gaze for a few seconds then tugged his arm free. 'So, what do you suggest?'

'I'd have strongly recommended not riling him up in the first place Mo, but that boat has now sailed,' Kell rubbed the back of his neck. 'You could just try talking to him.'

'Yeah, like that'll make any difference.'

'It's better than just being a sitting duck,' Kell shrugged. 'What's the harm in just saying that you'd like to sort things out.'

Mo sighed heavily as he weighed up his options, 'I dunno...'

'Tell you what,' Kell dug out his mobile, typed *'Davy Lilley Removals'* into the browser and handed it to Mo.

'I didn't know Davy had a removals firm,' Mo tugged an earlobe. 'It's a bit odd there is no photograph of a furniture van.'

‘Er, I don’t think it’s that kind of removals,’ Kell said. ‘Look if you want his number then there it is – up to you.’

‘What’s that plastic thing he’s lugging on his shoulder Kell?’

A cheerful-looking Abraham reappeared, tossed a phone to Kell and bumped into the back of Mo in his eagerness to have a gander at the image too.

He jabbed his finger at the screen. ‘That had better not be one of ours!’

‘One of your what?’ quizzed Mo with a sudden turn.

‘Body bags!’

***

Mo was more than surprised when Abraham offered him a lift. Kell looked somewhat puzzled too but he waited by the car’s back door while Mo dawdled. The *potential trap* notions that buzzed through Mo’s brain only intensified with Abraham’s widening grin. Mo didn’t have to get in. The sensible part of his brain told him not to. Shrieked not to. But something in his subconscious started to prod, and he found himself wandering over to Kell rather than hot-footing the hell outta there.

‘I’ll give you some money for a taxi if you prefer,’ Kell whispered as he handed Mo his phone back.

Mo hadn’t the faintest idea what was going on, but somewhat paradoxically that’s what made him slide into the back seat with a shake of the head. Something wasn’t right. And not just about Abraham’s sudden miraculous conversion to good cop, but also the police interview that had just taken place. But what? He kneaded around his sorry eyes with the heels of his hands. Nothing to do with the accusation of threatening Alex. Or supposedly following her. Probably not even to do with the picture of her on his phone. Something else. Oblivious to Abraham’s ‘where to?’ question, Mo stared blankly at his phone as cerebral cogs clunked and cogitated. It was only when Abraham spoke again did the answer slot into place, like three cherries on an old-fashioned fruit machine.

'How about Shahzad's? At the very least you could be owed back pay,' Abraham suggested. 'If you want to get what's due to you then you're better off speaking to him in person rather than contacting him by phone.'

That was it. That was the niggle that Mo hadn't been able to shake about the whole interview shebang – the fact that his contact details were on Alex's phone. He had never met her previously and didn't know her. So how could she possibly have added him as a contact? Unless she wasn't the one to add him. And if that was the case then this begged the question *who did*? And more to the point, *why*? A chilling shiver rippled down Mo's spine as a crazy but terrifying thought hit home. *Could someone actually be trying to set me up for murder*? The sensible part of his brain cranked up the volume again, screaming at him to scarper. The not-so-sensible part had other ideas. If Mo *was* being set up, and Abraham was behind it, then just being in the car with him was a risk in itself. Then again so was being "safe" on the outside, but stuck passively in the dark.

What was the lesser of the two evils?

Mo closed his eyes and swallowed hard. 'Okay drive.'

***

Mo raised an eyebrow and wondered about the existence of a vanity gene being passed down as Abraham admired himself in the driver's mirror while Kell checked out his chiselled model pose in the passengers' sun flap mirror. Mo's mind drifted back to the party. Kell had been transfixed by his reflection in the kitchen window then too – his habitual narcissistic smiling self - ostensibly oblivious to Alex's sniping at Mo, or Mo reaction to it. For the life of him Mo couldn't remember his exact reaction. But he had reacted. Maybe a glower. Maybe a jibe. Probably both. He'd certainly pocketed the scissors. Moreover, if someone had been outside watching that night – something Mo increasingly felt convinced of – then whoever it was could well have seen all that through the lit-up window. Daggers. Threats. Reactions. ...But enough to set him up? Enough for murder? Mo gave his head a little jiggle to shake out the sheer absurdity of it all.

Try to shake it out.

What was even harder to shake was the fact that the smart money was not on a mere set-up, but on Mo as the actual murderer. Mo knew it. And he had more than just an inkling that Abraham knew it too - something that made the DI's sudden good cop reincarnation all the more puzzling.

'You know, I think we've got off on the wrong foot,' Abraham twisted around at the T-junction and smiled. 'It'd be good to get to know you more Mo.'

Mo turned to Kell, eyes narrowed. Kell raised his palms and shrugged.

'Kell tells me that you've applied to join the police and have also signed up for a distance university course. That's very commendable.' Abraham continued. 'Is that do you want to do with your life – policing? Or is it more academic?'

'Er...' Mo understood the question. It was Abraham he didn't understand. After some deliberation he eventually answered. 'Somewhat ironically, I've always wanted to be a detective, but if I can't get in the force then I'll probably do a degree and maybe move to the States at some point - maybe for good if I can persuade my mam to come with me. My grandmother was American and we've some family there.'

'How splendid.'

Mo bit a fingernail as he listened to Abraham's laugh and watched his eyes sparkle in the mirror. He looked at his phone again and bit a fingernail.

Something definitely wasn't right.

Probably some things (plural) Mo suspected.

***

'At your service sir,' Abraham clicked his heels and saluted as Mo stepped out of the car and headed towards Shahzad's shop.

Abraham cheerily swung the car door shut then followed in Mo's footsteps.

'It's fine DI Abraham,' Mo said. 'I've got this from here, you don't need to come too.'

‘Ah, but I do,’ beamed Abraham as he skipped past Mo and pushed the shop door open. An old-fashioned bell jingled. ‘I feel a personal responsibility to clear up any misunderstanding with your boss.’

‘Really detective inspector, I insist...’

‘No really Mr Blenkinsopp, it is I who must insist,’ Abraham chuckled as he moved into the shopfront. He spotted the rotund aproned butcher in the back room. ‘Ah, Mr Shahzad. A quick word if you please.’

Mo turned back around in the doorway but bumped into Kell as he brought up the rear. ‘Oh, to hell with it. What more is there to lose.’ Mo spun on his heels and joined the others in the back room.

‘You’ll be pleased to hear that your young assistant, Mr Blenkinsopp here, has done a fine job of assisting us with our ongoing murder enquiry, and we are now exploring other avenues,’ Abraham patted Mo on the back. ‘Also, the other things that I mentioned such as flashing, sexual assault and drugs have been cleared up too. You may therefore wish to reconsider your earlier decision and reinstate him.’

‘Er, right. I’m glad to hear it,’ Shahzad spoke into the end of a black pudding as if it were a microphone. Suddenly, he tugged an ear with one hand and tapped the black pudding on his chin with the other. Something whirred behind his thick round spectacles. ‘Hang on, what’s that about drugs? You didn’t mention that before?’

‘Didn’t I? Oh, let’s clear that right up now then if you don’t mind Mr Blenkinsopp,’ Abraham smiled as he stretched Mo’s arms out and patted him down. He stopped when he reached Mo’s shorts’ pocket. ‘What’s this?’

Abraham extracted a packet of white powder, opened it, sniffed it, then wet the end of his finger, dabbed it in the powder and tasted it. ‘Ecstasy if I’m not mistaken. No wonder you’re always such a happy bunny Blenkinsopp.’

Mo’s eyes toggled between Abraham’s jubilant expression and Shahzad’s and Kell’s looks of shock and horror.

'You swine Abraham!' Mo shrieked and kicked out as the DI cuffed him, getting a stiff elbow to the sternum for his trouble. He collapsed to the floor and curled up wheezing.

'Take him to the car constable,' Abraham had no patience for Kell's hesitation and barked, 'Now!'

A pair of eyes steamed in Abraham's direction, but they weren't the struggling Mo's.

'What are looking at me like that for Kell?' Abraham threw his palms up into the air and grinned.

Kell shook his head at Abraham as he helped Mo to his feet and silently led him through the door.

'Seven years if you're wondering Blenkinsopp,' Abraham wagged a finger with a smirk. 'You know, the maximum sentence for possession.'

Mo made a choking sound. It wasn't clear if it was the result of Abraham's physical or emotional blow.

'Oh, just thought,' Abraham added. 'A criminal record like this should also scupper your police force application and your migration plans for the US too. Such a shame for you. Ah well, not to worry. I'll still be here waiting for you when you eventually get out of the clink.'

***

As Mo's cell door *clunked* rather than *clinked* shut, the turning Abraham caught Kell's glower upon him. Big-grinned, he clacked up the tiled corridor towards him.

'What?'

'You know damn well what.'

'Sure I don't know...'

'Stop, I don't want to hear it.' Kell cut off Abraham's smiley-faced protestations with a raised palm. 'But I do want to know why you've got it in for Mo? I mean, what has he ever done to rattle your cage?'

'Ha, I get it,' Abraham pulled a wry smile. 'Blenkinsopp has been bleating to you about the time I roughed him up a bit at your old school one night. No doubt he left out the bit about the serious sexual assault on a young girl, or the fact that he came at me with his fists.'

'Serious sexual assault I very much doubt, and as for coming at you with his fists is concerned, I'm pretty sure he wouldn't have done that without reason either.'

'I can't say I know what you mean officer,' Abraham chuckled.

'That tealeaf, whatsisname, Bremner, came at you the other day too,' pointed out Kell. 'But only after you'd whispered something to him about his daughter. You deliberately provoked him so he'd attack you so you could justify your karate chop to his windpipe.'

'Self-defence,' smirked Abraham.

'Only by a very shaky letter of the law,' Kell ran his fingers through his hair, then lowered his voice. 'Look, Bremner I get. He stole that old lady's entire savings and now she's a bag of nerves and her life's a mess. But what I can't fathom is Mo... I mean why on earth...'

'Apart from the fact that a couple of months after our first encounter he fobbed his way into one of my press conferences posing as a *school reporter*,' daring to accuse me of heavy-handed bullying, and in front of the media and all and sundry.'

'Oh.'

'Well, I managed to talk my way around that,' said Abraham. 'And young Blenkinsopp got himself all tongue-tied, which helped, but not enough to keep the top brass from sticking their oar in, and not enough to prevent an ugly dint in my rep.'

'Even so, that must have been all of five years ago. It still doesn't explain why you've been on Mo's back ever since - and still are for that matter.' Kell shook his head. 'You know as well as I do that Mo's innocent over this drugs nonsense. If you had any morals, you'd let it drop and free him.'

‘Should I drop it?’ Abraham drummed his fingers on his tie as he contemplated for two seconds max. ‘Er ...nope.’

‘But...’

‘Look son, morals don’t keep baddies off the streets son, and who says it’s nonsense? Besides, Blenkinsopp is not as innocent as he’d have you believe. Evidence for Alex’s murder will crop up with his stamp all over it, mark my words,’ said Abraham. ‘I’ve been doing this for a long time, and I know a wrong ‘un when I see one. Indeed, if you care to check my long list of collars over the years, I think you’ll find that my instincts tend to be pretty darn good.’

‘I’m not denying that, but there is more to this Mo thing than mere suspicion,’ said Kell ‘Come on Dad. Be honest. With me at least. Why have you got it in for him?’

‘Hm,’ Abraham stroked his goatee. ‘In all honesty Son, I truly can’t put my finger on it either.’

‘Think...’

Abraham’s breathing became more pronounced, and his gaze wandered upwards as he pondered and ruminated.

‘I genuinely can’t say why, but staring eyeball to eyeball with him that night at his school was an eerily unnerving experience. Made me literally convulse and spontaneously cough up some phlegm it did,’ grimaced Abraham. ‘If you’re asking me to pinpoint why, then I guess the word that springs to mind is *revulsion*.’

‘Revulsion?’ Kell snaked his brow. ‘Revulsion at Mo and at what he might have done? Or revulsion at yourself?’

***

If Abraham did reply, then it got lost in the commotion as a gaggle of uniforms surged in and jostled to lock up a vehemently protesting bear of a man into cell number three.

Chapter Seventeen

After his brief stint in cell number two followed by a short interview, the charging process down at the nick proved a relatively straightforward affair. Mo protested his innocence but nevertheless signed the charge sheet and agreed to be summoned to appear at court in the not-too-distant future. It had crossed his mind to call Usman, but he refrained. He didn't want to bother the poor man yet again, and besides, fit-up or not, he had still been caught in possession, almost certainly, he deduced, as a result of Abraham slipping the package in his pocket when he had snuck up behind him to view Davy's website on Kell's phone.

Davy. Mo had forgotten about him. Maybe Kell was right. Maybe doing nothing with a thug on the warpath was sitting-duck-esque. But do what exactly? He massaged his eye sockets as his tired brain cells put in yet more overtime. He desperately needed some sleep. Amongst other things he'd surprised himself at the somewhat blasé way he'd dealt with Abraham. He'd put that partly down to physical exhaustion, partly to mental fatigue and party to just being sick to death of being on the defensive with a smug intimidator like Abraham. Really, it was well out of character. Even so, Mo didn't regret his behaviour. Moreover, he couldn't help but get a kick from seeing Abraham on the back foot for a change. That said, jousting with Abraham could be the least of his worries if there were any substance to the vivid nightmares he'd had recently. Were the police holding anything back? Possibly. But if so, probably nothing definitive. Abraham in particular would jump on the tiniest bit of evidence physically connecting him to the murder. What worried Mo possibly more than most of the other disconcerting circumstances and events was the blood that he had discovered on his body and clothes. That wasn't dreamt or potentially imaginary. It was nailed on real. And no matter how hard he banged his drained neurons he could not fathom how that could be safely explained away to anyone – least of all himself. Raking out the truth could be like opening Pandora's box. No matter how much he wanted to deny it, that was the chilling reality. Moreover, the way his world kept on crashing around him he wasn't holding out for much leftover titbits of hope either. Even so, hope or hopeless, he was determined to unravel the bloody clothes enigma before someone else did.

Just how he was supposed to do that was arguably an even bigger enigma in itself.

***

After just one hour's sleep in what seemed an eternity, Mo craved his bed like Santa on Christmas morning. His pace slackened to a plod as a couple of things continued to maul on his mind. Firstly, the fact that he was heading further *away* from his house, not *towards* it, bled his physical and emotional energy like a needy leech with bad bearings.

That was the first thing. The second thing was even worse.

Mo groaned miserably, dug out his mobile and typed *'Davy Lilley Removals'* into DuckDuckGo. He tweezed the website's image with his fingers to get a closer look at it.

'It *is* a body bag!' He muttered under his own breath.

Mo sighed heavily, let out a loud moan and psyched himself up with some knuckle raps. He hovered an index finger above the call symbol. Should he? Shouldn't he? These *lesser of two evils decisions* were killing him. He just wasn't sure how he'd succumb first - mentally or gruesomely physically.

Chapter Eighteen

'Room for a little 'un?' Kell winked.

Beth shuffled her dainty buns over to one side of the lounger and patted the newly evacuated space beside her. 'I didn't expect you back this early.'

Kell took one last look at his reflection in the shiny metal dumbbell that he'd curled all the way down garden and cosied in alongside her.

'I'm just on a short break, then I'm needed back at the station. It looks like it'll be a long night.'

Beth's stretched out her size 3 feet as far as they would go – so, just past six-footer Kell's knees. 'As you can see, I'm the little one.'

Kell tweaked his mother's bicep. 'Yes, you're tiny but trim and toned thanks to your rock climbing, swimming and Pilates.'

'Oh, Pilates. Thanks for reminding me. I'd better get a move on, or I'll miss my class,' Beth sprung to her feet and kissed Kell on the cheek and Davy on the beady eye tattoo atop his bald head. 'Gotta love you and leave you boys.'

From the comfort of his oversized lounger, Davy blew a kiss to Beth as she disappeared indoors, then clocked Kell shaking his head.

'What?'

'Does Mam know about your latest bit on the side?'

'What she doesn't know won't harm her,' Davy rotated his hams of forearms and admired his cobra tattoos. 'Besides, she can hardly talk after her thing with that Kevin guy.'

'You mean the nice bloke who she occasionally innocently chatted with at the village green?' Kell hissed. 'The one that suddenly disappeared one day, leaving his dog, his house and all his possessions behind.'

'Did he?' gaped Davy. 'Well, I never... Mind you, now and again yer do hear stories of people disappearing. You dabble in magic yourself, yer probably know a lot more about that than me.'

'Palming the ace of hearts is a far cry from making real people vanish off the face of the earth dear dad of sorts,' Kell retorted. 'And it's uncanny how those going missing tend to be people who've crossed you.'

'Can't say I've the foggiest what yer on about kidda,' Davy took a sip of his scotch on the rocks and chuckled. 'Besides, if I'd ever even put so much as a foot out of place, I'm sure that cuckoo Abraham would have charged me by now.'

'It's kind of hard to do that when witnesses clam up,' Kell countered. 'And I assume your *cuckoo* comment is another jibe at him being my biological dad.'

'For all of the two minutes that he's been in the picture.' The ice in Davy's scotch on the rocks did little to quell his fiery scowl as he took a big swig.

'He's been *in the picture* for about three years now, as well you know,' Kell said. 'He helped get me in CID, he doesn't charge me rent and he doesn't cause me grief.'

'For now,' snorted Davy. 'All of a sudden Abraham's got the son he always wanted, but the novelty will wear off, and when the honeymoon period's over he'll drop you like a stone, just liked he dumped yer pregnant mam at the altar.'

'It wasn't the alter - again, as you well know - they didn't know she was pregnant at the time,' Kell swept back his floppy mane and took a few sips of water. 'Look, I know that when Mam revealed that Abraham was my real dad it was a blow for you. I get that you'd feel like you were losing a son.'

'I should have finished him off when I put him in hospital that time.'

'And if you had then you'd be banged up for life,' Kell replied. 'Just remember, I'm grateful for what you've done for me – bringing me up as your own – and I do appreciate your continued *over*-generosity and stuff, but I wish you'd grow up where Mam's concerned, and also put this longstanding feud with Joe behind you.'

'That's not gonna happen,' Davy's eyes hardened. 'And you should watch out for him. I wouldn't trust him as far as I can throw him.'

Kell scratched his stubble. 'Can I ask you something... with my policeman's hat on?'

'Is this official?'

'Let's call it semi-official.'

'Semi-official along the lines of if I let something slip, you'll feel obliged to dob me in?'

'Have I dobbed you in yet?'

'Have I ever let anything slip yet?'

'I might notice things,' Kell said. 'Comings and goings at strange hours. Bulky packages. Handlers in hoodies. That kind of thing.'

'That's kinda vague kidda,' Davy smiled wryly. 'Are you able to be more specific?'

Kell sighed and shrugged.

'So, I've a side-line delivering to persons unknown. Probably for Amazon,' replied Davy. 'And my removals business is simply A-to-B relocation stuff. If anything, it's more of a public service. Nothing sinister. Nothing traceable. And nothing for you to worry yerself or your precious conscience about.'

Kell tapped a fingernail on a tooth then nibbled it.

'It's about the park isn't it?' Davy said.

'How did you know?'

'You were wondering about Alex's body being found under my tree and whether I had anything to do with it.'

'Well, yes actually,' Kell admitted. 'So, did you?'

'No,' Davy slid a giant hand along his long pointy beard. 'But I did wonder about that myself when I saw pictures of the scene and Abraham's TV interview. You've got to say, it's a bit of a coincidence. Almost if someone was trying to set me up. And especially since Alex was an ex of mine, before I met your mam.'

'But why would you kill her?' Kell crinkled his brow.

'Alex was no saint. Far from it. She rubbed plenty of people up the wrong way. Including me,' said Davy evenly. 'But I haven't seen her since before you were born. Warned her off ever clapping eyes on her ever again I did as it happens. And she's kept well clear.'

'Oh, why? What happened?'

'Let's just say that we had a falling out,' Davy's eyes flittered and fell. 'Nothing for your ears.'

'You mentioned a possible set-up,' probed Kell. 'But who'd be mad enough to set *you* up?'

'Well, I wouldn't put that past Abraham. He hates my guts and had previous with her too.'

'*Acquaintance* is how he put it, but yeah he gave that impression,' Kell cogitated in silence for a while. 'As for setting you up is concerned, it's a crazy suggestion, but...'

'But what?'

Kell nibbled a knuckle as he pondered.

'This is just between us... okay?' Kell caught Davy's eyes and waited for his nod before proceeding. 'Well, Abraham did set Mo up today - with drugs.'

'Pisswizard?' chuckled Davy. 'Couldn't have happened to a nicer pipsqueak. Just how do yer know him anyway? I've never seen yer with him before.'

'I've never really hung out with him before, he's always been a bit of a loner,' said Kell. 'But when he turned Muslim - or even before that actually – bullies at our school used to gang up on him.'

'And he'd wet his pants and run away,' Davy smirked.

'No, he'd square up and take them on,' Kell sighed. 'Used to get the crap kicked out of him pretty regularly until...'

'Oh, hang on, I remember now,' Davy interjected. 'When yer battered that Bradley kid yer said it was because him and his cronies kept picking on a lad a few years below you.'

'Yes... Mo,' Kell rubbed his knuckles. 'Anyway, Bradley got the message. We've since Mo and I swapped numbers without actually calling each other, but we do chat on the rare occasions our paths cross.'

'Well, I'll do a damn sight more than chat with him when I get my hands on him,' growled Davy. 'Have yer seen the dent in my c...'

Davy's words trailed off as his death march ringtone emanated from his garden *'office.'* He clambered to his feet, stretched his 6'10" frame and turned to the shed-cum-pub.

'Sorry kidda,' business calls.

Kell knew the score. He nodded upwards and headed indoors. Just before he closed the patio door behind him Davy called out.

'If yer looking for someone with motive to kill Alex, then ask Abraham about her dead daughter, Jade.'

***

Davy's mush was usually hard to read, especially covered in a footlong thicket of red whiskers as it was. On the other hand, his lively blue eyes frequently gave the game away. Today was no exception, and they creased up and positively glistened long before his bass chuckle worked its way up and out of his oesophagus, like some sort of sonic-optical echo.

He listened to Mo's voicemail message again, possibly to double-check that he had heard it right the first time, but more likely just for the fun of it. He replayed it a third time, and unable to contain himself any longer, spat a response out loud, accompanied by raucous laughter.

'So, yer wanna to *sort this out once and for all* do yer young'un?'

Davy enjoyed sorting things out. Arguably it was what he did best. He always said that his favourite kind of fight was one played by the rules. And especially when his opponent was the only one playing by them. He pulled out a drawer, closed it, ran a finger back and forth across the scar on his neck, then finally pulled it open again.

His trusty studded knuckle-duster freshly extracted, he slid it on like a silk glove and kissed it reverently, like he used to kiss his late pit-bull, Python, RIP.

Chapter Nineteen

Haze Bond was very cosy thank you very much. Cuppa, biccie and fluffy pyjama bottoms, she could have been all set for bed if she wasn't sat opposite Debbie Harrison down the nick.

'You say left the party an hour or so after Alex,' said Debbie. 'Where did you go? And was that alone?'

'Well, I didn't pull if that's wha' yer gerrin' at. More's the pity,' Haze's pink-violet-shadowed eyelid winked. 'Just went 'ome on me tod din I? Maybes about half twelve or so.'

'You live quite near the park don't you?' quizzed Debbie. 'You didn't see anyone in the vicinity did you? Or did anyone see you for that matter?'

'Well, I don' live quite as far as the park,' Haze stretched her long muscular legs to the side of the table. 'And nah, I didn't see no one, and I dunno if anyone saw me... I was pretty mortalled wan I?'

'What about Alex's boyfriend. Mr Downing?' Debbie asked. 'Have you seen him recently? It's just that we've tried his number numerous times already without a response.'

'E'll be up in Jockland probablies. 'E works there dun 'e?' Haze slurped her tea. 'Unless 'e's back in town I suppose.'

'So, do you know Mr Downing?'

'Course I know Deano,' Haze grinned. 'Me and Alex were besties were'n we? Besides, 'e was shaggin' me before they got together innit?'

'And that didn't bother you?' Debbie arched an eyebrow. 'Or make you jealous perhaps?'

‘Naa, not me bestie. Share and share alike was our motto innit?’ Haze laughed. ‘Now that Deano’s another story innhe? Green-eyed with a temper on ‘im. Glad to see the back ‘o ‘im wan I?

‘I see,’ Debbie jotted down some notes. ‘So, would you say that Alex had reason to be afraid of Dean?’

‘Well, she did put it about din she?’ Haze’s brown permed hair jumped around her shoulders as she chuckled. ‘But naa, he doted on ‘er and she only ever played the field when she was back in town an ‘im up in jockland din she? Alex might ‘av been loose, but she wasn’t daft.’

‘But what if Dean discovered she’d been unfaithful?’ Debbie asked.

‘Well, that could‘ve been dodgy but she said nowt to me, so I doubt ‘e knew, but it’s possible, I guess,’ Haze munched a biscuit. ‘She was gonna leave ‘im anyways wan she?’

‘Oh, and why was that?’

‘Well, Deano was ‘andy inasmuch as she never ‘ad to work, ‘e bought ‘er nice togs an’ ‘e kept ‘er in tequila, but she was just usin’ ‘im till a better option came along.’

‘Such as?’

‘She was due another windfall wan she?’ Haze machine-gunned crumbs across Debbie’s notes. ‘Loads more than the first one she said. Then she was gonna leg it somewhere ‘ot. Benidorm or Ibiza or summit.’

Debbie underlined the word *windfall* and put a big question mark after it. ‘I don’t suppose she told you where this windfall was coming from?’

‘Naa, clammed up when I quizzed about it din she?’ Haze knotted her big oblong face. ‘An us besties an all. ...Though if yer ask me it’ll likely ‘ave ‘ad summit to do wi’ Jade innit?’

The DI appeared at the windowpane and Debbie waved him through.

‘Sorry Ms Bond,’ Debbie turned back to face Haze as Abraham entered. ‘What’s this you were saying about Jade?’

Abraham sat down opposite Haze and locked his frosty eyes onto hers. 'Yes Ms Bond, what's all this about Jade?'

'Er, nowt,' Haze stared at her false nails and fiddled with them. 'Dunno innit?'

***

'As far as you are aware, do you know of any reason why someone might attack Alex?' asked Abraham. 'Or wanted her dead.'

'Well, she 'ad – and dumped – a couple of hubbies an' more than her fair share of ex's din she?' Haze glanced at Abraham then quickly looked down, 'Used t' 'av 'em dancin' on a string she did. I'd have *died* for her figure... Jesus, wharamah sayin'?'

Tears suddenly flooded down Haze's round cheeks. Abraham leaned forward and handed her a tissue. 'I share your tragedy Haze. But rest assured we'll get the scum who did this.'

'Soz,' Haze wiped her eyes and blew her nose. 'Can't ger over it can I? Yeah, she was no Mother Teresa, but she was me bestie. And I've no idea who'd wanna kill her... and especially like *that*.'

'I know it's difficult,' Debbie passed over another tissue. 'But if you have information about who could be responsible then you must tell us.'

'Well, she 'ad a huge fallout with Davy Lilley, but that was over twenty years ago. She also said that Mick Braithwaite 'ad her by 'er throat one time. Swore blind he almost killed her,' Haze sniffed. 'That was maybes three years ago.'

'Interesting,' Abraham sat up straight. 'Had Lilley or Braithwaite been pestering her lately?'

'Naa,' Haze said. 'Though we did bump into Mick at that party the other night, but that was pure chance. Alex said that she 'adn't seen 'im before then in donkey's.'

'Do you know if Alex ruffled any other feathers?' asked Debbie.

‘Well, I did wonder about summit,’ Haze chewed her lip then fiddled with some of her gold neck chains. Debbie encouraged her with a nod. ‘Well, it’s about the way she died innit? You know… decapitated.’

‘What about it?’

‘Well, it’s just that she ‘ad a thing about them lot, yer know, Muslims din she?’ Haze’s eyes toughened. ‘She ‘ad nowt against anyone, yer blacks, yer Asians and wotnot, but for some reason – an’ she never said why – but she definitely ‘ad it in for yer Muslims. Now and again she’d just blow ‘er top and rant on about ‘em, and to ‘em – like the right mouthful she gave this poor lad at the kebab shop; effing and blinding an’ shakin’ her fist… and just ‘cos of too much garlic sauce… or so she reckoned.’

Abraham looked from Haze to Debbie and back again.

‘I don’t suppose she knew anyone at the mosque?’

Haze shook her head.

‘Or someone called Blenkinsopp?

…Mohammed Blenkinsopp.’

Chapter Twenty

It was a five to ten-minute hop from three-quarters of the way up Grange Road to Ward Jackson Park. Droopy-eyed Mo took twenty.

The park detour was the last thing he wanted. 10000 steps a day they say. He'd seemingly done that tenfold, some of it almost literally in his sleep.

Exhausted or not, he found the crime scene without any bother. The tell-tale tape had since been removed, but several bunches of flowers laid out by some bushes near a tree gave Mo more than just an inkling of where it had been. He slapped his sides and blew out a big breath as he trudged over; an attempt to stir some life back into himself. If there were any clues still hanging about then he needed all the wits he could muster to weed them out, and especially with those other things hanging about; his uncertainty about his own innocence, a feeling that he had been followed, and doubts about some of the evidence against him such as his mobile number on Alex's list of contacts. *Was someone really trying to set him up?* Shattered though he was, something within told him that he needed to be on the front foot and not just hang about like a... he looked over to the pond. ... a sitting duck.

***

After thirty minutes mooching and poking around amid the flora and fauna on his hands and knees Mo finally discovered something – namely that this policing malarkey was a lot harder than it looked. Certainly, a sharp TV sleuth would have spotted, analysed and deciphered one, two or more virtually imperceptible clues by now – linking a tiny grain of black chernozem soil to the Russian Steppes, the KGB and a distant descendant of the cousin of one of the Cambridge Spy Ring. Alas, all Mo had unearthed for all his troubles was a toffee wrapper, some duckling down and a dog turd. Strictly speaking, that wasn't quite true. He too had noticed the same rectangular indentation in the ground as Abraham and SOCO, but whereas he reasoned that the police would already have a handle on its significance (or otherwise), Mo could only scratch his head and wonder.

Yawning, he crawled over and slumped next to the tree. Did he really want to continue searching? Unequivocally not. It wasn't just the fatigue that was gnawing away at him, but dread and realisation that if there were any clues to be had then they'd long since been bagged up and carted off to some evidence room. He'd already been over the scrub with a fine-tooth comb - was there really any point to going back over the same ground? Almost certainly not. Was there any value to just accepting his losses and staggering home to bed? Plenty – it beckoned his withering soul like a dessert oasis mirage. It was just that if there was even the tiniest bit of truth to be had, the most minuscule clue that could prove his guilt or innocence either way to himself, then Mo would be kicking himself from here to kingdom come if he missed it. Sighing, he leaned his back against the tree and resigned himself to scouring the scene at least one more time. Well, after a ten-minute breather...

He ran his palm over the rough undergrowth and got a splinter in a fingertip for his trouble. He tweezed it out with his teeth and a droplet of blood surfaced. Mo closed his eyes and took in the sound of leaves rustling in the gentle breeze, some kids on skateboards and a quacking duck – possibly a disgruntled drake lecturing his chick on the importance of good feather upkeep.

Mo stretched his arms behind his head and blindly ran his fingers across the tree's bark. After a while he stopped what he was doing and shuffled around to examine whatever was under his index finger. It was hard to tell by touch alone, but it felt like a carving. A fresh one. When he did lock his eyes on it, they no longer drooped, but bulged and widened, while more than just a jitter juddered through his veins as he traced the inscription.

MB I

Chapter Twenty-One

'Do you just sit on your backside and eat and drink all day?'

Gran's quip was delivered with a smile, but there was something in the tone that suggested that she was serious.

'Yep,' Duty Sergeant Matty Black popped another crisp in his mouth without looking up from his newspaper. 'What are you up to anyway? I thought you were supposed to be interviewing Mick Braithwaite with the DI?'

'The DI has decreed a recess due to Braithwaite's arseholiness,' Gran swiped a few crisps. 'If indeed there is such a word.'

'In Braithwaite's case I'm sure there is,' Matty said. Right on cue a din emanating from Mick's holding cell kicked off. Pounding fists, threats and effing and blinding. 'That's a turnaround he was fine when you brought him in.'

'Yes, well, that was me,' Gran said. 'Mick and the DI seem to rub each other up the wrong way.'

'What about the interview,' asked Matty. 'Have you made any progress yet?'

'Not really, he's admitted that he had a run-in with Alex on Catcote Road, and he's owned up to the bad blood between them, but he's denying everything else – most vehemently - as you can hear for yourself.'

'Do you have anything on him?'

'She attacked him in the vicinity, so there is motive and opportunity,' said Gran. 'And we'll be testing his clothes for Alex's blood and DNA as well as checking Alex's body for traces of Braithwaite, but if all that comes back negative then we've got diddly squat other than circumstantial evidence.'

'So, no murder weapon?'

'No sign of one as yet, and according to the DI, Mick is habitually *more of a bare-knuckles kinda hoodlum*. But that doesn't necessarily mean he is incapable of murder or doesn't have any weapons stashed away somewhere. 'There's even a rumour that one of his false legs doubles as switchblade.'

'What? gaped Matty. 'Did you check it out?'

'Yep, he handed them over with a wink and an amused grin earlier.'

'And?'

'He probably started the rumour himself for a laugh,' said Gran. 'I spent 30 minutes prodding it and fiddling with the bolts while he scoffed and picked his nose.'

'Find anything?'

'Me no. But Mick unearthed an unfeasible number of bogeys,' Gran took a slurp of Matty's tea uninvited. 'Urgh, you've put sugar in it.'

'What about Blenkinsopp?' Matty took back possession of his Mr Messy cup and grinned as he added yet another sugar lump. 'He's been in and out of here like a yoyo.'

'Yes, I heard about the drugs,' Gran sighed. 'I asked Kell about that and he just shook his head at me and told me to *don't ask.*'

'Tch,' Matty shook his blond head as well.

The station door clattered open and Jerzy hurried through towards gents. Aftab ambled in a few seconds later and leaned over the public side of the reception counter. He too nicked some of Matty's crisps. 'Don't mind me. As you were...'

'If you are talking about the murder,' Gran addressed Matty without minding Aftab one little bit. 'Then unless we find a weapon with his prints on it then anything we have on him is all just circumstantial too.'

'Who is this *his?'* Aftab enquired. 'Mo, Mick or someone else?'

'Blenkinsopp,' Matty replied.

'Ah,' Aftab crunched. 'If you are talking about Mo then there is one thing.'

Matty raised a physical eyebrow alongside his verbal 'Oh aye?'

'It could be Mo will have a perfectly reasonable explanation,' said Aftab. 'But me and Jerzy have searched high and low at his place, including the back garden and bins and stuff, and the funny thing is that we couldn't find head nor tail of these chinos, shirt and Hush Puppies that he was supposedly wearing at the party.'

'That is odd,' Gran concurred. 'Some would even say suspicious.'

'Yes, you'll have to let the DI know Aftab,' said Matty. 'Although, I'm pretty sure he was wearing Hush Puppies when he left here. If the last couple of days are anything to go by, he'll be back again tomorrow, and we can nab his shoes then.'

'Or better still,' Gran ran a hand through her curly grey locks. 'You and Jerzy can get yourself back in the vicinity and extend your search for the garments to the neighbouring bins and gardens.'

'Yeah, we can pop back round again in a bit,' Aftab said. 'But I thought Mick Braithwaite was the prime suspect now?'

'Well as things currently stand, he's a slightly more likely candidate than Blenkinsopp,' Gran said. 'But Blenkinsopp is still in the frame. He'd had cross words with the victim and admits to following her, or at least he admits to heading in the same direction as her. He's by no means in the clear yet, and especially not if something else crops up.'

'Like a bloody blue and white shirt,' offered Aftab.

'Like a bloody blue and white shirt, like a weapon, or in the words of the DI, like *being up to no good on the Islamist crackpot front.*'

'Funny you should say that Gran,' Matty thumbed backwards through a few pages in the local newspaper. He stopped at pages two and three flattened them out and turned them an angle so both Gran and Aftab could read the content. 'Here, what do you make of that?'

'Oh, MI6 are issuing heightened warnings of Islamist backlashes following the latest in a long line of tit-for-tat killings. This time an ultra-right-wing loner with a rifle at a Swedish mosque,' Aftab read. 'Are you saying that you think Mo is gun-toting vigilante Gran?'

When Gran didn't answer Matty chipped in, 'Maybe a sword-toting vigilante. What do you say Gran? Do we nab Blenkinsopp for sword or gun-toting vigilantism?'

'I wasn't actually looking at that article. But it's no joke. We may be nabbing Blenkinsopp for more than just that before long. Sorry about this Matty ...' Gran separated the first couple of sheets from the rest of newspaper, spun around and headed briskly back towards the CID offices. '...But I'm going to have to commandeer this.'

Gran was halfway back down the corridor and before Matty realised the full implications of her actions.

'Oi! The sport is on the reverse sides. You've taken that too!'

Chapter Twenty-Two

DI Abraham plonked himself uninvited on Audrey Melrose's desk, his legs akimbo. His eyes fixed onto her tied back sandy frizzy hair then wandered further down as he spoke.

'So, any progress on the numbers yet?'

'Not really,' Audrey crossed one arm over her chest and raised the other to her chin. 'Mick was born in December, so the twelfth month, and his flat is number 98 Wynyard Lane. He possibly gets the number 14 bus to the gym, stuffs his gear into locker 82 and does 58 bicep curls each day with 12kg kettlebells – but even if he does it's all just random stuff.'

'Yes, we need the common factor.'

'I'm aware of that sir,' Audrey heard a door open and looked pleased as she turned to see Gran enter. 'And I'm exploring possibilities.'

Gran signalled Abraham over to her desk at the other side of the room.

'Keep up the good work sergeant,' Abraham brushed Audrey's arm with his thigh as he dismounted the desk in a clumsy pommel-horse-esque manoeuvre.

'What is it?' he asked Gran curtly.

'Here,' Gran spread the newspaper on her desk and flattened it with a small palm. She lowered her voice. 'What, do you make of that?'

Abraham glanced down and scrunched up his nose. '*The Damned are booked to play at The Studio next Monday. It's the original line-up with Dave Vanian, Captain Sensible and Rat Scabies.* What's this? Are you taking the piss Grantham?'

'No, not that. There's this,' Gran tapped on the headline about the Islamist backlash warning and then prodded another article. 'But this is the one that really caught my eye.'

'Huge crowds and parking chaos anticipated as the Tall Ships event is set return to town in July,' gaped Abraham. 'That's just three months away.'

'Yes,' Gran flicked through her notepad and flashed the *Imam / ginger lad (sounds like) Tall Ships boom!* page in front of Abraham, who nodded in silence.

'I know you said you want real evidence not hunches or guesswork, but more and more things keep pointing to a possible terrorist angle. Do you still maintain that this jihadi-style element to the murder is a coincidence?' Gran tapped the newspaper features again. 'And especially if you also factor in this '*Tall Ships boom!*' thing as well as this Islamic backlash thing.'

'Look, I know what I said in the incident room, but that directive came from the chief super, not me.' Abraham ran a finger along the word *'boom!'* in the notebook. 'Pen-pushers don't really grasp the value of gut feelings. All they want to do is cover their squeaky-clean arses.'

Abraham led Gran over to the kitchenette. He felt the kettle. It was already quite hot, but he flicked the switch anyway and it rattled into life.

'All this terrorist stuff is more uncorroborated instinct rather than actual evidence. I know that, and you know that. But...' Abraham beckoned Gran closer with a bendy finger. His murmur could just about be heard above the almost boiled kettle. 'Holme-House prison is full of scum that would still be terrorising the streets if it wasn't for officers following our intuition.'

Gran rubbed her pointy chin. 'What are you saying patron?'

'I'm saying that while we do need to be sending out the right messages and be seen to be doing everything by the book, it's *my* case, and as far as

I'm concerned, my gut out-trumps the chief super's arse,' Abraham said. 'Privately I've had this down as an Islamist thing all along.'

'It's certainly an avenue that's hard to ignore,' Gran plonked two mugs down on the counter.

'Alex's best mate Haze has also just stated that Alex was anti-Muslim and very public about it,' continued Abraham. 'She can't remember Alex having dealings with anyone at the mosque, and she says she'd never heard Alex ever mention Blenkinsopp, but it doesn't mean there is no connection.'

'That's pretty flimsy though,' said Gran. 'It's not like having actual physical evidence tying Blenkinsopp to Alex.'

'Agreed,' Abraham said. 'But Debbie's just shown me an old *introduction to Islam* booklet that was found at Alex's flat.'

'But I thought you said that she was *anti*-Islam.'

'Alex was. But this was her daughter, Jade's, booklet. She tragically died not long... not long afterwards.' Abraham took a few moments to look away and wipe an eye. 'Guess who gave it to her?'

'Not Blenkinsopp?'

'Yes, Blenkinsopp. There's even a signed and dated inscription to Jade from him inside the cover. Apparently, they used to chat together at playtimes.'

'How do you know that?'

'Debbie was three years above them at their school,' Abraham said. 'It seems Jade and Blenkinsopp were both loners taking some solace in each other's company.'

'Hm, loners tend to be quite impressionable,' mused Gran. 'How did she die?'

'She...' something caught in Abraham's throat. 'She apparently committed suicide. Downed a bottle of vodka and jumped off a townhouse roof on a building site.'

'And this all happened after Blenkinsopp gave her this booklet?'

Abraham nodded. 'If Alex somehow associated Jade's death with her sudden interest in Islam, then it goes some way to explaining her deep-seated anti-Muslim views.'

'And if Jade was one of Blenkinsopp's few friends, then vice versa with him,' postulated Gran. 'Say for example, Jade had been feeling vulnerable and had been bad-mouthing her mother before she suddenly died - it'd explain how Blenkinsopp, with the help of his cronies or some Islamist cell, could be out for revenge on Alex. They could have been planning this for ages.'

'Yes, though talking of cells, it's a bit unusual that no Islamist extremist group has claimed responsibility for the beheading or for victory over the West yet, but it's early days, and besides, it may serve their purpose to lie low and keep shtum until they've completed their mission.'

'You mean more atrocities to come?'

'Atrocities? Yes. You can count on it Grantham,' Abraham flung two teaspoons down next to the mugs. 'Unless we nip it in the bud first. It's one reason why the chief super is leaning his sizable bulk down on my neck for a quick arrest.'

'I could have another word with my contacts,' said Gran. 'But there hasn't been as much as a whisper yet.'

'It's a shame it's still not the good old days or I'd have already hauled Blenkinsopp, Ishmael and Ahmed in - away from prying eyes,' Abraham rubbed his knuckles. 'Used to get so many crims singing like canaries in the far cell we could have set up a pet store side-line.'

Gran eyed Abraham over the rim of her glasses. 'But times have changed.'

'Not just times, but also protocols. Top-down sissy pandering and political correctness now don't just stretch to tiptoeing around rainbow-ribboned minefields and prisoner, religious and civil rights,' Abraham huffed. 'If the chief super had his way, then it'd also prevent us from arresting crooks in the first place.'

'An exaggeration surely,' said Gran.

'Not really. Take the chief super for example. What does he even know about frontline detective work? Or taking on adversaries with a bit of nouse? Zilch times FA squared. That's what,' scoffed Abraham. 'As I told some of our guys in the canteen a couple of weeks ago, with the chief super and the bluebottles in charge I'd be able to commit the perfect crime, leave flashing neon clues, and still get away with it.'

Gran raised an eyebrow and a crooked smile.

'Publicly, we've got to tow the company line on the both the *political* and the *keeping all lines of enquiry open* fronts, but between you and me, it's all BS Grantham.'

'So, what do you suggest doing about it?'

'Make the right sounds – at least in public,' Abraham continued. 'But behind the scenes stir things up, snout around and dig up dirt on Ahmed, Ishmael and Blenkinsopp. As soon as we get something concrete on any of them, we'll pounce.'

'What if any of them doing a runner in the meantime?'

'It's possible, but I doubt it. For starters, Ishmael and Ahmed don't know that we're wise to them. Unless that changes then they've no reason to run. In the meantime, we can monitor them. As mentioned, it could be that they are mere tiddlers who will lead us to the really big fish – and a spectacular collar.'

'And what about Blenkinsopp?'

'That's different. But I can't see him running either,' Abraham stroked his whiskers. 'If he legs it then he might as well just tether a giant neon ball and chain to his ankle flashing, *I'm guilty!* He'd get about as far as the end of his street. No, his only real option is to stay put and front it out.

'So, you are suggesting keeping tabs on Blenkinsopp too?'

Abraham's eyes gleaned ravenously, like a vampire about to pounce on a limp, defenceless virgin.

'*Especially* Blenkinsopp!'

Chapter Twenty-Three

Rather than head directly for the park exit, something drew Mo towards a nearby section of railings. He grunted with effort as his worn-out limbs hauled him over. Unsure what he was looking for he crouched down and examined the hotchpotch of bare soil and tufts of grass. Still none the wiser he creaked upright and scanned through the rails, past a mature willow towards the funny shaped tree and the bushes where Alex's body was discovered. He couldn't explain it, but all of a sudden, a chill froze his bones like the *Beast from the East.*

Or a blast from the past.

***

Ten minutes later he found himself suddenly stopping and scratching his head again. This time by a hedge-flanked gate of an impressive detached dwelling. Georgian, he guessed. A big, unusually shaped black and white thing anyway, with leaded windows, a prominent wooden rectangular door and a brass number plate by its side. Number 101. A prime number. Mo wondered if the owners realised it was a prime number. And a unique prime number at that. Was that one of the numbers that had been circling his subconscious? Maybe. Maybe not. The number 14 seemed to ring a bell. Or was it something else?

He sighed heavily.

Yet another enigma he was utterly clueless about.

***

Just 400 metres later, Mo took to walking on the sides of his feet to counteract the onset of blisters on his soles. No one hitchhiked in these parts, but he stuck his thumb out anyway. To hell with it, jobless and soon-to-be skint or not, if a taxi stopped instead of a kindly motorist, he was jumping in regardless.

As it happened it was a newish VW Beetle plastered in seemingly 1970's filth that stopped. A cloud of smoke bellowed from the driver's side window followed by a hairy face and a gap-toothed smile.

'Hey, you're the dude from the party,' Serge turned to his passenger and tweaked a knee. 'Look Kez, it's *him* from the party.'

Kerry turned, gave Mo a brief friendly wave then exhaled another long flume of smoke. 'Hey.'

Mo wafted away some smoke and peered into the car. His overcast eyes fell on the hippie and his beanpole girlfriend and brightened with recognition. 'Ah yes, I remember you.'

'Jump in dude,' Serge enthused. He took a drag of Kerry's roll up and offered it to Mo as he slid onto the back seat.

'No thanks,' Mo declined politely. The car stunk like an ashtray and the multitude of cigarette butts littering the floor told him just why. Even so, Mo felt a rush of gratitude. Not just for the relief for his sore feet and weary limbs, but also because after all that had gone on lately, it was a wonderfully refreshing reminder that, no matter how it seemed, maybe, just maybe, the whole world and his dog might not be all out to get him after all. 'Which way are you going?'

Serge looked over his shoulder and eyed Mo while simultaneously accelerating. 'Judging by the way you look man, we're going whichever way you are.'

***

As it happened, the way in question turned out to be pretty much in the same direction. It turned out that Serge lived above a shop on Brenda Road, just five minutes away from Mo's house.

Serge again turned to face Mo as he drove past St Cuthbert's church, 'Will somewhere around here do you okay?' Kerry giggled and jolted the steering wheel to avert bashing into a Volvo's wing mirror.

Mo gripped his seatbelt and nodded eagerly. 'This is just great. Thank you so much.'

'Glad to be of service dude,' Serge screeched to a halt and depressed the clutch with one foot while revving like mad with the other. Jaded as he was, Mo bolted out like a coiled red-headed krait. 'Hey, we're having a few jars in The Causeway after I drop the car off home. It'd be cool if you like to join us.'

'Maybe,' Mo raised a palm to receive Serge's hi-five through the window then yawned and stretched. 'But probably not.'

***

As Mo traipsed back to his house, he felt his phone vibrate in his pocket. Possibly a boring text message from Saboor. Although probably not if the events of the day were anything to go by. He yawned again and told himself that regardless of whatever it was, it could wait until tomorrow.

It wasn't the first error of judgement Mo had made today. And it wouldn't be the last either.

Not by a long chalk!

Chapter Twenty-Four

'Is that you Mo?'

It was a well-worn rhetorical question that greeted his entry. After all, who else but he and his mother had a key? Untypically, Mo ignored it and headed straight up the stairs instead.

'Mo-oh?'

'Urgh,' Mo moaned as he flopped facedown onto his rickety old bed. 'Yes Mam. It's me. I'm going to have forty winks if it's okay with you.'

'No wait.'

Mo grumbled from somewhere underneath his pillow as Mary's panting and her familiar slow, heavy footsteps got louder with each stair that she climbed. The door scraped open and a wheezing sound combined with the creaky floorboards to signal Mary's approach. Mo felt a tap on his legs. He sighed, then shifted to the wall side of his bed.

It was better than have his mam squash his legs.

'You look different?' the bed sagged and groaned as Mary lowered her planetary posterior down on it as gently as she could. 'Your hair. Your clothes.'

'Yeah well,' Mo mumbled a stifled response. 'Maybe a new look will bring me more luck than my old one ever did.'

Mary let out a little sigh and nodded. 'Where have you been son? Your bed hasn't been slept in.'

'I've been out.'

'Yes, but where?'

'Just out!'

Mo didn't usually sound like a stroppy teenager.

But right now he did.

'The police have been around.'

Mo turned his head, peeked out from below his pillow, then flung it aside and straightened up. All of a sudden Mary had his full attention.

'Police? Here?'

'Yes, that nice young man who you know, Aftab, and a colleague of his,' Mary said. 'Why did they come here looking for your clothes Mo?'

'Oh, I was just helping them with their enquiries,' Mo's casual response was in stark contrast to his heart that suddenly batted like a spring-loaded punchbag. 'It turned out to be a bit of a misunderstanding. Er... they didn't find anything by any chance did they?'

'No...' Mary felt Mo's breath wash over her as he exhaled. 'But I did.'

'Eh?'

'I did Mo. *I* found your clothes,' Mary spelt it out for Mo with probing eyes and a prodding finger. 'I put them in a bin at one of the houses on Patterdale Street.'

'What did you go and do that for?'

'Because they were soaked in blood son,' Mary took hold of Mo's shoulders and gave him a good shake. She looked him up and down with bubbling eyes. 'Why was that? And what are you hiding?'

'I don't know why. I was drunk. And I'm not hiding anything,' Mo roughly wriggled himself free of his mother's grasp. 'And you shouldn't have hidden them. It'll just give them more even reason to be suspicious of me.'

'I thought I was helping.'

'Well you weren't,' Mo spat. He rattled a temple with a knuckle then threw his hands up into the air. 'And what a stupid place to put them anyway. In a bin in the next street up from ours. That's one of the first places they'll look if they ever come back. I'm going to have to go out and retrieve them myself now.'

'Sorry son, I didn't know what to think,' Mary down bit on a nail, paused, and then looked up. 'But with all that's been going on in the news, you know with that poor lady in the park and all that...'

Mo felt his mother's hesitation and steeled himself for the inevitable question.

'You definitely didn't have anything to do with that did you?'

Mo sunk down and reburied his head in his pillow. Yes, he was tired, but that wasn't the main reason for turning away. He simply just couldn't look his mother in the eye right then.

'I met her at Saboor's party, which is why I'm on the police's radar,' Mo mumbled into his mattress. 'And I know it looks bad. I've been walking around all last night trying to get my head straight. But if you're asking me if I killed her, then the answer is no.'

Ten seconds later, confused and disturbed by the subsequent silence, Mo rolled back over and sneaked a glance at his mother through a gap in his pillow cocoon. The one eye of Mo's that was visible had a hint of fire, but behind a blurry sheen. Mary took some time to examine it before finally returning a slight but satisfied smile.

Mo's word was good enough for his mother it seemed.

Mo surreptitiously uncrossed his fingers behind his back. His own word seemingly not good enough for himself.

***

'I wanted to talk to you anyway,' Mary reached for Mo's hand. Mo twitched and retracted it, as if his mother's fingers were electrified. It wasn't so much the actual touch as the surprise that it came from her. 'It's about today.'

'What about today?' Mo yawned, closed his eyes and clawed his pillow closer still.

Mary placed both hands on her lap, looked down and fiddled with them as she mumbled. 'My appointment.'

'Appointment? What appointment?'

Mo rolled onto his side and faced the wall. Several seconds passed in silence, save for the breathing. Then a dozen or so more, save from the breathing, ...and the sniffs. Mo sharp spun over and flipped around so he was side by side with his mother on the bed. Tentatively, he touched her nails then gently stroked the length of her fingers.

'*That* appointment,' Mo's heart looped-the-loop then divebombed. 'Sorry Mam, I've been so wrapped up with myself that I completely forgot about you. I'm so selfish. How did it go at the hospital?'

Mary gently pulled her hand free from Mo's grasp, wiped her eyes, then replaced her palm on top of his. She turned to face him and slowly shook her head as tears trickled down her cheeks.

'No!' Mo cried. He sprung to his feet and wrapped his arms tight around her as far as they would go. 'No Mam! No!'

'I'm sorry son,' Mary wept. 'It's back again. In my stomach this time.'

'But they can treat it? Right?' Mo lifted his mother's chin with a finger and made a semblance of an attempt at a smile as he wiped away her tears. 'You can beat this Mam. Just like the last time.'

'But that's just it son,' Mary's tears suddenly stopped, as if someone had turned a stopcock. She dried her face with quavering fingers then shook her head solemnly. 'I'm tired. I've had enough. I really don't think that I do want to beat this.'

***

Mo collapsed on his knees in front of his mother and clamped her palms between his, in prayer.

'No Mam, please,' he implored. 'You can't just give in. You've got to fight. You've just got to.'

Mary sighed heavily and coughed as she struggled to her feet. 'Sorry Mo, I'm tired. I'm going to bed.'

'No, not yet,' Mo tugged at his mother's hands. 'We need to talk about this.'

'Not now son,' Mary pulled her hands free. 'Tomorrow maybe, but I doubt it'll make any difference.'

'No, now Ma...' Mo's words trailed off at the sound of banging at the door.

'What a racket!' Mary shuffled to the window and looked down. Abruptly she twisted back around and stumbled, gaping-mouthed and wide-eyed, half on Mo, half on the bed.'

'What is it?' Mo gasped as he wriggled upright and helped his mother struggle to her feet.

'The police,' Mary shuddered then scuffled out of the room. 'I can't deal with this son. I'm going to bed.'

'The police?' Mo gawped. 'Mam, please don't go. What if it's more trouble for me?'

Mary paused on the threadbare-carpeted landing. 'Sorry son.'

'But Mam...'

Mo watched helplessly as his mother scurried to her bedroom without even looking back. She waved away his protest with the back of her hand then clacked the door shut behind her. A split second later the letterbox clattered into life at the foot of the stairs.

'Argh,' Mo pounded his knuckles on his skull again and thumped down towards it.

Chapter Twenty-Five

Abraham shoved his palm through the door the moment it opened.

'Shoes!'

Mo looked down at his feet then returned a knotted brow gaze upon Abraham.

'Now!' Abraham barked impatiently, motioning Mo into action with a bendy finger.

Mo put his hands on his hips, stood stock still and studied Abraham's reddening face and contorted expression.

'Didn't you get as far as two syllables at ape school inspector?'

Abraham balled his palm into a fist and bore his eyes into Mo's. Mo leaned against the doorframe observing the transition as Abraham's sneer turned into snorts, then into a sigh, then into an ironic laugh.

'Very funny Blenkinsopp, but I'll tell you what's even funnier...'

Mo stretched his arms above his head and yawned elaborately.

'Me arresting you for perverting the course of justice,' Abraham smiled. 'Up to you of course.'

Mo peered down, then nonchalantly bounced off the doorframe with his shoulder to right himself. He kicked off his shoes without looking at them, preferring instead to hold Abraham's stare. Abraham held out his palm again but Mo ignored it and took a scruffy pair of trainers from a little pile in the hallway and sat down on the bottom stair.

'There you go Joe,' Mo said as he strapped on the old scuffed trainers without looking up. 'I've got nothing to hide.'

Mo smiled inwardly as Abraham bent down to pick up the Hush Puppies. Alas, his little personal victory proved short-lived, and he groaned inwardly once Abraham responded.

'That's good to hear. So, you won't mind me confiscating your PC too then?'

Mo held Abraham's gaze through slit eyelids, high noon stand-off style. He could sense the sweat on his neck as he cogitated. A voice in his head barked a warning, but for the life of him he couldn't work out why. Finally, he let out an exasperated sigh, turned and trudged up the stairs.

'I want it back soon mind.'

***

Unplugging all the cables, putting them in a bag from the kitchen, and carting them and his computer down to Abraham's car gave Mo time to think. There was nothing untoward on his PC, and he'd already given his Hush Puppies a good clean the day before. Nothing wrong with that. He habitually kept his stuff clean and tidy. That's just normal. Indeed, once he'd retrieved his other clothes from a bin up the road, he'd thought about giving them a good 60 degrees wash too, but on reflection, he decided that the right thing to do would be to take them to the police station unwashed.

'Be sure to take care with it, and I want it back soon remember,' he reminded Abraham as he carefully laid his desktop PC flat in Abraham's boot. He slid the computer further towards the centre and started to offload the cables from his bag into the boot too.

'I don't want your manky cables too!' Abraham hissed. Mo shoved them back in his bag and Abraham clunked the boot shut before finally deigning to answer. 'You'll get your PC back *if* and when I'm good and ready, and not a second before.'

Mo opened his mouth to argue, but realised it was probably a lost cause so instead he swivelled around and started walking away.

'Going anywhere?'

'Yeah,' Mo waved his red cloth bag without looking back. 'I've had a recent setback on my gear front, so I'm off to get a ginormous great stash of coke.'

Even Joe Abraham couldn't prevent himself from laughing at that riposte.

***

'Actually, Blenkinsopp. Come back a minute.'

Mo sighed and trundled back. 'What is it now?'

'I couldn't help remarking a disgruntled tinge to your tone just now. 'Perhaps you feel hard done by, or even,' Abraham laughed at his suggestion. 'That I somehow set you up with the drugs.'

'No somehow about it!' Mo spat. 'You know damn well you did.'

'Blenkinsopp, Blenkinsopp,' Abraham smiled as he edged up to Mo's ear. 'Of course I did. But knowing it and proving it are two completely different animals.'

Mo's eyes widened. 'I know that. I'm just surprised you've even admitted it at all, and especially to me.'

'But it's you especially that needs to know.'

'Eh?'

'Of course,' Abraham sneered. 'You've had confirmation that I've done it once. You need to know that I can do it again. Say for example if the evidence in the case of Ms Hobbs' murder doesn't quite add up to nailed-on conviction material then it could *ahem*, be given a helping hand.'

'And what if I didn't do it? What then? You'd send down an innocent man?'

'Innocent? You? You're in it up to your eyeballs. Apart from all the circumstantial evidence, no one gets rid of their clothes without reason. In your case, I also can't help but notice that you've recently given your shoes a damn good scrub. I wonder if you've considered the fact that the ground was damp that evening? As such we got some good shoeprints. Some very much like yours if memory serves me right. Don't worry we'll check thoroughly for a match. We'll also test the rest of your clothes when they turn up. If they are out there somewhere then we'll find them, and if there's just one drop of Alex's blood on them then I'll have you. We've already found something of yours at Alex's flat, but this would be physical evidence linking you not just to the victim, but to the scene of the crime, and the actual crime itself. And just so there'll be no squirming your way out of it with your top lawyer buddy Ghosh. I dare say I could also rustle up a bit more insurance on the evidence front, as well as one or two witnesses as a nice little bonus, God knows I've plenty of lowlifes under the cosh who could easily be knelt on.'

'And you'd do that? Kneel on them?'

'Why not? The chief super is kneeling on me to make an arrest ASAP. He's very keen on evidence. And as we know, I've a knack of supplying just that.'

Mo's mouth said nothing, but his eyes smouldered.

'I know what you're thinking. Will I go as far as helping the evidence along in something so serious as a murder enquiry? And maybe I'm bluffing,' Abraham winked. 'But just maybe.'

Abraham paused and stroked his goatee. 'Tell you what though. I'm a fair man. I'll do you a deal. If you can prove someone else did it then I'll let it drop.'

'Me prove it? You're the copper,' Mo spat. 'What do I know about policing? What evidence do you have on anyone else? What other clues do you have? It could take months. Years!'

'Should I supply you with classified police information?' Abraham pondered the question with a tap to a tooth. 'Alas, I'm not at liberty to divulge classified case information to a hoodlum like you Blenkinsopp.'

'But...'

'And oh yeah,' Abraham smirked. 'I'm due to give a media conference at midday tomorrow, and I intend announcing an arrest one way or another. So, you've got around 19 hours from now. Cheer up Blenkinsopp, you're going to be famous!'

Mo turned around without a word and started walking up the road again.

'I must say, I would have expected more of a reaction,' Abraham called out.

'I don't know why,' Mo muttered. 'Catch a killer with no clues and zero intel within the space 19 hours or go down for murder myself – that kind of crappy deal is par for the course. Just another day in the life of Mo Blenkinsopp.'

Chapter Twenty-Six

Mo picked up his pace. As hard as it was, he had to try to put Abraham's ultimatum out of his mind and focus on the next task at hand. In this case that involved finding his bloody clothes before the cops and then handing them in himself, possibly even to a different police station – or better still, a different police force - and insisting that they are tested without passing through DI Abraham's hands first.

Yet another nagging doubt started to pinball around his sore brain, but he couldn't put his finger on it this time – unlike a niggle he'd had a couple of hours earlier. He wouldn't swear to its authenticity, but he'd had a very hazy vision of looking through park railings that night and hearing a voice and a scream. He'd actually toyed with telling Abraham about it, but now, on reflection was super relieved that he hadn't. That admission, real or imagined - and regardless of his actions, guilty or innocent - would be enough for Abraham to gleefully tie Mo to the murder scene. Could the scream have been Alex? The shiver down his spine said yes. What about the voice? Was it her voice? Someone else's? Or even his own? Was there even a voice? And could he have climbed the railings and fell headfirst into the bushes as Abraham had suggested at his interview? The shiver down his spine quaked and intensified. Possibly. Quite possibly.

He glanced around and spotted Abraham's car still parked up. Was Abraham watching him intently in the rear-view mirror? He couldn't just turn around and go home now even if he wanted to. He pressed ahead. It was still daylight, so not the ideal time to go rummaging around strangers' bins for clothes caked in blood. Then again, the alternative of venturing into people's gardens after dark with a torch was arguably dodgier still. He rubbed the back of his neck, scanned around, then plonked some litter into his bag. His plan, if you could call it that, was to nonchalantly flick up the lids of some of the bins as he walked along Patterdale Street, throw in some litter as cover, and make a mental note of the bin that contained his clothes. If he didn't locate the right bin on the first attempt, then he'd then refill his bag and repeat the process every thirty minutes or so until he struck lucky. As long as he knew which bin to look for, he reckoned he could come back after dark and niftily extract his clothes semi-blind.

Mo took a deep breath and set forth. Some of the wheelie bins stood just behind the low walls that separated the gardens from the pavement, whereas some were right up against the houses. Mo aimed for the bins nearest the pavement first, not only because they were the easiest to get to, but also because his mam, more likely than not, would have chosen one of the closest bins too.

He flipped up the first lid, threw in a Twix wrapper, took a peep and continued on his way. He passed a few houses before lifting a second lid chucking in a crisp packet and taking another peek.

'Mo, what are you up to?'

Mo's heartrate suddenly shot up like a rev-counter at Silverstone. Trembling, he turned around. Then around again.

'Over here!' A few gardens away on the other side of the road a wrought iron gate swung open and Aftab's head popped out. He got up off all fours and stood up tall, closely followed by Jerzy, both sprouting refuge sacks, like bobbie binbag beanstalks.

'Oh, hi Aftab,' Mo's facial expression seemed pleased to see Aftab, but his body language didn't, and he dragged his feet trundling over, looking down and around and anywhere but in the detective's eye.

'You still haven't answered the question,' Jerzy glowered hard and unblinking. 'And what did you put in that bin over there.'

'Oh that,' Mo ran a hand through his waxed red hair then tugged an ear lobe. 'It was just a crisp packet. I've not eaten much all day, and I'm no litterbug.'

'What have you got in the bag?'

'Just the usual,' Mo gave it a pat like a faithful dog.

Jerzy's eyes narrowed and he moved forward. 'Mind if I take a look?'

'Be my guest,' Mo's voice sounded indifferent, but he felt his hands shake slightly as he held it open.

'What have we got here? A pumpkin, some computer leads, a mouse and assorted bits of litter,' Jerzy scratched his floppy blond hair. 'That's *the usual* is it?'

Mo pulled a crooked smile and looked over to Aftab.

'I'm more of a broccoli, TV aerial and bubble wrap kind of shopping bag guy myself,' quipped Aftab.

Mo's spirits warmed a tad at Aftab's friendly smile. For a moment he considered telling him about hearing the woman's scream at the park as well as Abraham's horrendous ultimatum. He'd always had Aftab down as a good guy. Maybe he could help? Mo was feeling more out of his depth by the minute and needed all the assistance he could get. That was for sure. It's just that... He bit on a nail as he dithered.

'So, what are you doing around here Mo?' asked Aftab with a raised eyebrow.

Mo clocked Aftab's sidewards glance to Jerzy. On second thoughts, maybe confiding in Aftab wasn't the best plan Mo decided. Instead, he just blurted out the first thing that came into his head. 'I said I might meet someone at The Causeway. I'm heading there.'

'It's a bit of a roundabout route,' Jerzy studied Mo who sensed his gaze and folded his arms across his chest. 'It would have been quicker to just go straight along Brenda Road.'

'Yeah well,' Mo shrugged and started out again in the same direction as before. 'If you really want to know I've been avoiding the main drags, what with Abraham's persistence in rounding me up, fitting me up and pissing me off.

There was some truth in that.

But just some.

***

Once he was out of earshot Mo let out a whoosh of relief at the thought of getting away without getting caught or arousing suspicion.

Back in the garden of number 93 Patterdale Street Jerzy tied another rifled refuge sack back up again and returned it to another wheelie bin. He nodded over his shoulder towards Mo as he rounded the bend then turned to face Aftab.

'Did you buy any of that?'

'Nope you?'

'Nope.'

'Abraham's going to love it when we tell him.'

Chapter Twenty-Seven

A mile and half away Kell knocked on Ishmael's door and waited for it to open. He flashed his ID card and tilted it upwards towards Ishmael who habitually bowed his head whenever it was near a doorframe anyway.

'Good evening sir, I believe you've already spoken to my colleague DC Harrison earlier. I was hoping we could have a word. Just some routine questions,' Kell nodded towards the hallway. 'Inside if you don't mind.'

Ishmael fixed a stare on Kell, his feet remained rooted to the front step. The only thing that actually moved was his mouth, chewing on something, like a giraffe chomping acacia leaves.

'Sir?' Kell's tone seemed part rhetorical interrogative, part imperative. Either way, it didn't appear to have much effect on Ishmael. However, just as Kell tapered his eyes, raised an index finger and opened his mouth Ishmael turned around and stepped inside.

'Come.'

***

'DC Harrison said that you confirmed that Mohammed Blenkinsopp came here around midnight on Saturday,' Kell wandered around the simple, compact living room and ran one finger first across the windowsill then another over some books on the battered five-shelf unit. A coating of dust blackened one of his fingertips. 'Midnight is a bit of a strange time to come calling.'

Ishmael shrugged, moseyed over to the fireplace and stretched his tubular arms down to each extremity of the old-fashioned mantlepiece.

'What was the nature of his visit?' Kell took out one of the books and flicked through a few pages. 'It's just that he's been assisting us with our enquiries on a very serious matter. I'm sure that you'd want to do the same – being a very serious matter and all that.'

Ishmael straightened his back and, almost unfeasibly, stretched his dark arms further still, like a kapok tree - sending the sleeves of his ill-fitting brown suit riding practically to his elbows. His bald head remained stock still, but his big black eyes followed Kell as he wandered around the room. Kell stopped in front of a black cloth banner pinned to the back wall above a tatty two-seater sofa. He rubbed his jaw as he studied the funny white writing. He bent an eyebrow then crinkled the other. If he really wanted to decipher the gobbledygook then he needed to be rubbing a genie's lamp, not his stubbly chin.

'As explained to your female colleague, it was a chance encounter,' Ishmael said. 'I invited Mohammed in, we spoke briefly and then he returned home.'

'Surely you mean headed back across the green towards Catcote Road, rather than *home*?' Kell corrected. 'You don't actually know where he went when he left here. Or do you?'

'No,' Ishmael set stony eyes on Kell. 'But any implication that Mohammed had anything to do with that murder is unfounded.'

'I'm not implying anything, but do you know that for a fact Mr Kipkeita?' Kell returned Ishmael's stare with interest. 'I'd be very interested to know just how if you did.'

'I just know,' Ishmael was the one to break eye contact.

'So, when you happened to just bump into him at an ungodly hour practically on your front step, he didn't perchance have a weapon on his person did he?' Kell chuckled ironically. 'I don't know, something like a great big sword for example?'

'No, he didn't,' Ishmael replied blankly.

'And I don't suppose that you have... I don't know,' Kell unhurriedly scanned the room. 'Something like a great big sword here by any chance do you?'

'No, I don't,' Ishmael swept a huge palm towards the hallway. 'Now if that's all officer, I have matters to attend to.'

'Certainly, I won't keep you. Just one last thing if you don't mind,' Kell smiled like a long-lost buddy as he dug out his notebook and pen and laid them on the small computer desk in the corner. 'If you could just jot down your telephone number that'd be great. It'd save us from coming here and disturbing you if we have any other questions.'

Ishmael fixed a stare on Kell, nostrils fanning. Without breaking eye contact he strode over and took the pen. As he scribbled down his number Kell moved to reoccupy Ishmael's recently vacated spot. He ran his hand along where the ornately tiled mantlepiece met the wall, then stepped back and admiringly took in the view.

'The electric fire is a misfit, but they don't make mantlepieces like that anymore.'

Without a word, Ishmael held out the paper with his number for Kell and examined him with narrowed eyes.

'Thank you for your assistance Mr Kipkeita,' Kell made his own way out. 'You've been most helpful.'

***

Ishmael watched Kell drive away from a gap in the thick curtains. He retrieved his ancient Nokia from his jacket pocket and readied himself for another battle with first-generation predictive text. He got as far as navigating to Mo's number and clicking to write a new message, but after a few minutes of deliberation he binned the message. Despite running over things again in his head. And again, for a second, and even a third time, he still wasn't quite sure what had just taken place himself.

Chapter Twenty-Eight

For the second time in the day, Mo was back on his blisters, detouring. This time to a spot opposite Burn Valley. He massaged his legs but wasn't really thinking about his weary limbs or tight calves, instead he was ruminating over this *MB I* engraving thing while keeping half an eye on the big old house with blue and white spotlights running down from the roof. One that bore an uncanny resemblance to a place that Kell had previously described to him as the one he shared with Abraham.

True, his colander-esque recent memory could hardly be classed as reliable, and admittedly, the *MB I* etching could have been carved with the scissors that he'd taken from Saboor's kitchen – no need for a sword. But even so, this whole thing sat very uneasily with him. His initials or not. Memory or no memory, Mo just felt someone else's hand at play. And foul play at that.

And if so, then who?

And, just as importantly, why?

***

He backed into the shadows of an overhanging branch as he weighed up the pros and cons of the insane idea of breaking into Detective Inspector Abraham's house. On the one hand, if he got caught – something which was more *probable* than possible - then Abraham would throw the book at him for sure. On the other hand, if there were clues to be had, and he missed them, then the odds were that he'd be arrested for murder in... he checked his watch ...just 18 hours' time.

Truth be told, he couldn't, hand on heart, say that he knew for sure if foul play shrouded the case - let alone if he was being set up for murder. Coincidences did happen after all. However, the fact that the hairs that stood up on the back of his neck whenever he thought about it suggested that there was something in the crazy notion. And if so, then one candidate's smug grin and icy eyes didn't just spring to mind, but shook and slapped it about to boot! A person who had not only threatened him less than one hour ago, but who had also encouraged, nay, all but *coerced* him to go digging for evidence.

'Okay Joe,' Mo whispered to himself as he crept edgily down the drive. 'If you insist.'

***

Yet another of his mounting nags resurfaced as he neared. Abraham had mentioned that something of Mo's had been found at Alex's flat. Rack his brains as he might, he just couldn't fathom what on earth the DI meant by that. Either way, it had more than just a foreboding ring to it. He wiped some sweat from his forehead and made a mental note to add it to his growing *'to investigate'* list.

Trudging the house's perimeter, Mo cringed with each branch snap and crunch of gravel. Backing into and bashing his head on a hanging basket with a loud 'ouch!' hardly classed as textbook *casing the joint* material either, but the minute or so's subsequent silence at least confirmed Mo's suspicions that the house was probably empty. He greeted the apparent lack of CCTV and the absence of guard dog teeth marks on his butt as welcome bonuses too.

What the hell. Mo gave the front, back and garage doors energetic rattles. He pulled a crooked smile and scratched his head. Had he really expected the local force's finest to be lax on the lock up front? No, of course not. It was always going to be a long shot. He scanned the windows and the alarm box. Battened down and primed. No surprise there either. A brick through a window remained one possibility.

And it did cross his mind. But not for long. Yes, he wanted to have a good snoop around inside for clues, but not really at the expense of vandalism. Besides, the alarm was almost certainly hot-wired direct to the police station.

It was the scraggly end of a compromise, but Mo settled for a gander through all the ground floor windows. He yawned as he scanned the living room. It wasn't clear if this was due to his own exhaustion or the room's dull décor. Either way, he spent a little while longer peering through the next window. Eyes straining, he couldn't quite make out the wording on the papers on Abraham's desk, though on reflection, they looked more like household bills than case documents. Abraham's PC was switched off, so that yielded nothing new either. He scanned the pictures on the wall, a small bookcase, a compact filing cabinet and various bits and bobs dotted around the room including a penknife, a diary and a camera with a zoom lens.

Mo spent a few more minutes peering through a sparsely furnished dining room window before coming to the kitchen at the back of the house. The first thing that hit him was the knife on the worktop. He'd handled a butcher's knife often enough over the years to recognise one when he saw one. Of course, just because Abraham owned a butcher's knife, it didn't necessarily translate that he'd kill someone with it as a means to set Mo up. Besides, extremely sharp as they were, a short thing like a butcher's knife didn't strike Mo as a beheader's weapon of choice.

Mo contemplated his findings as he approached the garage. Yes, Abraham had a penknife, and he *could* have etched *MB I* on the tree, but so could plenty of others – including himself. Similarly, Abraham *did* have a butcher's knife in his kitchen, but so did many thousands of householders. It didn't mean anything.

'Face it, there's no evidence to suggest that Abraham has it in for me enough to set me up for murd...' Mo's self-mumbling tailed off as he peered through the garage window. He gaped like a gobsmacked gibbon as evidence to the contrary hit home.

Chapter Twenty-Nine

As he traipsed towards The Causeway, Mo's mind ticked over like a jittery psychological timepiece with super-hiccups - racing from thoughts to prickly notions to doomsday scenarios ad infinitum. Far from *getting away with things,* it had now dawned on Mo that his escapade with the bins had just made matters monumentally worse. Firstly, the penny had dropped that even if Aftab and Jerzy hadn't suspected him earlier – something that on reflection he doubted - then the fact of the matter was that there was no way he could go back looking for his clothes now. That particular stable door had been whacked to smithereens by a bolting band of horses. Worse still, there was nothing he could do now to avoid arousing (yet more) suspicion. They would surely find his hidden clothes. They would run tests on the blood. And if any of it matched Alex's then he was doomed. Even if it didn't match then the odds of retaining his liberty were still now hanging from thinner and weaker threads. Then there was also the matter of a nagging doubt that he couldn't place earlier. Now that he had put his finger on it - the jihadi video on his PC - he wished he hadn't, because it was like pressing a nuclear detonator. Certainly, his head felt like it was about to explode. And those little threads of freedom were going snip, snip, snip, snip, snip.

Almost as soon as he put a finger on that particular doubt another one surfaced. He began to feel like a little Dutch boy scrambling to plug holes in an increasingly crumbly dam. This latest niggle related to Abraham's comments and his ultimatum for Mo to solve the case within just...Mo checked his watch, ...17 and a quarter hours. If Mo hadn't killed Alex – something he wasn't even sure of himself – then the fact is that someone else must have. If so who?

Abraham seemed the prime contender, but a personal grudge against Mo going back to a school ground spat is one thing, but surely not enough for Abraham to murder someone else over? It sounded ludicrous, but Mo felt he needed to mull over the possibility, nevertheless. Just assuming that Abraham *was* the killer, then he was hardly going to arrest himself. He'd want someone else to take the fall. If so, then a set-up had to be considered as a distinct possibility. Little wonder then that he'd initially taken the sight of his peppered mugshot glued to the dartboard in Abraham's garage as proof of Abraham setting him up. That made sense in his state of shock at the time. However, on reflection, it wasn't so black and white. It merely confirmed what Mo already knew - Abraham had it in for him. Yes, it reinforced Mo's conviction that he should take Abraham's ticking clock timebomb seriously, but it didn't prove that Abraham had killed anyone or even done anything to tamper with the evidence against him for murder – yet!

A likelier potential killer was probably someone from the party anyway. Saboor, Kell and his new girl could be ruled out as they never left the house, but any one of the other partygoers could have followed Alex and killed her. The North African guy kept slipping in and out of his conscious. Had he been at the party? He looked pretty shifty. And some of the partygoers, male and female, looked downright dodgy to say the least. He had recognised some older lads from his school including that thug McCabe and his glue-sniffer pal, Jizzo – who looked like he'd since progressed to harder drugs. And what about Alex's lanky female-prop-forward-looking mate who had given him the evils as he had left? She had some menacing stare on her. Thinking about it, she'd given Alex the evils too. But that was probably just because Alex had left her on her tod with Jizzo hovering. A more likely killer candidate would have been Davy Lilley, had he not left wide-grinned and slathering all over his fancy woman. Then again, that Mick bloke had motive after Alex's attack on him. Opportunity too. But on the other hand, he had no weapon on him as far as Mo could remember.

His mind slipped back to Abraham again. He wouldn't put anything past Abraham. But killing someone? And what motive could he possibly have? Besides, he hadn't even been to the party, and it was hardly likely that Abraham would just coincidentally bump into Alex in the middle of the park after midnight. Mo shrugged off that thought as grabbing at straws rather than anything based on facts and rationale. Moreover, if the killer was someone other than Mo, it still didn't explain his vivid dreams about lying on top of a headless woman's body. If they were indeed just dreams. Certainly, the blood on his clothes and body suggested something both very gruesome and very real. If so, then how could even a muscleman like Mick, or anyone else for that matter, miraculously transport Mo on top of Alex's body without Mo or anyone else noticing? And why would even the most insane of murderers want to do that anyway? None of it added up. Indeed, all the sound posturing always came back to the same conclusion – *the only logical suspect is me!*

Mo hung his head, sighed heavily and changed direction towards the police station.

***

Glassy eyed, he suddenly stopped after 200 metres or so. Something else bothered him too. Something about his phone. And it scratched and refused to budge in amongst all this cerebral turmoil. He couldn't be 100% certain, but he would swear that something about his phone was different when Abraham retrieved it earlier.

If that niggle still sported a big question mark, then there was another one that kept resurfacing that was far clearer cut. How come *his* contact details were on Alex's phone? The more he thought of it the more it bugged him. He'd racked his brains and remained convinced that he'd never met her before. Moreover, they had barely exchanged half a dozen words between them. Things kept pointing back to the same question. Could someone be really trying to set him up? Again! For murder this time! Abraham? Someone else? Apparently, it was Debbie who checked Alex's phone. Surely not Debbie? Or could there be another explanation? Something possibly unrelated to the murder?

Either way, it felt like there was either something else going on or someone was out to get him. Mo swivelled on his heels and set out back towards The Causeway again, scanning around en-route. Ever since he'd sensed that someone had been watching him the night Alex was killed, he'd been wary. And all this wariness was making him weary.

After another five minutes of trundling, Mo came to a halt. He slowly raised his head up past *The Causeway* sign then up to the grey, cloudy, miserable sky. He clawed and rasped his hair as he wondered what in Allah's almighty kingdom he was going to do.

He marched forward emphatically. He knew exactly what he was going to do.

Drink was what he was going to do.

Chapter Thirty

A pert butt butted the door open.

'Gran says Dean Downing has been in touch,' announced Abraham.

'Yes, he works offshore as a diver and missed my initial calls, but has since got back to me. He sounded genuinely shocked when I told him about Alex. I also spoke to his boss who confirms that Dean has been offshore for three days, so has an alibi...' Audrey's voice trailed off as she watched Abraham struggle to back into the office with his briefcase in one hand and something else in the other.'

'Pressie for you, courtesy of Blenkinsopp,' Abraham turned around, smiled then promptly crunched his teeth together after dropping Mo's PC on DS Melrose's desk from a height with a clunk and a clang.

Audrey studied his changing expression and tutted.

'What?'

'I know what that's about,' she waved a finger in the direction of Abraham's face. 'Dropping Blenkinsopp's computer gave you some sick kind of satisfaction. Possibly he asked you to be extra careful with it. So, you drop it. Then once you do, you realise something. Oh yeah. The metallic clatter signals that you may well have just shattered evidence – evidence that treated delicately could have put him behind bars. But oh dear, DI Joe Butterfingers has just made whatever it was disappear into some kind of binary black hole.'

Abraham laughed out loud, doffed an imaginary cap and applauded. 'I knew there was some reason why I put you up for promotion.'

Shouts and the sound of hammering fists on a cell door resonated up two corridors and into the open CID office. The DI and his sergeant turned towards the source of the din.

'Abraham, I know you're there. Let me out!' Mick yelled. 'You've no right to keep me banged up.'

Abraham smirked. DS Melrose pulled a crooked smile of her own.

'I know that look too.'

'Oh yeah?'

'Let me see,' Audrey teased her silver stud earring and studied Abraham's eyes. 'You've reasonable grounds to bring in Braithwaite so you question him. Notwithstanding the usual verbal abuse and the current racket, he's been quite compliant. Surprisingly so. He's handed over the clothes he was wearing on the night in question. Ones that appear wrinkled and grubby, but not, at first sight, blood-stained. Or if they do indeed contain blood then it's nowhere near as much blood that'd be consistent with chopping someone's head off. Anyway, he answers all your questions – waiving his right to a solicitor I should add - and he admits his run-in with Alex on the night in question, he admits his whereabouts in the vicinity of the park, he even admits that they sometimes came to mutually-delivered ugly blows when they were a couple. But what he doesn't admit is anything to do with her murder. Indeed, he denies it most vehemently, and most vociferously – as you can no doubt attest to this very instant.'

'Open up!' Mick's roared and ramped up his banging.

'You've no actual evidence of his involvement in the murder – it's just circumstantial - and deep down you suspect he'll be given a clean bill of health once all the forensic results come in. Really, you've got zilch in terms of actually proving he's committed any crime whatsoever.'

Mick laid into the door with his forehead as well as his fists, 'I've not done nothing!'

'Except perhaps a grammatical crime in the crackdown on double-negatives,' Audrey added.

'Very good,' Abraham clapped again. 'But you got all that stuff about circumstantial evidence from Grantham.'

'What if I did?' Audrey moved Mo's PC to one side. 'Besides, I haven't finished yet.'

Abraham rasped his whiskers and swayed a palm before him. 'Pray continue.'

'So, you're going to let him go,' she said without even looking up as she tidied her desk. 'You particularly dislike Braithwaite. He particularly dislikes being locked up. Keeping him in the cells longer than is necessary is a win-win for you and your twisted ego. So, you'll make him wait, you'll gloat on his suffering and once your threshold is reached, you'll let him go. My money is within the hour.'

'Threshold?' Abraham contorted one side of his goatee. 'What threshold?'

'Either you'll get bored, or he'll get too noisy and disturb your tea break or something,' Audrey looked up at Abraham with a gleam in her eye. 'So, which is it?'

'Well done sergeant, it's probably a bit of both,' Abraham laughed and clapped for a third time. 'And I probably couldn't put up with another full hour.'

Audrey picked up her mobile phone and reading glasses, stuck her thicket of hair under the desk and beamed to herself as she put her belongings in her handbag.

'Besides, between you and me, Blenkinsopp is still the main suspect,' Abraham tapped on Mo's PC as Audrey retracted her head out from under her desk. 'I want you to scour this thing.'

'For anything related to Alex's murder and numbers enigma I presume?'

'And any Islamist extremism link too.'

'So, you *do* think Alex's murder is related to that?' Audrey raised a neatly trimmed eyebrow. 'Do you have any evidence?'

'Nothing concrete as yet,' Abraham loosened his shirt collar. 'But I'm not ruling it out, and I wouldn't put Blenkinsopp past it.'

'So, what do you want me to check?' said Audrey. 'Emails, correspondence, browser searches, visited websites etc?'

'Yes, I'm not sure if it's worth checking his image and video files too. What do you think? I mean, even Blenkinsopp isn't dumb enough to leave us a file hanging around with ha...' Abraham chuckled. 'Him waving a bloody sword around!'

'Yeah right,' Audrey laughed. 'Even so, I'll go through it, video files and all, with a fine-tooth comb. Rest assured, if he's got anything even remotely dodgy on it I'll find it.'

'I wouldn't expect anything less from you DS,' Abraham said in all sincerity.

'But my shift was officially up two hours ago, and in theory at least, I think I'm still entitled to the odd slither of actual life,' Audrey slid her chair back. 'So, it'll be tomorrow morning now.'

As Audrey rose, stretched and yawned, Abraham couldn't help himself from ogling the bellowing of her generously proportioned bosom.

'Know what I'm thinking now?' he smiled.

'Yes,' Audrey whacked him with her handbag. 'Pervert!'

Chapter Thirty-One

'Drink! ...I need a drink!' Mo banged on the bar and a mop of thick brown curly hair popped up, closely followed by a puffy red face and a buxom-less barmaid holding a dirty wet cloth.

'A big one!' Mo added. Either he didn't notice the frosty stare behind her oversized glasses, or he didn't care.

The barmaid slapped down the cloth and pulled her best artificial customer-is-always-right smile as some dirty splashes speckled Mo's bare arm.

'A big one of what?'

'Er...' Mo hadn't thought that far ahead. He looked up and down the rows of pumps and optics and scratched the back of his head. 'Sorry, it's my first time in a pub.'

The barmaid drummed her sovereign-coin-ringed fingers. 'Whenever you're ready.'

'A pint of your finest ale wench if you please,' Mo dragged up a line from a film he vaguely remembered. A line probably delivered by a portly, bushy-side-burned country sort in a period black and white. 'And a finest ale chaser. With cheese and onion crisps. And a salt and vinegar chaser.'

'Are you for real?' The barmaid pulled a face like she'd just sucked a plum that was either sour or rotten, but she couldn't decide which.

'Hey!'

Mo felt a tap on the shoulder and turned to the sight of a slight, hairy man doing up the flies on his dangling black jeans.

'You made it after all,' Serge sniffed his hand and offered it to Mo. 'Cool man. We're over there.'

Serge nodded towards Kerry in the small back room then sauntered over and snuggled in beside her with a nibble to the ear and slap to her thigh. Kerry tittered, sucked on a straw and gave Mo a wiggly-fingered wave.

Mo turned back to the barmaid. 'And two more finest ales for my erstwhile saviours.'

The barmaid squashed an eye, leaned over and prodded Mo's flat chest through his thin black vest. 'How odd.'

'What is?' Mo said.

'You,' the barmaid made a little pointy hat shape with her eyebrow and gave her curly-topped head a shake as she pulled the first pint. 'You're odd that's what.'

***

Mo set the tray down on the table that was only slightly bigger than the tray itself and started to carefully offload the drinks.

'I get the impression that the barmaid was pleased to see the back of me.'

'Well, *we* aren't,' Serge high-fived Mo. 'Serge Francis Milligan. Enchanted to make your acquaintance.'

'Kerry,' Kerry high-fived Mo too. 'Or just Kez if you like.'

'Mo Blenkinsopp,' offered Mo as he set down a drink for both Serge and Kerry then sat down opposite them. 'Pints of finest ales for my erstwhile saviours.'

Kerry sniggered then sucked her Bacardi through her straw. Serge shoved their two glasses of ale back over to Mo's side of the table, beside his existing two. 'That's ace of you man, but we don't drink that stuff. I'm more of a snakebite guy, and I've nearly a full pint left anyway. But all the more for you eh.'

'Sorry, I should have asked first,' Mo pushed the crisps over to the other side of the table. 'But at least have some crisps.'

'Cheers dude, don't mind if we do,' Serge ripped open both bags and he and Kerry tucked in while Mo took a swig of the first-ever pint in a pub. He scrunched up his eyes and pulled a face, not unlike the barmaid and her sour/rotten plum. 'What's up man? Don't you like it?'

'Er,' Mo took another swig and sported a similar but not quite so tortured grimace this time. 'It's cost enough and I'm jobless and pretty skint so I'm going to damn well like it if it kills me.'

Serge and Kerry laughed coarse, differently pitched smokers' laughs and both clunked glasses with Mo.

'Way to go!' Serge beamed. 'So how are things hangin' man?'

'Oh, things aren't hanging particularly well at the moment Serge I'm afraid.'

Kerry mumbled something through a mouthful of crisps. Mo deciphered it as '*How come*?'

'Where shall I start?' Mo took a long drink of his ale, massaged the back of his neck and yawned. 'Well, I've hardly slept, eaten or drunk anything for the last 48 hours. I've also got a banging headache.'

'Oh, sorry to hear that Mo,' Kerry rummaged around her handbag and offered Mo a couple of pills. 'Here, take these.'

'What is it? Paracetamol?'

'Of sorts,' Kerry tittered.

'So I'm starving and knackered, but those are good things,' Mo yawned again, popped the pills into his mouth and washed them down with another big swig. 'Or at least in comparison to the other stuff.'

Serge and Kerry looked at each other then back at Mo.

'What other stuff?'

‘Well, notwithstanding something terrible I’ve just learned from my mam, I blew whatever chance I had of a girlfriend and most of the town thinks I’m weirdo-in-chief…’

‘Not us man,’ Serge coiled Kerry right up to him, stroked her long hair and kissed her cheek. ‘Right babe?’

‘Right babe,’ Kerry echoed.

‘Hang on, I’m not finished yet,’ Mo gulped down some more ale. ‘My nose is busted, I’ve sores on my blisters, I’ve just been sacked, I’ve ruined my chances of ever emigrating to the States, my best clothes are currently residing in a wheelie bin, and the local police enforcer has not only just had me on a trumped-up drugs charge, but he’s constantly dragging me down the station for everything from walking on the cracks in the pavement to flashing my bits at kids in the park – though to be fair to him on that score, I was in the bushes with my pants down at the time.’

‘Ow!’ Kerry cracked her pretty blond head on the table leg as she fell about, giggling like a ticklish hyena.

‘You’re the ma…aan man,’ Serge helped Kerry back into her seat and high-fived Mo.

Mo took another big glug of one of his pints, glanced at his phone and pulled a glum face.

‘Yes, a marked man.’

***

Alcohol is a funny thing. Sometimes quite literally. In Mo’s case, a couple of pints was all it took to transform him from sulking sourpuss to chatty Cheshire cat. Or so it seemed anyway. Either way, he was in a more contented place now than he had been all day. All weekend. Pretty much forever in fact. *Escapism* some may argue. That very thought even flashed across Mo’s mind. He quickly dismissed it. The way things were heading he reasoned that he should get as much escaping in as possible now - before cell doors, bolts and barbed wire got in the way. He drained the rest of his second glass then put it underneath the table next to its first, equally empty, counterpart.

***

If the previous 24 hours had dragged by, weighted down like Marley's chains by his thoughts, troubles and tribulations, then Mo's time with Serge and Kerry had whizzed by, as if he had been pinged through a temporal vacuum. Before he knew it, the two empty glasses were four and Mo was on his way; bumping past rickety tables, negotiating tricky lampposts and meandering along the pavement en-route, bag still in hand, to Serge's flat above his shop.

'Oh, I didn't know you were a t...tattooist,' Mo grabbed hold of Serge's upper arm to steady himself.

'I am usually. I just couldn't be arsed today.' Serge pointed to the shop's *closed* sign, fiddled around with the key in the lock and pushed the door open. As Kerry passed through in front of him he patted her bum. 'Or maybe I was just more interested in someone else's arse.'

'Way to go,' Mo nicked one of Serge's own lines.

'I'll do one if you like - a tattoo that is. Mate's rates,' Serge said. 'How about a scorpion?'

'Gee, thanks S...Serge. But no thanks,' Mo admired Serge's priorities, or at least his lack of capitalistic ones. And his heart lifted at the simple mention of a word that most people take completely for granted – *mate*. 'It's really good of you, but I'm not really a tattoo person.'

'No worries,' Serge flashed a gap-toothed smile through his beard. 'So, are you coming in Mo? We've got pizza and snakebite.'

Mo squinted at his watch and deliberated as the cogs in his soggy brain hammered out the semblance of a message.

'S...sounds good, but I'm not sure it's such a good idea Serge. If I'm not careful this may well be my last night of freedom,' Mo steadied himself on the doorframe. 'More alcohol might stifle my investigative faculties, and according to my reckoning, I've only got about fifteen hours left before DI Abraham fits me up for murder.'

Kerry giggled so much she tripped down a few stairs and bashed into Serge, setting him off into a fit of laughter.

'Don't tell me. ...I'm the ma...aan,' Mo toggled his gaze between up the stairs and outside. He tugged an ear and sighed heavily before trudging up after Serge and Kerry. 'Pizza and snakebite you say?'

Chapter Thirty-Two

'Who'd you think you're looking at?' Mick snarled and raised his elbows in readiness to bulldoze his way through the bottleneck at the station door if necessary. 'Outta my way!'

Jerzy stood his ground.

'Masur,' Abraham's grinning head appeared behind one Mick's cannonball shoulders. 'Let the gentleman past.'

Jerzy backed away to allow Mick passage into the street. Mick turned back to face Abraham who wiggled a few fingers.

'Thank you for helping us with our enquiries. Do keep in touch.'

'I'll do more than touch you,' Mick snapped.

'Dear oh dear,' Abraham tutted. 'Is that presage?'

'No,' barked Mick. He turned his back, raised a middle finger and set off hobbling away. 'It's a warning!'

'What's that you've got behind your back Masur?' Abraham gestured towards Jerzy. 'And it damn well had better be Blenkinsopp's clo...'

'No, we didn't get his clothes,' Jerzy cut in and thrust out a cardboard box sporting a big toothy grin. 'But we did get pizza.'

Abraham's eyes sizzled. He balled a fist and hammered the box down to the pavement. 'You useless...'

A chuckling Aftab spilled around the corner with some boxes with actual pizzas in them, rather than the mere empty box that Jerzy had. Abraham's eyes sparked as he clocked the bloody contents of the see-through plastic bag atop the boxes. 'Is that what I think it is?'

‘Pressie courtesy of Blenkinsopp,’ Aftab said. ‘Well, in a roundabout, highly clandestine kind of way.’

‘Pressie courtesy of Blenkinsopp,’ Abraham recalled his earlier quip to Audrey with an enthusiastic grin. ‘Just be careful not to drop it on my foot!’

***

Abraham’s mood was still very much upbeat by the time Kell rolled into the boisterous CID office some fifty minutes later. Kell swiped a large slice of the pepperoni pizza on Jerzy’s desk and mumbled, ‘What’s going on?’

Abraham jiggled the transparent evidence bag containing Mo’s bloody clothes right in front of Kell’s nose.

‘Blenkinsopp,’ he smiled. ‘That’s what.’

‘Hm…’ Kell tapped his cheek contemplatively. ‘And do you happen to be pleased by this by any chance DI Dad?’

‘Pleased?’ Abraham aimed a can of lager at Aftab and Jerzy who back-peddled as froth sprayed about. ‘In *raptures* more like!’

‘Oh, you might not want to hear about my other news then,’ Kell bit his lip. ‘I don’t want to burst your bubble.’

‘News? What other news?’ Abraham’s grin disappeared like a dessert snowflake. He slapped the can on a desk, splattering his white shirt and yellow and black tie in the process.

Aftab nodded to Kell’s twitching jawline. ‘He’s winding you up sir. Just look at him, he’s dying to laugh.’

Right on cue Kell burst out laughing. ‘Ok then, perhaps it is news that you might want to hear.’

‘About Blenkinsopp?’

‘Yep.’

‘To *my* liking? And not *his*?’

Kell chomped some pizza and licked his lips. ‘Oh yes, I think it’s to your liking alright.’

***

'Out with it then!' Abraham snapped impatiently.

Kell slid an A4 piece of paper across the desk and examined the printed '*To do*' list. He looked up at Abraham. 'I'm presuming Audrey wants me to check the ones with a 'K' next to them, is that right?'

'Give me that,' Abraham snatched the list away and gave it a glance. 'Er, yes I think so. But first things first. What about this news?'

'What would you say,' Kell slid the chair back and plonked his Timberlands on the desk. 'If I told you that Ishmael had a bloody big sword, but now he doesn't - what would you say to that?'

'I'd say I want to kiss you.'

'And what would you say if I told you that Mo didn't have a bloody big sword at the party but, lo and behold, by some strange freak of nature he had one in the vicinity of the park of all places, just an hour or two later?'

'I'd say is there a law against incest?' Abraham bent over and planted a noisy wet smacker on Kell's forehead.

'But hang on,' Abraham sprang back to attention and stroked his goatee. 'I can't see Ishmael just offering all of that to you on a plate. How do you know all of this? And just how kosher is it?'

'Tch, DI Dad, DI Dad,' Kell shook his head mockingly. 'I'm a detective. That's what I do. Naturally, I employed some of my amazing powers of detection.'

'Oh damn,' Abraham sighed. 'You had me excited for a moment there.'

'Seriously,' Kell gave a crooked smile. 'Ishmael was acting all weird with his arms stretched out and his feet rooted bang in front of his fireplace. So, I got him to shift over to his desk on the pretext of writing down his phone number so I could have a closer snoop.'

'I *was* joking,' Abraham said. 'Good thinking son... And...?'

'And there are two wall brackets and the distinct outline of a sword. That's what he was trying to conceal. It's there in black and white. Well, not black and white exactly – more dust and faded sky-blue paint – but it's there alright. Not only that, but he has loads of Islamist stuff on his walls as well as his bookcase. Oddly, he's even got bumf on fertiliser laying around. I know I'm just a rookie and you're like Hercule Poirot or something, but to me it looks dodgy with a capital D.'

'You might have something,' Abraham tapped a tooth.' But it's still just conjecture. *Suspect A might have had something shaped like a sword at some unknown point in history*. It could be an oversized stick of rhubarb for all we know.'

'I'd concur,' said Kell. 'If it wasn't for what Mrs Asher-Regis told me.'

'And who's Mrs Asher-Regis when she's at home?'

'You asked me to do some door-to-door enquiries in the vicinity of the park.'

'Yeah, and?'

'And most of the locals were in the land of Nod and oblivious that night, but Mrs Asher-Regis said she was woken by someone having a pee in her garden. She says around 12.20 am.'

'Is that it?'

'Here's the thing,' Kell continued. 'She described the culprit as a dippy looking gangly lad with red hair and a blue and white shirt.'

Abraham bared his teeth wide. 'Blenkinsopp!'

'Sounds like it,' Kell said. 'But that's not all. Apparently, the reason she was awakened was because he was drunkenly shouting numbers out loud.'

'What?' Abraham's eyes sparked fireworks. 'Like 58, 12 and 14?'

'Nearly,' Kell said. 'She's a bit hard of hearing and couldn't make out exactly what he was rambling on about until she got out of bed and up close to her window. The only numbers she says she definitely heard are 12, 13 and 14.'

'That's pretty damned close.'

'Yep, pretty damned close' Kell nodded. 'Although, it could just be a coincidence and it doesn't explain the other numbers. Then again, when you take the other thing into account then...'

'Then what? And what other thing?'

'Then you can't help thinking the worst,' Kell said. 'I mean, she couldn't swear to it. She says saw it clearly enough, but not all of it if you see what I mean?'

'Kell!' Abraham swiped Kell's feet off the desk and rattled him in his chair. 'Stop talking in riddles man. What did she see?'

'I asked her if there was anything else unusual about the garden intruder, and initially she said no, but I sensed her hesitate, so I pressed her.'

'And?'

'And she said that it was probably nothing, but it looked like the lad had a shiny pointy thing sticking out of the top of his coat.'

'The sword?' Abraham's eyes broadened.

'Like I say, she wouldn't swear to it,' Kell said. 'But on reflection, she did say that it could possibly have been the tip of a sword.'

'I knew it!' Abraham shook a fist triumphantly. 'Debbie even noticed a cut under his chin earlier. It all ties in.'

'H..hold yourrr horrrsesss,' Kell's words juddered as Abraham grabbed his shoulders and shook him like a cup final goal scorer. 'It's suspicious but it's still not proof.'

'The proof will come through tomorrow morning when the lab guys have tested his clothes for Alex's blood,' Abraham beamed. 'You can be sure of that.'

'Maybe.'

Abraham crumpled his brow as he examined his options for all of one second.

'Maybe nothing, we've enough on him for an arrest now,' he decreed.

Abraham extended a finger and shooed his subordinates into immediate action. 'Dehwar, you and Jerzy get yourself down to Blenkinsopp's place pronto and haul him back here. The murderous scum is going down!'

***

'Don't you think you're being a bit hasty?'

Abraham contorted his face and stabbed squinty blue eyes at Kell.

'Eh?'

'Well, it's just, you know, after what you said this morning,' Kell cocked his head at an angle and looked up at Abraham. 'You know, about acting on *evidence* rather than *guesstimates*.'

'Ah. I see where you're coming from,' Abraham pulled up a chair. 'But this is more than just a guesstimate. Everything pointed to Blenkinsopp before. We just couldn't place him at the scene. Your little chinwag with good old Mrs Asher-Whatisname has since put paid to that – with bells on.'

'By *bells,* I take it that you're talking about the sword and the numbers.'

'Yes, I'm talking about the sword and the numbers.'

'But that's my point,' Kell said. 'It's not like we have a real, actual blood-drenched sword in our possession, and it's not like it's a hanging offence to utter a couple of numbers in someone's garden.'

'Kell, I've been solving intricate, tortuous crimes since before you even worked out how to use a potty. And I've been doing it extremely successfully as it happens.'

'I know that.'

'Well, take it from me,' Abraham looked Kell in the eye. 'When I have a gut feeling about a suspect, I'm pretty much always right.'

'Pretty much?'

'Pretty much, yes.'

'So,' Kell steepled his fingers. 'Not 100% of the time then?'

***

Abraham tugged on some whiskers on his upper lip, tapped his tooth and looked towards - but not really at - Kell.

'Look, I'm not saying, you're wrong,' Kell said. 'In fact, you're almost certainly right. All I'm saying is that it might be good to have a bit more insurance before you go all gung-ho on the actual arrest front.'

Abraham tapped a couple of fingers against his taut stomach a few times while his eyes moved upwards and to the left.

'And especially if the chief super is on your case about not rocking the politically sensitive battleship,' Kell added.

'I still want him bringing in,' Abraham said. 'But maybe you can boot up that PC of his in the meantime and maybe have a mooch around for some insurance. If Blenkinsopp is going down, I want him to stay down.'

'Yes sir DI Dad sir!' Kell slid Mo's PC next to Audrey's and started swapping the cables over. 'I'll get onto it straight away. Is there anything in particular you want me to check for?'

'Things on Audrey's list. Numbers. Images. Videos. Anything dodgy. Anything semi dodgy. Anything remotely semi dodgy. Pretty much everything in fact. She said she'd give it a thorough once over tomorrow morning, but there's no harm in getting a head start now.'

'Gotcha.'

'Oh,' Abraham added. 'Get on the blower to Dehwar and tell him there's no need to go as far as to actually arrest Blenkinsopp just yet. He's a pain in the arse but is generally compliant and as I said to Grantham, if he does try to run, he won't get very far, and it'll just prove his guilt. A simple request for him to accompany them back to the station to help with our enquiries should suffice for the time being.'

'Sure.'

‘Then when the lab guys come back in the morning with a match for Alex’s blood, we come down on him like a thunderstorm of rhinos.’

Chapter Thirty-Three

The cloak of nightfall began to flutter around the scattering of moonlit clouds, giving them a bluey-silver tinge. Down at ground level lampposts buzzed and flickered into life, ready for another eight-hour stint. Aftab and Jerzy's shifts had long since slid into double figures. Jerzy yawned, turned off the ignition and lit up a fag.

'What was that you left on Gran's desk?'

'Oh, just an IOU for a lemon tart. She likes them and did me a favour earlier,' Aftab flashed the scrap of paper with a phone number and the name Anaya Dhanial. 'Gran says I've an admirer.'

'You?' Jerzy's face scrunched up. 'An OCD bore swathed in M&S cobber?'

'Rather that than a messy scruff with stained jeans,' Aftab transferred some of Jerzy's strewn sweet wrappers and a cigarette butt into the ashtray. 'And is it too much to ask to tidy up after yourself?'

'Oi!' Jerzy shivered as Aftab buzzed down the window.

'Well, it stinks in here. And if you insist on wearing hole-infested T-shirts...'

Jerzy huffed and grabbed his jacket from the back seat. 'What's the score with Gran Anyway?'

'She's half French. Her dad's English.'

'Yes, I worked that out for myself,' said Jerzy. 'But is she even a gran?'

'I don't think so,' said Aftab. 'She's not even as old as she looks.'

'Probably just a bit older than you then,' winked Jerzy. 'You've got to be what? forty?'

'Yeah, yeah,' twenty-seven-year-old Aftab refused to rise to the bait.

'I know Gran only arrived here a week or two before me,' Jerzy continued. 'But it's weird how she's like Mrs Popularity with everyone already.'

'Not everyone.'

'Ah, the DI you mean.'

'You've noticed too,' remarked Aftab.

'So, why's that then do you think?' asked Jerzy. 'A clash of policing styles?'

'They are both pretty unorthodox, but it could be a factor,' Aftab stroked his trim moustache. 'Personally, I think it's more a matter of her being so popular and the fact that she gets results that grates on the DI. It's like he's miffed that she's breezed in and is already stealing his thunder.'

'Abraham's record is pretty damn good though,' said Jerzy. 'She's still got some way to go on that front.'

'True,' Aftab nodded. 'His instinct is usually top-notch.'

'Abraham's had Blenkinsopp in his sights for this murder pretty much from the start,' Jerzy mused. 'And the more we dig the more it seems that he might have a point. I can't wait to hear Blenkinsopp's explanation for all the blood on his clothes.'

'Yes, all that certainly didn't come from the cuts on his arms,' Aftab paused a moment before continuing. 'But there could be an innocent explanation.'

'Yeah right,' scoffed Jerzy. 'I know he's a mate of yours from the mosque, but just how well do you know him anyway?'

'Mo keeps himself to himself most of the time,' Aftab ran long bony fingers through his short black hair. 'But I do know that he's just sacrificed a year doing a crummy job that he hates just so he can save up for university – a mostly online/remote degree, so he can stay at home and take care of his mother.'

'So, he's had a hard life, with no dad and a dysfunctional mother,' précised Jerzy. 'It wouldn't be surprising if he felt aggrieved with his lot. Maybe try to redress the balance somehow?'

'If that's an affront at Islam, then the principle behind Islamic morality is love – not just for God, but for all God's creatures.' Aftab elucidated. 'It's not about *redressing balances*, but about treating our fellow man with respect to please Allah, the one and only God.'

'It was a question, not a slight. And what you say is all well and good for the vast majority,' Jerzy said. 'But I'm sure you're aware that all religions have minority elements that take things to the extreme.'

Aftab locked eyes onto Jerzy. 'And by *all,* I take it you mean Islam?'

'Jeez, you're touchy today Afty... I didn't say that. As just one example, there are plenty of Christian extremists knocking about. Like in some places in the US. It's just that you do hear about impressionable youngsters being led astray...' Jerzy let his statement hang.

'I guess Mo has been knocking around with Ishmael a lot lately,' contemplated Aftab.

'And just what do you know about this Ishmael?'

'Not a lot,' Aftab admitted. 'He turned up about a year ago from somewhere in Africa and he and Ahmed have been like Tweedledum and Tweedle-dee ever since.'

'So, no one really knows his background or just what he's been bending Blenkinsopp's ear about,' said Jerzy. 'What do you make of that, the bucketful of blood on Blenkinsopp's clothes, and the fact that it's highly likely that Ishmael gave Blenkinsopp a sword the night Alex Hobbs was decapitated?'

'Doesn't look great.' Aftab shuffled his brown loafers in the footwell. 'I did have one thought, but it's not exactly in line with the *treating my fellow Muslim with the brotherly love and respect* narrative that I touted earlier... In fact, it's a bit sneaky.'

'Sounds good,' Jerzy's greeny-blue eyes glinted.

'I don't know...'

'Well, run it by me at least.'

'Okay, well, earlier I got the impression that Mo's mam was worried about him. And not just because we were at their house searching for his clothes. The way she flittered her eyes about and gnawed her nails, I dunno, it felt like she had something really heavy weighing on her conscious,' Aftab hesitated. 'I just wonder... *If* Mo is up to something on the Islamic front, and his mam knows anything about it, then if we approach her from an angle along the lines of '*we believe that someone at the mosque has been approaching impressionable young men'* with a view to say '*fighting a holy war'* then if Mrs Blenkinsopp does have any information, then if she offloaded it to us we could set about '*nipping it in the bud before her one and only son ships out to the desert with a phrasebook, a one-way ticket and an AK47.*"

Jerzy rubbed his jaw. 'Lie and pressurise her into dropping Mo in it you mean?'

'Well, if you put it like that...'

'No Afty, it's great,' Jerzy beamed. 'I bet Blenkinsopp's got all sorts of suspect skeletons in his cupboard. Maybe even the odd scrap of key evidence too. Your little plan could work a treat jangling something loose.'

***

Jerzy's floppy blond fringe flapped in the slight breeze as they strode down Mo's garden path yet again.

'This front door's due a lick of paint,' he remarked as he clanked the knocker.

'Not just the door,' Aftab added with a nod to the mottled drainpipe and flaky black windowsills. He dug his tingling phone out of his jeans and clicked to accept the call. 'Yes?'

Jerzy stepped back from the doorstep and cricked his head back. 'All the lights are off. Surely they are not in bed already?'

Aftab shrugged lopsidedly with an ear still glued to his phone. Jerzy knocked again, pointed to his watch and mouthed 'It's only quarter past nine.'

'It looks like no one is in. Or at least no one is up,' Aftab relayed to Kell on the other end of the line as Jerzy tried rattling the letterbox. 'My guess is that Mo is still at the pub – if that's where he really went - and his mam's in bed. What does the governor want us to do?'

As Aftab waited for Kell to confer with Abraham, Jerzy hunkered down and called through the letterbox. 'Mrs Blenkinsopp, it's DC Masur. Can you please open up? We need a word with you... About Mo...It's important.'

Up in her bedroom Mary Blenkinsopp eyed the scrap of paper with the smudged numbers and the word *jihad* and opened her mouth to speak, but after a few seconds she rolled over, buried her head under a pillow and muffled her sobs.

Jerzy was just about to try again when Aftab tapped him on the shoulder, snapped his phone case shut and motioned towards their car. 'We have to check The Causeway for Mo.'

'What if he's not there?'

'If Mo's not there then the governor wants us to give him a lift home.'

'And then we can knock off for the night?' Jerzy yawned.

'What do you think?' Aftab sighed wearily as he fizzed open another energy drink.

***

Thirty minutes later Aftab and Jerzy headed for their car again. This time outside the station, and with Abraham in tow.

'So, he was there then?' Abraham unapologetically bumped Jerzy out of the way and shuffled into the front passenger's seat. 'At The Causeway.'

Jerzy slid in the back with concertina legs and a tut. 'Yes, the barmaid was most definite. It sounds like he made a bit of an impression. She describes him as '*a geeky clown in rapper clobber*'. And '*a not quite there nut job*'. She asked if we were there to arrest him for crimes against normality.'

'If only,' Abraham chuckled. 'They'd throw away the key!'

***

Not long after dropping Abraham off, Aftab and Jerzy were parked back in front of Mo's house. This time just watching. A few minutes into the wait Aftab's phone rudely broke the silence, vibrating clean off the dashboard as an encore.

'That's odd,' Aftab said as he closed down the call. 'The DI says that when Mo shows up we need to tell him that we've found his bloody clothes, and if he wants to clear his name then he'll have to come to the station for some lengthy questioning with Gran.'

'And what if he doesn't want to accompany us back to the station?' asked Jerzy.

'That's the weird thing,' Aftab scrunched his nose and rasped his stubble. 'I have to grin, say that we'll be camped outside of his house all night and then stare at my watch and say *tick, tick, tick...*'

Chapter Thirty-Four

A few miles south, in a snug corner of their sumptuous house, Beth Lilley slipped her Macmillan's bookmark in the latest Louise Welsh novel. She padded into the hallway in her fluffy pink slippers and matching dressing gown.

'Davy, I'm making a hot chocolate and taking it up to bed,' she called. 'Do you want one?'

Davy ducked his head through one of the doorways all booted and suited in jeans, studs and black leather waistcoat. He clacked across the wooden floor, pulled his wife into his hip and playfully ruffled her hair with the back of a huge ring finger. 'Cheers doll, but I'm off out in a while. Just a bit of business to attend to. It shouldn't take long. You get yerself to bed.'

'What time do you think you'll be back?' Beth asked. 'I'll probably be asleep if it's late.'

'It shouldn't be that late,' said Davy. 'I want to get there an hour or so early, so I'll probably leave before eleven, and I dare say I'll have it all done and dusted in ten minutes max, so I should be back not long after midnight.'

'Oh, I'll be fast asleep well before then, Beth yawned as her phone pinged. 'Ah, that's appropriate timing, Kell wishing me goodnight.'

'Don't worry doll,' Davy winked and patted her bum. 'I'll tippy-toe my way in as quiet as a mouse.'

'Hm, hobnailed sewer rat more like!' Beth pulled a crooked smile and traipsed away tapping a reply to Kell.

Two minutes later the sound of a punchbag being battered reverberated from Davy's home gym to the kitchen where Beth stirred her hot chocolate vigorously. The clinking spoon failing to tune out the sound of Davy's heavy blows and ominous chuckles.

By the time Beth trundled back down the hallway, steaming cup in hand, Davy's punches were barely audible – largely drowned out as they were by the sudden addition of booming thrash metal licks, hammer-ons and power chords.

Beth tapped on the door. 'Goodnight Davy.'

No reply. He probably didn't hear her. Beth tapped on the door again. Louder. 'Goodnight Davy.'

No reply. He can't have heard her. Beth swivelled around and headed up the stairs.

Somewhere behind the door, Davy eyed the crude effigy he'd cobbled together from old small and large punchbags. He gripped the rag-turban crowned head with one huge hand and applied finishing touches in the form of two black felt-tip eyes.

'Should I?' Davy hovered the pen a few inches under the eyes and air traced a downward curve. He paused a couple of beats then air traced an upwards curve. 'Or shouldn't I?'

After a few moments' deliberation, he drew the upwards curve. A sad face as opposed to a happy one.

He then spun sharply around and sent the head flying with a ninja donkey hind leg kick.

'Good riddance pisswizard,' he smiled. 'Good riddance!'

Chapter Thirty-Five

The smell of donner kebab reached the CID office a good dozen seconds or so before Gran did, sporting a garlic sauce moustache.

'What are you doing here?' she raised an eyebrow and checked her watch. 'At ten past ten.'

'I could ask you the same thing,' Kell tickled the wheel on the back of the mouse. The jumble of letters on the screen flickered and scrambled down. 'Anyway, isn't it obvious?'

Gran ambled over and hovered over Kell's shoulder. 'Let me guess – Blenkinsopp.'

'You've got it in one,' Kell continued scrolling, slowly but surely. 'The DI asked me to check out his PC for anything suspect.'

'Yes, I called the DI earlier while I was staking out Ishmael, and he filled me in on the latest developments.'

'So, anything of note happening at Ishmael's?' Kell asked.

'Erm, I think he went to the bathroom at one point before bed.'

'Oh, so hardly Islamic State.'

'I'm sure Osama Bin Laden had the odd pee and forty winks too.' Gran ran her donner under Kell's nose. 'Maybe even the occasional kebab.'

'Smells good,' Kell stretched. 'I might nip out and get one after I've gone through the next folder.'

'So, how's it going with Blenkinsopp's computer? Any luck?'

'Just mountains of nerd and reams of geek – have a look at all these files. It's like he's a digital hoarder. His hard drive is not so much a data warehouse as a national binary stockpile. He's got files on everything from pre-GCSE school homework to dark matter theory. There are thousands of files – maybe hundreds of thousands.'

Kell's phone rang. While he retrieved it from his pocket and jabbed the accept button Gran took the opportunity to take over mouse control, tweak the wheel and scan the screen.

'Hi, what's up?' Kell pressed his back against the hard-plastic chair, puffed out his chest and twisted it from side to side. 'Yeah, I'm still going through it. I was just telling Gran that it's crammed with all sorts of crap... Nah, nothing yet, I could be here all night and still hardly scratch the surface. What?... No, I'm not planning on an all-nighter, I'll give it another couple of hours then head home. What about you?... Ah, diddums. Do you want me to check in on you when I'm back and tuck you in?... Ha!... Goodnight DI Dad.'

'I'll be turning in too soon if Blenkinsopp doesn't volunteer himself for questioning tonight,' Gran pushed the mouse back over to Kell. 'It's been a long one, and tomorrow could be even longer. Any more thoughts on the numbers by the way?'

'Just thoughts. No answers,' Kell sighed. 'I've tried searching for numbers on Mo's PC, and there are thousands of hits. There's everything from online shopping receipts and old maths homework to bus timetables and even documents that basically just describe numbers.'

'Eh? Such as?'

'Such as this,' Kell clicked on the file named 13.doc and started reading. *'13 is the sixth prime number and the smallest emirp – an emirp is a prime that is a different prime when its digits are reversed...* He's got files like that on loads of numbers.'

'Including the numbers found on the body?'

'Yes, but that doesn't explain anything, and especially since the vast majority of such files pertain to completely different numbers that were not on the body,' Kell said. 'It points to him being a bit of a nerd, yes, but no jury would convict him of murder on the basis of this.'

'Do you have any other thoughts on the numbers?'

'It's like the DI suggested earlier,' Kell shrugged. 'It could be one of any amount of things, or it could even be completely random.'

'It sounds like Blenkinsopp is a bit of a trainspotter,' Gran said. 'The DI would probably interpret that as him and his pals are planning to blow one up.'

'What do you think?' Kell asked.

'Something's going down,' Gran bit into her kebab and shrugged. 'But just what exactly...'

'Well, as you know Aftab and Jerzy are waiting to pick Mo up as we speak. Trains are just one of the things you could quiz him about,' said Kell. 'I'll also add train numbers to Audrey's list and I'll also keep working through Mo's PC tonight, but five numbers is such a small sample to work from. Another set of numbers could give us a better steer on any pattern.'

Gran pushed the flats of her hands into her furrowed brow and groaned. 'Be careful what you wish for Kell. Be very careful what you wish for.'

***

Gran took the mouse and clicked on the 'videos' folder. The screen filled with file icons. 'Have you checked these out yet?'

'I had a quick look, but as you can see...' Kell scrolled down. 'There are tons of them both in cloud and on his hard drive. It'll take at least a couple of hours to go through them all.'

'Hm... you did say that you'd be here for another couple of hours,' Gran said. 'Can you prioritise the video files? And give me a bell if you discover anything even slightly suspect.'

'Could do,' Kell rubbed his neck. 'But the DI did mention checking out the numbers first.'

'I suspect that was a suggestion detective constable, not an order,' Gran tapped the screen. 'And I'm ordering you to prioritise the video files.'

Kell stretched his muscular arms, interlocked his hands and cracked his knuckles. 'Whatever you say sergeant.'

Chapter Thirty-Six

Davy usually came early to recce the place. To sniff around. To crush any naïve helping hand hiding in the bushes. Not just nip them in the bud – physically and botanically speaking - but to squish them like the pathetic little slug that they surely were. It wouldn't be the first time that a would-be hero lurked in the leafy shadows. Almost certainly not this time, but Davy had learned from experience that it paid to be careful. He checked his watch. 11.16 pm. Later than he'd normally arrive - but no cause for concern. Not with that scraggy green runt. Davy smiled to himself. That wet weed would come alone - unwise, unprepared and unaware. Perhaps with a set of tiddlywinks in his shorts pocket. Or marbles. Or whatever kindergarten fad kids settled scores with these days. That's assuming the tyke had managed to settle a score ever before in his pitiful life. Unlikely. It was almost enough for anyone to feel sorry for the lad. Almost enough for someone to take it easy. Davy lowered himself down with his back against the base of his punchbag tree, stretched out his legs and swung one ankle over the over. He hummed a tune, picked at his nose and observed a willow branch sway in the gentle breeze. Slowly and sedately like a slothy arboreal waltz. Not as sedately as his heart, but slowly and serenely nonetheless. He rolled some whiskers between his digits. In his line of work, it didn't do to overlook threats. To allow acts of disrespect to go unpunished. To let bygones be bygones. That kind of thing was neither good for business nor the natural order of authority.

Then again...

He tapped one of his two gold teeth with a fingernail.

Davy wiped something from his eye and scanned around the park - past the pond, beyond the little café and towards the spot where his little niece

Amy had burst out of the bushes the previous day; teary-eyed, wet-knickered and scarred for life.

No, there would be no taking it easy.

No way!

***

Not long afterwards, and after no more than a cursory patrol of a few bushes in the vicinity, the bearded man-mountain stabbed a huge index finger at the normal-sized smartphone that always looked so tiny in his hand. A familiar *whoosh* sound told him the message had done just that – *whoosh* into thin air ...destined to magically rematerialize on another mobile a few miles away in less than the time it took him to pocket his phone and dig out his *insurance*. He weighed up his prized metal-studded companion in his palm then, as usual, shoved it back in his jeans. As much as he loved it, most jobs just didn't require any insurance. Well, at least not for him - Davy Lilley. Besides, as he'd occasionally explained to associates, 'insurance somehow took away the sport.' However, as he swivelled back towards the tree something caught his attention. With a raised eyebrow he squatted down and examined something he'd never noticed before... the *MBI* etching.

He'd have been hard-pressed to explain why, but for whatever reason, Davy dug his shiny gadget out again, slid it over his knuckles and slapped it home with the heel of his other hand. He then stretched his huge frame and flexed his pecs. Still with his back to the tree, he loosened up with some right and left hooks then an ominous crack rung out as he unleashed another vicious ninja donkey hind leg kick at the trunk.

Chapter Thirty-Seven

Mo couldn't remember passing out, or much else for that matter, but when something vibrating in his shorts pocket eventually tickled his senses he came to with a groan. He opened an eye and peeled off the side of his face that was stuck to the faux-leather armchair. A bombardment of sensations hit him instantaneously – his bloated stomach, his pummelling head, the smell of alcohol on his stale breath and the pain stabbing throughout his body, from the crick in his neck and the stinging face to the stiff lower back and the pins and needles in his feet. He moaned as he unfolded his limbs and sat up, if not straight, then at least nearer to vertical than an obtusely obtuse angle. He patted at a sticky patch on his shorts, suspiciously eyed a near-empty pint glass at his feet then sniffed at its snakebite remains.

His sorry brain cells started to hammer. Maybe snakebite related, or perhaps a solitary thought neuron pogoing to attract attention. He slowly creaked to his feet and stretched as he took in his surroundings – a sink full of tomato-smeared pots and sudsy glasses in the kitchen, a crumb-strewn, ring-marked table in the lounge/diner, and an eight-limbed snoring spider sticking out from the covers in the open-doored bedroom. He noticed a half-eaten pizza crust in the folds of his chair and popped it in his mouth rather than traipse all the way to the kitchen and the bin. Dry-lipped, he did the same with the last of the snakebite too.

He rubbed his blurry eyes and dug out his phone. The latest text was a brief *'How are yer daein' pal?'* from Saboor. But the message that had arrived thirty minutes or so earlier was from someone else, and on an entirely different matter.

'Oh hell, I'm going to be late,' Mo cringed. He rapped on his silly skull for forgetting. He'd noticed Davy's response to his own initial message while in The Causeway, but it had since slipped his mind. That first message, a summons to meet in the park at midnight read like an invitation to a royal garden party compared to the latest one that had arrived while he slept, '*Oi Pisswizard! Don't even think about keeping me waiting you f...*' He didn't bother scrolling down. He got the gist.

Mo considered tidying up before leaving, but on balance reasoned that spring cleaning was quite low on his current agenda. Besides the present obstacle (Davy), thoughts also resurfaced around Abraham's (now) 12-hour ultimatum - and he was no further forward with that either. He rasped his head with his knuckles as he mooted which problem he should prioritise, Davy or Abraham? Neither option filled him with anything other than dread. If there was ever such a thing as *on a hiding to nothing*, then this was it. Doubly so!

He tugged at an ear as he tried to dredge up yet another niggle from the murky depths of his misty mind. Something that had come back to bug him. Maybe something about a voice? Possibly a man's voice. Or could it have been something that he'd seen at Abraham's house? In the kitchen, or possibly the den. Not the penknife, not the PC... but the den spoke to him more than the kitchen... but in waning grainy gobbledygook rather than lightbulb Oxford English clarity.

He grabbed his bag and hobbled to the bedroom, still unsure and undecided even what to think - let alone do. He whispered 'thanks guys' before scuttling down the stairs, skidding halfway down and landing with a thump on his skinny butt.

***

Mo groaned as he ventured out into the night. His backside hurt but his thumping head ached even more. He massaged his brow with his fingertips and regretted not asking Kerry for another Panadol or whatever it was before leaving. He hiccupped and a feeling of nausea rose to the back of his throat. Another regret surfaced. Maybe he shouldn't have had that second snakebite. Or the first. Or the four finest ales for that matter either. He checked his watch and sighed. 11.54 pm already. It would take at least 30 minutes to leg it to the park, even if he managed to walk it in a straight line.

Something which he somehow doubted. He dithered, tottered, then spontaneously lurched out into the road and waved his bag about his nut like one of those airport ping pong bat types. Thirty thousand feet overhead a Lufthansa flight destined for Edinburgh carried on regardless. Down on Brenda Road, a yellow taxi swerved to one side and screeched its brakes.

'Are you on a death wish you dumb...' The taxi driver's words trailed off as he goggled at Mo.

Oblivious, Mo jumped in the front passenger's seat, slapped the last of his cash, £8.76, into the guy's hand and slurred, 'W..Ward Jackson Park my good man. Quick as pos, and you can keep the change.'

The driver, a 20s-something Turk in a Puma tracksuit dropped the cash into a pouch and set off at an amble. 'What? For a few coppers?'

Mo gurned and put his hand to his mouth. 'I feel shick.'

'Shit,' the guy cursed as he floored the Skoda Octavia's accelerator. 'Buckle up. I'll have you there in ten.'

***

'Er,' Mo scratched his ear and twisted his head back around. 'You've just gone through a red light.'

'Nah,' the taxi driver floored the accelerator and shifted into top gear. 'It was dark amber.'

Mo massaged his neck, face and pounding head. Without asking he prodded a button on the stereo and the drum and bass drone dropped to a whisper. The driver didn't argue.

'How come you're in such a hurry to get to the park anyway? It's not like it's open.'

'I've some businessh to attend to with *hic!* a certain Mr Lilley.'

'Jeez, not *Davy* Lilley?'

'The very s...same,' Mo slurred.

'Rather you than me!' The driver blew down at the hairs protruding from his T-shirt collar.

'It's cool,' Mo closed his eyes, pulled his bag to his midriff and wound his arms around it. A contented expression washed over his face. 'We're just going to s...sort something out that's all.'

'I *was* right. You *are* on a death wish!'

'Ha,' Mo gave a knowing little shake of his head. 'If he tries any funny businessh he'll have to face the consequenshes. He doesn't know what he's misshing with.'

The Turk rasped the side of his hair with a 'Z' etched into it. 'Well, I just hope you've got something sharper than a couple of lemons in that bag.'

'Erm...' Mo fumbled blindly around the red cloth bag and pulled out the pumpkin.

The driver's eyes boggled and bulged as he gaped. 'Jeez!'

***

The taxi wheel-spun away, leaving Mo with gravel spitting at his calves and the stench of burning rubber in his nostrils. The driver didn't even hang about for a tip. Just as well. He wouldn't have got one anyway.

Mo scanned around and a spark of... *something* hopped from one groggy brain cell to another. Unsure as to why, he headed towards the same section of railings as before. With each step, the knot in his stomach tightened as it slowly dawned on him that that 'something' was *recollection*.

His head whirling, Mo tossed his bag over the top into some bushes, then gripped the bars and tried to get some purchase with his foot on a knobbly bolt halfway up. It slipped and skidded. A bit like his memory. *Recollection*... He'd been here before. And not just today, but previously. ...Recently ...Somehow the railings seemed taller than the ones fading in and out of his conscious. Greasier too. As well as looser. And wobblier. And more jangly... Like the pounding pinball of a heart in his ribcage.

Could I really have climbed these very same railings on the night of the murder?

He desperately wanted to say no. Scream no...

Scream?

It might have been the loose bolt. It could have been the aftereffects of the booze buckling his legs. Or it could simply have been the brutal realisation that he *had* indeed been here that night. But one way or another, something suddenly sent him crashing backwards – without a word, or denial, or desperate plea of innocence...

... for salvation...

Falling, crashing...

Onto his head with a heavy *thud.*

***

Daunted, dazed and dented, by the time he eventually hauled his aching carcass and spinning head to the top, perched like a ginger emu on a line of giant nails, he'd almost forgotten why he was there. Almost but not quite. He gazed at, and beyond, the twenty-metre willow tree and saw nothing but bark, leaves and branches. Even so, something flickered in his eyes and sounds and visions flashed through his brain. A memory of a woman's scream. A shock of blond hair – there one minute, gone the next. Blood. Recollection. Red. Realisation. Recognition. Acceptance. Blood. Fear. Anger. Panic...

Whatever it was it tasered him into action. He sharp sprung from his squat, up through the vertical and across the chilled air, arms first, like a superhero flying squirrel. He caught hold of a high branch and swung with a warbled shriek, down and back up into the night, flailing and twisting before plummeting face-first into something or someone in the bushes next to a funny looking tree with forked branches.

Chapter Thirty-Eight

It felt like a minute. But it could have been thirty. The sensations pounding his being felt real enough though. The throbbing head and the stinging bones certainly leant towards reality. But then again, his subconscious could be quite the trickster. Whatever it was, the feelings seemed transient and the flashes fleeting and flummoxing.

Branches, blows and a beady eye.

Metal, mauling and mu....

His eyelids batted.

Fast. Then faster.

Then everything went dark once again.

***

It was another twenty minutes before Mo came out of whatever comatosed state he'd been in. He scrunched up his face, massaged his temples with the heel of his hands then edgily opened his eyes. Thousands of miles above him stars seemingly swirled like a fairy dust vortex in the spinning night sky. Hell, his head throbbed. So did his back for that matter. He let out a groan as he prised himself up from his prone position by his elbows. His arms hurt too. His neck cricked as he sleepily scanned down to his right and grabbed hold of the first thing that he could lay his hands on - some stick thing - to help himself up to his feet. 'Oof!' He wheezed as he awkwardly hauled himself upright, like a brittle nonagenarian. Somewhat on autopilot, he bent forwards, creaked back down and picked up his bag.

'Argh!'

Mo heard the noise. He was sure of it. Well pretty sure anyway. He even thought he had witnessed some strange blur accompany it, swiftly followed by a thud, a squeal and a clatter.

Mo blinked and rubbed his eyes as he stumbled forwards. His head continued to pound. Most of the stars he was seeing now were internal.

His mind was probably just playing tricks on him, even so, it appeared to him that there was something, or someone, fumbling about on all fours on the other side of the park railings. Whatever it was, he headed over.

'Mr Shahzad, is that you?'

The moonlit figure hiccupped then turned its chubby head upwards, 'Mo? Is that you?'

'What are you doing?'

'W..well I've ended up walking home from a function at the ... hic! Grand,' Shahzad said as he randomly patted the grassy pavement, head down. 'I tried f... flagging taxis but with no luck.'

'N...no, I mean w...what are you doing down on your hands and knees?' Mo slurred.

'Looking for my specs,' Shahzad raised his glassy eyes towards Mo. 'S...something bumped into me, or maybe it was the other way around, but either way, I took a tumble and my specs fell off. I can't see a bloomin' thing without them.'

'Here, let me help,' Mo stuck an arm through the railings and assisted Shahzad to his feet.

'You're a good lad Mo,' Shahzad hiccupped again. 'Sorry about earlier. You know...'

'It's okay Mr Shahzad,' Mo said. 'I don't blame you for anything. That Abraham knows how to shtick the knife in.'

'Oh, t...talking of knives,' Shahzad looked somewhat rockier on two feet than he did on all fours. 'DI Abraham called by again asking if I'd noticed anything out of the ordinary about you. I told him that I hadn't.'

'Thanks, but what has that got to do with knives?' Mo passed his stuff to Shahzad over the top of the railings then clambered up himself.

'That's the funny thing.'

'What is?' Mo squatted uneasily on top of the railings but still indicated to Shahzad to pass his stuff back to him.

'It was around shop closing time, and I was starting to clear up and wash everything down as I chatted with DI Abraham. I noticed your butcher's knife seemed to be mishing, and I mentioned it,' said Shahzad. 'I hope that d...doesn't cause any trouble.'

'I don't suppose you remember w...washing it before it disappeared, do you?'

'No, it won't have been washed by then.'

'S...so, it'd still have my prints on it. And did DI Abraham have the opportunity to...' Mo wobbled on the railings. 'Nab it himself by any chance?'

'Well, I did have my b...back to him at times as I was clearing away and whatnot,' Shahzad wiped some sweat off his brow with a handkerchief. 'I'd s... say that that was poshible. Why?'

'Why indeed? Perhaps an ulterior motive. One that has poshibly been carefully orchestrated for some time. One that may be tightening a noose further shtill around my neck as we speak. Bullies like him and Lilley think they can get away with murder. Well...' Silhouetted by the moon in the dusky night sky Mo straightened up and stood tall atop the railings. He raised his laden arms high and wide and cried, 'No more Davy Lilley! And to hell with you Joe Abraham!'

Shahzad moved backwards. Drunk and half-blind, he still had the wherewithal to sense Mo wobbling above his head. Mo howled like a wolf then jumped.

'Uh-oh.'

Both men looked down at Mo's feet, the source of the crunch. Mo stepped back, bent down and tentatively offered Shahzad his shattered spectacles.

'I'm sho shorry Mr Shahzad,' Mo said. 'I'll buy you a new pair. Just send me the bill.'

'You'll do no s...such thing,' Shahzad laid a heavy hand on Mo's shoulder and gave it a rough but kindly shake. 'Just walk me the remaining half mile or so home and we'll call it quits.'

***

'Just to let you know, there's no hard feelings about earlier, you know with my jo....' Mo's words trailed off as he noticed a full bells and whistles mountain bike laying abandoned just fifteen metres or so away. As they approached it, Mo scanned around, squinted, then crossed over the road to a shadowy figure hunched down in a driveway. Mo's knotted brow unfurled as recognition set in. 'Hi Stewie.'

'Er... hi Mo,' Stewie scrambled to his feet and made a beeline for his bike.

'Nice night for it?' Mo offered amicably.

Seemingly oblivious to both Mo's greeting and the fact this his expensive digital bike GPS gadget lay strewn on the ground, Stewie leapt on his bike and peddled away like Mark Cavendish with chronic diarrhoea.

'How strange,' Mo observed as his next-door neighbour, Stewie looked over his shoulder and almost kamikazed himself and his bike into a lamppost in the process.

***

After a laboriously slow and ponderous plod escorting the drunk and dis-dawdly Shahzad to his house, Mo tottered around and gingerly lumbered back to the main road, rubbing and prodding his many bodily ailments en-route. The latest huge lump on the top of his bonce was a different animal completely though, and that was way beyond his control. It throbbed so much it felt like he'd just headbutted Mars. His legs seemed to function, of a fashion, but something didn't feel quite right. In fact, plenty didn't feel quite right. Battered and bursting, he only got as far as the Georgian house when he pulled in for a pitstop behind the high hedge flanking its garden.

As he showered the vegetation more numbers zapped at warp speed from bleary brain cell to groggy neuron. Too quick for him to decipher much of it. Though the number 14 seemed to feature. Something else flashed by too. All blurry and blue. He saw as much through the weeny gaps in the hedge. Maybe an ambulance. Maybe not. While he pondered the possibilities another streak of blinking blue zipped by. Perhaps not an ambulance then. Ambulances tended to work alone. The hedge shuddered as something else zoomed behind it. Yet more blue. Then some more. Either fire engines or the police then. Mo scanned the night sky. No trails of light. No plumes of smoke. Just some moonlit clouds and the distant sound of a helicopter.

The police were hurtling towards the park in force.

Probably not for a picnic.

***

Mo turned towards the house. Number 101, with its big wooden door. Beams flickered in one of the leaded windows on the ground floor. Someone was watching television with the lights off. Quite loudly by the sound of it. The householder was probably half deaf Mo supposed.

He approached the source. Suddenly aware of the sound of his feet on the loose stones he slowed to a creep, edging closer and closer, hands chest-high and palms down, like a stealthy meercat. He cautiously peered through the window. No one in sight, just a TV's essences and rays dancing about in the dark. Some programme about space or the planets. One of the gas giants loomed into view, probably Jupiter Mo thought. It looked like an interesting episode. On another night, in a different lifetime, he'd be tempted to drag over the ornate wrought iron bench, park his butt, plonk his feet on the windowsill and take in the show.

Just not tonight.

Most definitely not tonight.

He wheeled around and took one, two, three steps back towards the hedge. On the fourth step, something grabbed his attention. A kind of beep, beep, beeping that he was familiar with. ...Yes, that was it ...BBC news intro sounds. He swivelled back to face the TV. He was right. The news was just starting. The planets thing was probably just a trailer on BBC News 24. Clive Myrie homed into view above a prominent 'breaking news' banner. Mo hurried to take a closer look.

His heart had started thumping even before he recognised the helicopter's overhead shots of the park, but it went into jackhammer overdrive when his face suddenly popped up on national television with 'Mohammed Blenkinsopp' in big bold letters underneath. Mo pressed his nose and hands to the glass and watched in horror as the newsreader told of a second murder and warned of a '*dangerous man on the loose*' who '*should not be approached by members of the public.*'

The images cut to a shot with a reporter's outstretched arm holding a fluffy microphone in the foreground as Kell and Abraham spilled out of a car and hastened towards the park, Abraham's yellow and black tie flapping in the breeze.

'No comment!' He barked. 'Other than we'll be out day and all night to catch this bas..., this *monster*, and bring him to justice.'

Mo was aghast. The frenzied neurons pogoing at the back of his brain told his legs to scarper and sharpish. Somewhere in the front of his brain either the message got lost in translation, or it somehow got out-trumped. Either way, Mo's leaden feet remained rooted. The only movement came from his thumping heart and his hands that made little squidgy sounds as they quaked against the windowpane. When he returned his gaze to the screen, he caught the remnants of Clive Myrie jabbering on about a tattooed face or something. Suddenly, Mo's photograph popped up again. One taken of him down the station a few months previously with a gormless, rabbit-caught-in-headlights expression. Only this picture had been altered and there was something blue curling down around the eyes to the top of each cheekbone. How odd. Mo took one hand off the pane and scratched his head. That was odd too he thought. Why were there were red streak marks on the window where his fingers had been? He stared at his reflection and saw his own eyes widen as he did so. What the hell was th...? Mo rubbed and squelched at his reflection in the glass. Then slowly and gingerly he traced a finger over the tender parts of skin on his face. The bits that perfectly aligned with the blue in his reflection.

'Noooo!' He howled and clawed at his likeness on the pane of glass.

Suddenly a head popped out in front of his on the other side of the window. A screaming head with no teeth and long white hair - flanked by ten wrinkly rigid digits on arms that flapped like a maraca madwoman.

'Argh!' Mo jumped back and scrambled for his stuff.

'Arghhhh!' Mrs Asher-Regis' ear-splitting scream out-trumped Mo's by at least 100 decibels.

Mo followed her petrified gaze down to his bag and his stick.

But it wasn't a bag.

And it wasn't a stick.

Chapter Thirty-Nine

Abraham was true to his word. Out all night - at the scene, conferring with Gina Lo, fending off the media, liaising with other constabularies, rousing the troops – physically in some cases - as Jerzy's sore butt could attest. Essentially, the DI was in his element and on the warpath, with him some sort of gladiatorial law enforcement general and Mo the fleeing foe. Within the hour transport chiefs had been issued with Mo's description and primed for vigilance. Within two hours Mo's photograph had been circulated to every port, airport and public transport company in the UK. If Mo wanted to escape Blighty, then unless an intergalactic spaceship happened to offer him a lift, the only other unvetted alternative was carrier pigeon.

Unsurprisingly perhaps then, the first breakthrough came fairly quickly, and fleets of squad cars following the GPS signal on Mo's phone converged on the A1 to skilfully snare their prey near Dishforth. Alas, the BA co-pilot in the Audi convertible eventually managed to convince the pursuers that Mohammed Blenkinsopp just wasn't them - if not by the proffered passport ID, then at least by race and gender - and Miss Ganesh was eventually released in time to fly her scheduled plane out of Manchester Airport to Goa.

***

'Just goes to show,' Abraham spat. 'That Blenkinsopp is a calculating sod. He knows exactly what he's doing. Or else why would he sneakily throw his phone into someone's car boot as they were preparing to leave on a trip?'

'What are you saying?' Gran asked. 'Guilty conscience.'

‘Conscience! That scum has the conscience of that Syrian leader, er... al-Bashatard,’ Abraham snarled. ‘We need to stop that Blenkinsopp before he can get his evil claws into any other innocent party.’

‘Bashar al-Assad,’ Gran corrected Abraham with a glare. ‘And with all due respect patron, you could call Davy Lilley a lot of things, God rest his soul, but I think even Davy himself would admit that *innocent* isn’t one of them.’

‘Yes, if the murderer were anyone other than Blenkinsopp, I’d be pinning a medal on him,’ Abraham ran his fingers through his silky mane. ‘But you know what I mean.’

‘Thinking about it, I did hear Blenkinsopp sort of threaten to kill Lilley once,’ Gran tugged an ear. ‘Lilley shouted *you’re dead!* from a bedroom window at Blenkinsopp who mumbled *not if I don’t kill you first!* under his breath. I only just caught it myself because I was a few feet away.’

‘*Sort of* threaten?’ Abraham snapped. ‘That’s yet more evidence and you’re yet another witness.’

‘To be fair though patron,’ Gran said. ‘I’ve heard you yourself threaten to kill Lilley as well. To his face, and far more vociferously.’

‘Well Blenkinsopp has beaten me to the actual deed now hasn’t he.’

‘Yes, well... I guess we don’t know for absolute certain that the victim is definitely Davy Lilley,’ Gran yawned. ‘Not until we find the actual head.’

‘Of course it’s Davy Lilley!’ Abraham snapped. ‘Even with the head missing the body is still over six feet tall. How many other people could it possibly be?’

‘You’re right of course,’ Gran backtracked. ‘But I’m just going by the book...’

‘No Grantham, you’re pussyfooting around and jumping on the chief super’s non-committal bandwagon,’ Abraham glowered. ‘Besides, Kell spewed up as soon as he clocked the cobra tattoos on both forearms. He sure as hell didn’t need a bearded baldy head to affirm that it was Davy Lilley’s lifeless body slumped in the park, soggying the undergrowth red.’

‘True,’ Gran nodded. ‘Davy was his dad after all.’

‘Not his *biological* dad,’ Abraham scowled.

‘No, his *step*-dad I mean,’ Gran backtracked for the second time in a minute. She moved the conversation at a tangent. ‘It was obvious Kell was rattled though. He barely said a word when I took him to his mother’s to for him to break the news and stay with her.’

‘It’s hardly surprising,’ Abraham took a slurp from his fifth cup of tea of the night. ‘The lad’s had a major shock.’

‘What was surprising,’ Gran checked her watch. ‘Was that he said he’d still be coming in as usual in time for your 9 am briefing. So, in two hours or so. I did mention that no one expected him to, and he should take at least a few days off, but he was most insistent. He’s determined to do his bit.’

‘That’s my lad,’ Abraham’s eyes twinkled. ‘Determined and doing his damndest to drive the last few nails in Blenkinsopp’s coffin.’

‘So, are you confident Blenkinsopp will go down for this once we nab him patron?’ Gran said. ‘He’s managed to squirm his way out of most things so far, and he’s got that hotshot lawyer friend of his too.’

‘Squirm out of it?’ Abraham belly-laughed for the first time since the whole thing kicked off. ‘With all we’ve got on him now, he can wriggle like a maggot with a hula hoop but a whole army of hotshot lawyers couldn’t save Blenkinsopp this time, and not just for Davy’s murder, but Alex’s to boot.’

Chapter Forty

On the surface the incident room appeared much the same as before; strip lights, white walls and plastic chairs straddled by pretty much the same bums in pretty much the same arrangements as the last time. The only real visible difference was the additional pictures, text and arrows on the now, even busier whiteboard. What was less obvious to the naked eye, but discernible to all those present nonetheless, was a force nine undercurrent of mixed emotions – hurt, indignance, resolve, tension and waves of spitting adrenaline.

...And concern.

'Are you okay?' Debbie sprang to her feet when Kell poked his pale face through the door. She gave him a hearty hug then held him out at arms' length to examine him. She took a tissue from her bag and offered it to him. 'Here, your eyes are all red.'

'No thanks Debbie,' Kell averted his gaze and waved the tissue away. 'I'm just tired that's all. Me and my mam didn't get much sleep last night.'

'Of course,' Debbie eased Kell into the seat next to her and rubbed the top of his back. Aftab, Jerzy and Audrey scurried to join them; passing on their condolences and fussing over Kell while Abraham stealthily removed a photograph from the whiteboard, the one depicting a close-up of Davy's bloody severed neck. He placed it face down on the table, cleared his throat and observed in silence as everyone returned to their seats and on full alert.

'Ladies and gentlemen, I'm aware that many of you have been up most of the night. We've a busy day ahead, and the clock may be ticking - so I'll cut to the chase,' Abraham tapped on the 'Victim 2' header on the board with his pointer. 'DNA and fingerprint confirmation should be in soon, but there is no doubt that the latest victim is well known to us all - Davy Lilley.'

Debbie gave Kell's hand a squeeze.

'There is also no doubt about the perpetrator. We're still waiting for the DNA results from the chewing gum and blood found at the scene, but in addition to irrefutable witness statements, Mohammed Blenkinsopp even left an Islamist card with his name on it as well as his own bag at the scene,' Abraham tapped on the newly photoshopped image of Mo. 'According to witnesses Blenkinsopp now has a tapering tattoo running around his eyes and down to the top of each cheekbone.'

Debbie slowly shook her head.'

'What's up Harrison?' quizzed Abraham. 'Do you doubt the evidence?'

'Erm, no. I'm aware of the evidence. It's overwhelming,' Debbie felt her cheeks redden. 'I just don't know what I'm finding harder to take in. The fact that Mo is a murderer, or what he's done to his face.'

'Who knows what goes on in the mind of a psychopath Harrison,' Abraham sniped. 'But at least the new developments mean that there is one less piece of the puzzle to spend precious time and resources on – we know the *who*, we just need to find out *where* he is as well as *why* he's doing this.'

'Surely the main thing is the *where*,' trumped up Jerzy. 'Once we've arrested him that'll be an end to it.'

'Yes and no,' Abraham tapped on a 'Next victim' red header on the whiteboard then the big '?' underneath it. 'We don't know what sick stratagem Blenkinsopp has up his sleeve. He could be stalking his next victim as we speak. Yes, we need to apprehend him ASAP, but we're currently working blind to some degree. If, on the other hand, we can work out the *why* then we may be able to pre-empt his next attack and nab him sooner, and before he strikes again.'

'Point taken,' said Debbie. 'But I wouldn't have thought it should take much longer to find him. Every force and his dog are out looking for him. Haven't there been any sightings yet?'

'Haven't there been any sightings yet?' Abraham shook his head ironically. 'There have been lots Harrison! If you believe them all then he's been everywhere from potholes in the Pennines to singing on the main stage of *We Are FSTVL*.'

'You always get some one-off crank calls,' chipped in Audrey. 'What we really need are some consolidated sightings – you know, at least a few people saying exactly the same thing.'

'We've had that too,' said Abraham. 'Half a dozen or so reports of Blenkinsopp getting up to no good with a big beardy acquaintance of some bespectacled wiz.'

'You mean Davy Lilley,' said Aftab. 'He was a big beardy bloke.'

'Indeed he was,' agreed Abraham. 'Alas, the big beardy bloke in this case turns out to be some character in a film. Apparently, various members of the public have confused Blenkinsopp with the ginger wizard friend of Harry Potter.'

'Hm, but surely there must be some clue as to his whereabouts though,' said Audrey. 'If not by physical sightings then at least by CCTV, card payments or ATM usage for example.'

'There's nothing,' Abraham jabbed his pointer hard into Mo's photograph. 'Nothing yet at least. But he'll slip up at some point. That's a certainty. We just need to ensure that he slips up before we do.'

'You mean we had better catch him before he kills again,' asked Jerzy.

'Precisely that,' said Abraham. 'Grantham is monitoring Ishmael and the imam. This thing has all the hallmarks of jihadi killings. It could be that Blenkinsopp is just their puppet and that they are pulling his strings.'

'And if so, the next murder might well be imminent,' added Jerzy.

'My thoughts exactly Masur,' concurred Abraham. 'It's time we went on the offensive, not just with Blenkinsopp, but also Ishmael and the imam. I want you and Dehwar to meet up with Grantham and bring them both in. In addition to intel on the murders, they could also let slip Blenkinsopp's whereabouts.'

'That could be a bit tricky,' Everyone turned to face the returning Gran. 'I tailed Ishmael to the mosque for morning prayers. He and the imam both went in alright. It's just that neither of them came out with the rest of the congregation, and inside it's empty. It's just like they've disappeared into thin air.'

'Like Blenkinsopp you mean?' snarled Abraham.

'Erm, yes,' Gran mumbled. 'Like Blenkinsopp.'

***

Abraham crashed his fist on the end of the table and his seventh cup of tea in eight hours catapulted through the air.

'This is another reason why we need to know the *why*,' he snapped. 'Even once we catch Blenkinsopp, we still need to get the full SP on any accomplices, puppeteers and potential new targets. For all we know once Blenkinsopp falls someone else will just take his place.'

'Do you really think he's in cahoots with some Islamist cell?' asked Aftab. 'Might he not just be acting alone?'

'He could be Dehwar. All the indications are that he committed the murders alone, and on the surface, they do look like independent acts,' Abraham said. 'But as you know, it isn't unheard of for impressionable young Muslims to fall under the spell of persuasive extremists.'

'Mo has never struck me as a raving extremist,' Aftab tugged an earlobe. 'He hardly says a word down at the mosque.'

Abraham shook his head and tutted. 'It's always the quiet ones you have to look out for.'

***

'Anyway, regardless of possible associates, we still need to establish the *why*. And there is a pattern in these murders somewhere,' Abraham tapped on a picture of Davy's bare torso. 'It's the same MO as the first victim. Beheading with one, possibly two, extremely sharp instruments.'

'Do we have anything back on the murder weapon - or weapons plural - yet?' asked Audrey.

'Yes and no,' Abraham replied. 'The largest blade has yet to be pinned down, but Gina believes that the smaller cuts were made with a butcher's knife.'

After a brief exchanged-glance-filled silence, Jerzy popped the question that everyone was probably thinking. 'Like Blenkinsopp's you mean?'

'Well, that's still missing,' Abraham snapped. 'But I wouldn't bet against it. Would you?'

Jerzy lowered his head, and his floppy fringe curtained his eyes. 'I suppose not DI sir,'

'Anyway, returning to the MO,' Abraham tapped the board. 'Again there are several, seemingly random, numbers written on the body in blood. In this case, 56 on the lower belly and 101 on the back of the right hand.'

'101?' remarked Kell. 'It's probably not related, but that's the number of Mrs Asher-Regis's house on Wooler Road, where Mo was at.'

'And Alex's house was number 56,' Gran piped up.

'What about the other numbers?' Abraham tapped the board twice. '87 on the left shoulder and 104 on the right shoulder, both with a little line, squiggle or possible arrow or something on top of them.'

'That's a bit weird,' said Aftab. 'Mo himself lives at number 104.'

'Hm, and Mick lives at 87. There could be some sort of connection with houses,' mused Audrey. 'I could run some checks.'

'Thanks Audrey. By the way, Kell made a start on trawling through Blenkinsopp's PC before the events of last night,' Abraham turned towards Kell. 'Do you have anything to report?'

'Nothing of note,' Kell shrugged. 'I did have a scour before we all got called out last night, but with the ton of files he has on his computer I only really scratched the surface.'

Audrey looked at Abraham who nodded his approval and she made tracks towards the exit. 'I'll get to it straightaway.'

'You pair,' Abraham jabbed a finger in Jerzy and Aftab's direction. 'Search Blenkinsopp's house again, as well as the places of any other known associates. Remember that that friend of his, Patel, also has a shop as well as a house. Make sure that you thoroughly search both. You can also get yourself down The Causeway again when it opens and do what you can to track down that couple he was seen with there.'

'Sir,' Jerzy and Aftab rose in unison and bounded out.

'Kell if you're feeling up to it can you go and help Audrey. Just do whatever she asks.'

'Sir,' Kell hastened to the CID office.

'Debbie, I want you to make another appeal for potential witnesses and also liaise with the bluebottles and authorities both locally and nationally. Make sure that if Blenkinsopp so much as pops a nostril out of his purported pothole then I'm the first to know about it. Well, me and armed response.'

'Armed response?' Debbie's eyes ballooned. 'Is that really necessary?'

'What?' Abraham's bark was accompanied with an incredulous glower. 'That *maniac* was last seen waving a sword around after decapitating his second victim Harrison. As far as I, and the general public at large are concerned, Blenkinsopp needs taking ASAP and *dead or alive*.'

Debbie opened her mouth to respond but Abraham shooed her out of the room with a venomous scowl.

'As for you Grantham, I want you to move hell and high water to track down Ishmael and the imam and pronto.'

'About that,' Gran closed the door and sidled up to Abraham. 'I've had a thought about that 'boom!' thing. Maybe Ishmael, Ahmed and Blenkinsopp weren't talking about the Tall Ships *event,* but The Tall Ships *pub* – you know, the one over Clavering way. If they are planning an attack on that then it mightn't be a matter of months away. It could be any time now!'

'Oh hell,' Abraham bit on his filed fingernails. 'The Tall Ships *pub.*'

'I think it's time we called Special Branch patron,' Gran pulled out her mobile but before she could even swipe the screen Abraham batted it out of her hand and it bounced across the floor.

'This could be huge. A serial jihadi murderer and a possible Islamist bomb attack. And in our backyard! If anyone's going to thwart them and get the collar for this then it's going to be me,' Abraham eyed Gran coughed then added. 'I mean *us,* not some nansy pansy cockney.'

'I can't say I agree with this,' said Gran. 'I'd like it on the record that I wanted to escalate this.'

'I'm in charge of this case and I'm not interested in what you think Grantham,' Abraham sniped. 'Besides, what are you so worried about anyway? It's only Blenkinsopp with the *possible* addition of a little old man and someone who can't even source a suit that fits. You get yourself out and about, keep tabs on the Tall Ships pub, and track down the imam and Ishmael. You can leave Blenkinsopp to me. The snare is closing in around him and believe me, Harry Potter's mate or not, no amount of wizard wand-waving is going to get him out of this one.'

Chapter Forty-One

Abraham's front door had had numerous previous owners, but it wasn't until he moved in that it started to scuff in the middle and fray around the edges. He jabbed impatiently with his key and finally got the lock to turn. He barged through to the hallway shoulder first and slung his briefcase on the floor. It had been 38 hours since he had last slept. Knackered and then szzzome. He tugged his jacket off and flung it at the wall. Knackered *and* angry. Without looking he backheeled the door shut with a clatter. Knackered, angry *and* pissed off. He slowly stomped up the stairs, steaming irises eyes under droopy eyelids. After running a bath and traipsing to the bedroom, he flopped down on his bed face-first. He ironed out some creases in the duvet with the flat of his hand then groaned at the effort of having to roll all of two feet to put his mobile on charge and retrieve the remote from the bedside cabinet. He flicked a button and cringed as a shot of himself filled the bedroom TV screen – a rerun of an earlier media briefing outside the station.

'Detective Inspector Abraham,' called out a tiny mighty mouth with grey fuzzy hair that matched her microphone. 'This very morning you stood on these very steps and told the world that you had identified the serial killer. You promised that you would have him *behind bars with enough evidence to convict him till Doomsday - very soon, possibly by teatime.* You even staked your reputation on it. It's now 6 pm and it transpires that not only is the killer still very much at large, but that his whereabouts are still a complete mystery to you. Is it true that you haven't got the faintest idea where Mohammed Blenkinsopp is?'

Abraham hurled a shoe at the TV and by design, or more likely luck, he connected with the power button and the screen went black. Just as well.

He hadn't believed his own response the first time around. Three and a half hours later his lies would ring hollower still.

Pissed off, but too bushed to even raise a scowl, he at least managed to force himself off the bed and trudge through to the bathroom. Wearily he dumped his clothes in a pile and, closing his eyes, slid under an indulgent layer of bubbles.

Barely had he brushed his butt with the loofa than he dozed off.

***

Fifteen minutes later he was rudely awoken with a blob of marmalade up each nostril. He sneezed, squirmed, slipped down, spluttered, coughed, then scrambled to sit up straight.

'You!'

Mo set his small tray complete with mug of tea and slice of toast down on top of the toilet cistern, sat nonchalantly on the seat and proceeded to toss and catch the heavy four-slice metal toaster - precariously close to the tap end of Abraham's bath.

Abraham wasn't normally lost for words, but such was his astonishment that he just gaped like a gobsmacked guppy.

Suddenly he lurched forward.

'Whoa Inspector Clouseau,' Mo swayed out of his reach in one direction then twisted sharply back around and dangled the toaster over the bath. Abraham's startled eyes followed the toaster's extension cable out of the bathroom and to somewhere along the hallway. 'Yes, it is plugged in, just in case you're wondering. Do you know what would happen if I dropped this in the water?'

Abraham froze, jaw dropped, half-in, half-out of the bath.

'To tell the truth, I'm not totally sure myself,' said Mo. 'I've been looking it up on the computer in your den. Apparently, it's probably not fatal in modern houses as most have ground-fault circuit interrupters installed these days, but many old houses like this still don't have GFCIs.

I've had a snoop at your plugs and electrics and my guess is that yours still doesn't. If not, then in all likelihood you'd be paralysed by the current as it passes through your body, you'll get stuck in the tub, and you'll be electrocuted to death.'

Abraham's eyes whirred. His cheeks, flush from the hot bath, suddenly paled.

'Of course, we'll never know for sure unless we try it,' grinned Mo. 'I'm game if you are?'

'You wouldn't dare,' Abraham glowered.

'Wouldn't dare what? Drop the toaster? Or wouldn't dare chop someone's head off in cold blood?'

Abraham hesitated, gulped, then slowly eased himself back beneath the bubbles while Mo took a slurp of tea.

'You'll never get away with it.' Abraham sat back up straight, jutted out his whiskered chin and pointed a finger. 'Put the toaster down and stick your hands up. You're under arrest.'

Mo laughed long and hard. It felt like a release of sorts. It was a struggle to remember the last time he'd laughed at all, let alone as heartily as this.

Moisture dripped off Abraham's brow. It could have been the hot water, but Mo suspected otherwise.

'Put the toaster down and stick em up!' Mo turned around, took a bite of his toast then turned back round to look at Abraham. 'It's not the wild west Joe. And you're not Wyap Earl. You're not even Deputy Dawg.'

Abraham wiped his forehead with the back of his hand.

'In fact, you're not the great detective, what is it you call yourself?' Mo picked at a crumb at the side of his mouth with his tongue. 'Oh yes. *Super Dick*. You're not Super Dick,'

Mo followed Abraham's line of sight. 'Yes, it *is* your shirt, and yes, they *are* your jeans. Pretty good fit don't you think? Thanks for the borrow. My clothes were somewhat dirty.'

'Somewhat bloody more like!'

'Quite, they're in your linen bin. You may need some of that stain removal stuff then put them on a 60-degrees cycle.' Mo noticed Abraham lower his gaze. 'Yes, they are *your* slippers too Joe. Quite snug and pretty comfy, but rather niffy. You never wash your slippers Joe?'

Abraham didn't reply, but took a sharp intake of air through his teeth and glared at Mo.

'Tut, tut,' Mo continued. 'It's basic hygiene Joe. You really need to take more care.'

Mo flicked up the toaster with one hand and simultaneously twirled it, basketball fashion. 'And your diet's no better.'

'What the hell do you know about my diet?'

'I know that the mushrooms in your fridge are four days out of date.' Mo slurped his tea loudly and licked his lips. 'The ones I had this morning were fine, but you're risking it Joe if you finish the others off. Going mouldy and all sorts.'

'You'd better not have been going through my stuff,' Abraham snapped. 'Why are you here? And just how did you get in anyway. I'll be adding attempted murder and breaking and entering to your escalating charge sheet.'

'Really DI, patience. One question at a time if you please,' tutted Mo. 'Firstly, *of course* I've been going through your stuff. You've been going through mine. It's only fair don't you think? And if you want to know why I'm here it's because you invited me.'

'Eh?' Abraham gawped. 'I did no such thing.'

'Well, maybe not directly as such,' a mouthful of crust caused Mo to mumble. 'But when you stood alongside Kell on the news last night saying that you would be *out night and day* hunting for me I said to myself *that's handy, there's an empty house just around the corner then*. And as I was covered in blood and dog-tired at the time, it just seemed like too good an opportunity to pass up.'

Abraham moved his jaw, but nothing came out.

'It's a nice bath by the way, and a comfy bed too come to that,' added Mo. 'Best night's sleep I've had in ages.'

'I thought someone had been on my bed,' scowled Abraham. 'The duvet was creased.'

'What can I say? Ironing it wasn't top of my list of priorities,' Mo pointed to the sash window. 'As for your other questions, I didn't break in, you left this window open, and it was an easy shimmy up the drainpipe. I must say, I was a tad surprised that you hadn't set your house alarm. Not that I'm complaining. Told you it was practically an invitation. If you like, I can ask Sergeant Black down at the station to give you a leaflet on home security.'

'You patronising little shit,' Abraham balled a fist. 'The alarm would have been on and the window would have been shut properly if I hadn't had to urgently rush off to the park on a small matter of you beheading someone!'

'I'd appreciate it if you'd mind your manners,' Mo said, tossing the toaster even higher this time, and catching it only at the second attempt, just above Abraham's feet. 'Whoops! Butterfingers.'

Abraham snapped his feet to his knees, not that it would have saved him. 'What do you want Blenkinsopp?' he retorted. There was defiance in his voice, but also a distinct quiver.

'What do I want?' Mo placed the toaster on his knees and sipped some tea. 'That's simple detective inspector. I want the truth.'

***

'What do you mean you want the truth? The truth about what?'

'Well, it's all well and good you standing there on national television and telling the world that I'm a serial killer,' Mo said. 'But with all due respect Joe, you're not what I would call the most trustworthy person around, are you? I mean, what real evidence do you actually have?'

'Are you serious?' Abraham cackled. It wasn't clear whether the cause of his laughter was nerves, bewilderment or something else, but judging by the look on Mo's face it wasn't the reaction he'd wanted.

'Deadly,' Mo paused for a couple of moments. 'If you forgive the pun.'

Abraham studied Mo's features and demeanour. Yes, Mo was holding his stare, but through doleful eyes. Yes, his cross-legged posture seemed cocky and confident, but if so then why was he fidgeting on his butt and pulling at his fingers?

'My God, you're serious, aren't you? he chuckled. 'Sure, why not...'

'Come on then,' Mo prompted with a roll of the fingers after a few seconds silence. 'What are you waiting for?'

'I'm just wondering where to start,' Abraham smiled ironically. 'We could be here all night.'

'In that case, you had better hurry up with the abridged version detective. Before you shrivel up like a naked mole rat.'

'Okay then, let's start with Alex,' Abraham said. 'You photograph her, make threats to her about losing her head, follow her to the park, kill her, engrave your signature *MB* mark at the scene, you also get covered in Alex's blood then hide your clothes in a bin and give Aftab and Jerzy some cock and bull story.'

'Yeah,' Mo's voice croaked. 'I know it looks bad, but...'

'But what?' Abraham creased his eyebrows. 'There is nothing you could possibly say in mitigation or defence. Witnesses affirm all of this. We've irrefutable DNA evidence. You've no alibi. You were seen with the murder weapon in the vicinity. And you were even overheard shouting the numbers.'

'What numbers?'

'You know very well what numbers Blenkinsopp,' tutted Abraham. 'The witness is half deaf so didn't catch them all, but no doubt they were the same ones that you wrote on the body in Alex's own blood - 12, 14, 58, 82 and 98.'

'I don't know anything about those numbers,' Mo scrunched up his nose.

'Really?' Abraham raised his eyebrows. 'Are you sure they have nothing to do with some deranged Islamist plot? We know your buddies Ahmed and Ishmael have been up to no good and now they've miraculously vanished.'

Mo's eyes buzzed as the jihadi video on his PC flashed through his mind. 'I don't know anything about that,' he said somewhat hesitantly.

'But you're admitting everything else then?' probed Abraham.

'No. Well yes and no,' Mo said. 'There's some truth in all of it, or at least most of it. But I don't remember killing her. And I don't remember anything about numbers.'

'How can you not remember killing someone?' Abraham shot Mo an incredulous glare. 'It's not the kind of thing you're likely to forget.'

'I was drunk,' Mo said. 'I remember some bits, but there are some distinct gaps. Things have just been coming back to me in a sort of drip-by-drip piecemeal fashion. And I'm not even sure if everything I remember is actual reality, or just dreams.'

'Bullshit,' Abraham sneered. 'If you killed someone then you'd damn well know about it.'

'Well, I do suspect that I was at the park, and on reflection, I do recall climbing the railings,' Mo grated his teeth together and shifted his eyes upwards. 'And yes, I may well have found my way on top of her headless body, and I suppose you're right about my clothes being drenched in blood, and okay, I did have a sword, but I don't remember killing her.'

'Yeah, yeah,' Abraham tutted. 'What about Davy Lilley? I suppose you'll be saying you didn't kill him either.'

'That depends,' Mo tugged at his bottom lip. 'Do you have any evidence against me for that too?'

'What planet are you on!' Abraham roared, his laughter warbling as he shook his head. 'We've enough to convict you ten thousand times over!'

'Oh,' Mo said.

'Yes, *oh*. Oh with Big Ben sized bells on.' Abraham whistled.

'Evidence like what though?

'Okay, I'll play along,' Abraham cracked a crooked smile. 'But just so you know, we both know you're as guilty as hell on an arson charge.'

'So?'

'So, it's the same MO isn't it?' Abraham ran some fingers through his wet hair. 'You intimidating the victim in public. And even threatening to kill him.'

'Eh?'

'Don't play the innocent,' Abraham tutted. 'I understand your exact words to Lilley during one of your set-tos with him were '*not if I kill you first.*'

'Yes but...'

'But nothing? There's no point denying it,' Abraham scoffed. 'DS Grantham overheard you. Moreover, in Lilley's case, we also have telephonic evidence of you luring him into the trap of meeting you.'

'Yes, to sort things out.'

'Well, you did that alright,' Abraham sneered. 'With another sharp fatal blow to the neck followed by your usual bloody numbers ritual – this time 56, 87, 101 and 104. Just what's all that about anyway?'

'No idea,' said Mo.

'Let me guess. You just happened to be drunk again and everything's all rather conveniently cloudy.'

'Well, yes, now you mention it,' said Mo. 'But I wouldn't say *all* of it – just some.'

'Do you see the recurring theme here Blenkinsopp?'

'I know what you're getting at,' Mo exhaled heavily. 'But do you have any *actua*l evidence besides a dubious threat and the fact that we both ended up in the park?'

'What? Besides yet more cast-iron DNA evidence of you at the scene? Not to mention changing the inscription on the tree from *MB I* to *MB II* – and with traces of your own blood on it I should add - not to mention the discovery of your *Allah is Great* card by the body too. The one inscribed '*Welcome to the brotherhood - Mohammed Blenkinsopp.*'

'What?'

'You heard,' Abraham jibed. 'Oh, you left your bag at the scene too by the way. The same one I saw you with. Your computer cables and stuff were still in it. The cab driver who took you there not only revealed that you were heading to the park to *sort Davy Lilley out*, but he also identified the pumpkin.'

'There must be loads of people with pumpkin's in bags,' Mo argued. 'It could be anyone's.'

'It's not Halloween!' Abraham jeered. 'And even if it was, I doubt anyone else would also have a letter from your mother in the pouch.'

It was now Mo's turn to gape.

'We also found your fingerprints in Lilley's blood on another startled witness' window,' Abraham continued. 'Oh yeah, and there is also the fact that you were seen by yet another witness stood right next to Lilley's body – again your clothes caked in blood. It's some hobby you've got there Blenkinsopp, I'll give you that!'

'Witness? What other witness?'

'Stewie Allision. He was adamant that he recognised you, even with your new tattoo disguise.'

'It's not a disguise,' Mo argued. 'But hang on, Stewie... yeah, it's coming back to me now, I do remember seeing him at the park. His girlfriend lives around there somewhere. So, he remembers me does he?'

'Remember you?' Abraham cried. 'Of course he remembers you! How could he not? What with you holding your sword next to the headless body one minute then waving the weapon about your head while stood on top of the railings the next - shouting '*No more Davy Lilley'* and howling like a werewolf!'

'Ah, but for all Stewie saw I could have just stumbled upon Davy's body. You know, like an innocent passer-by,' said Mo. 'I don't see how he could, in all honesty, point the finger at me as the culprit.'

'Are you taking the piss?'

'No,' insisted Mo. 'Really, what could possibly have given him the slightest reason for him to believe that I was the killer?'

'Maybe the fact that you stood there, bold as brass, telling him it was *a nice night for it*,' Abraham bellowed. 'With your big sword in one hand and Davy's severed head held upside down by his pointy red beard in the other!'

***

'Congratulations, you are truly world-class when it comes to taking the biscuit,' Abraham's shaking head wobbled like it was coiled. 'Arise Sir Bourbon Blenkinsopp! They'll probably make you tea lady in Broadmoor.'

'So, I did kill them?' Mo hung his head and his eyes quickly glazed over.

'Yes. Felicitations, you're a damned certified nut job,' huffed Abraham. 'Now if you don't mind waiting outside a minute, I'll get dressed then I'll escort you to the station.'

'I did it,' Mo sniffed and slowly rose to his feet. 'I'm a killer.'

'Yes, you are,' Abraham tapped his goatee as Mo headed for the hallway. 'Hang on, pass me my trousers will you.'

Mo bent down and plucked them from the pile of clothes on the tiled floor. 'What for?

'I just want to get my handcuffs that's all,' Abraham said. 'We don't want you doing a runner while I'm getting changed do we?'

'No, I suppose not,' Mo jangled the trousers, took hold of the handcuffs and trudged up to Abraham who thrust out a palm and bounced it.

'Come on, give them here Blenkinsopp. Your number is up.'

Mo slowly lowered the handcuffs and Abraham snatched at them, but just as his fingertips brushed the metal Mo flung them away and lunged for the toaster.

'*Numbers!* The numbers thing just doesn't add up,' Mo jiggled the toaster above the bath. 'I'm actually a quite a numbers buff. If it really was me who had daubed those numbers, then I'm pretty sure I'd have remembered it. But I don't. And if I didn't write those numbers then maybe I didn't kill anyone either.'

'Of course you did Blenkinsopp!' Snapped Abraham. 'Haven't you listened to a word I've said? Now, put down your electrical appliance and kindly hand over the cuffs.'

'It just doesn't add up,' Mo repeated. He dropped the handcuffs into the bath and ordered Abraham to slot them around the chunky metal bridge that joined the two old-fashioned taps together. 'Cuff your feet to that thing. Something's not right.'

***

Abraham protested. Most stridently. But after another slip of the toaster and a last gasp grasp from Mo, he hurriedly chained himself to the taps.

'Where are you going?' Abraham called after Mo. 'You do know that Kell will be back any time now don't you?'

'Nice try Joe, but he's hardly likely to leave his newly widowed mother all by herself,' Mo said without looking back. 'And don't you worry. I'm not going far.'

***

Mo had seemed to hit a raw nerve earlier when he'd told Abraham that he'd been mooching through his stuff. He'd reacted angrily. Then again, Abraham was naturally an angry kind of person. Or at least he was in Mo's experience. With others perhaps Abraham was joviality personified. Either way, Mo couldn't help wondering if Abraham had anything to hide? And if so, would he manage to uncover anything before either Abraham managed to free himself, Kell came home, or the police net finally closed in on him? ...As it surely would. ...And every waking second clawed that inevitable nightmare closer still.

He set about retracing his steps. In Abraham's bedroom, in the kitchen and then through to the small den. He traced a finger across the limited volumes on his window-sill-cum-bookshelf. A Jeremy Clarkson autobiography, a Chris Ryan novel, a DIY manual, a book on photography and even a hardback on Islam. What was Abraham doing with a book on Islam? Mo scratched his head and recalled Abraham's comments about *Ahmed and Ishmael being up to no good*. The DI had been researching the enemy, no doubt. He opened it at random and noticed some marks in pencil. He felt an urge to read through some passages; about hope, truth or justice. Or possibly about untangling your neck from a strangling manhunt noose. The last one, Mo knew, was desperate wishful thinking, but he did take time to locate a passage about hope. *Whoever hopes to meet with their Lord then let him do righteous deeds.* Mo sighed. Was chaining a police officer to his bath righteous? In all honesty, Mo couldn't say that it was. He rubbed some soft whiskers on his jawline then thumbed through some pages until he found something about truth. *Do not mix the truth with falsehood*. Who had been the most truthful here? Mo or Abraham? He skimmed through some more text. Suddenly his eyes locked onto the word *justice*. He silently mouthed the phrase, *Be ye staunch in justice*. Mo put the book down and picked up Alex's murder case files that he'd earlier found in Abraham's briefcase. He briefly skimmed through them again. *Staunch in justice.* Something Mo couldn't put his finger on made him re-examine the files in closer detail. Then afterwards, unsatisfied and niggled but still none the wiser, he plonked himself down again in front of Abraham's PC.

Come on Mo, think man. You're missing something.

Truth be told Mo didn't know what that something was, or even if it actually existed. But something ate away at him. Something that had either prodded his subconscious earlier - here or possibly elsewhere - or else there was something much larger about this whole shebang that he just wasn't seeing.

One thing he *did* see as the PC booted up and MSN's home page automatically loaded, was a prominent headline, '*Nationwide manhunt for killer Blenkinsopp heightened.* If Mo was indeed missing something, then the time he had to fathom it was quickly running out.

***

Abraham closed his eyes, snorted and cursed under his breath. He thrived on control, yet here he was, chained to his own bath, in his own house, by the very person who he'd promised the nation would be in custody by now. He'd staked his reputation on it. If he didn't nail Mo for the crimes he'd so assuredly and so publicly accused him of then it'd be his head, not Mo's, on a plate. If he didn't deliver, then he'd surely have to resign. Not that he'd be sacked or physically forced to resign. He'd had a very successful career as well as a long and distinguished record until this point. Even so, he'd never be able to hold his head high ever again in these parts, or for any other force for that matter. Hero to laughingstock in one fell swoop. He pounded the bathwater with his fists and yanked, yanked and yanked again with both hands and feet. He tugged, splashed, twisted and swore as he tried again and again – and failed again and again - to free his bound feet. He paused for a minute or so. Recuperating and taking stock. He eyed the clunky metal bridge that the cuffs were chained to and slowly curled up his legs. He filled his lungs full of air, held it, then in a flash attacked it with an almighty double heal kick.

His eyes creased and watered and he bit down on his thumb to muffle his shriek of pain. Traditional features like that were rock solid and build to last. His heels would be shot and his ankles down to the bone before the tap/bridge anchor gave way. 'Damn you Blenkinsopp,' he cursed defeated under his breath.

What could he possibly do to escape? Shouting would do no good. One of the reasons why he'd bought this detached house was because of the notable distance to his nearest neighbour. Besides, a booming cry for help wouldn't go down too well with whoops-a-daisy toaster boy downstairs. It was hopeless. He twisted on his side and half of his face and mouth sunk under the suds. Notwithstanding his sinking career, he was drowning mentally and physically too. He silently screamed then abruptly coughed and spluttered upon swallowing some soapy water. Suddenly he sat up straight, his eyes flickering. He chewed a fingernail and mumbled to himself. 'I need a plan B'.

But what?

***

The sound of Mo's footsteps preceded him as he climbed the stairs. Abraham shoved the loofa back underneath his legs to hide it. After almost two hours in the bath, the thick layer of bubbles had long since dissipated. He'd spent the last hour or so trying to fish his trousers over with the loofa. Not to cover his modesty, but to get his mitts on the handcuffs' key in his trouser pocket. He'd stretched every sinew of his limbs and torso in attempts to reach it, but no matter how much he tried, time and again the loofa never quite made it – falling short by a tantalising two or three inches.

'Sorry, I wasn't thinking. How rude of me. Would you like some tea and toast?' Mo set down his tray and placed a cup of tea on the side of the bath. He then dropped a couple of slices of bread in the toaster and plunged them down. The toaster fired up and its orange glow reflected in Abraham's startled eyes. Mo noticed. 'Well, I did tell you it was plugged in didn't I Joe?'

Abraham swallowed hard.

'I've been checking your browser history, amongst other things. You browsed this on your most recent online session,' Mo took a sheet of paper from the tray and flashed it at Abraham. 'Care to explain this Joe?'

The DIs eyes widened, fell then hardened as he clocked the picture of a small teenage girl with a pretty face but all skin and bone.

'That's Alex's daughter, as you well know.'

'Nonsense, it's Jade Quigley' Mo tutted. 'I knew her well. She was pretty much the only person I ever felt close to in school.'

'Two loners finding refuge in each other?'

'To begin with,' Mo admitted. 'But it was more than that. We had something... a bond... not romantic, but something... real... well, until...'

'Until she jumped off a roof,' Abraham's voice creaked.

'Pushed more like,' Mo angrily retorted. 'True, she may have been the one to jump, but she wouldn't have been up there in the first place if it wasn't for the living hell that was her home.'

'Tell you about that did she?'

'Not a dickybird other than her stepdad was a *waster who'd run off* and her mam was *difficult*,' Mo muttered. 'I tried probing for more often enough, but she clammed up tight each time. Even so, it was easy to spot the signs and read between the lines... the marks on her arms, the tremble in her voice and the fear in her eyes whenever the going home bell rung.'

'So, you tried to comfort her by filling her head full of your Islamic nonsense.'

'It's far from nonsense,' Mo snapped. 'And it was a real comfort to her if you must know... Hang on, how come you know about that?'

'You signed the Islamic book you gave her,' Abraham locked his eyes onto Mo's. 'The one we found at her mother, Alex's house.'

Mo scrunched up his nose. 'Alex's surname wasn't Quigley, but Hobbs. It says so in your case notes.'

'You almost sound convincing there Blenkinsopp,' Abraham chuckled ironically. 'But as I'm sure you are already fully aware, Alex reverted to her *Hobbs* maiden name after the waster ex-husband did a runner, but Jade kept her surname,'

'What?' gaped Mo. 'I never...'

'Save it Blenkinsopp,' scoffed Abraham. 'We know all about your close relations with Jade. Your precious Debbie was the one to rat you out. I've also just been doing some extra digging on Alex myself, and it transpires that you were spot on about her being a difficult mother – though *difficult* is a gargantuan understatement. And I fully agree with your *pushed* insight too. Little wonder poor Jade topped herself. And no wonder whatsoever that you felt aggrieved. Angry. Enraged. It's what's called *motive*, and in this case, it's clear that you've got mountains of motive. Most juries would send you down on that basis alone. But of course, when you also take into account the witnesses and the vast quantities of circumstantial and cast-iron physical and DNA evidence...'

Abraham let his statement hang in the moist bathroom air while Mo's mind boggled and a gobstopper of a lump built in his throat. He clamped sweaty palms over watery eyes for ten seconds, ...twenty ...thirty...

Silently, Mo gathered a couple of sheets of paper from the tray and placed them on the toilet seat.

Abraham nodded towards them, 'What's that?'

'Oh those,' Mo said. 'Just some printouts from your computer. You don't have much A4 left though so I'll probably just take the hard drive when the paper runs out.'

'You do and I'll kill you!'

'Funny you should say that Joe,' Mo turned the top sheet over revealing a selfie of Abraham with a smiling blond woman. 'You didn't mention that you knew Alex personally. You kept that very quiet you dark horse. And to think, you made quite a song and dance about me having a photograph of her on my phone when you yourself have one of her on your home PC! Do your police colleagues know?'

'None of your damned business!' Abraham snapped.

'Ah, but you see, you've made it my business,' said Mo. 'I mean, I didn't know her from Adam one minute and yet the next you are accusing me of her murder.'

'Of course you killed her,' cried Abraham. 'The evidence is irrefutable. Who else could it have possibly been?'

'Funnily enough, I've been asking myself the same question,' Mo flicked his eyes up and tapped his chin pensively. 'And I've concluded that it could well have been you.'

'Me?' Abraham laughed. 'On what grounds!'

'On the grounds that you obviously knew her a lot better than me, most victims tend to know their killer, and you only live a two-minute jog from the park. For all I know you could well have arranged to meet her, killed her, then legged it back here before anyone was any the wiser. I mean, there are no police CCTV cameras around this leafy part of town as far as I'm aware. There's also the question of a woman's muffled scream and a man's voice that I heard at the park. Initially, I doubted my own memory, but bit by bit it's been coming back to me. I only caught a faint snippet of the voice. A hushed 'be quiet.' But I *did* hear it. And at the spot where Alex was murdered. I'm quite sure that it was a man's voice. On refection, *your* voice.'

'Pish!' Abraham laughed louder than normal.

'It's nothing of the sort,' continued Mo. 'And it's your case files that's pish. For example, from your notes, I see that your own interpretation of the pathologist's report is that you believe that Alex was raped.'

'A perfectly natural conclusion given the bruising.'

'That depends on the bruising,' Mo said. 'There significant marks were on the *sides* of her upper arms. But if someone was raping her, she'd have had more bruising on the front of her upper arms - as her assailant pinned her down.'

'Like you know the first thing about crime scenes,' Abraham scorned. 'You've no idea what you're gibbering on about.'

'It's true that I've no real crime scene experience,' Mo admitted. 'But I've seen the photos, and it's sound postulating. I think the marks on her arms came from someone grabbing her and shaking her about. It's probably why she tried screaming and why you subsequently hushed her up.'

'What kind of fantasy fairy-tale world are you living in? If she screamed then no doubt it was at the sight of you wielding your sword of death. And as far as hushing her up is concerned, then you achieved that most categorically with a bang to her head followed by gruesomely severing her neck,' Abraham sniped. 'Get your facts right Blenkinsopp. You're spouting fanciful drivel, not hard evidence. And notably, *all* the real evidence points conclusively to you – and you alone.'

'But does it?' Mo's eyes bore into Abraham's. 'You say that you *have telephonic evidence of me luring Davy into the trap of meeting me*. But has anyone at the police station tried tracing telephonic evidence of you luring Alex into the trap of meeting you?'

'That's preposterous,' Abraham sneered. 'But yes, Alex's phone has been checked, and there is no record of anyone arranging to meet her late that night.'

'How convenient,' mused Mo. 'Interestingly, I've checked your phone to see if a certain *Alex* is listed as a contact. And there isn't.'

'There you go then.'

'On the contrary,' said Mo. 'All it means is that you deleted her as a contact recently.'

'Pish!'

'Not at all,' Mo continued. 'You see, you do still have her as a contact in your Outlook application on your PC. It would have synced and updated when you next attached your phone, but clearly you overlooked doing that.'

Mo didn't wait for a response from the gawping Abraham, but instead continued. 'That's a bit of a coincidence Joe. I wonder what the odds is of your chat messages being deleted from Alex's phone too? Wouldn't it be very strange - some would say suspicious even - if it transpires that you were deleted as a contact from her phone in the 48 hours following her untimely demise?'

'Crap and double crap!' Abraham's Adam's apple slowly descended, and he fiddled with the end of his nose.

'Is it?' probed Mo. 'My recent drugs charge is living proof that you are not beyond manipulating evidence when it suits you. 'If you have the front to plant class A drugs on an innocent party in the goddamned police station of all places, then I dare say that clicking a button on a dead person's phone should be a piece of cake in comparison.'

'If you're playing the sleuth then you're an amateur one,' Abraham tutted. 'After the evidence has been bagged up at the scene it gets locked away and I don't get to touch it.'

'You'd find a way,' argued Mo. 'You may have even deleted it at the scene. You probably used her thumb to unlock it.'

'Amateur,' Abraham ridiculed with an ironic tut. 'The phone technology relies on electric charges in people's thumbs - which dead people don't have.'

'You could have knocked her out, used her thumb and *then* killed her,' Mo postulated. 'You could even have guessed her password. A birthday is common. If you knew her you could have used that.'

Abraham tutted again and shook his head.

'Anyway, you mentioned my lack of an alibi. What about you? Do you have one?'

'No,' admitted Abraham.

'How very convenient DI. I dare say you don't have an alibi for Davy Lilley's murder either.'

'Nope,' Abraham smiled crookedly. 'I was right here on my lonesome. But then again, I'm not the one who threatened both Davy and Alex, killed them, got covered in their blood and was seen with the murder weapon in the vicinity.'

'Yes, and that brings me onto my next point,' Mo steepled his hands. 'You keep referring to the sword as the murder weapon. I just don't buy that. You don't have it, so how do you know it's the murder weapon? It's pure conjecture. In fact, you've got a couple of big sharp knives in the kitchen yourself. They'd be perfectly capable of doing the job.'

'You're grabbing at straws Blenkinsopp. Tiny little ones that the tooth fairy feeds her even tinier dolls with. 'We've more than enough proof – forensic and otherwise - to convict you even without the sword. Recovering the sword will be the icing on the cake, not a game-changer.'

Abraham stared at Mo. Mo stared back. In between them three feet of electronic pulses, charges and neurons jousting. The toast suddenly popped up. Without a word, Mo spread both slices generously with butter and marmalade and plonked them next to the tea. Very slowly, he overturned the other A4 sheet. Abraham averted his gaze at first. Spuriously so. Perhaps suspicious after Mo's accusations, or by the way that Mo had silently and very deliberately made of show of turning it over. Abraham veered his head one way but with twitchy eyes.   Would he? Wouldn't he?...

***

...Well, at least not at first. At least not while Mo was still in the room. At least not until Mo had started down the stairs. Abraham looked at it then alright.

Mo looked on too. Furtively and through the crack in the door before bounding down the stairs – this time for real; eyebrows raised and eyes igniting.

***

Abraham's ankles were red raw and starting to bleed by the next time Mo bounded up the stairs an hour or so later. Again, Abraham hid the loofa before Mo entered the bathroom and dropped a leather sports bag on the floor.

'You going anywhere?' Abraham asked.

'Much that I've enjoyed your hospitality I wouldn't want to outstay my welcome. But I'm not going just yet,' Mo said. 'I've had another good mooch around, I've some bits and bobs in the bag and I'll confiscate your hard drive after I've gone through more of your files. You'll get it back once you give me my PC back.'

'You little sh...'

'Shh, I want to talk to you about this,' Mo shushed Abraham with a finger to his lips then took the upturned A4 sheet from the toilet seat and held it in front of Abraham's face. 'What do you have to say about this Joe?'

'Nothing, it's just a picture of a dress.'

'Ah, but it's not just any picture,' Mo countered. 'It's an old, poor-quality picture that looks like it has been scanned. It's not like the digital ones that you get these days.'

'So, what if it is? I've never seen that picture before. It's probably just one of many work files I bring home.'

'A perfectly reasonable response,' remarked Mo. 'And if it wasn't for the fact that I found your work laptop downstairs in your briefcase, and it's full of work stuff, whereas your personal PC isn't, then I'd be inclined to believe you. Oh, that and the little fact that I clocked your reaction when you saw that image. You definitely recognised it. And it wasn't just recognition in your eyes, but surprise, shock and fear.'

'Believe what you want, you'll be banged up by morning anyway.'

'It's quite a distinctive dress isn't it Joe? Unusual colouring and an even rarer pattern. I recognised it straightaway myself too. My mam doesn't have many photographs of her childhood, but she is wearing this same dress in one of those. She once told me it's the favourite dress she's ever had.'

'So what? Your mother had a dress. Big deal.'

'But it's not *just* the dress,' said Mo. 'It has been taken from behind and at some distance. Notice too the leaves in the foreground and the pond in the distance. This photograph was taken at the park, from behind a bush, and probably without the subject's knowledge.'

'So what?' Abraham repeated.

Mo fixed his eyes on Abraham's. His voice caught as he spoke. 'It's just that my mam once told me that when she was young, a guy, ten years or so older than her, offered her a lift home from the park.'

'Very chivalrous of him,' remarked Abraham.

'Well, it would have been,' said Mo. 'If he hadn't instead driven to Crimdon Dene and tried to rape her.'

'Attempted rape?' Abraham's expression steeled. 'That's a very serious crime. I hope she reported it.'

'Unfortunately not. She says never got his name, didn't take note of the car's registration and was too shocked and scared to do anything other than run away and hide among brambles bushes.'

'Well, it's not too late,' offered Abraham. 'If she remembers anything else then if she comes to the station we'll certainly take it seriously, and follow it up.'

'That's just it,' Mo shook his head. 'I doubt you would.'

'Of course we would!' Abraham said. 'Why ever wouldn't we?'

'Because detective inspector,' Mo threw up the toaster, it banged off the ceiling and he only just managed to catch it on the way down. 'I think the would-be rapist is you.'

'Me? How utterly ridiculous,' Abraham laughed, possibly nervously, possibly for real. Mo sometimes found it difficult to tell. 'What on earth has possessed you to come up with that crazy, outrageous notion?'

'It's not that crazy,' Mo proffered. 'You're about the right age, and the girl in the dress has her back turned, but it could be my mam, although it could easily be someone else too.'

'Well then!'

'It's just that even if the girl isn't my mam, then that still takes nothing away from your look of shock and horror when I showed you the image,'

Mo said. 'But my guess is that it *is* my mam and you're petrified you've been rumbled.'

'Bollocks!'

'Well, we'll soon find out. Smile for the camera...' Mo zoomed in on Abraham using the DI's own phone and clicked the button. 'I'll show her this and ask her myself. I'll get the truth out of her.'

'Truth?' Abraham sneered. 'The truth is you're deranged! But, by all means, please do run along to your mam's house. We've got officers keeping tabs on it, you'll be nabbed and hauled away in chains before you're halfway down the street.'

'So what if I get arrested. If I'm guilty then I'll deserve what's coming to me. If I'm innocent, then with Allah's blessing I'll be spared. Right now, I'm more concerned about getting justice for my mam.' Mo dropped the toaster on the floor with a clang, paused, put Abraham's phone in the bag, then shouldered it. 'That said, I don't trust you lot. If I want justice for my mam then I'll need legal assistance. I'll go and knock Usman up. He only lives ten minutes from here and he'll come to my mam's with me.'

'You don't need Usman Ghosh for us to take any allegations seriously. And we've sensitive female officers at the station who can give her support,' said Abraham. 'It's very touching that you'd put your mother first. Gallant even. But would she do the same for you?'

'Of course!'

'Hm,' Abraham's eyes danced as he smiled. 'Are you sure about that Blenkinsopp? Are you really sure?'

***

Mo trundled, rather than bolted down the stairs. He had things on his mind. Plenty. Maybe he wouldn't leave just yet. He wanted to mull things over a bit more. Amongst other things he hadn't decided what to do about Abraham yet. Besides, it wouldn't do any harm to do a bit more snooping. He hadn't really checked out the drawers properly yet, other than the one for utensils near the chopping block. He rummaged through the other drawers with their tea towels, coasters, cup-cake moulds, food colouring bottles, candles, nutcrackers, kebab skewers, chopsticks and other assorted tat. He then finished up with Abraham's PC before mooching through the desk cupboard and some files; adding a few more bits and bobs to the bag.

***

Abraham's eyes had sparked as soon as Mo disappeared down the stairs. He'd long since planned what he would do if he ever got the chance, and now the opportunity had arisen he would do his damndest not to waste it. Quickly, he'd reached down for the toaster that Mo had carelessly left within his reach and he'd unplugged it from the extension cable. He'd then cast the plug-end like a clunky fishing line on top of his trousers and gently teased it back. He'd cursed as the plug scratched along the tiles back towards him. He'd tried again. And again. If only he could free himself then he could capture Mo singlehandedly and triumphantly parade him in front of the media and watching world. He'd tried again. And again, cursing as each failure brought the alternative of defeat and the additional humiliation of being found chained naked to his bath ever closer.

Now, as noises rang out from downstairs as Mo rifled through his home, Abraham continued to try and continued to fail each time. He hadn't expected it to be easy, but it was proving impossible. The plug reached the trousers just fine, but there was no grip, so each time it simply slid off the cloth when he tried winding it back to him. Doors banged and drawers rattled downstairs. There was a grating metal on metal sound too, like a knife being sharpened. Abraham's heart quickened, but rather than rush, he forced himself to do the exact opposite. He steadied his hand as best he could, took aim and launched the plug, in a twisting motion this time, as well as higher and further than previously. This time the plug landed at the waist-end of the trousers, metal pins down. They snagged on the belt. Abraham bit on his lip, exhaled long and slow. Then, ever so carefully, he teased the cable ...and the plug joggled...

...the trousers seemed to budge a tiny fraction towards him...

***

Somewhere in Mo's subconscious, he sensed change; be it a change in the atmosphere, a tiny tremor on the ceiling or the sound of dripping water as Abraham stood up and stepped out of the bath. Either way, by the time he got to the foot of the stairs Abraham was already rushing onto the landing towards him, cracking the electric cable like a whip and sending the end with the heavy toaster crashing down on top of Mo's skull, sending him sprawling and twitchy like a gangly electric eel.

'I see you're cowering before me again Blenkinsopp,' Abraham cackled as he bent over the prone Mo and grabbed the toaster. 'Just like that time at your school.'

'Who's cowering?' his head still hammering like a punching speedball Mo blindly took a swing at the naked Abraham's calf and missed. 'Besides, you wouldn't kill me. I'm not armed.'

'Ah but I've reasonable grounds your honour,' Abraham kicked the leather sports bag by Mo's side. 'For all I know you're just about to pull a gun, knife or fertiliser bomb on me!'

'Eh? It's a bag that I found in your own den,' Mo gurned, clawed at the sticky patch of blood above his ear then unzipped the bag. 'Take a look, it's just got your phone in it, my case files from your briefcase and printouts from your computer in it.'

'So what?' Abraham raised the toaster head height. 'You're a double murderer attacking me in my own house. No one at the CPS is going to prosecute, and no judge in the country would convict even if they did.'

'You wouldn't dare,' Mo frenziedly rifled through the bag praying for a gun or knife that he knew wasn't there as Abraham raised the toaster high above his head with a laugh that Mo read as both *insanely exhilarated* and *evil* in equal measures.

'Wrong!' Abraham roared as he bared the clunky metal toaster down towards Mo's head.

***

The pitch and tone of the deafening shriek suggested that it wasn't one of surprise, shock or horror – but of agonising and excruciating pain.

Abraham toppled over on one side and the toaster dropped harmlessly to the floor. If the toaster had ultimately proved harmless then the same could not be said of the bag's zipper, sandwiching and crunching the DI's genitalia as it was, like a metal toothed piranha.

Mo staggered to his feet, groaned and uneasily jostled through the front door. He paused on the step and momentarily considered retrieving the bag currently bashing around Abraham's meat and two veg as he staggered back up the stairs. Instead, Mo darted back in, grabbed Abraham's briefcase from the hallway then hurried back out into the night.

***

The sensible part of Mo's brain screamed at him to leg it the hell out of there, so it probably wasn't too chuffed when he instead skidded to an abrupt halt just thirty metres away, at the end of the driveway. He turned around and scratched his head. Why wasn't Abraham bearing down on him? For a moment or two, the non-sensible part of his brain tried to persuade him to go back to the house. He wavered, unsure. Suddenly, Abraham appeared at the bedroom window. Big-grinned, cocky and, apart from the bag, starkers. He wiggled something in his hand. Mo couldn't make it out at first, but he sharp spun on his heels and raced away when the penny did drop.

He couldn't be sure who Abraham had just phoned, but he somehow doubted that it was the pizza delivery man.

Chapter Forty-Two

After just another fifteen metres or so Mo suddenly put the brakes on and stopped, hands on hips, heart thumping and mind whirling. His sensible head was telling him to run, but some other part of his being weighted his feet down like size 10 lead-lined anchors.

As he caught his breath, he gazed up at the full moon together with the stars that bejewelled space like sparklers on Bonfire Night. He inhaled deeply, savouring the wonders of the heavens, the hoot of an owl and the moist night air - fully aware that it might be the last opportunity he had to do so for decades.

A few minutes later he found himself wandering along the gravelled-dirt path that hugged the little stream in Burn Valley. He ambled. Gently. Unhurriedly. He stopped to watch a squirrel scoot up one of the trees. It looked alert. Maybe it had clocked the owl. Maybe it wasn't even an owl, but the distant hubbub of sirens. Of the police coming to take him.

He sat down cross-legged on the most moonlit of three benches, closed his eyes and breathed in and out through his nose. Relaxing. Waiting. Thinking. Something dug into a buttocks a tad. He wriggled a small book out of his back jeans pocket and flicked through the semi-intelligible scrawl of figures and shorthand of sorts. In his haste, he had left his bag of goodies dangling around Abraham's person, so besides the hard drive that he already had tucked away in a front pocket, this little book was all that remained of Abraham's things in his possession. Well, that and his briefcase. He wasn't even sure why he'd gone back in for that. After all, it no longer contained Abraham's work laptop or his case files, and he had skimmed through the remains of its contents a couple of times already. It contained nothing really of note; a diary, some pens, a virtually blank notepad, some receipts, documents relating to expenses, an overtime sheet, some crime leaflets, and a scrap of paper with the header 'Windfall?' then '*Dean Downing – boyfriend*' and '*Haze Bond - best friend*' written next to two telephone numbers in neat writing. Probably female writing he deduced.

Mo set the briefcase by his feet then scanned trunks and foliage for the squirrel. He hoped that it was alright. He too knew the feeling of being hunted. And he didn't wish that on anyone. And especially not a cute little critter with a fluffy tail.

His mind wandered to some of the things that Abraham had said. Things that they had both said. He bit a nail as he pondered Abraham's suggestion that Ishmael and Ahmed could be leading an Islamist plot. In addition to being the mosque's imam, Ahmed also worked as a hypnotist. Maybe he had hypnotised Mo? That could explain why Mo appeared to be at the centre of both murders without remembering the details. Was it possible to unwittingly kill under a state of hypnosis? Mo swallowed hard as he reasoned it was. Maybe Saboor was right about Ahmed and Ishmael after all – and that was without Saboor knowing anything about the jihadi video!

The thing about the inscribed '*Allah is Great*' card also wrangled. Mo had thought there was something not quite right about his phone after Abraham gave it to him back at the police station. He had been looking at the phone itself, but perhaps he should have been looking at the *case* instead. He couldn't swear to it, but he thought that the card was in his phone case before Abraham had taken his mobile, but not afterwards. Could Abraham have swiped it and planted it at Davy's murder scene to incriminate Mo? Conveniently slipped in among the undergrowth during the forensic inspection perhaps? Abraham had proven that he wasn't beyond planting evidence, but did Mo really think that Abraham had killed Davy? In all honesty, no. Did he think that Abraham had killed Alex? His mind flashed back to Abraham's smiley selfie with her. The pair struck more as bosom buddies than mortal enemies – so no, Abraham probably didn't kill her either. *Probably not* anyway. Did Mo think that Abraham would have killed him with that toaster just minutes earlier? The back part of his brain barked yes, but the front part ahhed and tutted. It could have been a bluff. At least that's what he tried to tell himself.

Did Abraham really think that Mo had killed both Alex and Davy? It certainly appeared so. And what was all that about the numbers? What were they again? Numbers were one of his things. He did fit that particular geeky profile. But with everything else that had been battering his brain recently, for the life of him he couldn't even recall all the numbers Abraham had mentioned, let alone remember writing them in blood. *Think man!* Mo nibbled a bit of chewed off fingernail. There were a couple that ended in eight. Fifty-eight and er... eighty... no *ninety*-eight. That was it. He was pretty sure. Sort of. Even so, the possible significance of a couple of numbers was undeterminable. He needed more to go on. Mo rasped his skull and tried to summon other niggles to the forefront of his mind. Answers to the labyrinth of riddles were there somewhere in amongst all the detail, he was sure of that much. ...He just seriously doubted that he'd be able to scratch the surface – let alone get to the bottom of things – before the cops carted him off to the clink.

And that was only a matter of time.

...A rapidly dwindling matter of time.

He focussed on the task at hand again. Thoughts about his contact details being on Alex's phone resurfaced. Previously, Mo couldn't reconcile that. But now, thinking about it, Alex could have got Mo's number from Jade's phone. But why? One possibility sprung to mind. Jade had previously told him that her mother vehemently opposed Islam – or at least vehemently opposed Jade's interest in it. Could Alex have somehow blamed Mo for that? And for Jade's death? Maybe Alex had been the one watching Mo from the shadows? Had she planned to take revenge on him? Had she attacked him while he was sozzled that night? And if so, did he kill her? Mo nibbled the end of his finger and noticed some blood under a nail. Quite possibly Alex's blood. His hand trembled as a memory knocked him for six – the feeling of despair, rage and anger that he'd felt when he'd heard of Jade's death. Anger at Jade's mother. A person whom until Saturday, he'd never even seen, let alone met! And why had he been so incensed with her exactly? Truth be told he didn't know. All Jade ever told him about her mother was that she was *difficult* – and that's hardly a reason for rage to rumble – let alone erupt. ...But rage had certainly rumbled at one point. ...Mo hated to admit it, but he couldn't deny Abraham's accusation of him having motive. And not just for Alex, but for Davy too.

Mo's spinning mind flittered to the missing butcher's knife as he tried to make sense of other doubts. His knife going walkies from Shahzad's screamed set-up. And it wasn't the only thing. Something else that he couldn't put his finger on scratched the same itch. Something in Abraham's house. Possibly more than one thing, that he had seen, smelled or touched...

But what?

Other things still bedevilled him too. A minor detail that he had missed. A little piece of the puzzle that could be staring him right in the face. Or maybe it was the bigger picture itself that he was missing. He cast his mind back, not only over the potential stitch-up and the big, salient recent events, but also over the seemingly minor incidents and happenings that joined the dots. The things. And the people; Alex, Davy, Mick...

Mo tapped a fingernail against a tooth. *Mick*. That's one thing that had subconsciously struck him earlier. According to Abraham's case files, the T-shirt retrieved from Mick matched the one he was seen wearing on the night of Alex's murder. Apparently, it was relatively clean but smelled of bonfire smoke. Judging by the report's briefness, that can't have struck the police as odd. But it did Mo alright. For starters, Mick's T-shirt was wet and looked fairly grubby when he'd seen him flat on his back in the street. Also, it should have smelled of *cigarette* smoke from the party, as well as whatever alcohol was in the bottle that Alex had attacked him with. Mo thought he remembered blood on it too - presumably from Mick rolling on the broken shards of glass. Mo tapped his tooth some more and pondered not only why Mick had given the cops a lookalike T-shirt, but also what he might have done with the real one. Did Mo think Mick had set him up? It was hard to fathom how – let alone why... Did he think Mick could have killed Alex and be hiding his tracks? That seemed a possibility. Then again... the state Mick was in that night...

Mo examined the scrap of paper again. The *Dean Downing – boyfriend* entry didn't mean much to him, but he couldn't help wondering if the *Haze Bond* in question happened to be the 6-foot muscular woman who had given both him and Alex wicked stares as they'd left the party. If so, could she be involved in any way? Could she have been the person, not Alex, whom Mo had sensed watching him? Certainly, she could have easily slipped out after him that night.

Mo turned his attention back to other people; Davy, Abraham, Debbie, Davy's bit on the side, Shahzad, Ishmael, Ahmed, Serge, Kerry, that North African guy, Debbie... Even another police officer besides (or in addition to) Abraham could be involved, or indeed central, to the entire affair. Mo knew from a brief discussion with Aftab at the mosque one time that Aftab abhorred Islamic extremism and everything that it entailed. True, it could all be a front, but Mo didn't think so. Similarly, while Kell was his nemesis, Abraham's son, he had always come across as a good guy at school. He'd even helped Mo out a couple of times with bullies and it wasn't so surprising when he became a policeman. Also, thinking about it, Kell had even turned Alex down; staying put and spending the night at Saboor's with that new girl of his. Aftab's colleague with the blond hair though, Jezzy or something, ... could he be trusted? He did seem particularly intent on meddling into Mo's affairs (and his bag for that matter) when they were searching all the bins. And the way he looked at Mo... There was possibly more than just suspicion in that regard. As for Debbie... well Mo dismissed that notion just as soon as it arose. But what about DS Grantham? She came across all good cop, but she seemed pretty close to Abraham...

Whether it was the people, the events or the whole shebang, not for the first time Mo couldn't shake off the feeling that everything just didn't add up. He looked down at a slug and pondered out aloud. 'Either I'm guilty or someone has stitched me up like a kipper and has got me by the short and curlies.'

The slug edged along in silence. If it had an opinion on the matter it was keeping it to itself.

'And if I have indeed been set up then whoever has done it has pulled off a work of absolute genius. Hell, I'm the only real suspect, and *all* the evidence points to me. Me! Just how is that even conceivable? Unless of course I'm guilty,' Mo closed his eyes. 'It's just that...'

***

Mo opened his eyes, rubbed them and did a double-take, as if he had dozed off in his thoughts and was only just drifting back to normality now. Not that any of this was normal. Just how long had it been since he'd left Abraham's? Five minutes? Ten? Twenty? It felt like at least twenty. Maybe thirty. But if so, how come he wasn't already trussed up inside the back of a paddy wagon? Mo caressed his sore brow. Yet another enigma. Yet another unanswered question. There was also another. The one he didn't want to revisit. The one about his mam and Abraham's snide inferences about whether or not he could trust his own mother. Sure, his mam had her issues. Way more than her fair share. And yes, she could hardly be called stable, or even a typical mother. If anything, Mo was more of a mother to her than she was to him. But despite all her many failings, and regardless of all the other things she couldn't give him, Mo was sure of one thing - that she truly had faith in him. Indeed, all the way from infancy through to adulthood she was the only one who ever did. And misguided or not, her unwavering faith had had a profound effect on him – providing an armour of conviction that protected the crumbly, insecure doubter within. Intangible or not, it had somehow magically kept him together all these years, through the bad times and... well... the bad times. What on earth did Abraham know about her? If anything! ...Of course Mo could trust her. He would bet his life on it.

She was his life after all.

He looked down and realised that he had blocked the slug's passage. He placed the offending soft leather briefcase on his crossed legs and subconsciously fiddled with a tab as his mind meandered down new paths and the slug inched slimily towards the undergrowth. He didn't realise it at first but tweaking the tab had released a front pouch. He hadn't noticed that before. Mo extracted a handful of photocopies. The first few were just more receipts. The last one, on the other hand, set his heart thumping and his hands trembling like Beethoven with Parkinson's.

***

'No!' He shrieked. He ripped the sheet up into half a dozen bits, balled them up and punched them through to the centre of a rose bush. 'No! No! No! No! No!'

Mo booted the briefcase up into the air like a rugby fly-half, sending more papers scattering. He buried his smouldering cheeks in his sweating hands then stomped around in circles, yanked at his hair and squared up to a tree before headbutting it and collapsing in a heap.

With all the racket, if the cops didn't know where he was before then they probably did now. Not that Mo seemed the slightest bit interested. After a few minutes nursing his head and wiping his eyes, he crawled back over the rosebush, and gingerly set about retrieving the ball of paper.

Tentatively, he set about piecing it back together. Willing himself to be mistaken. Praying that he'd got it wrong. But he hadn't got it wrong. It *was* a copy of the letter Abraham had told him about. The one found in the red bag belonging to his mam that he'd unwittingly left next to Davy's body. Mo Shook his head as he read it again, scattering tears onto the words already stained red by the blood from his gashed hands.

Abraham was right about the other thing too. He couldn't trust his mam. He screamed out loud that he'd '*never trust that treacherous, deceitful woman ever again!*' What had she ever given him apart from headaches, dejection and an abject misery gene? All that crap about faith, it was all just bullshit. A Himalayan-proportioned fanciful fib. Why else would she write a whistle, no, a *fog-horn*-blower letter to the police warning them of her *potential Islamist terrorist son*? Mo ran to the tree and punched it so hard the bark chipped off. Beyond the fauna, blue and white lights clinked and flashed up Elwick Road, heading towards him.

This was it.

His time was up.

***

Except it wasn't.

Mo scratched his head with his non-throbbing hand and watched the blinking lights fly straight past him and, as far as he could make out, towards Summerhill Country Park. Come to think of it, he'd heard sirens earlier too, and that convoy of blues and twos hadn't stopped either. Why had they all raced straight past Burn Valley? And what was taking them so long to arrest him? Yet more questions! Mo stuffed the ripped-up pieces of his mother's letter in his pocket. He'd be the one asking *her* questions real soon. And demanding answers! He punted the briefcase over a bush and more thoughts swirled around his brain as he quick-stepped to the exit. ...About bloody clothes in bins, about other clothes, about his mam's exploding eyes, about her shutting him out, about her ton weight on his back, about numbers... and letters... He had another quick flick through Abraham's little book. Something detonated behind his bulging eyes. Mo clenched his fists and pumped his arms, higher, faster, harder as he broke into a run...

Chapter Forty-Three

Kell clicked a switch to respond to the controller on the other end of the radio.

'Sorry, there was a sighting of Ahmed and Ishmael, so we've been following up on that.... Yeah, we collared them, locked them up and have just headed straight back out now... Eh?... Oh, something about holding a vigil for a very sick parishioner in a house round the back of the mosque... Yeah, a cock and bull story no doubt. What?... yeah, we're on our way.'

Kell flicked on the flashing lights and banged on the dashboard. 'Come on Dehwar,' 'It's an urgent request. Put your foot down. I promise I won't arrest you for speeding.'

'Everyone else will be there by now,' said Aftab. 'They might not need us now.'

'Even so,' said Kell.

Aftab floored the accelerator and the Mondeo surged up Elwick Road. Then suddenly swerved. 'What the hell was that?'

'Hit the brakes,' yelled Kell. He jumped out and was six feet back down the road even before the car had come to a complete halt.

***

'Oh dear God. Kell, are you okay?' Aftab, if not immediately, then very quickly recognised the object in Kell's hands. He squatted down beside him and gently rubbed Kell's shoulder then stretched out his hands. 'I can take it. I mean *him*. I mean...'

'Davy's head you mean.'

'Yes that,' Aftab retracted his hands when a bubbly-eyed Kell showed no sign of releasing it. 'More numbers I see. 19, 86, 88 and er... what's that?... 110. I don't suppose you've any idea what these signify either.'

Kell creased his pale face, swallowed and slowly shook his head as he tried to take in the chilling enormity of this latest discovery. 'But cars have been up and down this road all day long, as have we,' he finally muttered. 'I think someone deliberately put Davy's head in the middle of the road, and recently.'

'Mo?' Aftab's question was at least three-quarters rhetorical. 'We'd better take it back to the station.'

'I don't know who, what or why, but I strongly suspect that whatever's going down requires more immediate and urgent action than just popping back to HQ,' Kell started running to the car, blood slopping out of Davy's head onto his clothes. 'My gut's telling me that someone's in serious danger!'

Chapter Forty-Four

Mary had barely caught a fortieth of a wink since Mo's disappearance, and now spent most of her waking hours glued to both the sofa and BBC News 24. Now, by candlelight, she was watching yet another rerun of Abraham's charade on the station steps when the letterbox burst into boisterous life.

'Mo!' Mary cried. She hadn't been quick on her feet for going on twenty years, but she hoisted herself up and shuffled to the window in under ten seconds. In the meantime, the letterbox continued to rattle. She edged the main curtains aside and eyed the rattler as he squatted down, face stuck to letterbox and whacking the door with a flat of the hand. 'Mo!'

***

Single parent, Stewie Allison was habitually a good sleeper, but ever since his (quite literal) tête-à-tête with Mo the previous night he'd hardly slept a wink either. Just seeing someone nonchalantly holding a severed head like that was already the stuff of nightmares, but living next door to the barbaric perpetrator was infinitely worse. Of course, he'd reassured his ten-year-old daughter that the big bad man next door would never be coming back. It's what the police had assured him, and he'd pretty much bought it – along with a door chain, an extra heavy-duty bolt and a baseball bat.

When he first heard the din next door his heart suddenly thumped at double the rate of the clatter. He'd pulled the sheets over his head initially, but when the rattling continued, he'd got up and peeked out of the window, just as he had done thirty minutes or so previously when he'd heard wheels spinning and realised that the hitherto ever-present squad car had suddenly scarpered. The gap where the car had been parked remained, but down at number 104, there in the shadows, a stooped figure impatiently whacked at the door with the flat of his hand. 'Mo!' Stewie gulped. He instinctively put his fingernails to his mouth to chew them, but instead they just jigged on his teeth like a tarantella with tap shoes.

***

Mary wheeled around, knocking the TV off the MDF unit in her haste to reach the hallway. The ensuing smash and bang only adding to the continuing letterbox clatter. Panting, she turned the lock and stood back as the door banged on its hinges as he darted in.

***

Stewie grabbed his phone and had just punched in the first *nine* when a terrified shriek rang out. *Mary*. Instinctively, and without a seconds' thought, he bounded down the stairs, fumbled with his key, grabbed his baseball bat then yanked the door shut behind him. Swiftly but stealthily he hopped over the small wall that separated his garden from Mary's and edged up to outside the living room window.

Peeking through a small gap in the heavy curtains that were further filtered by nets it took a while for his eyes to adjust to the dark room. Dressed in only his boxers, he tapped the second and third *nines*, and held his breath as some invisible electronic pulses scrambled through thin air to magically connect the call.

'Emergency services, which service do you require?'

'Police,' Stewie replied, barely above a whisper, his eyes still scanning the lounge with its flickering candle, smashed up TV and someone's back intermittently obstructing his view. 'I'm outside Mo Blenkinsopp's house, you know the murderer. I heard his mam scream. I've got a baseball bat but... What's that? ...Wait for the police? ...How long will that be? I'm certain that she's in danger... Are you sure? ...Hang on, it's gone all quiet... Now they are moving around. He's got his back to me... Pardon? ...Yes, I'm sure it's Mo! I've known the lanky so-and-so since he was a nipper. Besides, I clocked his new tattoo from my bedroom window... What's happening now? Well, like I said, it's gone quiet, but they are shuffling about and rocking a bit from side to side. It's so dark, it's hard to see. I think they are hugging... Yes, *hugging*... Wait. It can't be hugging. They are faced the same way, both with their backs to me...And what's that? Oh my God. Hurry!'

***

Stewie only just caught a sense of the figure as it bounded past him and stormed inside, but he certainly heard the door bang on its hinges again.

'....Yes, a blade. He has got her from behind and has it to her throat. Also, someone has just run in.'

'Put down the knife Blenkinsopp, the game's up!'

'Did you hear that too? ...It's DI Abraham. ... Sure? Yes, I recognise his voice... Now they are struggling. All three of them... Pardon? Hang on a min, I hear something... Yes, I see them. The car's thundering up the street... They are piling out. It's Kell and another policeman... They're sprinting inside...'

Suddenly an eerie, ear-splitting shriek cut through the night. It boomed, reverberated then slowly died into ghostly silence.

'...Y...yes. Sorry ...I'm s...still here,' Stewie croaked.

'... Please send an ambulance too.

... As quick as you can.

... She's not moving. ... I...

...I think she's dead!'

Quartz

Chapter Forty-Five

Mo looked down to the gutter as Kell's eyes stabbed at him. Apart from one quick, purely *police business* call, the two hadn't exchanged a word since Mo's clumsy attempt at an apology for his part in luring Davy to his death. True, Kell had gallantly rushed to Mo's mother's rescue. *Attempted* rescue. And so soon after Kell's own stepfather's gruesome demise. But Mo wasn't so naïve that he didn't get that Kell would be bitter. Might be aggrieved. Could be looking for someone to blame. Or throttle. Or pound. ...to a pulp. But as far as Mo was concerned a physical battering would have been preferable to Kell's cruel '*shove your apology up your pisswizzard loser backside*' riposte.

Kell shot Mo another glacial salvo as he spun the Mondeo around and zoomed off all blues, twos and choky exhaust fumes.

Mo couldn't help himself from watching. And pondering. He wished he could do U-turns too, and turn back time. He thought back to recent events and all the crazy twists bumps and meanderings. Another niggle gnawed. Par for the course recently. This one was something to do with the night, *that* night, when his world caved in - or got better - depending on how you looked at things. Bumps, twists, meanderings, interpretations bang, bang, bang ad infinitum ...

As Kell's car disappeared around a corner Mo could only sympathise. How could Kell respect Mo when he couldn't even respect himself? Look where his impious actions had got him. Where they had got his dear departed mother. Sure, he could point a finger of blame at the alcohol. But he'd swallowed it as easily and readily as the drink had consumed him. Led him astray. Wobbled his compass within. And despite warnings!

Walking between Ishmael and Ahmed, Mo draped an arm over each of their shoulders and pulled them in towards him.

'I don't deserve you,' he declared. 'But I'm so glad you have my back brothers.'

***

Saboor looked over the rim of his glasses and wiggled his fingers. Mo wiggled fingers back, left an index finger upstanding and mouthed, 'One minute.' After several pats on the arms and flashes of teeth Ahmed, Ishmael and a twenty-something North African man offered outstretched hands which Mo batted away and trumped with beefy man-hugs.

'Who's that wae Ahmed and Ishmael?' Saboor asked as Mo approached his outdoor table at the park's café.

'Oh, that's Zaid,' Mo plonked himself in a metal chair. 'He's been living rough for a few months but finally plucked up the courage to come into the mosque and ask for help. Ahmed's letting him stay at his place.'

'That's good of him,' Saboor tugged on some whiskers. 'Maybe I got Ahmed and Ishmael all wrong.'

'You weren't the only one jumping to conclusions,' Mo took a sip of Saboor's Fanta. 'I even had doubts of my own at one point, and the police thought they were planning a terrorist attack.'

'Wow, how come?'

'I guess they had their reasons,' Mo shrugged. 'Buying fertiliser in bulk probably didn't help.'

'They did what?'

'For their new venture,' Mo explained. 'It's a florist's with the proceeds going towards for the mosque and good causes. They are calling it *Tall Ships Blooms*. It's the thing I was helping them with. I designed the website and fliers, but they swore me to secrecy until it was all signed, sealed and ready for launch.'

'Ah, I think I've seen the groundwork started. I'm guessing it's the one on that bit of wasteland by The Tall Ships pub.'

'That's the one,' Mo said. 'They've been updating me about it on the walk up from the mosque just now, while for my part I've been humbly apologising about getting them mixed up in... well you know ...stuff.'

'Ah, *stuff,*' Saboor rearranged his glasses. 'I've been reading about just that very thing. Damn shame the trial clashed wae ma operation tae remove the metal pin in ma leg. I'd have loved a front-row seat!'

Saboor ironed out the newspaper and held down the flapping pages with his can of Fanta at one end and his tuna panini at the other. He read out the headline in matter-of-fact monotone, but he said it with a grin. 'Triple murderer top cop Abraham sentenced tae three life sentences.'

While Saboor read silently Mo leaned back in his chair and smiled as a toddler cheered when her excited labradoodle contorted mid-air to catch a frisbee.

Saboor eyed Mo. 'Yer've a really nice smile Mo. Shame it only comes out once in a blue moon.'

Mo shrugged. 'I guess I've not had much to smile about lately.'

'Yer can say that again. I'm sure that being the subject of a national manhunt isn't exactly an erm...' Saboor's nodded towards an elderly couple walking arm in arm. 'A stroll in the park.'

'Not quite,' Mo placed a hand over another corner of the rustling newspaper.'

'And especially not wae... yer know, yer mam and all that too...'

'I know what you mean Saboor thanks.' Mo dropped a few breadcrumbs by the big bunch of flowers by his feet. A pigeon waddled over and started pecking. 'I'm going over to her grave again later if you'd like to join me?'

'I can't today Mo. I've a hospital appointment,' Saboor patted his sticks. 'But next time. And, who knows, by then I may even have dispensed with these damned nuisance contraptions.'

'That's great Saboor,' said Mo. 'And who knows, your hit-and-run driver's days of liberty could be numbered too.'

'I'm not holding ma breath on that.'

'Yeah well,' Mo said. 'Justice will out.'

'Don't yer mean, '*Truth* will out.'

Mo stood up, laid a hand on each hip and thrust his pelvis forward. 'Truth, blood, guts and stubborn coffee stains, with the crime-fighting, grime-busting, non-biological Blenkinsopp super detergent of justice!'

'It's still highly unlikely and I'll believe it when I see it,' laughed Saboor. 'But thanks for the thought, ...and the image!'

Saboor tapped his fist against Mo's and returned his gaze upon the newspaper article.

'It says here that Abraham killed yer mam to stop her reporting an alleged attempted rape from years ago. Is that right?'

'Pretty much,' said Mo. He raised his arms above his head and stretched from side to side. 'What else does it say?'

'Well, part of it is already common knowledge. The stuff that hit the headlines,' Saboor tried a lateral stretch and got about a fifth of the distance Mo had managed before he winced and gave up. 'Yer know, stuff like the fact he had it in for yer, and that he killed Alex and Davy and made it look like jihadi killings so that ye'd cop the blame.'

Mo wiggled the front of his black vest and fanned his chest. 'Yes, he also saw me on the park railings when he was there with Alex on the night of her murder. According to the prosecution that made me a potential witness and gave Abraham yet another reason for wanting me out of the way. DS Grantham even testified that Abraham accurately described my antics on the park railings during an earlier interview – albeit I later remembered that I fell headfirst on the *pavement side* of the railings, and not into some park bushes.'

'How come he went after yer mam and not you then?'

'That's a point Abraham's defence raised too,' Mo said. 'Me clocking him at the park was just my word against his, whereas my mam had something she could use as real evidence against him – potential DNA on the dress she'd kept but had never worn since her rape attack. Besides, by attacking my mam dressed up as me he was killing two birds with one stone – eliminating one accuser and discrediting and almost certainly incarcerating the other.'

'Look at this,' Saboor gaped. 'An artist's impression of a clean-shaven Abraham dressed in yer cargo shorts and vest.'

Saboor took a bite of his sandwich and turned the paper around so that Mo could study the mock-up image of Abraham with a blue tattooed face. 'Uncanny resemblance eh Mo?'

Mo raised an eyebrow and his pupils widened.

'Yes, I was somewhat gobsmacked at his get-up myself,' said Mo. 'But not as much as when I saw Abraham with a blade to mam's throat and him shouting at *me* to drop the knife that *he* held! He hadn't bargained on me returning, so he improvised when I arrived with approaching sirens outside. If Kell and Aftab had arrived just moments later then they wouldn't have seen Abraham cut my mam's throat as I tried to wrestle the knife away from him. Instead, no doubt Abraham would have tried to knock me out, change clothes, force my prints on the knife and cry wolf.'

'What makes yer think that?'

'Not just me, but the prosecution and jury too,' Mo said. 'Firstly, Abraham didn't just sneak up to the house... well, there was no CCTV of him driving to the nearby alleyway where he left his car, so he was careful about not being seen *driving* dressed as me, but once in the open, he had brazenly strutted up to our house, safe in the knowledge that he'd just sent the officers watching it on a wild goose chase. Moreover, he purposely clattered at the front door. He wanted someone to notice him, or rather he wanted someone to *think* that they had seen *me* – as Stewie Allison had inadvertently assumed.'

'Oh!'

'Not only that, but Abraham even brought a change of clothes with him,' continued Mo. 'If I hadn't turned up, he'd have just donned his clean togs, pretended that he was the first at the scene and that I'd killed my mam and scarpered.'

'Hang on,' Saboor raised an index finger. 'Ma mind is boggling wae all of this.

Did I hear yer right a few moments ago? Did yer say that yer actually tried to wrench the knife away fae that lunatic? Yer could hae been killed.'

'I doubt it, Abraham had staked his reputation on catching me, sending me down and hanging me out to dry.' Mo said. 'For some deranged reason he wanted me to suffer. And suffer badly. But not kill me. ...Well, *probably* not.'

'Madness!' Whistled Saboor. 'Where did he even get yer clothes from? If they were indeed really yours?'

'Yes, they were mine alright. And he got them from the linen bin.'

Mo smiled to himself. Everyone, including the police, assumed that Mo meant *his* linen bin, not *Abraham's* when he said that. It was partly Abraham's own doing of course. If he had just played ball when he was caught with the metaphorical smoking gun, then his ex-colleagues might have taken him a bit more seriously. As it was, Abraham had panicked and had persisted for days in slinging wild accusations, not only about his purported innocence but also about Mo's supposed guilt. By the time Abraham changed his tune and swallowed enough of his pride to mention Mo's appearance at his own house then it merely sounded like just another in a long line of fantastical fairy tales.

'He must hae seriously had it in for yer tae go tae such extremes,' Saboor said.

'Yes, I've been wracking my brains to try to understand just *why me*. I still can't make any sense of it now, just as I couldn't the first time his volcanic eyes gored into mine that day at school.'

'Yer, and even just the fact that he'd shaved his trademark goatee off and dyed his face blue says a lot about him and his dastardly plan.'

'Well, his flimsy goatee soon grew back and the dye was just some food colouring around the eyes to look like my tattoo. His red hair was also food colouring, but you're right, it does show intent,' Mo agreed. 'Actually, Debbie spoke up about this at the trial. People do tend to notice tattoos, sometimes more than the actual person themselves. Apparently, even the park flasher's victim only really noticed the guy's tattoo, not the flasher himself. Abraham played on this.'

'And then some!' Saboor shook his dark locks then turned back to the newspaper. 'It says that *the now-disgraced detective persisted with his vendetta against Mr Blenkinsopp at trial, accusing him of not only attempting to set him up for all three murders, but also planting false incriminating evidence*. Planting what Mo?'

'He somehow has it in his head that I managed to plant the butcher's knife that killed my mam on him for each murder,' said Mo. 'Oh, yeah, he maintains this allegation even though it has blood from all three murder victims on it – while the only fingerprints on it were his. DNA evidence from Abraham was also found at each murder scene.'

'So, where dae yer come intae all this, apart from him wanting to set yer up again?'

'Abraham claimed it was my knife from Shahzad's butcher's, and that I'd stolen it.'

'And was it?'

'Well, Mr Shahzad had reported it missing,' said Mo. 'But he later found it under a unit in his shop.'

Saboor silently read the next part then laughed as he continued, '*When asked by the prosecution how Mr Blenkinsopp had planted evidence and set him up, the self-styled "super detective" defendant was forced to admit that he "didn't know", but that it was a "fit-up" and that Mr Blenkinsopp had broken into, and had stayed at Abraham's own house for 24 hours while he was the subject of a national manhunt. Abraham further asserted that Mr Blenkinsopp had threatened him with a toaster while he was sat on the toilet.'*

Mo rocked in his chair, unclipped his black plastic sunglasses from his vest and slid them over glinting eyes. 'Tch!'

Saboor carried on. '*In summing up Judge Barratt-Hall described Abraham as a venomous racist with a pathological obsession with Mr Blenkinsopp that began while Mr Blenkinsopp was still at school.*

Sentencing Abraham to three life sentences Judge Barratt-Hall commented on both Abraham's lack of remorse as well as his relentless persecution of Mr Blenkinsopp and his continued accusations against Mr Blenkinsopp of the first two murders, despite his cast-iron alibi for the first one.'

'One thing,' asked Saboor. 'How come the police didn't unearth any alibis during their initial investigation?'

'Well, Abraham was adamant that he'd examined all police CCTV. But...' Mo cringed. 'It's a bit embarrassing.'

Saboor's eyes widened. 'Oh aye?'

'Well, apparently one of those big houses at Elwick has CCTV,' Mo rolled his eyes. 'It seems that it caught me doing naked yoga in the rain in the back garden. The owner wasn't too chuffed when she came back from their holidays, pressed play and caught an eyeful. She sent a copy of the footage of it complaining to the police.'

'Hang on,' Saboor laughed, 'Yer were doing what?'

'Lotus position mainly,' said Mo. 'I've seen the footage. I had my eyes closed and I'm not quite sure if I was meditating or asleep.'

'Yer what?'

'Lotus position, you know, the cross-legged pose. Plus some warrior poses. And tree.'

'Tree?'

Mo stood up, placed the sole of his grey Converse shoe on the side of the opposite leg's inner thigh, extended the bent knee outwards and raised both arms upwards, like a ten to two position on a clock. 'Tree – how it should be done.'

Saboor remained seated but raised his arms in solidarity, 'Shrub!'

'My tree pose was particularly shocking that night,' Mo smiled wryly. 'I was wobbling all over the place and toppled over into some bushes at one point.'

'So that's where yer got all those cuts from?'

'Do you know,' Mo rasped his fingernails against his new, number-one-all-over haircut. 'I'm still not quite sure myself. Like I told you before, I had a bit of a memory loss after my first ever dalliance with alcohol. I could have cut myself in those bushes, or the garden wall I climbed over may have had some jagged bits, or I could have possibly done it at Ward Jackson Park. I definitely climbed into the park at some point, but CCTV has me at Elwick from 1.20 am till 3.10 am, which coincides with Alex's confirmed time of death – hence the first alibi. There was no need for an alibi when my mam died as Abraham was caught red-handed in the act holding the murder weapon from all three killings.'

So that dream yer had about falling on top of a dead body. It was nae a dream after all?'

Mo shooed away a wasp. 'No, it's reality. I must have stumbled over Alex's body when taking a shortcut through the park on the way back home. DNA results show the blood on my clothes matched that of Alex.'

'Macabre!' Saboor contorted his round hairy face. 'No wonder yer were the prime suspect.'

'Yes, and being seen with a sword didn't help either,' Mo said. 'I later recovered it from the bush I'd stashed it in and handed it to the police myself. The cops had initially thought that it was the murder weapon, but it couldn't have been. It just wasn't sharp enough. You can buy fairly blunt swords engraved with Islamic inscriptions online, and Ishmael lent me his.

This one deals with faith and temptations. I suspect it was Ishmael's way of nudging me to keep on the straight and narrow.'

'Yer should hae listened,' said Saboor. 'It might hae steered yer away from the evils of booze.'

'That's so true. The Quran says that alcohol contains some good and some evil, but that the evil is greater than the good,' Mo sighed. 'I would never have got into such a disastrous predicament if I hadn't been so weak in the first place.'

'Aye,' Saboor agreed. 'And I take it that this sword yer on about is the one yer'd told me yer'd lost?'

'Yep, when I mounted the park railings on the night of Davy's murder, it nudged a memory that I'd previously tossed it high up into a tree,' said Mo. 'It wasn't visible among the mesh of branches - which is presumably why the police missed it - but I had a conviction that it'd still be there, so I flung myself onto a branch to free it and in the process, I inadvertently divebombed head-first on Davy's decapitated body.'

'Gruesome!' Saboor gurned.

'And then some!' Mo cringed.

'So why did Abraham want Alex dead?' Saboor asked. 'And Davy too fae that matter.'

'Well, he still denies everything,' Mo said. 'But the prosecution did speculate based on certain facts as well as statements from fellow police officers and other witnesses.'

'Such as?'

'Abraham had a chequered history with Alex going years back. Alex's best friend Haze told the court that Abraham had pressurised her to reveal something she'd been sworn to secrecy about – namely that Abraham was the father of Jade, Alex's daughter.'

'Why would Alex keep that from him?'

'Haze was asked that very question in court,' said Mo. 'She reckoned that Alex was petrified that Abraham would have forced her into getting rid of the baby if he'd known the truth.'

'Isn't that just speculation?'

'Yes, and Abraham venomously denied the assertion in court,' continued Mo. 'Even so, the prosecution construed it as motive – arguing that Abraham wanted revenge, not just because he'd missed out on Jade growing up, but also because he somehow blamed Alex for Jade's death, aged just 13.'

'Poor wee lassie,' Saboor muttered sombrely.

'The prosecution also argued that me introducing Jade to Islam also constituted motive for him setting me up,' said Mo. 'Abraham was an anti-Islam racist. DS Grantham not only testified to that, but he also suggested that my involvement with Abraham's dead daughter – however innocent – would be like a red flag to a raging bull as far as the DI was concerned.'

'What about his motive for Davy's murder?' Saboor probed.

'Well, Abraham also had quite a thing with Davy's missus before she married Davy. Indeed, it came out in court that Abraham had very nearly married her himself,' Mo explained. 'According to some, Abraham had always regretted their split, and was jealous of Davy, not just for marrying his old flame, but also because of the relationship Davy had with Abraham's biological son, Kell.'

'What dae yer think?'

'There could be truth in all that, and by all accounts bad blood abounded between Abraham and Davy,' said Mo. 'Moreover, Aftab also testified that he'd witnessed Davy winding Abraham up about the powerful bond he had with Kell and threatening to use that to wheedle Kell away from Abraham and back into his fold.'

'Dae yer believe that?'

'Yes,' Mo nodded. 'Kell even told me once that Davy was being extra generous towards him since Abraham's arrival on the scene.'

'But is all that enough fae murder?'

'The jury thought so,' Mo said. 'And Aftab did confirm that Abraham had threatened to kill Davy. Also, several officers including Debbie backed up the prosecution's assertion that Abraham had it in for me.'

'That was good of Debbie,' Saboor flashed his beautiful pearly teeth and winked. 'Maybe there's hope for yer wae her yet?'

'Nah,' Mo wiped an eye. 'All she did is corroborate the facts. It was all purely professional. Nothing personal. Alas, that pipe dream well and truly popped ages ago.'

Saboor nodded and gave his friend a rub of the shoulder. 'Yer'll find someone one day soon.'

'It's cool. If all this death and mayhem has taught me anything it's that there is a lot more to life than finally finding a girlfriend,' Mo smiled. 'Besides, I've unfinished business.'

Saboor crumpled his bushy eyebrows. 'Such as?'

'Such as assorted mental battering rams pounding my head shed,' Mo tapped his temple. 'And I've still doubts and questions.'

'Like?'

'Like *Why me? What the hell just happened? Why this whole thing at all? How? Am I still missing something?* And *what next?*' Mo tapped his teeth with a fingernail then gnawed off the end of another. 'Essentially, my mind is boggling and it's literally doing my nut.'

'I hear yer,' sighed Saboor. 'But the sensible thing would be tae just let it lie and tae leave things be pal.'

'You're probably right, and if recent events are anything to go by then I'm dreading what I might unearth by digging.' Mo spat out a bit of nail. 'Maybe it's the lesser of two evils, but I do need to dig.'

Saboor slowly shook his head, with a crooked smile.

Mo didn't smile back.

Chapter Forty-Six

As Saboor limped away Mo skirted the pond and sniffed the flowers reflectively. He had asked the florist for a colourful mixture, and that is exactly what she had given him. Marigolds, gypsophila, bluebells, carnations and chrysanthemums. His mam had loved flowers. He knew that for a fact. Flowers and butterflies. What he wasn't so sure of was what her favourite flower was. Lilies, roses, geraniums, daisies, buttercups, begonias - she seemed to like them all. Just as with everything else in her life, she wasn't one to fuss, and seemed easy to please.

Mo ran a finger across his bristly scalp, around the corner of a whispery eyebrow and down to where blue inked lines curved and tapered across an angular cheekbone. Would his mam have approved of his new look? Probably not. Would she have given him grief about it? Highly unlikely. She too had known dark times. Had made mistakes. Possibly even more than Mo. And her own upbringing and teenage years had been tumultuous to say the least. Even so, she had been the one to, if not let her demons rattle her mind, then at least somehow fail to prevent them from running riot. Tainting her clarity. Draining her energy. Sapping her will. Getting the better of her. Taking over the reins.

Right up to her death Mo had taken his mother's lack of interference in his life as a sign of indifference. There were times when he'd shouted at her. Chided her impassiveness. Mistaking it for a lack of care. Now, on reflection, and to his shame, he concluded that he'd got it all wrong all those years. That she did care. That she did have an opinion. But Mam being Mam she probably just thought who the hell was she to pass judgement when she was so screwed up herself. Maybe that was the reason why she never actually sent the letter that she'd addressed to the police. While he'd never know for sure, Mo chose to believe that, in the end, and despite all the evidence to the contrary, she didn't send it because she really *did* have faith in him.

Mary Blenkinsopp had never been one for money, possessions or physical affection. She wasn't proud, she wasn't vain, and she never seemed too fussed about what other folk thought. There were times when Mo had thought that the two of them lived in completely different worlds on either side of the thin wall that divided their bedrooms. But now, as he brushed the petals against his nose, he felt a closer connection with his mother than he had done for a long time. Since he was the shy little boy running to hug her legs at infant school gates.

'Who needs a girlfriend?' Who needs looks? Who needs a job? A career? An iMac Pro with dual-core processor and 128 gig memory?' he said to a squat red-faced man unfolding a fishing keep. The guy scratched his scaly brow then returned to his business without a word. Just as folk used to do when his mam rolled out the occasional odd one-liner out loud.

Was he turning into his mam? Would that be such a bad thing? Would his mam have wanted him to end up like her? On reflection, Mo decided that she most certainly wouldn't. Yes, she was a screw-up, and she didn't always see the bigger picture, or the suffering she caused others. Caused Mo. But she wasn't selfish. Not really. Or at least not always. Not on purpose anyway.

There were times when Mo had hoped, had dreamt, that his mother would regroup. Reengage. Kick her personal hell into touch. Some people do that – right? But in all their years together Mary had never struck Mo as a fighter, but more a passenger. Not clinging onto life's coattails and gripping on for a white-knuckle ride, but more an almost unwitting participant, being slowly edged along the conveyor belt to the inevitable. Like one of those amusement arcade machines where the coins inch and shuffle, bit by bit before tumbling down into the unknown.

Not that Mary was oblivious to it all. The fact that she had moved his blood-stained clothes showed awareness, concern and even a degree of lucidity; well-intentioned, though mistaken as it was.

Lucidity, Mo gave a little chuckle at the irony of the thought. That said, on reflection he reckoned there were definitely some beams of light in amongst all that cerebral fog. His mam might not have fought tooth and nail to combat it, but she was conscious of the fact that she was losing her own personal battles. The demons and the Prozac nibbled away. Dictated. Got what they wanted in the end. But the same little voices also gnawed at Mo's brain now too with yet more questions. It was Abraham's hand on the blade, but did her death stem from Mo? There could be no denying that he had been the harbinger of turmoil and woe, but could the Grim Reaper's appearance on Mary's doorstep be stacked firmly on Mo's shoulders too? What must she have been thinking of in her final moments? Could he have saved her?

Mo had an inkling about where he might possibly get some of the answers from. Possibly. But did he even want to go there? If the answers weren't those that he wanted to hear it could trigger a guilt trip of galactic proportions ...Mo clamped his eyes, gritted his teeth and tried to shake the thought that didn't bear thinking about right out of his head.

Tried.

And what about his mam's terrible secret. Why did she keep it from others? From everyone? From him! What would he do with it? Release it to wreak ruin like a revengeful biblical twister?

Maybe!

These last few months Mary hadn't just appeared physically distant from her youthful self, but mentally more fragile than Mo had ever known her to be. She hadn't said it, but the signs were there. The mumblings. The frequent scratching of her fingers and knuckles. The lost, doleful look in her regard.

'I'm sorry Mam,' Mo wiped an eye. 'I should have noticed. I should have done more.'

Mo raised the bouquet up above his head, almost eclipsing the sun, save for a bright haloed outline.

'I love you Mam,' Mo said into the bunch of flowers as if it were a microphone to the heavens. He exhaled deeply, let the bouquet drop down to his side and whispered into the wind. 'But I'll be damned if I'm going to be like you.'

***

Mo raised an eyebrow as he took a shortcut across the grass. Totally oblivious, a seemingly besotted, clean-shaven Aftab carried on strolling arm in arm with a pretty young lady. Suddenly, Mo stopped, rubbed his chin, and doubled back across the grass again. He teased a white carnation from the bouquet, laid it by the bushes where Alex's headless body had been found then continued on his way.

Leaves rustled and the wind ruffled Mo's shorts and bellowed his vest as he walked along the narrow-shaded path that skirted the road next to the park. A couple holding hands detoured out into the gaps in the traffic rather than rub shoulders with Mo. He didn't look back himself, but something somehow told him that it was exactly what the man and woman were doing themselves. Mo was acclimatising to this kind of thing. That and the whispers. Well, he himself had wanted people to notice him. There was no denying that. Just not necessarily like this. Mo brushed one of the marigolds against the tip of his nose, and walked the next fifty metres savouring the fragrance, eyes closed.

His route to Stranton Grange Cemetery and Crematorium took him past his old school. Inwardly Mo cringed. Every time he passed the gates it always unlocked vivid memories and triggered a gush of emotion. Even now, five full years later, the very thought of that evening remained excruciating. The most agonising part wasn't all that calamitous mess with Debbie on the dancefloor, but later in the car park when, floundering on the tarmac, he'd looked up and the arriving Debbie witnessed his embarrassment – not his roughing up at the hands of DI Abraham, or the deplorable thing that Abraham had done as he cried out – thank God – but the mortification of a glassy-eyed little boy, so tongue-tied as he faced his crush, that he'd rolled over, snotty-nose-first into a puddle, rather than meet her eye. Hell, the puddle might just as well have been of his own making. True, he did roll back over ten seconds later and called her name.

But she had already gone.

He shook his head and not for the first time cursed himself for being a solid gold prize idiot.

His habitual route was the straight one, south along Catcote Road then east down Brierton Lane, but today, on impulse, he turned down Oxford Road and decided to take a more zig-zag route instead.

A dozen minutes into the diversion he heard a familiar giggle and looked up and noticed Davy's ex-bit on the side's bedroom window ajar. He glanced roadside and clocked a black BMW 3 Series with shiny spoked wheels where an equally shiny Range Rover had stood in the not-too-distant past. She hadn't wasted much time in moving on. Mo kicked a bit of gravel for old time's sake and carried on his way.

Within himself, Mo felt a new person. A better person. Did that mean he would also lay a flower on Davy's grave?

Hell no!

Dance on it maybe.

***

For some reason, it was less windy in this part of town. A meteorologist would explain it with science, isobars and a pointy stick. Mo chose to interpret it as a sign of respect for the dearly departed.

The cemetery was busy in its own semi-silent way. The odd car inching respectfully down the narrow driveways, middle-aged sons and daughters walking arm in arm with an elderly relative, and handfuls of young kids - tiny fingers in big hands - whispering questions and inexplicably behaving without really knowing why. A temporary unspoken truce before sugar-induced hostilities recommenced.

Mo overtook a pink-haired woman pushing an elderly gentleman in a wheelchair and turned down one of the rows. He continued to the far end, knelt down and started to pick withered flowers out of a small urn by a marble plaque.

'Looks like I've got you all to myself today Mam.'

Mo removed the urn's brass plate, fished out a plastic bag containing a small pair of scissors and began cutting down the stems of the fresh bouquet, then inserting each flower individually.

'What do you think about the plaque?' he gave it a rub with his vest. 'I ummed and ahhed about the inscription for ages. I wanted something original. Maybe about your struggle with life. Or the cruel ending.'

Mo took a few flowers back out of the urn and trimmed them down yet further.

'But Saboor said that inscriptions like that *just wasn't you*. He suggested something simple instead - *Mary Blenkinsopp, Beloved Mother, Rest in Peace* – I reckoned it was too clichéd at first, but then thought of you and decided that Saboor was right. Clever clogs that he is.'

Mo ground down on a fingernail.

'Mam, I've been thinking. I think if I really want to discover myself then I won't do it here,' he picked up a flower stem and put that between his teeth in place of his fingernail. 'But I don't want to leave you. Besides I've no idea where I'd go. And with my track record, if I went it'd almost certainly bound to be an unmitigated disaster...'

He spat his tongue out and picked at some floral fibres with his thumbnail.

'But I just...,' he lay down flat and closed his eyes. Sounds filtered in from various directions. A bee filling his boots. Soft footsteps on gravel. A two-stroke motorbike somewhere on Brierton Lane. Mo felt something on the back of his hand. He opened his eyes and bent his head forward. Gently he moved his hand up to in front of his nose, and for a while, he and the peacock butterfly examined each other in silence. Mo seemed bewitched by the eyespot markings on the butterfly's orangey-red wings, and as for the butterfly, well Mo somehow got the feeling that she was perfectly content, and very much at ease in his company.

Mo kept his hand still and slowly brought his mouth up until his lips brushed the butterfly. He closed his eyes. A slight popping sound accompanied his kiss. And when he opened his eyes again the red, orange, black and white was already fluttering past the brown bark, towards the green leaves and the blue sky beyond.

***

As he traipsed to the bus stop on Stockton Road, the question around Mo's future resurfaced and wrangled. It wasn't something that he was going to shake off any time soon. If tomorrow was an unknown then next week, and the next sixty years come to that, remained a mystery in a labyrinth of whereabouts woolly.

As for today... Mo took a deep breath and prepared for yet more trouble and perturbing new brushes with the law.

Sort of.

Chapter Forty-Seven

'What the hell are you doing here?' Abraham growled. His fellow inmates and their visitors turned in unison and watched Mo give prisoner number 87669969 a big friendly wave and grin.

'Well, I had hoped they'd let me in your cell Joe.' Mo scraped back the plastic chair, turned it the wrong way around and sat down. 'I could have stuck on the toaster and enjoyed a nice little chinwag from the comfort of your en-suite toilet. You know, for old time's sake.'

'Piss off Blenkinsopp,' spat Abraham, starting to rise. 'I've got nothing to say to you?'

'Tch,' Mo rested both elbows on the back of the chair and cradled his chin in his palms. 'You had plenty to say about me at your trial Joe.'

Abraham ignored the comment and stood up. 'Guard.'

One of the prison officers, a heavy-set 40-something with jutting ears looked over. One end of his virtually interlocking eyebrows snaked upwards. 'What is it Abraham?'

'I'd like to go back to my cell.'

The guard cursed under his breath, grunted then peeled himself from the wall that he'd been leaning against. At the same time, Mo reached into his pocket, slid one of the contents onto the table and coughed.

Abraham started to stride away but couldn't help himself from looking down. Mo turned the photograph of the girl in the patterned dress around, 'Don't you want answers Joe?'

Abraham remained rooted to the spot; his eyes fixed on the image.

'Well?' the guard snapped. He clicked his fingers. 'Oi! Abraham. Either sit down or get here – *now!*'

Abraham looked over, raised a palm and sat back down.

'Ok then,' he rocked back in his chair and stretched, the tightness in his facial muscles visibly relaxing as he reverted to accustomed inquisitor mode. 'Let's start with the obvious – who is she? Because she sure as hell isn't your mother.'

'I know you recognised her, I saw it in your eyes the first time I showed you the picture,' Mo said.

'The dress might have caught my eye, but it's not your mam. Do you think I'd want to hump a revolting two-ton hippo like that? I'm Joe Abraham. Women are queuing up for me. Gorgeous ones. Shapelier ones. Slimmer ones.'

'Not anymore!' Mo's mind went back to the moment in Burn Valley when he had recalled the look of sheer horror on his mam's face as she fell onto him after looking out of his bedroom window. Originally, he put it down to the fact that she was falling, but she'd said it was *'the police'*. It was one of the niggles that had bounced around his brain, but he couldn't put his finger on at the time. Abraham had been in plain clothes. How could his mam have known that he was a policeman unless she already knew him? That she was already terrified of him. That defining realisation set Mo desperately hurtling into action that night.

'I know recognition when I see it.'

'That body language mumbo-jumbo. You're not Derren Brown you convoluted prick Blenkinsopp. You're just a low-life crim loser playing detective – a poor man's Hannibal Lecter.'

Mo laughed at the analogy and clapped. 'Good one Joe, but you're the caged convict, and you are the one who's been wearing a mask all these years – it's just finally slipped right off – and not before time.'

'I know a snivelling, conniving low-life when I see it,' Abraham sneered. 'And don't think I haven't worked it all out now.'

'Worked what out?'

'You planned it all along, in cahoots with your loopy mam,' Abraham snorted. 'That's why she hesitated and dithered when I asked her if she intended to accuse me of attempted rape.'

Abraham rocked forward and stuck his face inches from Mo's nose. He smelled of coffee and something sweet. Mo guessed rhubarb crumble.

'Do continue,' Mo said unblinking.

'I could see her confused and lonely little brain cell working,' Abraham tapped on a temple then circled a finger slowly around it. 'Ticking. Computing. Gradually figuring it out.'

'Figuring just what out may I ask detective inspector?'

'How best to help you. Even when she said it ...,' Abraham imitated Mary's faltering voice. *'Oh yes I'm er... going to report you for erm ...attempted rape*, it was fantasy. She had trouble even stringing the words together. You could hear the doubt in her intonation alone. She had zero conviction in what she was saying. It was artificial. Contrived. Claptrap!'

'Of course she faltered! Who wouldn't? You had just barged in, disguised as me toting a bloody butcher's knife!' Mo snapped. 'Also, she'd held off reporting you for two decades, no doubt scared of the consequences of accusing a ruthless, corrupt police officer, but after you barged in it no doubt ran through her mind – possibly even as potential leverage to try to help me.'

'I don't cut deals for the likes of you.'

'And I wouldn't want one. But it could have been something she weighed up in the few seconds she had to think. Or maybe she just decided she wanted justice at long last,' Mo rubbed his chin. 'Anyway, why did you attack her if you didn't believe her?'

'Were you actually at the trial?' Abraham curled his lip. 'Like I said to the judge, I didn't attack her as such. I just wanted to warn her off.'

'What?' Mo's eyes narrowed. 'Dressed up like me and with a butcher's knife?'

'Yeah well,' Abraham rubbed his face between his palms. 'I thought it'd give her an extra shove in the right direction. You know. To do the right thing?'

'Right thing?'

'Yes,' Abraham coughed up some phlegm and bore into Mo's eyes with his habitual air of confidence, just had he'd done that night at school when he'd pressed down over Mo and landed a bullseye when young Mo had cried out. At such proximity both could see the reflection of their own eyes in each other's pupils, but this time Mo didn't snap his head away as he had done then. ...Five seconds, Ten. Twenty... Mo felt his heartbeat gradually slow as his gaze deepened, losing himself and his thoughts for a while before becoming aware of the solidity of his own regard as Abraham's irises flickered in the periphery.

An almost imperceptible little shudder rippled through Abraham's head and shoulders. An eye socket twitched and a vein on his temple bulged and started to pulsate. He continued to stare with increasingly fidgety eyes for a few more seconds before turning away and looking down. He recoiled into the folds of his chair then rummaged through a pocket and spat into his handkerchief.

'The right thing?' Mo repeated. 'You've quite a spaced-out view of right and wrong Joe. I'll give you that.'

'I'm the wronged party here,' Abraham clenched his fist and thumped it on the table quite forcefully. Too forcefully. Conversations stopped. Heads turned. Abraham ran a finger around the inside of his shirt collar, looked over to the jug-eared guard, and raised his palm for the second time and mumbled, 'Sorry.'

'Is that an apology Joe,' Mo smiled wryly. 'It's been a very long time coming but...'

'That wasn't for your benefit, as well you know pisswizzard,' Abraham sneered. 'As I was saying. I'm innocent and I'll prove it at the retrial.'

'Good luck with that,' Mo said. 'But in own vocabulary, I'd say that you're erm... *banged to rights!*'

'Look Blenkinsopp,' Abraham pushed his heels down and his calves backwards and his chair made a grating sound as it scraped the tiled floor. 'I've had enough of this. I'm going back to my cell. I've no idea why you're even here. I'm the one who's supposed to be obsessed with you. Not the other way around. Are you just here to gloat? Is that it? What is it that you want with me?'

Mo stood up, turned his chair so that it was the right way around, sat down again and pulled himself right up to the table. 'I want the same as you Joe.'

Abraham's nose squinted. 'Eh?'

'Answers,' Mo said. 'I thought we could help each other out.'

'Why should I tell you anything Blenkinsopp?'

'Quid pro quo Agent Abraham,' Mo's eyes twinkled. 'Quid pro quo.'

He may have been wrong, but Mo thought he detected the tiniest of smiles form across Abraham's lips. He took this, and the subsequent lack of any protest, as an invitation. Mo bowed his head slightly and swept an open palm before him. 'Be my guest. After you.'

'Okay,' said Abraham tapping a fingernail against a tooth. 'Did your mother (A) really believe that I was guilty of attempted rape? And (B) would she have reported me for it.'

Mo checked behind his shoulder, put an index finger to his lips and leaned forward. He whispered, 'This doesn't go any further than between us two. But (A) no, and (B) I doubt it.'

'I knew it,' Abraham snarled. 'You and your mother. Bloody liars both of you!'

Mo sat back up straight and watched the capped volcano that was Abraham's fury boil, sizzle and come as close as it could come to exploding without risking a stretch in isolation. Mo tapped out a beat on the table while he waited for the rage to peter out.

'My turn I believe,' he said eventually. 'I'd like to know whether you pushed the blade, or my mam pulled it?'

'You were there!'

'I know I was there Joe,' said Mo. 'But it was impossible to tell. My view of the blade was obscured, and it all happened so fast. Only you know if you pushed it or Mam pulled it.'

'So you're effectively saying *did I kill her or did she commit suicide?*'

'Effectively, yes.'

Abraham slowly patted his chest several times and made a point of gradually scanning the room.

Mo gave a slight nonplussed shake of the head. 'I'm not wearing a wire if that's what you think.'

'I know that,' said Abraham.

'What then?'

'Dunno. Maybe I'm just wondering why the hell I should tell you anything at all.' Abraham stretched and laughed, 'No comment officer.'

Mo felt his neck redden. If his blood was boiling, he didn't want to show it. He turned his head away, deliberately slowed down his breathing and let his eyes wander around the visiting room. What is it they said? You can smell fear. And the strain was evident. Behind the jittery eyes. In the over-exaggerated gestures of coolness and comfort. In the electric sensation currently tasering Mo's body. *Front and bravado.* That's what Mo put it down to. Even the guards played up to their part in the pantomime. Steely stares, bulldog barks then long drags on cigarettes at break times that never come soon enough.

Mo's mind returned to his time at Abraham's; toaster in hand and slippers on feet. The little red hairs on the back of his neck spiked to attention as he remembered his clumsy attempts to catch the toaster. Abraham had no doubt assumed that Mo was probably just toying with him. Shamming an inability to catch a sizable inanimate object. And that had been on Mo's radar of intent. A show of supposed strength. A *show*, a message of control. Of intimidation. Albeit with an ultimate blunt edge. It is what he had played over in his mind during the long hours spent alone in Abraham's house. That was the theory. The reality was hands so shaky that twirling and tossing the toaster seemed the only way to mask his anxiety. And that was despite the medicinal tot of rum in his tea, and the big swig of whiskey that had preceded it. Sitting on the toilet had never been part of the plan either, but it had proved to be a useful prop when his jelly legs started to give way. Hell, the only reason he'd made Abraham handcuff his own ankles was because he didn't trust his own fingers to do the job properly.

Had he thought himself capable of pulling that bathroom escapade off? Or any such stunt again? The pool of warm vomit outside the prison suggested otherwise. Yet here he was. Blagging it. Blagging it and getting away with it. Blagging it and getting away with it and enjoying it. Again! He'd gone from a semi-invisible *square shit* to a face with a rep; be it tattooed possible murderer, the hunted lad turned hunter, or the crackpot nutter who'd halted a vicious gangster's car with his bare hands. Cool dude or crazy? Goodie or baddie? It seemed that people just weren't sure how to take Mo these days. And truth be told, neither did he. It was a whole new experience for him too. To be noticed. Looked at. Feared.

'I've another question,' said Abraham. 'How come you led me down the garden path about your mother about the attempted rape nonsense? Especially if you'd known it'd put her in danger.'

Mo shook out his reverie and scowled.

'Firstly,' he said firmly, loudly and with a deepening icy glare. 'I had no idea that you'd come after her with a butcher's knife. That's a humungous overreaction. And I would never have put her in such a position if I thought there was even the tiniest chance that even a sick vindictive fruitcake like you would go to such ridiculous extremes.'

Abraham opened his mouth to speak but noticed the pairs of eyes turning in his direction, and instead just settled for busying himself with his shirt collar again.

'Secondly, I had my reasons,' Mo lowered his voice and continued. 'One of which, I don't mind telling you was to set you up. Pre-emptive action in case you had any other threats up your sleeve.'

'I knew it,' Abraham snarled.

'You knew nothing,' Mo rebounded. 'I was in control, with you cuffed at the time. I was going to *"accidentally"* leave a hacksaw blade within your reach as I left your place; giving me enough head start to creep over gardens and hedges, sneak in the back of our house, and set up covert video recording with my tablet before you broke free. The first you'd have known about it was either when a cell door clunked behind you or your antics were plastered all over YouTube.'

'Eh?'

'Don't play the innocent with me. If I'd have disappeared into the night then I fully expected you to bomb straight over to my mam's once you'd freed yourself,' Mo glowered. 'But apart from letting you escape - leaving me just a couple of minutes' head start - my only mistake was thinking that your cop chums would come gunning straight for me.'

Abraham opened his mouth, but Mo cut in again before he could say anything.

'You watched me go into Burn Valley from your bedroom window. So why did half the squad cars in the county hurtle past it to the wrong location? The only possible answer I could come up with is that you didn't want me to get caught. Well, not until you had dealt with me, my mam or ideally both of us. It was also spurious that you gave me a tip-off about the squad car at my mam's house. I'd have guessed surveillance would be posted anyway, but why would you, the person in charge of my capture, tip me the wink? Unless of course, you wanted me to stay away, presumably so you'd get to my mam on your own, so I'd never get to ask her about you ...and I, and the police for that matter, would never hear her response – dead people don't testify!'

Abraham shuffled in his chair, 'Bullshit.'

'It's the truth and you know it,' Mo glared. 'It was only when squad cars kept zooming past Burn Valley that the penny dropped, and realising the imminent danger I legged it to my mam's.'

Abraham shook his head and shuffled some more.

'I know you've things to hide,' Mo continued. 'Things you'd like kept quiet or brushed under the carpet. I also knew you had opportunity for Alex's murder – a damn sight more than me it turns out. It was no secret that you had it in for me. And if you could have made me swing for Alex's murder it'd have made your decade, let alone your day.'

Abraham smiled, tutted and slouched in his chair – all coolness and comfort – then loosened a button on his shirt as Mo continued.

'So, I thought, do you know what, get the first punch in - best form of defence is attack and all that.' Mo brought his fists up to just below his chin. 'I thought let's see what the deranged loon has in mind. How's he going to try to screw me over next? Foolishly though I thought that you'd have the sense to show some restraint. To limit yourself to a warning off, a metaphorical twisted arm, or at a highly unlikely last resort, *physical* arm twisting – at which point I would have rushed out and laid into you before you could have even administered even a Chinese burn.'

Mo quickly jabbed a right hand and Abraham instinctively scrunched up his eyes and ducked behind his forearms.

'That's what I thought it might pan out like,' Mo retracted his fist. 'The last thing I expected was you bulldozing in, doolally, all guns blazing.'

Abraham laughed, a bit too long, then leaned forwards.

'Firstly, if you *ever* put your fist anywhere near me, I'll snap it off at the wrist. Got it?'

Mo smiled ironically.

'Secondly, if that was your cunning master plan then what the hell happened?' Abraham sneered. 'There was no multiplex screening at the trial and, if I remember rightly, no gay cavalry charging out of the closet.'

Mo bowed his head and muttered. 'I got there as soon as could once I realised the immediate danger.'

Abraham shook his head. 'You still pointed me in the direction of your mother after you'd called me a murderer. That's hardly doting son form.'

'I agree, it wouldn't be' said Mo. 'But get your facts right. I didn't call you a murderer at that juncture, did I? All I did was moot a bit of a wild hunch and highlight that you had no more of an alibi for Alex's murder than I did. Indeed, when our conversation took place, I didn't know for certain that you'd met up with her that night. I also didn't know all about your previous *history* with her either for that matter. Those were mere gut feelings, not hard facts. Similarly, at the time, even though I discovered that you had downloaded a photo of Jade, I had no idea that you were Jade's father until that all came out in court. If anything, prior to our chat, I was under the impression that I had more motivation and better opportunity than you.'

Abraham folded his arms.

'Also, when I raised the possibility of you deleting your chat and contact records from Alex's phone at the scene it was just wild speculation. I got goosebumps when the prosecution revealed that phone records suggest that this is what you actually did, and by using her password which was indeed her date of birth - which they proved you knew after finding 'happy birthday' wishes from you in text records.' Mo looked Abraham straight in the eye. 'When I first broke into your house, it was never about setting you up, or trying to nail you as a murderer. That never even crossed my mind.'

'So why then?'

'Same as now.' Mo shuffled in his seat too. 'I wanted answers. *Want* answers. Only then it was a desire to know more about the case that you had – or hadn't got –against me. You know, so I had a bit of intel, a few crumbs of knowledge, some pieces of information to help me string the puzzle together. With a clearer picture of the evidence, I would be in a better position to work things out for myself and to possibly build a defence; rather than just roll over and let you contort things, corrupt evidence and pin whatever the hell you wanted on me – and don't deny it. You know you wanted to.'

Abraham didn't deny it. 'But one thing you fail to mention is that you also broke into my house and quizzed me so that you could try to work out if *you* were the one who had killed Alex.'

'Yes, that too,' Mo shrugged. 'It was a skeleton I hoped I'd never find when I started unlocking doors and joining the dots. And if the answers uncovered a shadow of guilt over me then I'd have held my hands up and handed myself in. That's God's honest truth. Indeed, you yourself know how close I came to letting you cuff me. But it wasn't my DNA they found under Alex's fingernails was it Joe? It was yours.'

Abraham planted his heels again and rocked the chair back. 'What can I say? She's an old flame. A regular bonk. Big deal. We had sex in the park, and not for the first time. She liked it rough. It doesn't mean to say I killed her.'

'So why lie?' Mo eyed Abraham. 'Why didn't you mention that you'd seen her that night to either the investigation team - the team that you yourself led – or your subsequent interrogators?'

'Because why put myself in the frame when there was no need to? Besides, there was already my DNA on Alex's body that I could innocently explain away after I tore my mask off and tumbled over her to puke.'

'The prosecution called that *suspicious* Joe, not *innocent*.'

'Yeah, like they've ever witnessed a worm wriggling out of a friend's severed neck before!' Snapped Abraham. 'As for the fingernail DNA intel, my ex-colleagues conveniently held that information back. I'd have come clean if I'd known about that. Hindsight is a wonderful thing. But so what? It's still not proof that I killed her.'

'So, what about the other thing the prosecution pinpointed? The fact that Alex had previously accused you of a sexual assault?' said Mo. 'There was the suggestion that you'd wanted revenge for that – and that's motive.'

'What rot,' spat Abraham. 'Alex was no saint, and no goddamned virgin for that matter either. Yes, she made an *accusation* one time after we'd had a spat and she was swimming in tequila. But she *retracted* it just two hours later once she'd sobered up. That's a silly, quickly forgotten minor drunken reprisal. Not a motive.'

'Maybe. Maybe not. But tell me what happened that night Joe? Were you jealous that she wanted Kell instead of you? Did she turn you down? So you forced yourself on her?' Mo lowered his head slightly and glared up at Abraham past raised eyebrows. 'The prosecutor said that bruises around her wrists and arms could be consistent with rape.'

'I thought you reckoned it wasn't,' Abraham snorted.

'I'm not a pathologist. It might have been,' Mo shrugged. 'What happened? Did she threaten to see it through to the end this time and report you? For the sickening, disgusting rapist that you are.'

'Screw you Blenkinsopp!' Abraham sprung to his feet and poked his snarling face right up against Mo's. 'Screw you!'

'Sit down Joe,' Mo whispered.

'Are you deaf?' Abraham spat. 'We're done!'

Abraham spun on his heels and started stomping towards the prisoners' exit.

'Recognise this Joe?'

Abraham turned his head around towards Mo and the little black book he was fanning with his hands. 'How the hell...?' He made a grab for the book, but Mo was too quick and slid it down the back of his shorts.

'Hand that over pisswizzard. It's mine, as well you know,' Gnashing his teeth Abraham kicked the chair backwards, crashed down onto it and glowered at Mo. He thrust his palm across the table, 'Now!'

'Tch,' Mo shook his head slowly. 'You're a policeman Joe. Or at least you were. You should know better than most that possession is nine-tenths of the law. Ten-tenths in this case.'

Abraham bore his eyes into Mo's, but without effect.

'And you know very well where I got it from,' Mo patted the rectangular bulge stretching the back of his shorts. 'The shoebox at the back of your wardrobe. And, oh yeah, I do have a copy. Several in fact.'

Mo extracted and unfolded several photocopied sheets of paper from a pocket. 'You do know your scrawl is terrible Joe don't you? I hear there are educational programs in prison. Maybe you could take up, if not calligraphy, then at least elementary handwriting or something?'

Abraham wiped his forehead with the back of his hand and undid another button as Mo scanned the documents.

'And what's with all this shorthand Joe? 12/6/17, ?, pk, 16, bld, cvy, sht skt, av,7' Mo scratched his head and squinted. '22/7/17 sue wrd, fns, 18, bk, skn, fit, tght legns, 8.'

'No idea,' Abraham snorted.

'Really?' Mo said, scanning down the lists. 'There are an awful lot of entries here. All the same kind of shorthand. All in your own special drunken spider handwriting. It'd be some coincidence for you not to be aware of what you're writing about.'

'No comment.'

'And you don't strike me as the kind of detective who believes in coincidences Joe,' Mo continued. 'Ah well, lucky for you, I worked it all out.'

'If you say so.'

'Oh, I do say so,' Mo replied. 'It wasn't that hard really. You know, dates, names, locations, ages, hair colour, body type, other features and I presume the last digit is a score from one to ten on how you rated them in bed.'

'Oh, you are a smartie pants aren't you Blenkinsopp,' Abraham clapped ironically.

Mo ignored him and shook his head as he continued reading.

'I get why you're so obsessed with my little black book,' Abraham chuckled. 'It's because you're jealous. You're a pug ugly virgin with the sex appeal of a squid.'

When Mo showed no reaction to the bait Abraham continued. 'Anyway, there's no harm in a red-blooded male keeping track of, how shall I put it, *conquests*.'

Mo slapped a palm down hard on top of the photocopies. 'It *is* when twelve of the entries are for girls aged fifteen and under. And yes, I counted. One as young as 13 for Christ's sake. Not to mention all the ones with question marks instead of actual ages.'

Abraham writhed in his chair, looked around the room and turned back towards Mo. Finger to lips. 'Shh, keep your voice down dumb ass.'

'I'll say what I damn well like,' Mo said loudly. He turned a semicircle in his chair and returned gazes from prisoners, visitors and guards. 'And how I like!'

'Yeah. Sure. I'm not saying you can't,' Abraham held his hands up in surrender then slid as far across the table as he could while remaining seated.

Mo turned back around and folded his arms.

'It's just that it's not going to do anyone any good,' Abraham said in a hush. 'Shouting the odds about stuff like that.'

'Sit back and get out of my face,' Mo said.

Abraham instantly uncoiled and pressed his back against the chair but his shoulders, head and fringe all drooped forwards.

Mo tapped a finger on his upper lip.

'Firstly, don't treat me like an idiot,' he said softly. Beads of sweat glistened along Abraham's hairline. Mo noticed some grey that he couldn't remember from before. 'Secondly, be aware that I've all the image and video files from your personal computer as well as backups.'

Abraham opened his mouth to speak but Mo put a finger to his lips and continued. 'Thirdly, and you may be surprised by this Joe. But you're already facing three life sentences, and – despicable creep that you are – that seems about right to me. So, feel free to try to sway my mind if you like, but I'm considering an option of just keeping your disgusting little book and your sordid filthy movie files under wraps - at least for now.'

Abraham's mouth remained agape. His jaw wobbled but nothing came out.

'I think *thank you* are the words that you are looking for Joe.'

Abraham hesitated and ruminated before mumbling, Thank you.' He dabbed at some more sweat on his forehead.

'I think we're done now,' Mo said as he slid his chair back, stood up and turned around.

After three paces Abraham called after him.

'No wait a minute.' Abraham leaned across the table. 'Just one more thing. ...Please.'

Mo looked down at Abraham with narrowed eyes. '*Please?*' He tapped his cheek, gave the faintest of nods and sat back down.

'Could you pass on a message for me? You know, to Kell.' Mo detected a thin watery sheen to Abraham's cobalt eyes. 'It's just I've not had any other visitors to ask and he's not answered any of my calls.'

Mo exhaled deeply and rasped his spiky haircut as he observed Abraham, head inclined downwards, wringing his hands.

'Okay,' Mo said. 'What's the message?'

'Er, you know...' Abraham pulled at a finger and the knuckle cracked. 'That I tried calling him. That I miss him, and that I'm going to sort everything out so things will be back to normal for us. You know, after the retrial.'

'*After the retrial,*' Mo repeated with raised eyebrows and a sad smile. 'Anything else Joe?'

'Er, no I think that's it.'

'Don't you want to say that you love him?'

'Oh yeah,' Abraham's cheeks flushed. 'Yeah, that as well.'

'Certainly,' Mo nodded. 'Tell me Joe. What did it feel like when you found out you had a child after all those years? A strapping teenager.'

'It felt....'

'Good? Satisfying? A pleasant surprise?'

'It felt erm...'

Great? Terrifying? A pain in the ass?'

'It felt perfect. Like the missing piece of the jigsaw of life had just fallen into my lap. I'd always wanted a son. It's just that I never actually realised it until it belatedly happened.'

Mo tilted his head to one side and eyed Abraham from another angle as he stroked his chin.

'And now it's gone,' he said softly. 'You only get one chance at fatherhood Joe, and you blew it.'

'Maybe not,' Abraham's forced a hopeful smile. 'It might not be too late.'

Mo returned the smile with a crooked one of his own. 'Can I ask you one last thing?'

Abraham took a few moments then nodded.

'Why me?' Mo shifted uncomfortably in his seat. 'Out of all the people, out of all the real, genuine scumbag hoodlums in the world, why did you choose to pick on me? What did I ever do to you to deserve all the abuse, the hatred, the victimisation?'

Abraham stared blankly at Mo, swept back his hair and thought.

'Well?'

'I don't know,' shrugged Abraham. 'I honestly don't' know. There's just something about you. Something different. I can't put my finger on it. Maybe it's nothing personal after all. Maybe I just don't like the unknown.'

'*Nothing personal,*' Mo repeated as he rose. 'There's quite some irony there Joe. Maybe you're softening in your old age.'

'Nah,' Abraham sneered. 'I still want to crush you. Destroy you. More now than ever before. And one day I will – it's just I'm not quite sure why.'

Mo gave a tiny shake of the head then spun on his heels.'

'You know Debbie's there too, don't you?' Abraham jibed. 'In my little black book.'

'Goodbye Joe,' said Mo without turning back.

***

Mo slowed as he approached a parked Volvo up the road from the prison. He thrust both hands out and raised an eyebrow. He then placed both palms on the car's bonnet, pressed then retracted them.

Just a slight tremor and a bit of a smudge he thought as he wiped the mark off the bonnet with his vest. *That's progress.*

After twenty metres he stopped again and examined his hands for a second time. *Hardly a wobble*, he contemplated with a wry smile. *Careful you don't get a taste for this kind of thing Mohammed my son.*

Chapter Forty-Eight

Mo hopped off the bus by the village of Greatham. Separated from the town by barely a half a field, a few carrots and a signpost Mo somehow always seemed to feel its *villageness* as soon he left the main drag; the sudden absence of cars whizzing past, the stillness in the air, the few painted terraced houses that no one ever appeared to go into or come out of.

Mo had never been to the house he was looking for before, but he knew it was in Greatham somewhere. He stopped by the village shop-cum-post office and scanned around, immediately dismissing the terraced houses around the green and those intermittently flanking the road that ran back to towards town. The house he was looking for would be bigger, and more private. He carried on walking and in virtually no time at all came to a fork in the road. The shadowy single track to the left appeared more foliage than thoroughfare while the right fork offered more terraced houses that curved around a bend, with the probability of more houses and who knows what beyond.

Mo didn't need to know what. He veered to the left and stepped into the leafy darkness.

The lane, if you could call it that, was only long enough to host a handful of detached houses. The first one had a Fiat Punto in the driveway, the second one had miniature football nets in the garden and the third had a sign offering private yoga classes. He kept on walking. The next house had a ring of mystery about it; grey, grand and substantial it managed to make the row of towering elm trees in front of it look weedy and inconsequential, but Mo dismissed that one too, and on the '*Edelweiss*' name alone. The last house, Mo assumed, sat somewhere behind the 25-foot-high, ramrod straight hedge. He clocked the high-tech security cameras well before he reached the imposing wrought iron gate that they were perched above. He had seen gates like this before; ornate but hippopotamus heavy and impossible to shift unless someone flicked a switch on the inside, clicked the right fob on the outside, or drove a Sherman tank. What was different about this gate was the two cobras defiantly spitting out their tongues at him.

Mo stuck his tongue back out at them and pressed the intercom buzzer.

***

'Oh! I wasn't expecting you.'

Mo gave a wiggly-fingered wave and the gates clicked and swung out open. He craned his neck to scan the huge red brick property and felt the warmth of the sun on his face as he did so.

Crunching footsteps on the gravel got louder. Without looking around Mo whistled. 'That's some place you've got here Kell.'

'Yeah, well it's Davy's house really. *Was* Davy's house,' Kell corrected himself. 'I didn't even know you knew where I lived.' Kell didn't offer a hand to shake, but Mo wouldn't have noticed if he had.

'I didn't,' Mo replied without shifting his gaze. 'How many bedrooms? Six? Seven?'

'Eight,' Kell offered. 'Though a couple of them are pretty titchy.'

'I somehow doubt that. I bet your broom cupboard makes my bedroom look like a rabbit hutch.' Mo scanned around the estate. 'How the hell do you mow all that? And where is Tiger Woods?'

'He's in the rough,' Kell nodded towards a blue spruce where a wrinkly twig of man in brown overalls lay on his back precision-snipping. 'No seriously, our gardener does it all. We inherited him from the previous owners, and they inherited him from the owners before. He sort of comes with the house, and the garden is pretty much his life's work.'

Mo eyed the pristine lawns, the Giverny-esque pond and topiary that Edward Scissor-Hands-da-Vinci would have been proud of.

'Who is he? Capability Brown?'

'No,' Kell scratched his nose. 'He's called Bernie.'

'Of course he is,' Mo said just as a girl's scream rang out. He turned suddenly, wide-eyed.

'Ah,' Kell jabbed a thumb towards the back of the house. 'That's just Amy in the paddling pool.'

Without being asked, Mo marched around to the back garden and laughed. 'I've never seen as much grass as that before without a hundred head of cattle grazing on it.'

Kell hunched his shoulders.

'And that's not like any paddling pool I've ever seen. Mine was the diameter of a hula-hoop and patched up with Elastoplast. You could keep dolphins in yours.'

Mo waved as Amy jumped in again from the little diving platform and screamed in delight as she splashed into Beth's waiting arms.

'Hi Mrs Lilley.'

Beth turned, hesitated ever so briefly, then returned the wave with a smile. 'One...two...three!' She threw the giggling Amy up into the air and caught her. Amy wrapped her arms around her aunt's neck and hung on tight.'

'Your mam looks different Kell.'

Kell ran a hand through his hair. 'In what way?'

'There's colour in her face and a kind of freshness in her eyes,' Mo said.

'It's Amy,' Kell offered. 'She brings out the best in her.'

'She seems a lovely little girl,' Mo smiled. 'It's nice to see her happy too.'

Without smiling back Kell guided Mo back to the front of the house. 'Look, what are you doing here?'

‘All in good time,’ Mo gestured towards the gardener as he squirmed under the blue spruce, like a giant worm with secateurs. ‘It looks like old Bernie there is about to do a spot of botanical microsurgery, and I wouldn’t want to be responsible for him chopping off the wrong leaf.’

While Kell turned to look at Bernie Mo pushed the front door open.

‘Hang on...,’ Kell scowled and grabbed Mo’s arm.

‘Walls and gardens have ears,’ Mo nodded over to Bernie then surveyed Kell with steeled eyes.

Kell stood tall and rooted, breathing heavily through his nose. His strong grip gradually loosening as his eyes roved between Bernie and Mo. Before another word was spoken, Mo manoeuvred them into the house and clanked the door shut.

***

‘What’s this?’ Mo ran a finger over the troughs and ridges of some of the masses of publications in the bookcase that flanked the hallway. ‘I’ve heard of having a nose in a book, but you’re up to your armpits in them.’

‘Higher than armpits,’ Kell opened a door to reveal a floor-to-ceiling library complete with a small antique table and a *Whurther’s Originals* grandad chair. ‘You could drown in books in this house.’

Mo took a couple of long sniffs. The lingering whiff of recently sprayed eau-de-furniture-polish hadn’t quite snuffed out an underlying dusty stuffiness. He inched up to the titles and read. ‘Poetry, fantasy, biographies, history, ornithology, Greek mythology.’ I’m guessing this isn’t you den Kell. I don’t see too many comics or cartoon collections here.’

‘You’ve got me there, it’s Mam’s room,’ Kell tapped two books. ‘Although I did read these.’

‘Harry Potter? That’s almost PhD level for you.’ Mo climbed a few rungs of the sliding ladder and slowly pushed himself along, examining yet more contents. ‘Paintings, geography, crime, thesauri, cookery, religion, science, science-fiction, gardening, politics, antiques, nutrition, housekeeping, geomorphology, astrology, astrophysics... *astrophysics?*’

'What can I say,' Kell shrugged. 'Mam's a bookworm. I've been meaning to try some proper adult stuff myself, but you know what's it's like chasing villains and whatnot, I just don't get the time.'

Mo took out a few books and flicked through some of the pages. 'Very comprehensive. It seems like your mam has books on just about every subject going.'

'Yes, well she never really gets out much.'

Mo hopped off the ladder, flicked through an index box on the table then joined Kell gazing out of the window.

'It's a lovely view. Very pretty. And this room makes quite a peaceful inner sanctuary. I'm not surprised your mam spends so much time here,' Mo pointed to a charcoal drawing of the garden on an easel. 'Did she do this?'

Kell nodded to a miniature watercolour and a pencil drawing. 'Those too.'

'Very impressive,' Mo rattled the tin of pencils and charcoals on the table. 'Puts my matchstick men to shame.'

'Mine too.' Kell wandered over to the door and pushed it ajar.

Mo poked a finger in a rare gap on the shelves before joining Kell.

'How come you're here Mo?' Kell shoved the door all of the way open. 'Is this about that business you called the station about yesterday? Because if it is Debbie has it in hand and should be on the case as we speak.'

'That's great Kell, but no,' Mo crossed the hallway and breezed into the room opposite with another whistle. 'Wow! I'm guessing this was Davy's playroom and not your mam's.'

Kell shrugged and nodded.

'And what's that thing?' Mo pointed a finger back and forth along a wall. 'A multiplex cinema or a flat-screen juggernaut?'

'Good one Mo,' Kell said unsmiling.

Mo skipped past a bulky treasure chest and plonked himself astride the vintage motorbike. 'Some bike this is Kell. What is it?'

'It's a 1960 Triumph Tiger.'

Mo cranked the accelerator and made a revving noise.

'So why are you here Mo?' Kell crouched over the pool table and sunk a stripe. 'I mean, it's a bit out of the blue you turning up like this. It's not like you've been here before or we've had anything arranged.'

'Is that Kell the ex-schoolmate or Kell the policeman talking?' Mo took a cue and proceeded to miss a sitter over a pocket.

'It's both and neither,' Kell downed another stripe. 'I'm just curious, that's all.'

'Couldn't it be just a friendly social visit?'

'It's possible I suppose,' Kell aimed at a pot directly in front of Mo's crotch. 'But it isn't though is it?'

Mo looked into Kell's flickering green eyes. Were they jumping between the cue and object ball or something else altogether he wondered?

'I guess not,' Mo straightened up.

Kell let fly and the cue ball jolted up and caught Mo in the midriff.

'Dear me,' Mo laughed, 'Has something rattled your cage?'

Kell shoved the cue back in the rack with a clatter but without a word.

'I've a message for you,' said Mo as he examined the jukebox. '*Motörhead, ACDC, Metallica* ...'

'Oh aye?'

'*Slayer, Megadeath...*' Mo laughed. 'I had Davy down as a *Kylie Minogue* man myself.'

'What message Mo?'

'I remember this,' Mo made for the contraption in the corner. 'You brought it to do your magic tricks at the school talent show. The thing that sliced a poor innocent watermelon in half, but somehow let off Jamie McCabe scot-free?'

'My guillotine, yes.'

'Some performance that was. They had to mop the stage afterwards, some said it was more to do with McCabe wetting himself than the watermelon juice.'

'Well, it's a real blade,' Kell pinged it with a fingernail. 'But perfectly safe in the right hands. Not that I've used it in ages.'

'Are you sure?' Mo gave the steel a ping with a fingernail of his own. 'This blade looks brand new to me.'

'Na. 'Anyway, what's this about a message?'

'Oh that?' Mo took a small log from the fireplace, put it at the base of the guillotine and pulled the lever. The blade hurtled down like a rampaging Stuka and spliced it clean in two. He whistled, 'No wonder McCabe wet himself!'

Kell tossed the log halves towards the fireplace then drilled his eyes into Mo's.

'Oh yes,' Mo clicked his fingers and tapped his temple. 'The message. Your dad sends his love. Well, to be more precise he asked me to tell you that he loves you.'

'Joe?' Kell scratched his head. 'Joe Abraham.'

'Of course, Joe Abraham. Who else?'

'Yeah, of course.' Kell cleared his throat. 'It's just that he's the last person I'd expect you to be doing errands for, that's all.'

'Well, I wouldn't call it an errand,' Mo said. 'It's just that I had a cosy little chat with him down at the prison and I promised I'd pass the message on.'

'Oh right, thanks,' Kell motioned towards the door with his hand. 'It was good of you to come all this way to tell me that. It's a shame you hadn't just rang me instead, it's just that I need to get going soon.'

‘Places to go, people to meet?’

‘Precisely,’ Kell started to walk towards the door.

Mo remained stock still. ‘It’s funny that?’

‘What is?’ Kell fiddled with an earlobe.

‘You’ve places to go and people to meet, but it’s been weeks now and you still haven’t been to visit your own dad in jail.’

Kell pressed his toes down to flatten the corner of a rug. ‘Yeah well, to be perfectly honest I don’t think I’ll be seeing him again.’

Mo sat down on the bench underneath the guillotine. ‘Oh, why’s that then? I thought you two got on great. Like peas in a plod pod.’

‘Yeah well, that was before wasn’t it,’ Kell rocked back and forth on the balls of his feet. ‘You know, before it transpired that he was a racist serial killer.’

‘And there’s another funny thing,’ Mo said. ‘He’s still accusing me of setting him up.’

‘Well, he would, wouldn’t he?’ Kell spat. ‘He’s always had it in for you. That’s not going to change just because his sordid little plot didn’t pan out. He’s cornered and angry and if he can use you as a *get out of jail free* card he will.’

‘Anger manifests itself in different ways,’ Mo said. ‘Anger at being caught isn’t quite the same as anger at being caged.’

‘So what?’

‘So, if I were a betting man, I’d put my money on something else. A different source of rage,’ Mo scratched his chin. ‘Something more like a seething sense of injustice.’

‘You’re reading too much into it,’ Kell laughed, somewhat loudly. ‘Every scrap of evidence points to him not only committing those murders, but also trying to set you up for them. He even intimated to me – before it happened - that evidence for Alex’s murder would crop up with your stamp all over it. You’re the last person who should be defending him.’

'I'm not defending him,' said Mo. 'He's a nasty piece of work who is where he deserves to be.'

'Well then.'

'Just not for murder.'

***

'Eh?' Kell peered over the seated Mo.

'What I'm saying,' Mo stretched his arms up, almost touching Kell's chin. 'Is that Abraham is still convinced that I killed Davy and Alex.'

'Oh well let him think that. No one else believes you had anything to do with the murders anymore.'

'Yes, but the point is if he didn't kill them – and I didn't either, then that means that someone else must have.'

'What rot,' Kell laughed. 'A judge and jury convicted him based on clear evidence. Who else have you been spouting all this nonsense to?'

'No one. Just you,' Mo moved his hands onto the guillotine and slid them down the frame. 'But I'm right.'

'On what grounds? Kell's eyes narrowed and he ran a finger around the back of his T-shirt collar. 'The evidence is overwhelming.'

'Yes,' agreed Mo. '*Too* overwhelming.'

'You've got too much time on your hands Mo,' Kell put his fingertips to Mo's forehead as if gauging his temperature. 'Your imagination is running riot.'

'So, you think it's natural for a detective,' Mo batted away Kell's fingers. 'A successful, experienced detective, to leave so much evidence pointing directly at himself?'

'Yes,' Kell replied flatly. 'He's cocky, arrogant and thinks all criminals are dumb imbeciles and all coppers - apart from him – are bungling buffoons who don't know an arsonist from their elbow. He has even repeatedly openly boasted that he'd be able to commit the perfect crime, leave flashing neon clues, and still get away with it.'

'Hm, that's a convincing argument,' Mo mused with a rub of the chin. 'It's just a shame that it's claptrap.'

Kell knotted his eyebrows and exhaled heavily through flaring nostrils.

'Come on Kell. Cocky, overconfident and overestimating his own ability I get,' Mo continued. 'But your theory effectively suggests that Abraham is not only stupid, but so stupid that he deliberately killed three people then purposely left an obvious trail back to himself.'

'Yes, it's a classic double-bluff.'

'No, it's downright quadruple-bollocks,' Mo insisted. 'It's Hansel and Gretel revisited, only their pebbles and breadcrumb-trailed story has more substance to it than this threadbare Abraham fairy-tale. I mean, come on, would even a schoolboy killer leave his DNA-caked chewing gum next to Davy's body? It's quite literally overkill. Also, for Alex, I do believe that the skin DNA under her nails is genuine, and the result of rough sex, but would Abraham be so stupid as to leave one of his snotty tissues at the scene too? It's fantasy!'

'You don't know what you're talking about,' Kell countered. 'I get it through; you watch a few TV cop shows and all of a sudden you're Lieutenant Colombo.'

Mo responded with a crooked smile.

'Just one more thing, Mr Blenkinsopp,' Kell put on a woeful American accent. 'You've forgotten all about motive. Sorry for the bluntness, but my dad hated your guts and was dead set on making your life a living hell.'

'Granted, but not to the point that he'd sacrifice himself in the process. Again, you're accusing him of crass stupidity. And we both know he isn't that dim. Devious yes, manipulating yes, dishonest, underhand, untrustworthy – absolutely. But stupid, no. I agree there must have been a motive,' Mo sat up straight on the bench and eyed Kell. 'Just a different motive, and for a different person - the real killer.'

Kell shook his head again, 'Bollocks.'

'You're the detective,' Mo pointed to Kell. 'Who else had a motive to kill Davy or Alex?'

'No one else,' Kell shrugged. 'We checked. Apart from your run-ins with Davy and Alex, the only other common denominator is Joe Abraham. Once the evidence unfolded there was no point looking anywhere else. It's an open and shut case.'

'So you say,' replied Mo. 'But it doesn't mean to say there were no other links. Maybe you, or someone else, should have dug deeper?'

'What are you saying? Are you accusing anyone? If so, out with it!'

'Well, here's the thing,' Mo tapped his pointy cheekbone. 'I'm not sure that you have been as thorough as you could have been. What about your mam for starters? She was married to Davy and had previous with Abraham.'

'So what?' Kell sneered. 'Having an ex isn't exactly a capital offence.'

'Agreed,' Mo replied. 'But we both know that both Davy and Abraham played the field. And as you know; Alex wasn't shy in coming forward. Indeed, she struck as an *I want him, I'll take him, and to hell with the consequences* kind of woman.'

'That's not a crime either,' Kell said. 'Women's lib, equal opportunities and all that.'

'Even so,' continued Mo. 'It's a small town and the chances of Alex's path not crossing with either Davy, Abraham or both are pretty slim.'

'I guess,' Kell shrugged. 'But again, so what?'

'So, here's what I think,' Mo craned his neck back, so he was looking directly into Kell's eyes. 'I think the reason Abraham left your mam not long before the alter had something to do with Alex. My guess is that Alex had got her claws into him before the wedding and one way or another and that shattered all dreams of idyllic wedded bliss, and as a result either Abraham called the wedding off or your mam did.'

'You've had a shock, and you're imagining things,' Kell lowered Mo's head towards the wooden block at the foot of the guillotine. 'Here, have a lie down.'

Mo held himself up by his elbows and glanced around. 'Just making sure there are no bolts on the stocks!'

Satisfied, Mo went along with it and eased his neck into the wooden groove. For a moment, found it quite relaxing – until that is Kell suddenly snapped the stocks shut around Mo's head, flicked a hidden catch and laughed as it locked.

'What are you doing?' Mo staccato chuckled as Kell pulled the chord and the glistening blade rose and fixed into position directly above him with an eerie shudder. 'Are you aiming to do a hatchet job on me?'

'Just a bit of light relief,' Kell smiled as he raised Mo's legs and flattened them out on the bench.

'Now I know how that watermelon felt like,' Mo squirmed.

'Well, you do sound like a fruitcake,' Kell retorted. 'With all this unfounded drivel.'

'It's not all drivel,' Mo struggled to lift his head. 'And it's not unfounded either. I did a bit of digging of my own.'

'Yeah, and?'

'Well for starters, I found a listing for the wedding between Abraham and your mam in St Joseph's parish records but is marked as 'cancelled' a month or so before the big day. It had been due for 13th June 1998, a Saturday. Rainy by all accounts.'

'That's meaningless,' Kell scoffed. 'Mam had a lucky escape one rainy day. So what?'

'Well, it would appear to be meaningless, and certainly Abraham didn't twig the significance, but the dates don't tally.'

'Don't tally with what?'

'Don't tally with your version of events Detective Lilley. I'm afraid the game is up.'

Kell cackled and Mo caught his breath as Kell stood tall, leaned on the frame and the blade wobbled. 'Do go on Mo, I'm intrigued.'

'It's simple maths,' Mo closed his eyes. 'The date of the breakup - May 1998, plus 9 months at most, means that the baby your mam was carrying at the time can't possibly have been you.'

Mo heard a snort and felt Kell's breath wash over his face.

'You were born in April 1999, weren't you?'

In the absence of a reply, Mo continued. 'April 14th 1999. A day full of bluster and wind. Probably.'

He waited in silence, eyes closed for the full twenty seconds it took for Kell to respond.

'Mam had a miscarriage if you must know, it's not something she likes talking about,' Kell spat. 'Not that it's any of your business.'

'But you made it my business,' Mo replied quietly. 'In a roundabout kind of way granted, but it's all related.'

'You think you have all the answers Blenkinsopp,' Kell snapped. 'But you're still the same hapless chump who was punch bag for lads and a bag of nerves with lasses. You were green then, and even more clueless now.'

'Times change, people change Kell,' said Mo. 'Just look at your mam. She's like a woman reincarnated; smiling and splashing about in a period of *deep mourning*.'

'She's moving on. People do. Even you. There's no crime in that either. Besides, you've only seen her for all of ten seconds, and with the one little girl in the world that brings out the best in her,' Kell sneered. Come on then Einstein, I'm getting bored of your games, if you think you know something then out with it.'

'I'm no Einstein,' Mo chuckled, 'I'm no Columbo either. Not even his dog.'

'Well, we're agreed on something.'

'But being framed for murder, or murders *plural* to be precise, does tend to get the old brain cells jumping.'

'Yes, jumping to the wrong conclusions,' Kell huffed. 'Any theories you have are just blind guesses Blenkinsopp.'

'Possibly. But I doubt it. Did you know that Einstein used to visualise solutions to unimaginably complex problems,' Mo said softly behind closed eyelids. 'That's how the theory of relativity came to him. I think the ACDC electric current guy, Tesla had the same gift. A literal visionary visionary.'

'`So what?'

'I tried doing that myself. I've spent hours in bed and at the cemetery with my eyes closed, trying to visualise just what happened on the nights of the murders, and trying to make sense of this whole sorry business.'

'And?'

'Yeah, like I said, I'm no Einstein,' Mo flashed his teeth. 'I couldn't make head nor tail of it, which is why I went back to basics.'

'Which is?'

'Hansel and Gretel,' said Mo. 'One step, one pebble, one crumb at a time. Following the trail wherever it leads.'

'Which is?'

'I'm here aren't I?' Mo closed his eyes again. 'I only had crumbs to begin with. Crumbs, doubts, niggles. Call them what you will. Nothing concrete. Nothing watertight. Just dribs and drabs dripping away. Bit by Bit. Until pieces of the puzzle started to slot together, and pennies started to drop. Things kind of snowballed after that. Crumbs leading to pebbles and pebbles paving the way to well... dodgy dates, and dungeons in Greatham.'

'This isn't a dungeon,' Kell forced a smile. 'And nothing is dodgy.'

‘Feels like a dungeon,’ Mo gave the stocks around his neck a tap. ‘And it’s plenty dodgy. Take your explanation just now for example. Even if your mam had a miscarriage, the fact remains that, at earliest, you were born eleven months after she and Abraham split up. I’ve heard of overdue births, but this would be a tardy miracle of British Rail proportions.’

‘So what?’

‘It means Detective Lilley that you’re not Abraham’s son, and if that’s the case then you’ve been lying to both him and Davy.’

‘Nah,’ scoffed Kell. ‘You’ve muddled up the dates. Besides, we did DNA tests and both Davy and Abraham separately witnessed me place their sample in their own envelope and seal it.’

‘Yes,’ retorted Mo. ‘And half the playground saw you make a ping pong ball vanish from a plastic cup and reappear in Mr Frost’s jacket pocket. I’m sure your sleight of hand skills could stretch to a saliva swab swap.’

Kell neither confirmed nor denied anything. He just bore his eyes into the place where Mo’s own eyes remained somewhere behind his closed eyelids.

‘Talking of sleight of hand. I’m guessing – well, an educated guess - is that you somehow palmed the knife from the butcher’s and used it as a distraction. Abraham assumed I’d swiped it when Mr Shahzad told him it was missing, and given that two sharp murder weapons were deemed to be involved, it was only natural for him to assume that one of them was my work knife,’ Mo said. ‘But it miraculously reappeared clean as a whistle whereas Abraham was caught red-handed with another butcher’s knife splattered with blood from all three murders. Ironically, I think I even saw it myself when I was there at his house.’

‘So you *were* there? In his house?’ Kell’s eyebrows jolted up. ‘He was telling the truth about that all the time?’

‘Yep,’ Mo smiled. ‘Everyone seemed to think he was in cloud cuckoo land when he started accusing me of that, and I must admit I had a bit of fun playing dumb on that front. The bit about the bath and the handcuffs is also true.'

Kell gasped loudly enough for Mo to hear.

'Anyway, back to the knife,' Mo continued. 'Hiding it in plain sight. Did you just tell him it was yours? Did you even mention it at all? My guess is that you just left it lying next to the chopping board and wait for him to dab his prints all over it. I bet you couldn't believe your luck when he then took it to my mam's. Leaving the murder weapon in the kitchen of the detective leading the investigation, it's not only bold, but it's a stroke of genius Kell... Well, almost.'

'Almost?'

'Well, it would have been if you hadn't left any other clues pointing back to yourself. Well, more other bits of breadcrumbs than clues,' Mo replied. 'Take the book on Islam that they found in Abraham's house. The one the prosecution made so much fuss about at the trial.'

'And rightly so as it explained the mystery numbers written in blood on the victims' bodies.'

'So it did,' Mo concurred. 'The numbers of the surahs.'

'Surahs?'

'*Chapters* then, call them what you will,' Mo expanded. 'The fact of the matter is that the numbers weren't random but represented titles of surahs in the Quran that built up a picture. So, on Alex's body; 58 The Pleading Woman. 12 Joseph. 14 Abraham. 82 The Cleaving Asunder. 98 The Clear Proof.'

'Yes,' Kell nodded. 'That's typical Abraham. He's so cock sure of himself that he even incriminated himself in the clues and thought no one would ever work it out.'

'You did,' Mo said. 'As I understand it, you're the detective who cracked the code.'

'Yeah well, it was a stroke of luck rather than splitting the atom,' Kell shrugged. 'I was flicking through the book on Islam in Abraham's house and I noticed some markings. The names of some of the chapters were underlined and some of the numbers were circled.'

'In thick pencil?'

'Yes, as it happens.'

'Probably a soft pencil. A 6B pencil? The kind used by an artist.'

'Maybe,' Kell replied. 'I can't say I took much notice of the actual pencil. It's hardly important.'

'And I take it you also noticed similar markings next to the entries for the numbers found on Davy's body too; 87 The Highest. 104 The Slanderer. 56 The Inevitable. 101 The Striking Hour.'

'Yes, that's right. Abraham always hated Davy. He even threatened to kill him a day or two before actually murdering him.'

'How convenient,' Mo closed his eyes again. 'Did you notice any other markings in the book Kell?'

'No, why?'

'Oh, it's just that when I was at Abraham's house I checked out his tiny bookshelf and did think it odd that he had a thick, dusty hardback on Islam.'

'So?'

'So, he isn't the scholarly type. And he's openly displayed his hated of Muslims. Notably, a fifth of his book collection was on Islam,' Mo elaborated. 'Does that sound right to you?'

'Sure,' Kell explained. 'He was reading up on the enemy, probably drumming up more ways of how to frame you.'

'Possibly,' replied Mo. 'But that doesn't explain the pencil or the rubbing out.'

Kell curled up his nose. 'Eh?'

‘I thought I’d opened the book at random. But it wasn’t really random, the book opened at the page on surahs, probably because that’s the page it had been bookmarked. If you look closely then there is some smudging around some of the surahs,’ Mo buffed the bench with a fingertip and it made a squeaking noise. ‘As if someone had rubbed out some marks. Circles and underlining it seemed to me.’

‘So?’

‘So, I thought it was significant that there were markings for surah 4, The Women, and surah 65, Divorce. It’s as if someone initially intended to use these as numbers for clues on Davy’s body then changed their mind. Probably not to incriminate themselves.’

‘That’s news to me. It doesn’t mean anything anyway. Abraham scrawled something with a pencil then rubbed it out. So what?’

‘Well, there’s another funny thing,’ Mo clicked his fingers. ‘6B isn’t a typical pencil. It’s more something that an artist would buy in a specialist shop.’

‘Yeah, and?’

‘And Abraham isn’t an artist,’ Mo illuminated. ‘I can’t remember seeing a single pencil in his house, let alone a canvass and easel. Not like your mam for example. She uses 6B pencils. I happened to notice a couple in her library.’

‘Mam likes drawing, of course she has pencils,’ snorted Kell. ‘So what? Art isn’t exactly a niche pastime for the privileged. It’s enjoyed by thousands of people.’

‘So, if we got forensics down here and they checked the lead, or graphite or whatever it is these days, in your mam’s pencil and compared it to the samples on the book they won’t match? Is that what you’re saying? Because I’m pretty sure they would.’

‘How could you possibly be sure of a thing like that?’ Kell sneered. ‘Even if forensics could check such things, the odds of an exact match would be astronomical. Like Kim Jong Un becoming Pope, the royal family moving to Beirut or you finding a girlfriend.'

'Oh, I'm not so sure,' Mo said flatly. 'The markings on the book on Islam are dead ringers for those on other books in your library. The bold, marginally sloping straight lines and the ovals that go past 360 degrees to around 400 degrees in a slight concentric circle, tapering off in a little curly flourish. Both sets were done with the same hand alright. I'm sure of that.'

Kell snorted again and shook his head.

'There's also the question of the gap in the bookshelves,' Mo continued. 'That library is jam-packed full of books. I could only find one gap. Just big enough for one thick hardback. And guess what section it's in?'

'No idea,' said Kell. 'The astrophysics section? It sounds like a supermassive black hole in your theory.'

'I think it's more fact than theory,' rebounded Mo. 'And the fact that the gap is in the religion section, and that your mam's index cards indicate that there should be a copy of the 'Insights into the Quran' book on Islam sitting pretty on the shelf suggests that the book in Abraham's house came from your library.'

'You'd never prove it.'

'Maybe, maybe not,' Mo replied. 'But I dare say that with all the new-fangled technology these days, if there is any connection to be made then some bobby boffin could find it by fingerprints, bits of dead skin, stray hairs and such like. And failing that then I'm pretty sure a graphologist would verify the uncanny resemblance of the markings between the book bagged up as evidence at the station and those in your library.'

'Pish! You're clutching at fantasy straws Blenkinsopp.'

'You say that, and maybe you're right, a few squiggles on a piece of paper is probably not conclusive, even if my suspicions on that matter are confirmed.'

'Well then.'

'But then there's the murder weapon of course,' Mo paused before continuing. 'That's a completely different kettle of fish.'

'The knife has been examined from top to bottom in forensic detail,' Kell snapped. 'It has Alex's, Davy's and your mam's blood on it as well as Abraham's, fingerprints. This is well established already.'

'Yes, but the coroner suggested that for Alex and Davy's murders two blades were potentially involved in the decapitation; the butcher's knife has proved a match, but there's still the question of the other extremely sharp blade.'

'Yes, well that second one is still a mystery, if indeed there was a second weapon.'

'I don't think it's such a mystery any longer,' Mo tapped the side of the guillotine and held his breath as the blade wobbled above him. 'I think I'm looking right at it.'

'Rubbish! Call in forensics to check the blade if you like, it'll be as clean as a whistle.'

'I don't doubt it,' Mo agreed. 'As mentioned, it looks brand new. No doubt the blood-soaked, original blade is at the bottom of the North Sea by now. Even so, there'll be records of the niche purchase, as well as traces of the victims' blood, if not on the varnished wooden frame, then at least in the untreated exposed grooves that the blade travels down. That's an oversight on your part Kell. I'm surprised you didn't think of that. Or maybe you did? You talk about Abraham, but perhaps overconfidence has clouded your judgement too.'

Kell ground his teeth together and dug his nails into the heel of his hand.

'In fact, I can see a tiny splash of red in one of the grooves right now,' Mo tilted his head back in the stocks. 'There's no need for microscopes because at least one bloodstain is there. Minuscule but as clear as day. A pound to a penny says the base of your guillotine also matches the mystery rectangular impression I spotted at Alex's murder scene as well. I bet the base of your guillotine has traces of mud that match the park murder scenes too. The boffins would match that alright.'

'Just assuming, hypothetically, that this ridiculous fable of yours has legs Blenkinsopp,' Kell gave the guillotine a study slap. 'How the hell do you think me, or anyone else for the matter got this big thing all the way to Ward Jackson Park and back without arousing suspicion? It's ludicrous!'

'Er,' Mo waited until the blade had stopped trembling before continuing. 'Yes, I did wonder that myself, but then I noticed the new extra cuts in the top and bottom quarters of the frame. You can feel them just by running your finger along. The grain of the wood feels different to the joints in the middle. Coarser. Fresher. I'm guessing they haven't been there that long, probably only as long ago as you drummed up the basis of your plot. But the fact is that your fold-in-half guillotine has recently been converted into a fold-into-quarters model. Small enough to fit into a shoulder bag for example. Easy to cart around. No one any the wiser.'

Kell put his hands to his hips and stared down at Mo, heavy breaths and grinding teeth. Noises filtered through from the hallway. High pitched giggles and little feet running upstairs to the playroom. Kell listened as the footsteps faded and his gaze returned to the prone Mo. After half a dozen more seconds and a little chuckle, he began to clap slowly. 'Very good. I'll give you this Blenkinsopp, you're not as dumb as you look. But that doesn't say much considering you've unwittingly got yourself trapped, helpless and defenceless under an instrument of death. Actually, I take that back. You *are* as dumb as you look. Talk about landing yourself in the shit. You've just talked yourself into hell's putrid sewerage works.'

'You won't kill me.' Mo said flatly.

'Dumb *and* deluded!' Kell roared and banged his fist on the bench. 'Do you think I'm going to take Abraham's place in prison? Really? That just isn't going to happen. I guess this is goodbye Mo. I'd say it's been a pleasure knowing you but I'm just about done with bullshit for today.'

Kell made a cut-throat gesture, belted the blade like a punchbag and laughed insanely as it clashed, banged and clattered above Mo's head.

Mo jarred his head towards the door.

Kell sprang over to the jukebox and turned the volume to full just as Mo called, 'Mrs Lilley!'

'No one can hear you.' He sauntered back head-banging along to Lemmy from *Motörhead's* gruff rantings about a black card and placed his hand on the guillotine's lever.

Mo snaked and twisted in the stocks, reached his left hand up and flicked a small button up on that side of the guillotine's frame.

'Now, now Mo,' leave the little button alone. Kell flicked the button back down. 'Are you going to let all this nonsense drop?'

'No! Never!' Mo writhed in the stocks, legs flailing and hand desperately clawing at Kell's hand that protected the button. He yowled as Kell bent his wrist back, forced it onto the bench, then kneeled his full body weight onto it. Mo wriggled and contorted in an attempt to free it and he gawked as the blade above his head rattled, glistened and shook. With his left hand still stuck he frenziedly tugged at Kell's knee with his right hand, his head bashing around in the stocks like a pinball as his tugs frantically turned into slaps, shoves then a battery of punches. The guillotine juddered and the bench clanked and jumped as Mo lashed about and Kell cackled like a maniac. He caught Mo's fist in his palm, jammed it under the other knee and made another cut-throat gesture. Mo's eyes widened and ballooned to tree frog proportions as Kell applied increasing pressure on the release switch, like a trigger. Mo's shot a glance to the mirror on the wall and the reflection of the cleanly severed logs and his mind flashed back to the red splattered watermelon. He wanted to roar through his lion-sized gape but all he could hear were toothless grunts and fraught gasps as Lemmy's pneumatic bass pounded and thrashed and his own heart hammered and thumped and the trigger pulled and a crack rang out. Beth burst in with a piercing shriek, the door crashed on its hinges and the mirror plunged and splintered as the blade shuddered

...then plummeted down.

Chapter Forty-Nine

Beth shrieked like the Antarctic wind as the blade slammed home and blood spattered over her bare legs and feet.

Kell bounded over and caught his stricken mother in his arms just before her trembling limbs gave way.

'Why?' she pounded his chest hard with the flat of her fist.

'He asked for it,' Kell crunched over the broken glass and laid his quaking mother on the sofa. 'Coming here like a big brash know-it-all and throwing accusations about. He got what was coming to him!'

***

'Threatening me in my own house,' Kell spat as he gently picked out a shard from his mother's calf. 'Threatening to destroy everything we've worked so hard to pull off.'

'But you didn't have to go to such extremes,' rebuked Beth. 'It's not you. It's not us. And it's not what we agreed we'd do if things ever came to it.'

Mo tapped his head in a few places, just to make sure it was still there, then scratched it. 'I didn't *threaten* you with anything, and I didn't *know it all*. I still don't. All I had were some suspicions. I primarily came for answers.'

'How did you know I wouldn't kill you?'

'You don't have it in you Kell,' Mo said. 'I remember the crowd baying for that bully Bradley's blood when you had him pinned to the playground after he had whacked you with a brick. You just tossed the brick away as he'd begged for mercy and walked off.'

'But you thought I had it in me to kill when I flicked the button,' Kell said. 'You moron Blenkinsopp, it's in safety mode when it's down. I'd already switched it earlier when your eyes were closed. You were fighting me to try to chop your own head off.'

'Whoops!' Mo exhaled long and hard.

'You thought I was going to kill you though, didn't you?'

'Well, it did start to look pretty bleak,' Mo squirmed around in the stocks. 'It still doesn't look all that cosy to be perfectly honest.'

'Here let me,' Kell flicked the catch and released Mo.

'I must apologise for Kell Mo,' Beth said. 'We always knew it could come to this. We knew the risks and we know the consequences. Are you going to call the police? I suppose you must. Kell and I already agreed to go gracefully if discovered.'

'Just a shame you wouldn't let it drop,' Kell sighed heavily.

Mo stood up and stretched. 'Like I said, I came to find answers.'

Beth patted an empty spot on the huge sofa and Mo made his way beside her. 'If anyone deserves answers it's you. Where would you like to start Mo?'

'*Who? What? Why?* are as good a starting point as any.'

'I killed them both,' Kell piped up with raised hands. 'Mam had nothing to do with it.'

'*Kell*,' Beth's eyes bore into those of her son's, then softened. 'Please, the truth. Mo deserves the truth.'

Kell looked away and down.

'You must understand Mo,' Beth fidgeted with her hands and twisted her wedding ring. 'That I've always believed I'm a good person, a loyal wife, a loving mother.'

'No doubt about it,' Kell interjected vociferously. 'You *are* a good person, and a *fantastic* mam.'

Kell plonked down on a pouffe opposite Mo. 'One thing you've got to understand is the wretched, pitiful life my mam has had to endure all because of that, *those*, scum.'

'You don't have to tell me about Davy,' Mo said. 'I know first-hand that he was a nasty piece of work.'

'Oh yeah?' Kell snorted. 'Do you know about the rapes, the physical abuse, the mental turmoil?'

Mo let his eyes fall on Beth and he shook his head.

'Go on Mam, show him the cuts,' Kell pushed. 'The many bruises have since faded, but Davy has still left his mark all over her, inside and out.'

Beth shook her head and shushed Kell, but he encouraged her with a nod and imploring offspring eyes. After a bit more hesitation, and a tad more reassurance she stood up, loosened the gown around her bathing costume and let it slip to the floor, exposing twig-like limbs; burnt, scarred and abnormally jutting in places.

Mo gasped. 'Sorry Mrs Lilley, I had no idea.'

'Join the club! I was oblivious too,' Kell huffed. 'Well, semi-oblivious. I mean I thought something was up. *Knew* something was up, but you know how it is. When your mam tells you everything's just fine you believe her don't you? When she laughs about just tripping down some steps, you give her the benefit of the doubt. When she takes to sporting sunglasses because of *sensitivity to the light* you go along with it. In fact, you believe every last little white lie that comes out of her sweet quavering lips until one night when you're seventeen you hear a seven-foot bearded brute clattering down the stairs, slamming the front door shut then driving off. Nothing unusual about that. The difference this time is that there's a weird whimpering noise coming from the master bedroom. The one you've been explicitly told never to go into. But this time you do go in. You and the contents of your stomach soon wish you hadn't. But you do go in. You do see your own naked mother chained to a bedpost. You do see the red. On her. On the sheets. Behind your eyelids. Exploding in your head.'

'I'm...'

'Lost for words?' Kell broke in. 'So was I. So was Mam. But you told me. Didn't you? Eventually.'

Beth forced a smile and nodded silently, wiping away a tear as she replaced the robe and retook her place on the sofa.

'So, it turns out that my so-called father wasn't just a hoodlum, a gangster, call him what you will, but also a sadistic, rapist, control-freak bully who made my mam's life a living nightmare,' Kell flung a log at the cue rack and sent the lot clattering to the ground. 'She had a friend once. Kevin. Used to sit and chat with him, till one day he vanished.'

'Where...?'

'No one knows,' Kell shrugged. 'But you don't just leave your dog, possessions and house behind without so much as a by your leave? Do you?'

Mo shook his head slowly.

'Since then my mam has been terrified of talking to, let alone forming any sort of friendships with people,' Kell said. 'Little wonder she locked herself away here, even while Davy was making a mockery of her by shagging anything with lipstick and a pulse.'

'Is that where Alex came into all this?' Mo asked gently.

'Alex pretty much set this whole situation in motion,' Kell spat.

'For the four months or so I knew her, she became my best friend.' Beth chipped in solemnly. 'But she let me down.'

'*Let you down*?' barked Kell. 'She did a whole lot more than that mother.'

Kell booted at a pool cue by his feet. 'You said Mo deserved the truth, and the truth is she was a manipulative, scheming whore who, not content with prising the love of your life, Joe Abraham, away from you, also went as far as to set you up with the one man she was certain would put a stranglehold on you. And Alex knew that because he had all but had her in a noose around her neck too a few years beforehand. In fact, it later transpired that she only managed to rid herself of him by tricking him into believing she had AIDS.'

Mo turned his head and looked directly into Beth's eyes. 'Is that right?'

'Yes,' she nodded. 'Alex and I met in a bar and clicked straight away. We started going out together every Saturday night. Terrible twins knocking back tequilas and having a giggle. But that all got scuppered when I got pregnant. Alex dressed it up as empathy of course; *I can't drag you out boozing, what with the baby*. The dear, compassionate, apparent saint reincarnated. But it was all calculated. *You'll still come with me Joe won't you though? Just as friends of course. Don't want you getting any wrong ideas!* And the crazy thing is, that I went along with it. Encouraged it. Trusted him. Trusted them.'

Beth blew her nose. Kell snuggled in beside her and gently massaged her shudders.

'They kept the affair secret for a while,' Beth sniffed. 'But things changed. Joe changed. And there were signs. Humungous signs in retrospect.'

'How?' Mo asked.

'He made me have an abortion for a start,' Beth sobbed. 'My little girl. My beautiful little girl.'

'My sister,' Kell's eyes fumed. He wound his mother up to his chest and gently rocked her.

'I begged him not to make me do it,' tears cascaded down Beth's cheeks. 'But he was adamant. Probably with Alex's encouragement, he gave me some cock and bull story about it not being right for him to conceive a child out of wedlock. Bloody baloney I know *now*. Ah but then he had this beguiling, spell-bounding Joe-ness about him and when my head stopped spinning and my ears had stopped ringing from my own sobs, wailing and pleading I woke up and realised that he'd somehow just made me do the most terrible thing imaginable.'

Mo snorted and ground his teeth.

'Then, that same afternoon, he dropped me back home. Babyless and broken-hearted and hobbling up the garden path.'

Beth sniffed twice, wiped her cheeks then took a moment to compose herself. Fire and ice in her eyes.

'He didn't even make it over the threshold,' Beth caught her voice. 'Just plonked my bag on the front step, spun on his heels, jumped in his car and chuntered *oh yeah – you're dumped!* as he sped off.'

Certain words rushed to the tip of Mo's tongue, but he held his breath and chose not to say them.

'The ironic thing is that Alex was great. Calling me up, fussing around, making sure that I was if not alright, then at least I wasn't going to tether a lump of concrete to my ankle and hop off the pier. Though I guess I did teeter on the edge of such thoughts,' Beth went on. 'Fool I am. I thought she was being a wonderful friend, when all the time she was shacked up with my man. *Mine*. The one she'd stolen from under my very nose. And all that time she was the little blond pin that had burst my world.'

Mo shook his head and swallowed.

'And I was miserable, vulnerable and in a very black place. Otherwise, I'd never have gone along with it when she suggested I go on a date with one of her ex's, a certain Davy. She'd never mentioned him before. Ha, now I know why. But at the time she played him up and...,' Beth laughed out loud. 'It's so ironic now but at the time I thought *what the harm?* He didn't seem my type, and we had nothing in common, but he took an interest in me and I found the contrast between his Hell's Angels' look and his perfect gentleman demeanour quite alluring. And he could turn on the charm, and he knew how to treat a lady. It took a while, but I guess I even began to have some kind of feelings for him. Nothing like Joe, but *something* at least. Until...'

'Until?' Mo repeated.

'Until he snapped,' Beth put trembling hands over her face for a good few moments before lowering them again. 'It was my fault...'

'It wasn't your fault!' Kell broke in.

'Well, I blame myself to some degree, me and my shamelessness, but after numerous unanswered calls and text messages, Joe finally replied to one of them, and said he come around to my place to get the engagement ring back, 'Beth scrunched up her eyes and sucked up a sharp breath of air through her teeth. 'All I wanted was to show him how much I loved him, and how far I'd go to win him back. You'd do that for the love of your life. Right? Davy had only been in the picture for two minutes, and it's not as if I saw a clear future with him or we were a steady item or anything. Joe, on the other hand, well he was always the one for me. So, I told him that. Poured my heart out to him I said that I'd forgive him. That I'd still marry him. And that I still wanted to bear his children.'

'And?'

'And, well, he took the last part a bit too literally and we ended up breaking the bed.'

'Oh, I see,' Mo took in a breath through his own teeth too.

'Unfortunately, so did Davy,' Beth coughed. 'It cost me a few bruises and my first broken bone, but I managed to keep Joe's name out of it, even though I suspect Davy already knew. After that, we pretty much skipped the courting formalities and I went straight onto more or less forced marriage, semi-incarceration and long-term abject misery. And whatever the light at the end of the tunnel I held onto initially – well that just kept on getting smaller and smaller with each turning day. If anything, the green-eyed monster in Davy flared and bared his teeth more and more with each tiny transgression or trivial 'perceived' incident. If I hadn't got to him first, he would have killed me one of these days. I'm certain of it.'

Mo clasped his hands, gave a little shake of the head and sighed heavily.

'The hospital has Mam's records and there are X-rays if you want to check for yourself Mo,' Kell added.

Mo waved away the very thought with a shake of the index finger.

'But does that mean?' Mo hesitated. 'Does that mean that you are Abraham's son after all Kell? If your mam slept with him after the initial breakup, then the dates could tally after all.'

'Yep,' Kell shrugged. 'It's hardly anything to be proud of, but my real biological father is indeed the same person who treated my mother unspeakably and who also paid to have my unborn sister killed.'

'So, I was wrong about the DNA switching then.'

'Not really,' Kell explained. 'I didn't know who my father was either until we didn't a preliminary test using some strands of Davy's beard hair and discovered that it wasn't him. If it had been, I'd have switched the samples when we took them from Davy and Abraham afterwards. While we're at it I should own up to the fact that it wasn't Abraham who put your contact details on Alex's phone. My mam did that and it was me who gave her your number. Similarly, I palmed your *Allah is Great* card and gave it to Mam to plant at Davy's scene – purely to make it look like Abraham was setting you up of course. The same goes for the markings in the Islam book at his place. We didn't expect you to incriminate yourself up to your eyeballs!'

'It's true Mo,' Beth added. 'The rationale was that if there were circumstantial titbits from you at the scene, but it later transpired that you had an alibi, then it would pretty much prove that someone was setting you up. The last thing we expected was for you to get embroiled, and with motive, no alibi and swimming in damning DNA evidence.'

'By the way,' continued Kell. 'You were right about the butcher's knife too. Although sleight of hand didn't come into it. It was more a case of a good old-fashioned *stuffing it inside my jacket when no one was looking*. After Davy's death, I popped into Shahzad's as a matter of routine and slid it back under a unit when he wasn't looking.'

'And what about the butcher's knife at Abraham's place?'

'It's one we've had for years. Wearing gloves, Mam brought it back to the house after that first night in the park with Alex then snuck out with it again while Davy pounded punchbags in his gym to music. Mam's tiny, but a good climber. She knew the tree Davy would head for so lay in wait high up,' Kell continued. 'And after finishing Davy off she passed the knife back to me as I drove to Abraham's to pick him up. As you worked out, I left it on the chopping board next to some cuts of meat. But I swear I didn't know that he'd use it on your mam Mo. That was never part of the plan.'

'I believe you,' said Mo. 'It's lucky I'm now veggie otherwise I may have picked it up when I was cooking my dinner. So, what was the knife for? Just to set Abraham up with?'

'Yep, Mam's titchy and not the strongest. She couldn't have killed anyone with it,' Kell squeezed Beth's hand. 'Just a swift blow to the head with a rounders bat to disable them, a nick with the knife, then a click of a lever to set the guillotine blade hurtling down from a height. Over quick as a flash. And yes, I did get it converted so that it folds into quarters. You were right about that too.'

Beth tugged and clawed at one particular finger. Mo noticed that it was red raw. He clocked the deep lines on her brow too. 'One thing I must stress,' she said, 'Is that I do believe Davy's death was self-defence, and despite everything she had done to me, I wouldn't have even contemplated touching a hair on Alex's head had it not been for the risk to Amy.'

'Oh?' Mo arched his eyebrows. 'What don't I know about Amy?'

'It's what you don't know about Alex, Mo' Beth said. 'Not Amy.'

'Her drinking, and the consequences of it,' Kell took up the baton. 'Her drinking probably contributed to Abraham and Alex's split too. Well, that and the fact that neither of them could keep it in their trousers.'

'What do you mean by *consequences?*' Mo asked.

'Amy is my brother's daughter,' explained Beth. 'I'll be the first to admit that Mick has problems, issues and bad attitude pouring out of every orifice. He's no dad of the year, and never will be.'

'So, what then?'

'The point is that despite all his many shortcomings,' Beth closed her eyelids for a couple of seconds before opening them and continuing. 'My brother would never, never, sell his daughter, or deliberately put her in danger.'

'And Alex?'

'Ah Alex,' Kell rounded his sigh off with an ironic smile. 'Alex would serve up her own kid up on a plate to the Devil for the price of a bottle.'

'An over-exaggeration surely,' Mo commented.

'You'd think so,' Kell replied. 'Apparently, Abraham did get a tipoff a few years ago about Jade, but when he confronted Alex, she denied everything and either hoodwinked or sweet-talked him into not pursuing things.'

'What about Jade?'

'Alex was pimping her out to dirty old men,' Kell raged. 'She had some sort of deal going down with the owner of the Station Inn - free fags and booze downstairs in return for allowing some of the punters to,' Kell made air quotation marks, "*babysit*" Jade upstairs.'

Mo snorted heavily and clenched his fists tight as his eyes glazed over.

'It was effectively just hearsay and so no charges were ever brought,' Beth added. 'But after Jade's death the rumours never went away and one night Mick overheard a drunk bragging about *babysitting*. Unsurprisingly, he beat the truth out of the guy, grabbed Amy from Alex and marched her away in her pram.'

'It's the best thing he's ever done in his whole life for that girl, and notably Alex didn't lift a finger to stop him,' Kell offered. 'That was four years ago, and in all that time Alex didn't even ask after Amy, let alone send her a birthday card or drive a couple of miles up the road to see her.'

'Until around three years ago that is,' said Beth. 'Then she suddenly comes to see me, quite out of the blue. Before then I hadn't heard a dickie bird from her for over twenty years. Since before Kell was born. It's the first time she'd even been to the house, even though we are related through Mick.'

'She came to see you?' Mo rubbed his chin. 'Why you?'

'Well, truth be told our Mick has gone off the rails somewhat since his last tour,' sighed Amy. 'And even before he was invalided back to Blighty it was me who has been bringing Amy up.'

'You're like a second mam to her I bet,' said Mo.

'More like a first and only mam,' Kell gave his mother a tender peck on the cheek. 'No one loves that girl more than you, that's for sure.'

'Well, she *is* adorable,' Beth's lips tweaked upwards. 'Mick used to take her whenever he was back, but when he lost his legs that all changed. Initially, he'd visit here, or we would go around to his place or meet at the soft play, but before long he started making up excuses, telling lies, hiding behind his curtains. Shouting at us to effing *do one!* through his letterbox.'

'Oh!'

'Oh indeed Mo,' Beth said. 'And it just seemed to escalate from there. The drinking, the rage, the anger. He put that punter I mentioned in traction, but somehow managed to '*persuade*' him to drop the charges. Mick's out of control and needs help. I know that, and maybe even he knows that. He told me that he doesn't want Amy to be around him right now. Says he *can't be doing with her*. Says he's *not dad material*. He says a lot of things. Some truth. Some nonsense. Maybe he's just scared of what he's capable of – or what she might see. Either way, and as paradoxical as this sounds, I do believe he's putting Amy's best interests at heart. Which is more than can be said of Alex.'

'What about Alex?'

'Like I said, she turned up here one night stinking of booze and shouting the odds,' Beth closed her eyes and shuddered. 'She said that she'd heard that Mick was off his head on drugs most nights, that Amy was living with me – without her consent - and that she had come to take her back.'

'Oh?'

'That's not all,' continued Beth. 'I was alone in the house at the time. Davy was on some "business" and Kell was out at the time, not that she'd ever clapped eyes on him before. Naturally, she had given my side of the family a wide berth ever since that business with Joe. Anyway, while she was ranting away, I managed to covertly click to call Mick. He overheard her racket, rushed straight around and barged in like crazed stormtrooper.'

'And things kind of exploded from there.' Kell made a sound like a bomb going off and expanded his hands like a nuclear mushroom. 'Mick ended up shaking Alex wildly about by the throat and threatening to snap her in two. Mam had to trip him over, nab one of his legs and hurriedly bundle Alex down the past village to the dual carriageway where Mam managed to hail a taxi.'

'It was a cold starry night with a biting wind and heavy drizzle,' reminisced Beth. 'I don't know if it was that or Mick's attack that had sobered her up, but by the time we got to the dual carriageway she had gone from raving banshee to totally silent. Eerily silent. It was like a plunged dagger jammed my heart stone dead when she finally spoke, and then rampaging rhinoceroses pogoing on it by the time she'd finished.'

Mo knotted his brow. 'Why? What did she say?'

'It was an ultimatum,' Beth cupped her chin in her palms and shook her head. Mo noticed more scars on both wrists. 'Either I somehow bump Mick off – and she suggested I asked Davy to do that – *as if!* - or she'd get a court order for custody of Amy and she'd make damn sure none of us would ever see Amy ever again.'

'Did you believe her?'

'Absolutely,' Beth looked Mo straight in the eye. 'I tried to reason with her, I told her we'd heard all the rumours and tried telling her that the courts wouldn't allow it.'

'And?'

'She lit up a cigarette, took a long drag and admitted it all, as cool as you like. *Yep, it's all true. Jade needed to pay her way, just as Amy will if she lives under my roof. But hey, no crime was ever officially reported, and as far as the courts are concerned, I'm as squeaky clean as a snow-white mouse. Unlike that brother of yours...'*

'Like I said,' Kell spat. 'Pure scum. And that's not all.'

'Oh?'

'Yes,' Beth took a moment to compose herself. 'She said that as an alternative option to killing Mick, for the right price she might be willing to talk to the adoption people and sign Amy over to me.

'I think fifty grand should just about cover it,' she whispered as she slid into the taxi. 'Deano's got a new contract up in Aberdeen and we're going away for at least six months, probably more if his contract gets renewed. That's all the time you've got to give me everything I want - or else! Time is ticking. Tick, tick, tock!'

'So, you see what we were dealing with?' Kell said. 'Mam was left in an impossible position. Lose her brother. Lose Amy. Pay a ransom to just *possibly* save Amy – if you believed Alex would sign her over once cash changed hands.'

'And I take it that you didn't believe her?' Mo said.

'Not really,' Beth balled two fistfuls of her long black hair up in front of her face and sighed. 'But we paid her the money anyway.'

'Oh,' Mo's eyes narrowed. 'It's a lot of money. Did Davy give it to you?'

Beth and Kell both chuckled.

'Davy? You've gotta be kidding!' Kell crinkled an eyebrow. 'He was a very rich man, but Mam never saw a penny more than the pocket money pittance he used to allow her.'

'So how then?'

'With my share of the inheritance from my mother's house when she passed away around that time,' Beth explained. 'I actually received £85,000 but only gave Davy £35,000 and said there would have been more but for debts. I didn't elaborate on the fact that the *debts* weren't my mother's but the £50k due to Alex.'

'How come you gave Davy the rest anyway?'

'He was more than just a vicious bully,' Kell's eyes steamed. 'He was a megalomaniac control freak who thought, no, who *did* own every part of Mam – her possessions, her body, her mind.'

Mo shook his head slowly. 'And I'm guessing Alex subsequently came back for more?'

'Yes, around a year ago she demanded another £100k with the same ultimatum,' Beth wiped a tear with her hair. 'Kill Mick, lose Amy or cough up a fortune – which we didn't have, within 12 months...

...Or the alternative.'

'And I guess you chose the alternative.'

'What choice did we have? Time was nearly up on her ultimatum, said Kell. 'She buzzed our intercom a few days before we launched into action and held up three pictures; one with a red cross over Mick's head, one with a huge wad of money under the caption '10 days to go,' and one saying 'for sale' over Amy.'

'We just couldn't see any other way out,' Beth blubbered. 'For what it's worth, it was my plan, not Kell's. Though Kell did play a smaller part. For example, he rang me to tell me he'd called Joe and had baited him with the news that Alex was horny and heading towards the park...'

'Hang on,' Mo interrupted. 'I always thought that someone was watching me that night. Was it you?'

'Yes, well after Kell's call I drove over and watched Alex from a distance, but I couldn't help noticing you and Mick too. I then headed around the back of the park while avoiding CCTV,' Beth wiped some tears. 'Kell's only other involvement entailed setting things up so it looked like Joe was framing you.'

'How did you know that Alex and Abraham would end up in the park together?' Mo asked.

'I joined the police at 17 – primarily because I thought if I could somehow gather evidence against Davy, and protect a witness, or be a witness myself, then someday I could help get him banged up for life,' explained Kell. 'So, as a copper, I've known Abraham for some time.'

'But Abraham didn't know you were his son?'

'Not initially. I only *'reunited'* with Joe on the long-lost dad front when Alex hit us with the first blackmail demand - not just so I could move from uniform to CID, but also to gain his trust and keep tabs on him and Alex. Mam always suspected that they would never be able to keep their mitts off each other,' said Kell. 'After I moved in with him, I followed him on a few of his *midnight walks* to the park and copped eyefuls of them getting it on under Davy's tree. She and Joe had quite a regular thing going whenever she was back in town.'

'And I copped a few eyefuls that night with Alex too Mo – including you wobbling on the railings and tumbling back on the pavement side before you staggered away,' Beth said. 'I also overheard Joe suggest to Alex that the next time they had sex they should do it without a condom. Alex was a bit tipsy and quipped that the last time they did that she'd had Jade.'

'Ah,' Mo nodded.

'Joe was furious,' Beth continued. 'He shook her about and demanded to know if that and the rumours about Jade being sold for sex were true. She laughed it off as a joke of course, and Joe eventually cooled down a tad. But he was by no means convinced. He quickly got dressed and stormed off, promising to *get the truth out of Haze in the morning*.'

'And he did just that.' revealed Mo. 'I know because I quizzed Haze about it yesterday.'

'What?' Kell raised an eyebrow. 'How come?'

'Because of the timing issue.'

'Timing issue?' Kell's brow snaked.

'Yes, in court Haze disclosed that she'd told Abraham about Jade, but no one asked her when exactly,' said Mo. 'It was assumed she'd told him before the murder – giving him motive – but if that were true, I doubt that Abraham would have just shaken Alex about and given her a couple of bruises. So, my feeling was that Haze didn't spill the beans beforehand, and that Abraham didn't know the full truth, until *after* Alex had been killed.'

'I bet Abraham was livid when he finally got the truth,' commented Kell. 'Actually, thinking about it. Davy insinuated something about Abraham having motive involving Jade. I bet Davy will have had a fling with Haze too and she'd let it slip.'

'Maybe, but it'd have been before Abraham got the truth out of her,' said Mo. 'Abraham had threatened to put Haze's ex-con Dad away, and also make her life a living hell if she blabbed. Amongst other things, Abraham wouldn't have wanted word to get around that he'd failed to investigate the rumours, and that his blinkered blundering had cost his own daughter her life.'

'It was before my time in the force,' Kell caught Mo's eye. 'But you must know that I'd never brush anything like that under the carpet.'

Mo gave a little nod then turned to Beth as she took up the baton.

'Another thing you should realise is that Kell also did what he could to help you, such as dissuading Joe from arresting you when he was going to, deleting a jihadi video from your PC and dashing to try to save you and your mam when he realised you were in danger.'

Kell squeezed his mother's hand.

'The jihadi video was from an unsolicited source routed through an IP address in Alexandria, Syria. I'd jotted down some details, and was trying to find out who sent it before deleting it myself,' explained Mo. 'Believe me, I'm just as appalled at such atrocious acts as you - as are the vast majority of Muslims. It gave me horrendous nightmares. I once woke up shaking and covered in sweat. I might have even been screaming *Allāhu Akbar* too.'

Beth nodded and wiped a torrent of tears with the back of her hand.

I see you're distressed Mrs Lilley, it's understandable,' Mo got to his feet. 'I'll be on my way.'

Beth unburied her head from Kell's chest. 'And you'll tell the police?'

'Yes,' Mo coughed. 'I'm afraid I'll have to.'

'Yes, of course,' Beth nodded before snuggling into one of Kell's biceps and closing her eyes.

'Kell,' Mo motioned.

'Yes?'

'You're a policeman aren't you?'

'Er, yes.'

'Good,' said Mo. 'I've a crime to report. A double murder no less. A somewhat ingenious crime committed by the fair hand of scandalous ruffian, Beth Lilley no less, and ably assisted and abetted by her infamous, cad of a son, Kell.'

Beth opened her eyes again and exchanged quizzical looks with Kell.

'There,' Mo wiped his palms together then made strides towards the door. 'That's my civil duty done. I guess what the police do with this snippet of information is entirely up to them.'

'Beth knotted her brow and looked from Mo to Kell, 'I don't quite follow. Does this mean...?'

Kell shrugged.

'And what about this?' Beth motioned Kell to tip open Davy's treasure chest. 'We don't want his dirty money.'

Mo's gape widened and stretched as its contents spilled out across the floor.

'And there's lots more where that came from in his vault,' Kell added.

Mo took a while to take in the scattered and heaped bundles of fifty-pound notes. He'd never seen more than two or three single £50s before, let alone such a bounty.

'It's your choice,' Mo eventually said, turning the door handle. 'And it's just a thought. But I suspect that in a day or so there'll be news of numerous sexual abuse victims who will need counselling and support. You might consider a donation?'

'Of course,' Beth mumbled wearily. 'They are very welcome to the whole lot. We've never had any intention of touching a penny of it.'

Kell ran a palm slowly over his mother's eyes and covered her with a throw before joining Mo in the hallway.

'We didn't mean for you to become embroiled in all of this. The idea was just to make it look like Abraham was setting you up. I was as surprised as anyone when you failed to come up with alibis and everything somehow pointed to you.'

'I believe you,' Mo pulled at the heavy wooden door. 'But why me?'

'It was that night at the party. It just jumped out at me when I was looking at you and Alex in the reflection of the window.'

'Ah, so you were smiling at that revelation, and not yourself,' Mo stroked his chin. 'She'd had just given me the evils, told me to scram and called me a *square shit*. Damn rude she was, though my reflection told me that she did have a point. It's when I pocketed Saboor's scissors and decided to change both my hair and my entire look.'

'Yes, it was you and Alex giving each other daggers that set things off for me,' Kell explained. 'Mam and I already had the idea to kill Alex and Davy jihadi style and set up anti-Islamist Abraham for it, but looking at you in the reflection that night it just dawned on me that your involvement would be the icing on the cake, and hopefully the perfect nail in Abraham's coffin. God knows why, but he had it in for you, and that was common knowledge.'

Mo nodded. 'And I guess the fact that I'm Muslim and I'd also had run-ins with Davy and Alex that night was the cherry on the icing on the cake?'

Kell smiled impishly. 'Sorry Mo.'

'Well, you did rescue me at my mam's house I suppose.' Mo slapped Kell on the back. 'I haven't forgotten that.'

'There's something I haven't forgotten too,' Kell bowed his head. 'About the time you apologised to me... you were consideration incarnate, and me, well I'm appalled and deeply ashamed of my brutal *loser* dig at you.'

Mo patted Kell's shoulder. 'Think nothing of it.'

'But I do,' Kell pulled away and looked Mo square in the eye. 'I never meant a word of it. I swear to God. At the time I was just playing a wounded grieving son act. Anything else and I thought you'd twig. If there's anyone who should be apologising, it's me. Hell, I should be on my knees begging for forgiveness.

Mo felt Kell sinking down but grabbed his T-shirt and shook his head.

'You're twice the man I am Mo Blenkinsopp,' Kell straightened back up. 'Do you know that?'

Mo shook his head again. This time with a puzzled half-smile.

'About that night,' Kell turned to face Mo. Roughly the same height he looked straight into Mo's eyes from a matter of inches. Mo could feel them searching. Wondering. 'It was you, wasn't it? You who put those extra numbers on Davy's head, the ones that led me to your mam's house that night; 19 Mary. 86 The Night Visitant. 88 The Overwhelming Event. 110 The Help?'

Mo gave a wry smile and winked. 'Ah yes, that was another breadcrumb. In fact, it was the initial breadcrumb that got me thinking about your possible involvement. It didn't click at first, and certainly not in the heat of the moment, but when you did a U-turn and zoomed off earlier, it made me think back to that night, and how quickly you responded. Uncannily quickly. You must have done a sudden U-turn and mad dash that night too. Who else would have understood the code and come rushing straight to the house, other than the only other person who knew what the numbers signified?'

Kell nodded. 'You've got me there. But about that night. How come you were so sure that Abraham was going to go after your mam? According to him, it was to stop her from falsely accusing him of attempted rape. But why would she do that? And how could you be so sure he'd confront her?'

'Because…' Mo's voice caught and his eyes glazed over. 'Because I showed him a photograph that I was sure he would recognise. One of his victims. A girl in a particular patterned dress.'

'Victims plural? Not just one victim?'

'Oh yes,' Mo's jawline wobbled and he swallowed hard. 'Many more victims and the word *attempted* was a falsehood, in this case at the very least. Like I said. He's a nasty piece of work and deserves his fate.'

'You'll get no arguments from me on that front,' Kell concurred. 'But who was this girl? And what dress?'

'Just a waif of a girl from twenty years ago,' Mo said softly as he passed over the hearth. 'In a patterned dress. Flowers and butterflies.'

'Twenty years ago,' Kell eyes skipped, flashed and scanned under snaking eyebrows. 'I guess a lot can change in twenty years. Things. People. Appearances.'

'Yes,' Mo replied.

'Almost beyond recognition in fact.'

'To some observers, yes. Even completely,' Mo took a couple of steps down the driveway then turned around to face Kell. 'But maybe not to everybody.'

'No, maybe not.'

Mo looked up at the sky, squinted at the little yellow ball then walked back to Kell and held out his hand. 'I guess this goodbye.'

‘Goodbye or just so long?’ Kell asked. He took Mo’s hand, and changed the grip so that he curled and linked his fingertips like a chain and pulled him up close with a muscular arm.

Mo smiled enigmatically. ‘Who knows?’

Kell pulled Mo closer still, gripped his hand further still and whispered into his ear. ‘Well, you just take care of yourself Mohammed Blenkinsopp. Got it?’

Mo released Kell’s hand, gave a salute, span on his heels and crunched down the driveway.

‘Just one more thing,’ Kell called out in his dreadful American accent. ‘I underestimated you.’

‘Oh yeah,’ Mo replied without looking back.

‘Yes, you are as good as Columbo....’

Mo exited the gate, turned right and headed down the lane as Kell finished his sentence.’

‘...’s dog.’

Mo laughed all the way down the lane.

Chapter Fifty

As Mo eyed a big hedge on the 3-miles or so traipse back into town another little recollection chink finally dropped into place. Abraham was right, he *had* been chuntering numbers near the park that first night. The number of the big Georgian house itself, 101, followed by a slow boisterous count as he drunkenly watered its hedge. For the life of him, he couldn't remember just how far he'd counted to, but Abraham's 14 assertion certainly seemed plausible.

When Mo reached the town centre, he tapped across Avenue Road with a thick wooden stick that he'd picked up en-route. The street was pretty short in the whole scheme of things, but it outdid thoroughfares tens of times its length in terms of haphazard variety, with its jumbled walls, fences and brick structures sporadically scattered like urban centurion teeth.

Mo anticipated a potentially long wait and considered his options. Stand, sit on a wall further up the road, or just plonk himself down on the pavement. He plumped for the latter and settled into a half-lotus pose directly opposite the police station.

At 5.50 pm the west side of the street was partially shaded, and for some obscure reason, the wind seemed disproportionately stronger on that side of the road too. Mo's latest pair of shorts were nowhere near as baggy as the ones that had slipped down to his ankles in the park, even so, they still bellowed with each little gust, and goosepimples sprouted on each spindly leg.

Mo chewed a nail and contemplated why he was there and what he was going to do. He checked his hands a few times and seemed reasonably satisfied with what he saw. He also made another decision. To hand over Abraham's hard drive and little black book to the police. Yes, three life sentences were arguably already punishment enough. Even so, Mo reasoned that Abraham's many victims not only needed the specialist support that Beth's donation would help provide, but more than that, they deserved the truth. And justice. Whereas Abraham... we'll he'd made his bed, so he only had himself to blame if he had to lie in it.

Mo's mind kept returning to Jade, her gruesome end and her terrible secret. He wiped a trickling tear away, blew his nose and bitterly lamented his failure to grasp the real depths of her despair. Could the then 13-year-old Mo have saved her? Probably not. Almost certainly not. Even so, it wasn't going to stop him from beating himself up about it now. And probably for years to come. From over a thousand kids in school, Mo had struck up the greatest bond with Jade. What was the chance of that? He glanced at his hand and thought about Kell pulling him close as they bade farewell. If Mo had had but one guardian angel at school, then it was Kell. Was it all fate? Or something else?

As time went on his reverie drifted onto other things. His upbringing. His childhood. This town. It wasn't all bad. And there were plenty of people who were perfectly happy here. He knew that. He knew such people. *He* would have been happy here too if only... Ah, there were plenty of '*if onlys*'. Too many. And too much water under the bridge had passed. Besides, he was a different person now. *Different*. He looked different. He felt it. He was getting used to it. Even growing to like it. Mo tugged at an ear and wondered why the 'if onlys' still niggled him so much.

By 8.35 pm, *chattering teeth* and *pins and needles* had become the latest unwelcome additions to his niggles list. He shuffled his sit bones on the hard pavement and tapped a slow beat with the stick while bits of litter bounced along like urban tumbleweed. Mo yawned, gave his eyes a rest and just tuned into the sounds. In among the usual town centre noise of trashy bar music and disgruntled seagulls, Mo picked out another sound, one he'd heard several times over the course of the last couple of hours. The squeaky door hinge followed by a juddering clatter. Someone was either entering or exiting the police station. He opened his eyes, saw what he had been waiting for, and calmly rose to his feet and headed across the road.

‘Michael, we meet at last,’ Mo cheered. ‘Well at, least compos mentis.’

Mick glanced behind himself, looked at Mo again and scrunched his small grey eyes up. ‘Do I know you?’

‘Sort of,’ said Mo. ‘In a clinky blind date kind of way.’

‘Eh?’

‘Our voices met across a corridor and a cell wall.’

‘You’re him,’ Mick snared. ‘Blenkinsopp!’

Mo gave a wry smile, leaned the stout stick against his hip and tapped his hands together. ‘The very same.’

Mick puffed out his bodybuilder chest. ‘What the hell do you want?’

‘I come bearing gifts.’ Mo tapped the stick then twirled it around in his hands.

‘You’re off your trolly,’ Mick huffed and pointed a finger. ‘For starters, I don’t want anything from you, and secondly, I don’t even need a stick you dickhead.’

To press the point home Mick clunkily strutted a circle around Mo, eyeing him from every angle.

‘Ah,’ Mo stopped twirling the stick, threw it up in the air and caught it in one hand. ‘Well, it’s your choice, but it’s a shame as you’re going to need it shortly.’

‘What the hell are you on about?’ Mick’s laugh got hijacked mid-*ha* by his smoker’s cough. ‘Are you trying to threaten me?’

‘What was it you said you’d do to me?’ Mo closed his eyes and pressed the end of his index finger against his forehead. ‘Oh yes, *punch my teeth out right through my pimply arse*. It’s not the most eloquent turn of phrase I’ve ever heard, but if you want to try your luck then now’s as good a time as any.’

‘What? A weedy little prick like you!’ Mick cackled. ‘Do you know who I am? What I do?’

Mo leaned on the stick. 'Yes, you're the racist bully who deliberately mows down innocent people, leaves them for dead in the road then runs away and hides.'

'Oh,' Mick nodded. 'So that's what this is all about. Your Paki poofter pal?'

Mo silently revolved the stick around its tip on the pavement, his eyes fixed on Mick's.

'Not that it's any of your business,' Mick elaborated with more finger jabbing and some flying spittle. 'But I was just evening things out. You know, on account of your boyfriend's clan blowing me legs off in Helmand - I'm entitled.'

Mo stopped twirling the stick. 'Entitled?'

'*An eye for an eye* and all that,' Mick continued. 'That's what your lot believe don't' you? I know you're one of them.'

'Do you know,' Mo said softly. 'Servicemen and women do this country proud. They really do. Fighting wars, risking life and limb – literally in your case. They deserve the utmost respect.'

Mick's pointed finger drooped while subconsciously or otherwise he straightened his stance.

'Then again,' Mo took two paces forward, so he was in range of Mick's reach. 'It just takes one rotten egg like you, a childish xenophobic bigot, to throw his dummy out, do something selfish to an innocent man – a *good* innocent man - and it tarnishes the image that the public has of war heroes in general. And by that, I mean the real heroes, not moronic bullies like you.'

'Do you know how many people I've killed?' Mick snapped.

When the expected response from Mo failed to materialise, Mick answered his own question with three lots of flashing fingers.

'Thirty! One of them with my own hands!' Mick bared his assortment of chipped teeth, formed a fist and drew it under his chin. 'I bet you've never even had a fight.'

'Not one that I've won.' Mo admitted unblinking.

Mick slowly unfurled his snarl. 'Go on, on your way sunshine. I'm feeling generous.'

'You may not feel so generous when I tell you that it was me who put the police onto you. Your other threat, *I'll snap your legs in so many places you'll have to stagger to Mecca like a spastic* helped me link you with Saboor's hit-and-run. I followed you the other night and discovered that, lo-and-behold, you have a lockup near the scene housing a bashed-in car.'

'So, was it you who dobbed me in to the filth?'

'Yep.'

'Big mistake faggot, Mick growled noisily while covertly aligning notches in the top three bolts of his left leg. 'I'm gonna make you number thirty-one!'

'That's not going to happen.' Mo took a further pace forward so that he was almost touching Mick's fist with his chin. 'You see, I do believe in justice. Not necessarily an eye for an eye, but at least more than the measly six months stretch that you'll probably get once you've played your *disabled war hero with post-traumatic stress disorder* trump card in court. Meanwhile, my friend is stuck with a limp for life. So, I'm here for some fairer retribution. I've mulled it over and I think a gammy knee would be ideal, but since you don't have a knee, I'll settle for an elbow instead.'

'You're off your head!' Mick bellowed. In one swift movement he batted the stick from Mo's grasp with his left hand, twisted side on, and drew his other fist back. As Mick's shoulder recoiled to deliver a blow Mo anticipated the punch and weaved downwards. Mo felt the air whoosh just above his ear from the wayward blow. At the same time, he thrust an elbow while his assailant's momentum carried him forwards and it cartwheeled into Mick's gullet. Mick let out a stifled cry of pain while flinging his own elbow back sharply, catching Mo unawares to the back of the head. Mo gasped hard, grimaced and wrapped his arms around Mick's midriff. He sensed Mick's arm rise and turned up to see a fist forming above the tough man's head. As it came hammering down Mo hooked a foot behind Mick's stump and pushed, altering his position and causing the fist's trajectory to deviate a tad off course. It missed its target and skimmed Mo's upper back as the combination of his shove and the well-placed foot sent Mick toppling over backwards and down onto the pavement, with Mo crashing down beside him.

Mo was the first to react. He eyed the stick protruding from underneath Mick's side and, while flat on his back, quickly swivelled and planted his feet either side of Mick's hip and yanked at it, albeit unsuccessfully - jammed as it was under fourteen stones of metal and muscle. Grappling, grunting and too preoccupied, Mo failed to notice neither Mick's torso revolving nor the rapidly approaching fist. By the time it did register on Mo's radar it had already connected with his jaw; sending him head over heels backwards onto the road with the finally liberated stick clutched in his hand. While Mo gasped for breath, spitting out blood, Mick yanked off his leg, flicked out the knife and lunged at Mo. Still prone, Mo's eyes ballooned as the blade hurtled towards him. Instinctively he jabbed the wooden stick down to one side, like a white-water slalom canoeist, and rolled and rose in one swift movement as Mick's leg-cum-spear missed his head by a whisker. Mick's follow-through brought him plunging to the ground that Mo had occupied split seconds earlier. As Mo clattered down on top of him he whacked his forearm into the back of Mick's neck then stabbed the stick hard into his elbow joint – crunching bone and popping tendons.

Mick's piercing howl reverberated along the street.

***

Mo clambered up off Mick, taking care not to do any more damage as Mick squirmed on the ground and hugged his elbow in a panicky ham-fisted manner.

'You're dead Blenkinsopp,' He part growled, part winced.

Something in Mo's subconscious made Mo turn around. Mick's crazed eyes followed Mo's gaze and settled on Debbie who was observing proceedings from the police station doorway.

'Hey you,' Mick barked.

Debbie looked behind her, turned back around towards Mick and pointed a questioning finger at herself.

'Of course *you* Harrison you stupid...' Mick let the end of his sentence trail off and poked a finger towards Mo. 'Did you see that? This thug's just assaulted me.'

'Here you go Michael,' Mo smiled and threw the stick down at Mick's feet. 'Told you it might come in useful.'

Mick leaned forward, grabbed the stick and held it to his shoulder like a javelin.

'Hi Debbie,' Mo fished around in his pocket, flung a £20 note in Mick's lap and hailed over one of the cabs from the nearby taxi rank. 'See Michael, not everyone deserts an invalid lying in the gutter. For my part, I've called the police, in the form of the charming DC Harrison, and I've even arranged transport to the hospital. Ask them to sort you out with a psychologist while they're at it. No need to thank me - and yes, you can keep the change.'

Mick roared, flung the stick at Mo's head and cursed as Mo effortlessly batted it away with the back of his forearm.

'Tsh,' Mo tutted. 'There's gratitude for you.'

Mick barked at Debbie. 'I want him locked up Harrison. You're a witness. It's GBH.'

'GBH?' Debbie played with her earlobe. No, I think an elbow to the ribs and a punch to the face is more a case of ABH. Unless of course Mr Blenkinsopp also wants to add attempted murder to your charge sheet?' Debbie looked at Mo who smiled and shook his head.

'I'm not talking about charging me you imbecile,' Mick spat. 'It's that lunatic Blenkinsopp you need to lock up. 'He just attacked me and you're a witness, as well you know.'

'It's been a long day, Debbie rubbed her eyes, stretched and yawned. 'What with dealing with assorted low-life through a twelve-hour shift. All I know is that I saw you elbow Mr Blenkinsopp here, drag him down to the floor, punch him in the face, attack him with a blade, then fling the stick he offered to help you with straight at his head.'

'You bitch Harrison,' Mick glowered. He picked up his leg and aimed it at her like a cricketer targeting stumps.

'Tch, not the wisest move Michael,' Mo offered. 'Threatening a police officer at the local nick.'

'I'll have you for this,' Mick shook his leg viciously about his head. 'I'll have the pair of you for this. Just you wait and see!'

He twisted around, retracted the blade and flung his artificial leg to the startled taxi driver before shuffling into the cab; spewing threats and expletives every inch of the way.

Mo fumbled about in his pocket for a tip for the taxi driver, 'Sorry about Michael here, he's in a bit of a grumpy mood today. Let me check my wallet...'

Debbie hastened over, grabbed Mo's wallet, slapped a £10 note in the driver's palm then frogmarched Mo back to the police station. The door squeaked, juddered and clattered behind them as they disappeared inside.

***

'What the hell are you playing at?'

Mo started towards the row of plastic chairs but either he stumbled, or his legs simply just gave way en-route. One way or another he came crashing down headfirst, scattering the chairs like skittles across reception. He groaned, rubbed his ribs then wheezed hard as he clambered off the ground and dragged himself up into a seat. He coughed, twisted around to face Debbie and shrugged.

Debbie's sighed heavily. 'You do know he's a nutcase, don't you?'

Mo tapped his own head with a knuckle, smiled wryly and shrugged again.

'What can I say, I clobbered a cripple. Very politically incorrect of me. I hold my hands up.' Mo winced as he raised his arms. 'Would you like a signed confession?'

'Maybe next time. Almost certainly in fact,' Debbie upturned a chair and drew it opposite Mo. 'But promise me that there won't be a next time.'

Mo placed his hands between him and Debbie. They watched his hands tremble.

'I can assure you DC Harrison, that I'm no rush for a repeat,' said Mo.

Debbie shook her head, smiled dryly and tutted lamely. She pulled her chair closer to Mo's and instinctively Mo wriggled backwards into the recesses of the plastic. Debbie extracted her handkerchief, took Mo's chin between her thumb and forefinger and turned his face towards her.

'How come you're always in the wars Blenkinsopp?' Debbie asked as she dabbed the blood around his mouth.

Mo took one of his hands in the other. He could still feel it shake, but somehow it felt different to before. A more tingling kind of tremble. A niggling *if only* jumped on his heartstrings and slapped and sunk its teeth somewhere into his subconscious. It triggered sensations. Good sensations. Mo pulled his hands to his chest and wondered what quivered the most, them or his heart.

'Trouble just seems to follow me,' he eventually mustered.

'Hm,' Debbie hovered her hand next to Mo's side. 'May I?'

Mo scrunched up his nose, then the penny dropped. He nodded and carefully lifted his vest.

'You're all red,' Debbie said, gently running her fingertips over the peaks and troughs of his tender torso. Mo pulled his vest up further, completely over his head, and hoped that she was referring to his ribs and not his blushing cheeks.

Unable to see, Mo comically patted thin air with his palms. Debbie chuckled as she ducked to avoid her nose being flattened. When she bobbed back up her face was just inches away from Mo's cocooned one. Her eyes glistened. She kissed her fingertips and brushed Mo's raw chest ever so lightly, her smile widening as Mo's quivering intensified.

Mo inhaled deeply and, oblivious to Debbie's smile, felt one spread over his face too. He wrapped the vest closer to his face, closed his eyes and purred with pleasure. It wasn't until the 'Mm' had left already his lips that his utterance registered. He hastened to change it, 'Ooh.'

"Moo?' Debbie's pressed the heel of her hand against Mo's forehead, rocked back and laughed out loud. Mo lowered his vest somewhat sheepishly and felt the heat from his cheeks on the backs of his hands as he did so. After an awkward few seconds scratching his brain trying to drag up an explanation Mo just raised an index finger either side of his forehead and laughed, 'Moo!'

'You'll survive,' Debbie declared busy GP fashion.

Mo gazed into Debbie's eyes in silence and noticed for the first time that flecks of hazel, touches of amber and hints of blue speckled the green. His mind returned to his mother's grave, the trees and the sky above. By intuition or sheer coincidence, Debbie seemed to sense it too.

'Sorry Mo, it was insensitive of me to mention survival,' she said in a near whisper. 'I know your mother's death still must be incredibly hard for you.'

Mo scratched his head and sighed. 'Yes and no. Mam had such a tough life, what with one thing or another. I can't help thinking that she's in a better place now.'

'What about you?' Debbie said. 'You've had a hell of a hard time, not only with your mam, but with Abraham too. For my part, I can't help feeling guilty about not doing more to stop him from coming down on you like that. He's a sleazy, intimidating, nasty piece of work. I know it now for sure, and I had more than just an inkling about it at the time too. I should have done more.'

'Guilty by association?' Mo hesitated, then gave Debbie's shoulder the briefest of gentle rubs. 'Think nothing of it, Debbie. I know it was Abraham, Abraham and the whole Abraham so help me Allah.'

Debbie only half smiled but her eyes gleamed lock, stock and barrel.

Mo considered asking Debbie about what Abraham had intimated about him and her being lovers, but quickly banished it from his thoughts. He didn't believe it and wouldn't give Abraham the satisfaction of provocation – even in absentia.

'Anyway, what about you Mo?' Debbie said. 'How are you?'

'Despite all that's gone on - my mam notwithstanding – I somehow feel I'm in a ...' Mo clasped his hands and stretched 'I'm in a better place than I think I ever have been.'

'Are you sure?' Debbie traced one of the blue curved lines across Mo's cheek with a finger. 'It doesn't look like it from where I'm sitting.'

'Not a big fan of tattoos are you then Debbie?'

'That's neither here nor there,' Debbie said. 'It's just that it's such a big jump from...'

'From what?'

'From you before. The old you. You know smart, sensitive, sweet, wouldn't say boo to a goose to...'

Smart, sensitive, sweet. Another niggling *if only* somersaulted from the back of Mo's mind and slapped his conscious self hard to the face.

Debbie pulled at his vest, scrubbed his head and nipped a cheek. 'To this!'

'I'm still the same *me* Debbie.'

'No, you're not Mo,' Debbie let go of Mo's cheek, brushed down his vest and studied him. 'Maybe somewhere underneath the surface, bits of you are still the same, but there are parts of you that I just don't recognise. I'm not sure exactly who you are anymore.'

'Yeah well,' Mo tugged an ear. 'Truth be told, you're not the only one Debbie. I'm not quite sure who I am anymore either. Or who I've become or who I'm turning into. It's like I've been wound up like a spinning top then suddenly unleashed down some roller coaster mega-loop wall-of-death life detour. I'm still just getting my bearings now.'

'So, do you know where you are and where you are heading?'

'I know exactly,' Mo offered with a crooked smile. 'I'm at the centre of the whorling labyrinth of existence and I'm going to pick one of the countless paths at random and see where it takes me.'

'Oh, you're talking metaphorically.'

'Only to a point,' Mo said. 'I've no ties and no real idea what to do. The money from my mam's house sale is about to land in my pocket and the whole big bad world is in front of me.'

'You don't have to go,' Debbie stood up, wandered over to the information display on the wall and handed Mo a leaflet. 'And this is something that you certainly can do.'

'A police recruitment advert,' Mo gave a little chuckle. 'Well, I had always hoped to join up but...'

'You do know the CPS has dropped those drugs charges?' said Debbie. 'You've a clean slate.'

'Yes, I heard you had a hand in that Debbie thanks. But how can I join the force with a face like this?' Mo pointed to his tattoo. 'I've heard of the boys in blue, but this would be taking it to a whole new extreme.'

'I'm serious Mo,' Debbie persisted. 'There is no mention of tattoos on the advert, and I know first-hand that you're an exceptional detective. We'd be lucky to have you.'

'I don't know,' Mo snaked a smile. 'Maybe one day. ...We'll see.'

'The money from your mam's house sale will be enough to set yourself up with a nice little flat elsewhere in town. One without the scars and memories. ...Talking of which,' Debbie headed to the duty sergeant's desk. 'Matty can you dig out some bumf on victim support as well as police recruitment forms for Mr Blenkinsopp?'

Debbie turned and silently surveyed Mo while he studied the advert.

'About that night at the school disco...'

Mo cringed and covered his eyes with his hands at the phrase '*school disco,*' sending the leaflet looping through the air. 'I'm sooo sorry about that whole wretched business Debbie. I don't' know what I was thinking, asking you to dance. God knows what possessed me to think that I had any sort of chance with you.'

Debbie opened her mouth to speak but was cut short by a tap on the partition behind her. 'Is this what you're after?' She collected some paraphernalia through the gap in the partition from Matty while the main door clanged open and a gust buffeted reception. Debbie felt her cheeks burning despite the chilly blast of air. Eyes down, she bundled up the leaflets and forms as she spoke.

'But that's just the thing, I'm glad you did,' she said quietly with her back still to the room. 'Well, I would have been if you hadn't... well, you know.'

Matty pointed to his empty cup and wiggled it at Debbie from his side of the partition. She shook her head and bided her time while he traipsed into the back room. She spun around with a flashing smile and a wink. 'And who says you've no chance with me?'

The youth clutching a severed bike lock did a double-take to check that he was the only person in the reception before pointing to himself.

'Eh?'

'Wh...?' Debbie flung the papers up in the air and her eyes darted about the room.

'Hey!' The youth spat as forms and leaflets rained down on him. He let go of the broken bike lock and it clattered on the floor. 'What are you playing at?'

Matty darted back at the sound of the commotion, clocked the mess and rapped his knuckles against the partition. 'Oi Harrison!'

Debbie scratched at her hair like a dog with fleas, huffed then dropped on all fours and immediately set to work. As she fumbled about the door squeaked behind her, a squall hustled through and the papers scattered further still.

The young lad jiggled an eyebrow, got down on his hands and knees and crawled up to Debbie. He handed her an application form and whispered into her ear, 'Did you say what I think you said? That I've a chance with you gorgeous?'

'Of course, you've no chance with me!' Debbie snapped loudly. 'Get real!'

She craned her head around at the sound of a familiar judder as the station door clattered shut. 'What was that?'

The youth scanned around. 'Oh, it'll be that lad with the vest and tattooed face going out again. The one who went out chasing after something as I entered. He came back a few seconds ago, now he's scarpered again. He's not doing a runner is he?'

'Mo!' Debbie bundled the youth out of the way, scrambled to her feet and hurried to the exit. She yanked open the door, stumbled on the steps and crashed down onto the pavement. She clambered to her knees, looked both ways up and down the street, then both ways again.

'Mo' she called out.

But he had already gone.

Afterword

In her preface for *'And Then There Were None,'* Agatha Christie wrote this.

"I had written this book because it was so difficult to do that the idea had fascinated me. 10 people have to die without it becoming ridiculous or the murderer being obvious. I wrote the book after a tremendous amount of planning and I was pleased with what I have made of it. It was clear, straightforward, battling, and yet had a perfectly reasonable explanation; in fact, it had to have an epilogue in order to explain it. It was very well received and reviewed, but the person who was really pleased with it was myself, for I knew better than any critic how difficult it had been."

I'm not suggesting for one minute that I am Agatha Christie. She is a titan of crime whereas I'm a complete unknown, this is my first novel, and I couldn't even get an agent to read it, let alone a publisher! At the same time, I thought it might be interesting for readers to have a bit of background, and Agatha Christie's comments are part of that as they did inspire me to try to push myself and stretch my creative limits more than I might have otherwise done. My plan (if you can call it that) was to spice up crime with a touch of mystery, a sprinkling of humour and dollops of mayhem and wrap it up in an ambitious twisting plot. That was my aim, but at the time, I had no idea who the main protagonist would be or how he/she would fit into it all. Notably, while it was easy to toss in the word 'ambitious,' exactly what that entailed was an enigma in itself.

When I first had the idea of tying the protagonist to multiple murders with motive, damning (DNA and circumstantial) evidence and no alibi, but then flipping it so that a different character became the only suspect (also with motive, no alibi and damming DNA evidence), I thought that it sounded great as a concept, but was overly ambitious and almost certainly unworkable in practice. When I then toyed with the notion of taking it further still and flipping it on its head again so that the real culprits lay elsewhere, and with clues pointing to this right from the opening, then at that stage, I pretty much consigned the ludicrous notion to the realms of downright impossibility.

But what the hell. I thought I'd give it a bash anyway.

Butcher Boy Blue is the result.

Acknowledgments:

I am hugely indebted to Parul. If I was the creator of *Butcher Boy Blue* then Parul played a key part in shaping it; opening my eyes to genre method and giving me tools to add direction as well as extra sparks and tension with her nuggets of wisdom and brutal honesty.

Thanks too to Debbie. You only commented on the opening, but I never forgot your encouragement, and your words to help me get through the rough patches. The surname is different, but I named Debbie after you.

I'd have loved to ask Matty in person if he'd like to be included. Tragically, I was too late for that, but I thank his dad, David for his permission. Thanks also to Stewie and Audrey and for letting me use your names even though you didn't know what you were getting into. How mad is that? Talking of mad... respect to Kevin Feeney for converting the draft to a monotone AI voice and listening like that!

Finally, special thanks to Christèle, and not just for your comments, honesty, hugs and laughter but for your wisdom, support and for keeping me (relatively) sane in times of utter madness.

Some more notes

Purely for my own amusement, I chose not to name the town (or even mention the mighty Pools), though it's easy enough for you DuckDuckGo sleuths to work the town out. The street names are the same, there is a Ward Jackson Park (though in truth, fairly small) and there is also a Tall Ships pub - and at the time of writing it did have some wasteland nearby (not for long I suspect). The Tall Ships event really did come to town, but the only thing that bombed was the greedy council's plan to sting visitors by painting the town double yellow (apparently it cost them more to paint/remove the lines than they generated in hiked-up parking revenue). If so, it serves them right. I just rode down on my bike!

Why did I write a novel?

Bizarrely, it was never all about the writing. I had the (peculiar) notion that a novel might be a roundabout way to get more gigs for my music. I don't know if this ambition will ever be realised, but please feel free to check out my music at www.paulhichens.com. In particular, *Blueboy* is a song I wrote with Mo in mind. And if you happen to be some big shot global music impresario, or a small-time nobody with a tinpot venue and a passion for music then hey... you know where I am.

What next?

Another good question. With some encouragement from Parul, I started thinking of *Butcher Boy Blue* as a series. And I'm sure there are plenty of cavernous new holes for Mo to calamitously dig himself into. I'm curious about his next chapter(s) too. I enjoyed writing this - and not just the creative elements – but because weaving in mystery then tying up clues meant slipping into detective mode (of sorts) myself. Would I like Mo to wreak more havoc? Yes, but it was a many-draft, 5-year slog! True, I've learnt a lot and the next novel would be quicker, though a mountain of toil for potentially no reward. I initially wrote *Butcher Boy Blue* for music, not fame, fortune or recognition, but once I'd penned the first paragraph, a spark of hope ignited that maybe, just maybe ... I could possibly create something that some people might like. I guess I'm a tiny bit peeved that no agent wanted to read it – but only a tiny bit! I'm more interested in what real people think. As I write this, I've no idea how real people will perceive *Butcher Boy Blue*. I guess 'what next' depends on what people (like you!) think. Contact details are below, and I'm open to any comments (good or bad). If it does transpire that people want more, then that'll go a long way to ensuring more Mo mayhem!

Other books & films

I primarily wrote my mini-book, *'A Novel Experience – Writing Your Bestseller'* to give budding novelists a *worts and all* insight into the novel writing experience as well as providing tips, advice, practical sessions and real life examples. At the same time, if you are interested in discovering more about what went into the making of *Butcher Boy Blue* then you could find it very interesting (and especially since a lot more went into it than meets the eye!). It's available on Amazon for mere pennies. My CV book *The One Page CV* is published by Pearson Education, and my book *Stuff Strife, Gimme Life! Improve Your Job, Career and Work-Life Balance* is available in print, eBook and audiobook formats. I'm also working on some fun children's rhymes.

You can contact me via paulhichens.com, and if you just happen to be an adventurous filmmaker interested in bringing Mo to life on screen then drop me a line too – who am I to stand in his way? The lad could kinda do with a break.

Printed in Great Britain
by Amazon

40021009R00201